THE
REFLECTORY

DAN CASHMAN

Published by

Lion Bridge
PUBLISHING

Duluth   Edinburgh   Prague   Moscow

Cover design by FHS student Jordyn Gysbers with contributions from Heather Barnes and Hannah Herrig. Thanks to Dawn Cherwinka for her guidance and to John R. Waddle for his violin.

A special thanks goes to my parents, Mike and Bev Cashman. For everything they are and everything they do.

FOR KIM, MY ENERGY

The Days

"The changing of Bodies into Light, and Light into Bodies, is very conformable to the Course of Nature, which seems delighted with Transmutations."

—Sir Isaac Newton, inventor of the Reflecting Telescope
Opticks, 2nd edition (1718)

Saturday: Beware of the Tin Man

Chapter 1

Stonebrook Cottage, Minnesota's North Shore of Lake Superior

Alex Fitzgerald tried to focus on his phone interview but was distracted by the early-morning interruption coming his way. Through the November forest of pines and bare birch, someone lumbered downhill, one hand holding a bag, the other flopping with each step.

Phone to ear, Alex scampered across a clearing behind the vacation house for a better look: it was a short man—his belly bounced as his squatty legs churned, propelling a chubby torso over a footbridge that spanned a small river. Twenty feet away, the man spotted Alex and froze. His curly, graying hair was matted with sweat. An overstuffed plastic bag pulled taut against his hand.

Alex asked his interviewer to hold a moment, muted the phone, then asked the man, "Excuse me, but are you okay?"

The man's brow furrowed, he tilted his head to the side.

Alex held up his phone so the bewildered man could see it. "Can I call someone for you?"

Like a curious animal, the man tilted his head to the other side. His chest heaved as he labored to catch his breath. His big lips sucked in and blew out, kissing air like a fish out of water.

"What do you have in the bag?" asked Alex. He was beginning to think the man was deaf or did not speak English.

The fellow wiped at his nose with a forearm and replied in a quiet voice, "John Wayne."

Caught off guard by the odd reply, Alex almost laughed. The man must have gotten away from a group. Alex pictured a short bus idling in the parking lot at nearby Split Rock Lighthouse State Park and a headcount of special needs patients coming up one head short.

With eyes wide and nose sniffing, the man glanced around, and walked to within six inches of Alex. He could not have been over five feet tall and Alex was six-four so he had to look straight up. "It's not finished," the man whispered. "It's never finished … it needs someone." His voice was soft and breathy like a breeze in a field but his breath was foul, almost caustic, like rubber burning.

Alex took a step back. "Come again?"

The man touched Alex's forearm with a thick, dirty finger. "I left him for you."

Alex jerked his arm back. "Left who?"

"You will take him away in the boat," continued the man. He sucked in more clean air, exhaled more stench toward Alex.

"I'm sorry, but take who where?"

"Cannot, shannot, mannot ever tell," the man replied, shaking his head. Then to convince Alex, as if by merely uttering words he could make them true, he added: "you will seek, you will find."

Alex retreated a couple more steps, ready to escape. "Listen," replied Alex. "You have me confused with someone else. I'm not seeking anyone."

"You will seek."

Realizing he would get nowhere with further inquiry, Alex took another couple steps back. "Okay, I will seek. And, thanks. Thank you for leaving him for me."

Pleased with himself, the man pulled a cowboy hat out of his bag, placed it on his head, and started walking back toward the bridge.

"Wait," said Alex, perplexed. "You just … you just ran from that direction. Are you sure I can't call someone?"

The man stopped, turned, and then nodded over the river in the direction he was heading. "Beware of the Tin Man."

"Um hum, I will," replied Alex. *And Dorothy, too. Not to mention Toto. The wicked witch, though? She's cool.*

"Tin Man is dangerous. Very, very." The man's tone sounded more intelligent than before. As if a different person had spoken. Then the man-beast walked back on his path through dense pines and across his bridge. And, seemingly, back to Narnia.

When Alex resumed his phone call, the interviewer, a partner from a prestigious boutique firm in the Twin Cities offering $250K to start, finally asked the question that the past three interviewers had also asked: How had he managed to win four architectural design competitions in a row without having actually built anything yet?

"Well, Mr. Kupcho, I draft from a concept, not an end result ..." replied Alex, still breathing hard from his bizarre encounter. "I place myself in the center of a project and work from the inside out."

"You don't really know what your design looks like until you're done?" the ivy-league-educated interviewer pressed.

Deciding not to sugarcoat his answer because he was tired of talking, Alex let his answer stand. "No. It just ... it just comes together."

Mr. Kupcho expressed concern about hiring an unproven architectural genius. The coveted Minnesota Architect of the Year award had never gone to a rookie so he stressed the importance that designs should suit commissions. He mentioned budgets and schedules. And yet he offered the job, as had the others.

Alex hung up and gaped at the spot where the man had disappeared up the hill. A cold November breeze nipped at his face and he grimaced. Saving his marriage would have been so much easier in the Bahamas. Hot beaches, cold margaritas. Kate loved those things. Instead, they had to deal with fifty degrees and a foreboding hobbit with an astonishingly incorrect impression of the Tin Man. He knew his wife's thoughts on the cold temps and had a strong inkling what she'd think of the little fellow with the shopping bag if he came around again. He decided to keep the man a secret. If Kate became worried, they would have zero chance of getting close again.

Walking back to the cottage, fog sneaked inland from Lake Superior with its damp freshness smelling almost sweet. Inside the house's large bank of lakeside windows, he saw the fireplace at the end of the great room. At 20 feet high, it was an impressive floor-to-ceiling endeavor of rounded rocks. On the far side, a two-story library built into the wall held not hundreds of books, but thousands.

He recalled the phone call he had received from an East Coast attorney of the late John Mead who suggested he visit the man's estate for a week, free of charge. Sort of a last wish of the great man, the attorney had said. Alex had thought it was odd, because he had never actually met Mead. The reclusive architect had for several years guest lectured at the Thresholds of Architectural Theory seminar, but retired before Alex was even a student. Their only connection was that John Mead still graded the seminar projects, so the man would have been familiar with Alex's unique potential, and he obviously remembered him.

As if to entice Alex to stay, the attorney followed up the conversation a week later with a snail-mail letter that again offered up the estate with the line: "A secluded, old cottage with views of Lake Superior." The caveat at the bottom read, "Per John Mead, Stonebrook is more a thinker's getaway than a family retreat. No TV and no Internet. No pets."

A secluded, old cottage with views of Lake Superior, thought Alex with a smile. *Talk about undersell.* It was not a cottage in any sense of the word. On dozens of acres and surrounded by Split Rock Lighthouse State Park, the architecture of the century-old home had the look of a Victorian-era mansion. Half of the structure had two floors and could have housed a dozen people comfortably. The other half consisted of a great room and library suitable for a king.

Looking through the windows, he spotted Kate in a leather chair, reading. Instead of heading inside, he paused to admire her. His wife's long, brown hair was still messy from sleeping. The hell they had been through with the death of their nine-year-old son devastated her even more than it had him.

Michael, the boy who never learned to tie his own shoes, yet in six months of playing chess had become one of the best elementary school players in the United States. The boy who had a neurological condition known as synesthesia in which he saw colors in numbers—one was green, two was yellow—and could solve master-level Sudoku puzzles in minutes, yet could not read a book because stories were "too noisy" in his head.

Alex recalled the day of the car crash, the one time he had forgotten to make sure Michael had fastened his seat belt. When the texting teenager hit them head on, Alex's airbag deployed as Michael flew forward and in the instant their heads collided, Alex's life changed forever. It was as if the mind of his son continued and had passed through skin and bone into his own mind. When Alex regained consciousness, he had similar synesthesia-like perceptions. As the approaching ambulance siren wailed and Michael lay dying from the contusion, his brain hemorrhaging, it was as if transference had occurred, a gift had been given.

Two hours later at the hospital when Michael's heart monitor went flat, the classical song that was playing became a sensory kaleidoscope in Alex's head: dark-hued colors of rhythm splashed and musical notes popped open like bright blue flowers. His son's death tasted of black liquorish. Next to him, his wife's anguish, her love, smelled oddly of fresh-cut wood. His own aching loss felt like cobwebs on his skin.

Life, tenuous and fleeting life, was earthy and sweet like cinnamon.

The head-scratching psychiatrist he saw, at a loss for explaining how a thirty-four-year-old could see color in music and smell concepts, at last declared with an air of authority that it was a trauma-induced amplification of a genetic predisposition for synesthesia.

But Alex knew better. It was his son.

While these odd sensations of the condition dissipated in a few days, new perceptions and a feeling of sensory overload remained. Tasks, errands, everything—they all became so painfully difficult. No longer able to work in Information Technology because of its newfound hollowness, Alex went back to school and settled on a master's program in Architecture. It wasn't until he was working on his seminar project John Mead had graded that he found a purpose for his amazing brain. He could get lost while designing. Even on paper, the layout of a building could be so beautiful and rhythmic. And blue.

He saw himself dancing in the halls he created, spinning in his vaulted rooms with a Julie-Andrews-on-a-Bavarian-hill giddiness. Within architecture, his senses had an outlet and his overload started to ease.

Graduating as class valedictorian, the first-place prizes started coming: the Tristan Prize for Experimental Design, the Howser for Innovative Use of Space. The LapDog Werks, the Stanislaw.

And despite never having designed a single building that had yet actually been built, next came the prestigious Young Minnesota Architect of the Year honor, just four months ago. And now, the job offers.

Through the cottage's massive windows, he saw Kate get up from her chair, walk through the interior with a coffee cup in hand, and then out of sight. Still in her PJs, she emerged through the screen door off the kitchen, sniffed the air, waved at him, turned around, and walked right back inside. He loved her. So much.

After Michael's funeral two years ago, she had started exercising, started eating healthier. With a passion for Buti Yoga, her mind and body had become lean and strong. While her infectious belly laugh laugh was still absent and the sparkle in her eyes had faded, she was so lithe now. Ripped, even.

Alex rubbed his flat stomach. While she had lost twenty pounds of fat and added muscle through Buti, he had become gaunt. A former runner of marathons, he had a lean, muscular build before Michael died but was now merely lean. And he felt tired all the time, not his old athletic self, because he could not stop thinking about his boy.

There was a stretch recently when he had wanted their relationship to return to how it used to be, before Michael died, but he had given up on that. His wife's anguish, he knew, was infused with bitterness. While the car crash was not Alex's fault, he had been the one driving Michael home from daycare, and he had been late. If he had been on time, the texting driver who had crossed the median would not have hit them.

When Kate's mom died last month, he tried his hardest to be there for her, but she had closed him off. And that crushed him. Now he just wanted half of the passion they once had. A fragment.

At times, he thought it was guilt that made him unconsciously take on his son's debilitating synesthesia. Other times, he thought it was divine intervention, because when the raw synesthesia subsided, it was replaced by a subtler, enhanced cognitive ability that let him perceive things in ways most people never get the chance to experience.

Yet he was still so preoccupied. It was the simple things that blew him away, like washing a car. Hands submersed in soapy water squeezing a sponge, hot chrome parts glinting in the sun, rainbows, the smell of the steaming reflections. He would get lost in sensory overload and would have to lie down on the driveway or in the yard. It never failed that he'd be taking such a break when his mother-in-law drove up or a neighbor jogged by. "Hi," he'd say to them and get back up. Half the time they just looked the other way, pretending not to notice.

Kate popped out again, this time with a hat, gloves, and a scarf.

She walked up, sat down next to him, and put her hand on his knee. "Well done, Alex. This place is gorgeous."

"Thanks."

"How'd the interview go?"

"Got another offer," he said, almost awkwardly.

Kate nodded. "Congrats. Wow, three offers in one week. You should be Architect of the Year more often."

He smiled. "Guess I have a decision to make this week." He didn't give her any more details because he had already told her this most recent offer was with the coveted SinSol2 firm. But he wasn't sure he was stable enough yet to take a real job again. He had become an architect to create escapes. He wanted to design a world where his boy could come back to life and they could make a lemonade stand or a tree fort together. Build a place where he and his son were normal—a place where his wife still loved him. In other words, he wanted an imaginary world.

"Hey, want to come back in?" Kate asked. It's not too late for that breakfast in bed you promised me, is it?"

Alex hurried up the stairs to the second-floor bedroom of Stonebrook cottage holding an antique serving tray with crispy bacon, eggs, and coffee.

"Here we are," he announced to his wife, entering the room.

As Kate sat up in bed, he handed her a fresh cup of coffee. The old quilt she was under had an outdoor scene pieced together by dozens of squares, and her shape was right in the middle of a lake. He had a vision of water and fish cascading down her sides in a flood, washing away trees in the forest, and smashing the large quilt-cabin he saw on the quilt-shore. From the moment they had arrived, there was an aspect of the bedroom that struck him as beyond sensory, and therefore calming. And the library, too. They did something to his mind—calmed it, yet tugged at it.

Still snuggled in the bed, she read aloud the most recent entry from a guestbook she had grabbed from the nightstand.

Loved it here. Weather was nice.
—Nicolai Petrov

"Why would someone even bother to write that?" she asked. "Loved it here, weather was nice" she repeated in a mocking voice. She flipped back to the first entry in the book. "Now, here … sit down, Alex. Listen to this one."

Dear Guests,
    The night of the massive storm called the Big Blow was over one hundred years ago. Less than a mile from this cottage, the schooner-barge *Madeira*, a vessel half the size of the *Titanic*, separated from her steamship consort, the *Edenborn*. The 11-man crew of the unpowered *Madeira* was to ride out the storm at sea, but forty-foot waves pushed her, and at 5:30 a.m. she slammed against the cliff of Gold Rock Point.

DAN CASHMAN

If it weren't for one courageous seaman who
managed to time a wave and lunge for the top of
the cliff with a line, all would have been lost. He
rescued nine men. Caught aft side, the first mate
climbed the mizzenmast but went down with the
ship when, at 6:00 a.m., the steel hull of the
Madeira shuddered one last time against the cliff
and she broke in two.

As rain turned to sleet, the survivors trudged
down from the Point until they happened upon
Stonebrook's woodshed and they piled in for
warmth.

With the Madeira broken and sinking, the
Edenborn, whipped ashore a couple miles from
here. One man, pushed by a wave into the hold of
the vessel, lost his life. His mates scrambled to
shore and eventually found shelter at Tudor
House.

Several ships and many lives were lost that
night in what was, by all accounts, the second
worst storm in Great Lakes history. That night
prompted the construction of Split Rock
Lighthouse, right between Stonebrook Cottage
and Tudor House.

When the toll was tallied, the Pittsburgh
Steamship Company had on its ledgers the loss of
two men: one from the *Madeira*, one from the
Edenborn.

This is all according to historical record.

Yet with respect to the *Madeira,* with respect to
Stonebrook, ledgers and records … are dead
wrong.

Tudor House, now surrounded by state park
land, still stands. Duke, the old boy, is still there. A
park ranger carries in his food and cares for him.

As for Stonebrook … some among you reading this will have been invited, others not. Our Reflectory may remain undiscovered. Society today rotates faster, days are shorter. Life is still lavender, yet vacations are consumed in preoccupied rushes.

Here, things are different. Within these walls of white pine, and on these grounds, there is history. There are stories, mysteries, and puzzles. Here at Stonebrook, you may relax, but I invite you to ponder, to wonder, to think.

Turmoil is at hand.

For me. For you.

Mine: a falling, into tranquility. I shall scatter, resurrect. Yours, a rising; a call….

And another storm is gathering, another Big Blow.

—John Mead

Kate cleared her throat and fell silent. She closed the book and nibbled on some bacon. "So tell me again. Why did John Mead invite you here?"

Flustered by the entry, Alex did not answer right away. The statement that life was still lavendar meant that John Mead had synesthesia. "I don't know. He graded my Thresholds in Theory seminar project so he saw my design and the paper I turned in. And he probably read about my Architect of the Year award. I bet I received it right before he died."

"What's a Reflectory?" asked Kate. "Is that an architecture term?"

"Isaac Newton invented something called a reflecting telescope but I have no idea what a Reflectory is. Newton shocked the world with his little telescope because it proved for the first time that white light is really made up of a spectrum of colors."

Struck by the foreboding tone of the entry, yet not captivated by reflecting telescopes or Reflectories, Kate asked, "So what are we going to do? Ponder and wonder and think? Or relax?"

Alex mulled over the words: *Yours, a rising; a call.* What was that about?

"I know you," continued Kate. "You need to ponder and wonder and think, don't you?"

Alex knew they needed to focus on their relationship— that's why they were here. He picked up the guestbook. The cover was leather with an embossed blue violin; the paper inside was thick and rough. It looked homemade yet elegant, even the paper.

A storm is gathering, he thought. They both came here for peace, but perhaps what they needed was the opposite.

Perhaps they needed another storm.

Chapter 2

After breakfast, they took the most worn of the three paths that led to the lake, the one that angled to the right.

"Look, the woodshed!" Kate said. "Those sailors from the *Madeira* were in there! Can we peek inside?" She said this with an excited whisper, like it would be a mischievous thing to do.

Alex lifted the wooden bar from the latch, and then pulled. The light spilling through the open door was enough for them to make out a floor covered with bark and wood chips and, along one side and the rear, rows of stacked wood.

Kate inhaled deeply through her nose. "I just love the smell of cut wood!"

Within the familiar smell, Alex pictured the ten freezing, packed-in sailors hugging each other for warmth. He could see the pain in their eyes after watching a shipmate drown. They were like his own eyes after watching his son die, his own eyes that tormented him every time he looked in a mirror.

At the water's edge, they stood side by side on a beach of cobblestones. A few miles out, a cargo ship headed for Duluth. Northeast, past the boathouse, a lone seagull soared above the water, veered toward shore, and was joined by a second gull.

Alex tentatively moved behind his wife, wrapped his arms around her. Kate held his hands at her waist and craned her neck to peck his cheek with a kiss.

"Let's stay here," she said, as a gentle wave massaged the rocky shore. "Right here, like this…. This is perfect." She rose on her tiptoes and nuzzled the back of her head into his chest. "I'm sorry, Alex. For all my …" She was starting to say something about Michael, he knew, about how bad she felt for the anger she could not quite shake and for the forgiveness she could not quite give. He had heard it before.

He shushed her, not an abrupt shush but a soft one. He hoped she knew what it meant: *Kate, I know. I'm sorry, too. A hundred times a day, I'm sorry. Let's just leave this moment alone and not force the past into it.*

The pair of seagulls flew so close, they heard the flapping of sinewy wings against the air as the birds sped toward an outcropping of rocks down the shore.

He loved Kate so close, and loved that she welcomed his embrace. He wanted to say something romantic, but he had lost his romantic touch so he kept quiet.

"You sure we can only stay one week?" Kate asked.

"Afraid so."

"How much would a place like this cost?"

"No idea." Alex wondered how many hundreds of thousands or even millions of dollars it would take to buy Stonebrook: all the acres of land, the magnificent cottage, the lakeshore footage. He made a mental note of their life savings and sighed.

Finally, Kate said, "Alex?"

"Hmm?"

"I'm cold."

In the fireplace of Stonebrook's great room, Alex lit a fire, but then a draft of cold air poured down the chimney and started to fill the room with smoke.

"Alex, do something!" Kate said, fanning a hand in front of her face, and then she ran for the back porch to open windows.

At first, he became confused. In the past, urgent situations flustered him, but something was different here: *Action,* he thought. *Take action!*

He took a deep breath through his shirt and grasped a section of newspaper from a basket next to the fireplace. He rolled it up, lit it in the sputtering fire, and then plunged it like a torch up the flue. With a sucking sound, flames and smoke reversed direction and shot straight up the chimney.

Kate came back in, an arm over her mouth. "Hey, good job, babe. Guess I can close a couple of those windows now."

She turned back to the porch then suddenly clutched his arm. With an expression of shock on her face, she pointed outside.

Alex followed her line of vision and saw a tall man—a *huge* man—walking straight toward the cottage from the lake, an ax in hand. It was a situation, he thought, that smacked of the illogical, like a scene from a nightmare dropped into reality. Instead of chopping the back door down, the man veered around the side of the cottage toward the front. He was a shark, circling.

"What's he doing?" asked Kate. She clicked her fingernails together, as she always did when she was scared. "Alex, I don't like this—lock the doors."

After locking the three cottage doors, Alex glanced out front and saw a little yellow pickup parked in the driveway next to their Tahoe. "I don't see him…."

Kate screamed, "There he is! There he is! Out back again! He's carrying—something else now—" She squinted to get a good glimpse. "Wood! He's got wood!"

Alex came up next to her and Kate shoved a fire poker into his hand. She grabbed the end of a fireplace bellows with both hands like a baseball bat.

"He's like a Big Foot," she announced.

To Alex, the man no longer seemed to pose a danger. While somewhere past middle age, he looked boyish. His hair was a mop of black and gray, and unruly. His face was clean-shaven and blush-red from the outdoors. Almost comically, he wore a green wool sweater with leather shoulder and elbow patches, navy slacks, and brown sandals with white socks. The sleeves of his sweater ended a good two inches short of thin wrists. What struck him most were the man's downcast eyes. They were tired or timid. He was a far cry from what Alex imagined an ax-wielding serial killer would look like.

"Pretty snazzy outfit for a Big Foot," Alex replied as the man made his way toward the lake.

"Where's his ax?" asked Kate, still worried.

"Kate, he's harmless."

"You don't know that."

The man's long strides took him to the woodshed. He bowed his head and disappeared inside. Through the open windows on the porch, they heard hollow *chunking* sounds: pieces of split wood dropping on a stack. Then there was a series of smaller *chunks:* wood getting organized.

Alex pointed toward the shed with the poker. "See? He's just a worker guy. Bringing around firewood."

"But ... he's so tall."

Alex glanced down at his wife, wondering if she was kidding. "So am I."

"Yeah, but you don't tote an ax around with you."

Alex nodded. "Got me there." His wife, he knew, was a marvelous study of contrasts. Lone strangers made her uneasy and finding an unlocked door at night petrified her. Yet she had taken self-defense classes and firearm safety training; she could do intense sessions of Buti Yoga that he knew would leave him gasping on the floor. If presented with a fight or flight situation, her default mode would be fight. She could and would take a man down. He added, "Just wondering, though. That bellows in your hands. Is that supposed to protect us in some way?"

Finally Kate smiled back, relaxing a little. She innocently pumped the handles together, blew air in her husband's face. "I'll blow air at him."

Alex smiled at his adorable wife because he knew better. She would crack an intruder's skull with it.

The man reemerged, and Kate shoved Alex out to the porch to find out who he was, but the man's long strides already took him around to the side. He seemed to be in a hurry, and Alex guessed the man knew he was being watched.

Opening the front door, Alex stepped outside and waved as the pickup started. Alex said, "Hello?" but the truck was already moving. "Hello!"

Kate stepped outside with him as the truck sped off and disappeared in the trees at the bend in the gravel driveway.

In all the commotion, the fire had burned down to embers. Alex added a couple logs, and they discussed whether the man might return later in the week.

Kate lay on the couch with her smartphone. They had not brought their laptops and had agreed they would not recharge their phones. Hers would be getting low soon.

Alex picked up the guest book that his wife had brought down. He reread some of John Mead's entry and could not help but dwell upon one sentence in particular:

> Yet with respect to the *Madeira*, with respect to Stonebrook ... ledgers and records ... are dead wrong.

It implied a link between the *Madeira* wreck and Stonebrook. His dad had a book on shipwrecks of the Great Lakes. He thought about calling him.

At the bottom of the page, well under John Mead's signature, he noticed three words scribbled in tiny print. The words were in Latin. Kate had not mentioned the passage. Perhaps she hadn't even seen it.

Contemplata aliis tradere

It was the same phrase John Mead had written on the bottom of Alex's blueprint that he had turned in for his Thresholds of Architecture class. He had dismissed it then as one of those odd things the elderly do. Alex had taken a semester of Latin in high school and had forgotten nearly all of what he had learned except for the phrases *tempest fugit*—time flies; *e pluribus unum*—from many, one; *cave canum*—beware of the dog. He remembered *contemplata aliis tradere*, as well. It meant, "Handing on to others the fruit of our contemplation."

John Mead had contemplations he wanted to hand on. To whom? What was it he contemplated?

Alex tossed another log on the fire and then pressed a palm against a large, warm flagstone. He ran a finger over the gritty mortar between it and the surrounding stones as if the hearth itself had somehow absorbed the stories of this ancient cottage, stories his fingers could read like Braille.

Alex and Kate ate a late supper of steaks on the grill and shared a bottle of Merlot served in the canning jar glasses they found in the cupboard. Kate mentioned a drive up to Grand Marais in the morning but Alex had hoped to stick around the estate, maybe poke around a little. But he also did not want to spoil whatever was happening between them, so he agreed.

After dinner and cleaning up together, they perused books from the immense library. They had planned to make another fire so Kate could have s'mores, but she started to yawn. She gave Alex a goodnight kiss on the lips and went upstairs to bed.

Alone, Alex marveled at the thousands of books, all alphabetized. He was searching for something but had no idea what. Standing on the five-step ladder, he scanned the spines of several titles.

The 120 Days of Sodom by Marquis De Sade
Absalom, Absalom! by William Faulkner
The Adventures of Huckleberry Finn by Mark Twain
The Age of Innocence by Edith Wharton
The Age of Reason by Thomas Paine

He got down, walked over squeaky floorboards to the right-most shelf and kneeled on the floor to look at the last few titles.

Watership Down by Richard Adams
The Wealth of Nations by Adam Smith
Yertle the Turtle and Other Stories by Dr. Seuss
Zadig by Voltaire

He smiled at the inclusion of Dr. Seuss in such a collection. He pulled it, looked at several pages, put it back. Feeling sufficiently uneducated, he read titles here and there. Then, within the titles beginning with the letter C, he glimpsed one that gave him a chill:

Contemplata aliis tradere.

Pulling it, he saw a classic-looking cover: brown leather and ornate, gold lettering that smelled of dust and time. Leafing through the first several pages, he gathered it was either by or about the Dominican Order of monks. *Handing on to others the fruit of our contemplation* had evidently been their motto.

From the fifth or sixth page, a folded piece of paper fell to the floor. Alex picked it up and opened it. It was a note written entirely in Latin. He made out a word here and there, but he understood none of it. At the bottom, though, was a signature in English he immediately recognized:

John Mead

Go to your bosom: Knock there, and ask your heart what it doth know.

—William Shakespeare, Measure for Measure (1604)

Sunday: The Sailor's Stone

Chapter 3

The sun found a break in the clouds, and morning light streamed into the bedroom of Stonebrook Cottage. With eyes still closed, Alex shivered. He had never before had such a vivid, ominous dream. In it, he had been lying on a small inflatable raft in a tranquil bay, the lap of warm water soothing him. Ripples in the water formed beneath him, interrupting the peace, and he opened his eyes. The ripples turned into waves and his raft lifted and spun. The water turned cold and black, dark clouds blocked the sun, sleet pelted his body in a great tempest. An ice-cold wave broke over his raft, and he plunged into the water. He tried to swim but his feet were tangled in something. He went under, and down. Down into what, he did not know, because he woke up.

And thank God.

When he opened his eyes, he saw Kate lying just inches away on her side, her mouth slightly open, snoring softly.

Positioned in such a way, he noticed, she presented an even steeper incline for the quilt-lake than yesterday morning. He imagined water from the lake cascading down her Gulliver body in torrents. The rebuilt cabin would be re-destroyed. Lilliputian fatalities would be twice as high as yesterday.

Then Alex remembered the Latin note from John Mead and his heart quickened. He nudged his wife. "Kate?"

No answer.

"Katherine …"

She muttered, "What time is it?"

"I don't know. There's something I want to show you."

"Not yet."

"It's a note."

Kate opened her eyes. "For me?"

Confused, Alex replied, "No, it's from John Mead."

His wife plunked her head against his chest and then yawned loudly. "In that case, I'll need a shower first. And coffee. *Lots* of coffee."

Breakfast was blueberry muffins and oatmeal with banana slices on top. Alex liked the fact that the cast-iron stove had the word FAVORITE across the front. It was short and squat like none he had ever seen. Not even his great grandma's old stove back when he was a little kid compared. There must be a trick to using it that Alex had not yet figured out. *Finesse*, he thought, as he spooned out the runny, lumpy oatmeal. *That's what it takes. A cook with finesse who knows the hot spots and can stir or flip or turn at just the right moments. A cook who—*

"Happy anniversary, honey!" Kate entered the kitchen in her terrycloth robe and slippers, with her hair wrapped in a large white towel. In her hands was an envelope. She came up to him and hugged tightly. "Happy ten years, Alex."

In his excitement about the note and his idiotic preoccupation with the stove, he had forgotten today was the day. His card for her was still in his suitcase, still unsigned.

"Kate—" He kissed his wife and hugged her. His eyes moistened. He was sad for her because he was so incredibly inept. "Happy anniversary," he whispered in her ear. This week at the cottage, he had intended to do better. "I—your card. It's upstairs."

Kate shushed him softly as he had done to her on the beach. With a slight smile, she said, "I know. I saw it in your suitcase. And, thank you. It was lovely. Now, where's this note of yours?"

Alex told her to check the map table in the library as he pulled over-done muffins from the oven.

When she saw the Dominican Order book with the Latin saying on the cover, she said, "Hey, neat. The saying from the guestbook."

"The neat part's inside. Open it."

Kate started to thumb the pages and immediately found the slip of paper. She scanned down the paper and after a moment, she read out loud the only thing she could understand: "John Mead." She clutched her robe closed at her neck and swallowed hard. "Can you read any of this?"

"No. A few words look familiar but that's about it. We need a Latin-English dictionary."

"Think they have one in Grand Marais? And maybe a charger for our phones?"

"I doubt Grand Marais would have a dictionary. Too small. Two Harbors, maybe. At the library. As to the phones—"

"I know, I know," interrupted Kate with a sigh. "We agreed. No charging." She walked over to the dining room table, note in hand, and sat down. She cut off the blackened bottom of her muffin and then glanced at the note next to her plate. "We're not going to Grand Marais today then, are we?"

The Two Harbors Public Library was closed on Sundays, but they parked on the street in front anyway and walked down Waterfront Drive toward the harbor and the only bookstore in town.

At a corner, Kate pointed to a sign across the street and announced, "Hey, I'm going to get some coffee at Louise's Place. What kind of coffee do you want? Half-caf soy almond latte?"

Alex raised his eyebrows. His wife was teasing him. Unlike Kate, who knew the "palate acidity" of the different types of coffee beans, Alex always thought the term sounded like a painful dental disorder. All he knew about coffee was he liked it black, strong, and first thing in the morning. "It's almost eleven thirty, dear. After I find our dictionary, I'm going to have a beer right there." Alex nodded to an establishment on the corner next to Louise's, enticingly called, The Pub. "Then I'm going to solve our Latin mystery."

Kate laughed at him; it was her belly laugh, the one he loved. Her blue eyes that he swore used to change color with her mood and had for too long been stuck in a shade of dark blue, seemed to lighten. It was a moment of the vibrant Kate, the one he missed. Since arriving at Stonebrook, something about the place was allowing both their old selves to reemerge. Or maybe it was just the fresh air.

Paige and Turner Booksellers, sandwiched between a True Value hardware store and an American Legion, had a cowbell that announced Alex's entrance. Inside, towering stacks of books, magazines, and comic books almost made him duck and cover his head. The store was narrow but long, the dimension of a few bowling lanes. Packed shelves with jutting books constricted the long, narrow aisles. Hung from pegs on the wall behind the counter were three placards with quotes:

> A room without books is like a body without a soul. – Cicero
> The books that the world calls immoral are the books that show the world its own shame. – Oscar Wilde
> This is not a book that should be tossed lightly aside. It should be hurled with great force. – Dorothy Parker

The passages, positioned as they were at the front of the cave-like bookstore, seemed more like caution signs against literary avalanches rather than invitations to literature.

A hefty clerk stood up from behind the counter and nodded at his customer. His cheeks and nose were a patchwork of tiny dark veins and had a rough texture, like the underside of a leaf.

"So is there really a 'Paige Turner'," quipped Alex, "or is that just a catchy name for the store?"

"Sign says Paige *and* Turner," replied the man. "Paige passed on four years ago."

"I'm sorry." Alex assumed he was talking to Turner.

"What can I do for you?"

"Do you happen to have a Latin dictionary? I just need to translate a passage."

"Latin?" asked Turner as he ambled around the counter and toward the back of the store. His wide frame brushed up against several hardcover books in the photography/arts section when he stopped abruptly and turned around. "How about Greek?"

"No, *Latin*." Alex replied, smiling. "The passage is in Latin so I need a Latin-English dictionary."

The man harrumphed as if put off by his customer's unwillingness to compromise and then continued deeper into the store. Mumbling to himself, he scanned a section of dictionaries and foreign language textbooks. "Aha! Thar she blows!" One of his fat knuckles rapped the binding of volume 1 of a huge 2-volume boxed set, and then he squeezed around the corner to leave his customer alone.

Finding a folding chair in a nook of self-help books, Alex opened one of the massive books to start looking up words.

Before long, he heard, "You want to buy the dictionary?" It was Turner and he was peeking over *Men Are from Mars, Women Are from Venus.*

Alex looked at the price on the back of the box: $295. He had never seen such an expensive dictionary in his life. "I don't think I can afford it."

"I'll give you a deal."

"How much?" Alex asked.

"Ten bucks plus tax."

Back in the front, Alex glanced out the window: still no sign of Kate. *She must be talking coffee with Louise.* As Turner rang up the dictionary, he started in with small talk. "Yeah, bad ticker," he said.

"Excuse me?"

"Paige. She was stacking a batch of secondhand Clancy hardcovers when it happened. He was her favorite novelist of all time, by the way." He held his left hand up to his chest as he continued stabbing register keys with his right. "Goddamn heart attack." He pointed with his forehead to a bookshelf that now held a collection of *Harry Potter* books. "When she hit the floor, she bumped the shelf. A dozen copies of *Executive Orders* and the whole goddamn case landed right on top of her."

Turner squinted, leveled his eyes on Alex. "*Executive Orders* is eight hundred and seventy four pages."

"Oh my. I'm sorry," Alex replied, holding back a smile.

The register drawer, evidently sick of the abuse, finally sprang open. Turner dropped in Alex's cash and started sliding out change one coin at a time. "Her last words were 'Clancy is a,' then those goddamn red-white-and-blue books smothered her like a flag-draped casket."

"That's horrible," Alex said as solemnly as he could. Except it struck him as the funniest *goddamn* thing he had heard in months. Laughter expanded in his stomach and shot up his esophagus so quickly that he nearly gagged trying to swallow it down. Only by conjuring the image of ashen-faced *Madeira* sailors in a woodshed was he able to maintain the illusion of sadness on his face. He prayed that his watering eyes would pass for held-back tears.

"Her final words were really 'Clancy is a …'?" asked Alex, despite his better judgment. A snigger escaped his mouth that he tried to cover with a cough.

"That's right," replied Turner. He started to look at Alex suspiciously. "'Clancy is a …'"

"Is a what?" *Swallow, swallow, swallow.*

"Don't know. She didn't finish."

Oh, dear Lord, make him stop, thought Alex. Even the sailors in his vision started giggling and slapping knees.

Turner continued, "I called 911, I shook her and slapped her, but she never came to."

In a moment of silence—one man in somber remembrance, the other in stifled hilarity—the two men contemplated the poor woman's demise.

"Hope I go the same way, right here," added Turner. "Well, except for the Clancys. My preference would be a bunch of Kerry Caseys or Dennis Herschbachs."

Alex wondered what might have happened if he had come into the store asking for *The Sum of All Fears*, and this was the thought that put him over the edge. Unable to speak, he grabbed his books and ran out of the store just as Kate came around the corner down the sidewalk. His laughter, he saw, startled her. Then she smiled—no, she *beamed*. This made him realize that he had been turning into a Turner himself and that was the last thing in the world he wanted. For a moment Alex wondered if Turner was watching but decided he just didn't care. He had more laughter in his belly, a lovely wife, and a beer waiting for him at a place called The Pub. So he laughed. He laughed until he cried.

Inside the old brick building on the corner of Waterfront and 1st Street, The Pub had a burgundy-colored tin ceiling and hardwood floors. It was an Irish pub complete with green signs, clovers and Guinness beer on tap but what the owner brought for Alex was a pint of something called Surly Furious. As Kate scoured the menu for an organic salad option that she wasn't finding, Alex took a drink of the caramel-toffee ale and then started to scour the dictionary with an equal lack of success. Unlike English, Latin was considered an "inflected" language: a language that relied almost entirely on changes in the words themselves to indicate their grammatical function in a sentence. Same as in high school, he did not know what to do with all the endings on the stem words.

They ordered lunch and he returned to his task, hunkering over the Latin passage, when Kate announced, "My Lord, you look like a monk in a monastery. I've clearly lost you to a dictionary, haven't I?"

"Well," he replied, "that and beer." Undeterred, he took a sip of the Furious and continued working. The Latin message started with *Non omnis moriar*. He looked to his notes: *Non* was easy—it meant *not*. Omnis meant *all* or *every*. But how should he translate *moriar*? *Mora* meant *delay*; *morium* meant *character* or *morals*; *morior—to die, wither away, decay*; but *moror* meant *to stay, remain, reside, linger*. Which was it? Dying and withering or staying and lingering?

It was the ending of the word—what was it called, *declension*? It was the declension that was the key to the meaning of the entire sentence. Within the ending was the case, the gender, the number—the whole enchilada.

He ate lunch with his head in the dictionaries, and after Kate finished, she excused herself to go walk the breakwater that protected Agate Harbor.

Forty minutes later she returned to find him still at the table by the windows scribbling notes.

"Well?" she asked, plopping back down in her chair. "Any luck?"

"I'm sort of stuck. You want to hear what I've translated so far?" he asked.

"Does it make sense yet?"

"Not really."

"Then, no. I'll wait. Let's go back, Alex. I want to do some Buti."

Chapter 4

The stretch of Minnesota 61 between Two Harbors and the cottage ran along the shoreline of Lake Superior. It cut through woods, spanned streams, and tunneled through massive cliffs.

Exiting the northeast side of the second tunnel, Alex took in the scenery. It seemed as if they had emerged into something wilder. The trees were taller, the hills steeper, the streams wider, their falls more precipitous. The waves on Superior looked darker than they did near Two Harbors. Colder. Up here, they had passion; they hid secrets.

Around a sharp turn they saw the sign for Split Rock River ahead.

Quickly, they were upon the bridge over the river and he slowed the SUV. They looked to the right past the footbridge below that spanned the mouth of the river and Alex had a vision of what it had looked like the early morning hours of November 28, 1905. Half out of the water, the *Edenborn* was bashed and dented like a pop can kicked all the way home by an angry boy. He saw panicked men scrambling and jumping from the vessel to shore. Alex imagined this as if it had been captured on a grainy, black and white newsreel, the men moving in a jerky fast forward. Then all the men stopped. One of them stepped forward and looked through more than a century of time right at him. The man was speaking to him but Alex couldn't hear.

Just past the river, the road plunged back into forest. Alex scrutinized the trees on the lakeside, where the entrance to Tudor House, the place where the sailors had found their shelter, might be. He caught a glimpse of a narrow gap in the trees and saw an overgrown dirt road. In a second, it was behind them, out of sight.

A few minutes later, they turned into the long drive of Stonebrook Cottage and pulled up next to an old yellow pickup truck.

Before they got out, Kate reached for Alex's hand.

"Kate, he's just a worker here. I promise."

"We don't know that."

"Tell you what: you take the driver's seat and lock the doors. I'll go talk to him. How does that sound?"

"I guess. If he comes at you, run back and we'll peel out of here."

"*Peel?*" Alex smiled at her corny word.

She kissed him, a solid smooch on his lips. "Just be careful, okay?"

As Alex walked around the left side of the cottage, he felt like he was searching for a skinnier, older version of Lennie from John Steinbeck's *Of Mice and Men*. Out back, he'd find the childlike monster crouched next to a fire, eating beans with ketchup or stroking a dead mouse.

Suddenly, there he was, a mere twenty feet away. Walking directly toward Alex.

A knife in his hand.

Fear drew up tight like shrink-wrap and stole Alex's breath. The man wore gloves blackened by fresh dirt, and upon closer examination Alex was relieved to see that the man carried a trowel, not a knife.

"Hello," Alex said.

Perhaps because of his great height, the man stood erect and yet his body swayed, like a tower. One leg was bent at the knee to serve as a brace. A thin, gray scarf hung limply around his neck like a dead snake, but he was otherwise dressed the same as yesterday.

"In case you've been wondering," continued Alex, "my wife and I are staying here the full week."

The man had not yet looked directly at Alex. He scrutinized the ground between them, as if looking for something he had dropped there. Finally, he looked up—not at Alex, but a little off to the right. His large eyes blinked behind small, thick glasses. "That's nice." His voice was deep, but tentative.

There was a definite uneasiness about the man, thought Alex, as if he was not accustomed to people, not used to conversation. Perhaps he wished to be left alone so he could walk back to his truck and go about his business, whatever that might be. Tomorrow morning they would see him out back with a chainsaw. The next day he might be dragging around a wood chipper, and the day after that he'd have an armful of dynamite sticks or a machete as long as a hockey stick. All this would become routine.

So Alex tried to find out more. "My name's Alex."

"Hello."

"So, then … what's your name?"

"Shepherd."

"Nice to meet you, Shepherd."

"I mind Stonebrook Cottage."

"I see," Alex replied, nodding.

After another silence, Shepherd added, "Or … Paul." The tone of his voice had become warmer and softer. "Shepherd is just a nickname, and not my favorite. You may call me Paul." The man still did not look Alex in the eye but his gaze was getting closer—it looked to be on Alex's feet or legs.

"So what are you doing out here, Paul?" asked Alex. Kate would have applauded his directness because directness often went against his nature.

"Planting peonies."

Both men looked at Paul's dirty gloves and the man held them up as proof of his claim.

"Don't you do that in the spring?"

"Not peony bulbs. It's best to plant them in the fall. The air is cool and the soil is warm. The roots need to establish themselves."

Alex focused on a cluster of pine trees and the lake in the distance. It was awkward looking Paul in the eye because it seemed a violation of his personal space. "So you run this place, then?"

"Maintenance and upkeep. I clean inside between renters—make sure you have fresh towels and the like." Paul got a worried look on his face but continued staring at his gloved hands. "You out of fresh towels?"

"Nope, we're good." Alex glanced back at his wife and realized only he was in her line of sight—Paul was around the side of the cottage—so he gave her a quick, all-is-well nod. "Who owns Stonebrook, anyway?" he asked, turning back to Paul.

"No one, really. A lawyer from out east came around a couple months ago and told my mother that when the owner died—a man by the name of John Mead—they needed someone to fix it up so people could come and stay. Mother offered my services."

"The lawyer actually came out here?" asked Alex. "All I got was a phone call."

Alex was about to ask another question when Paul asked one of his own: "Have you seen the lake today?" The man looked concerned.

"Pardon?" Something in the man's voice suggested that he thought Alex should have known what he was talking about.

"The lake. Have you seen it today?"

"Oh yes, it's beautiful. It's a beautiful lake."

Paul turned around to consider the water, apparently confirming something he saw, and then turned back. "Not today. There's loneliness. Passion."

"Passion?"

"Superior needs to release every so often. She's quiet now, but she's gathering."

Alex got a chill.

Paul finally looked Alex in the eye. It was a jolt. Unlike scholarly men who have an aura of braininess about them—in their walk, their mannerisms, their facial expressions—with

Paul there were no such advertisements. And in his gaze, Alex caught the intended message as clearly as if the man had spoken it: *You see passion there, too, Alex. I know you do.*

The lake did seem passionate. But he could not explain why.

"Well, excuse me," Paul said. "I should get back to my chores." Then instead of continuing to his truck where he would come upon Kate, he turned and went around back again.

Back at the car, Kate looked agitated. She had not budged from the driver's seat, and her hands were gripping the wheel. As he walked up, she opened her door a crack and said, "What the hell was that? Are you okay?"

"Sure," Alex replied, startled. "Why?"

"Why were you swooning like that? I figured he must have shot you with a tranquilizer gun. And why were you looking all over the place when you where talking?"

"I'm fine. It's just … you'll understand if you meet him. He avoids eye contact when you're talking with him. And he has a hard time keeping his body still, I guess. Was I really swooning, too?"

"Yes. I thought you were about to pass out."

Alex was going to add that he figured the man was shy but realized that was not quite true. "Well, he's just a worker here. He's planting peony bulbs right now. Come on, let's go in."

Alex sat on the couch with the Latin passage, the dictionary, and the Stonebrook guest book. He reread his efforts at a translation. He erased, penciled in changes, tried to force some sense into it.

Kate decided to do her Buti Yoga workout later and instead had pictures of their three-week European honeymoon strewn over the dining room table. Alex walked over and checked her progress. Their three days in London was neatly condensed to two scrapbook album pages, and adorned with tiny British flags and Big Ben stickers. She was moving on to Alnwick. By the end of the week, she would likely have their honeymoon done.

Alex strolled through the great room to the back porch and saw Paul in the distance. Evidently done with his peony bulbs, he was now stooped over a sapling, wrapping wire meshing around its trunk. When he stood, his tall body dwarfed the tiny tree like he was Paul Bunyan. Then he picked up a stack of mesh sheets and a burlap sack, and disappeared in the dense trees to the southwest.

"Kate," announced Alex, not taking his eyes off the spot where Paul disappeared, "I'm going outside."

He found the narrow path through the trees, and a minute later heard the murmur of a brook. Then he saw Paul. He was on the ground, sitting cross-legged, tapping a wooden stake into the soil. At first, Alex kept his distance, not certain if he should disturb the man, but then he took a deep breath and walked right up.

"Hi," he said, kneeling. He felt foolish, like a naïve boy scout watching a troop leader. "What kind of tree is that?"

Paul pulled out two lengths of twine from his sack and two four-inch long pieces of a garden hose, set them on the ground, and then hammered another stake. *Tap-tap-tap.* "Northern white cedar."

"What's the screen going to be for?"

Tap-tap-tap-tap. "Protection."

"From what?"

Tap, tap. Tap-tap-tap. "To keep the white-tailed deer away."

Alex brushed his hand across a swath of moss on the ground. He plucked up a bit of the mint-green matter. "I don't mean to sound cruel or anything, but why do we care if the white-tailed deer eats the northern white cedar?" He held the moss up to his eyes, inspecting it. "They need to eat, don't they?"

"But they can eat them elsewhere. Cedars are good for cooling canopies over waterways and they help prevent erosion."

"Same with other trees, though, right? What about maples or birch or oaks?" Alex tore at the moss, sniffed it. It smelled like dirt.

"But once established, the northern white cedar lives for centuries. Up to five hundred years. When it does finally die and fall into a river or brook, it provides cover for fish for decades because it rots so slowly."

Alex looked at the water flowing before them. "What kind of fish does this brook have?"

"Not much of any kind lately … too much fishing in Superior, too many deer, and too few northern white cedars along its banks.

"You know," continued Paul, "it's not actually even a brook. According to the Department of Natural Resources, it's a river, but folks around here have always just called it Stonebrook because the cottage has been here as long as anyone can remember."

Paul strung the twine through the garden hoses, wrapped the hoses around the sapling trunk, straightened the tree, and tied the twine pieces to the stakes. He started to wrap wire meshing around the trunk. He did all this expertly.

"What do you hear in it, Alex?"

"Hmm?" Alex had been staring at Paul's fast hands.

"What do you hear in this brook? What does it tell you?"

"I don't know … I hear water. Movement." Alex tossed a pebble into the water and it made a quiet, high-pitched *plop* sound. "Why? What do you hear?"

"Laughter," Paul replied. "The laughter of little girls. A brook has innocence. It is unassuming and playful." He tilted his head toward Alex, but his vibrant eyes stayed on the water before them. "Can you see it?"

Alex swallowed. "See what?"

"Life. The *essence* of life. It is captured in a brook—in *this* brook. Born in mountains, it nourishes the forest, feeds the lake. It starts from nothing, carries with it potential, ends into something grander."

"Sounds like a riddle," Alex replied. He stretched his legs out and extended his arms behind him so that his palms were to the ground. Despite feeling silly doing so, he loosened up his mind a little bit: he closed his eyes, envisioned two girls jumping from stone to stone across the brook. They were peasant girls from an earlier time; perhaps centuries ago, because they wore dresses of drab, rough wool. Their bare, muddy feet hopped and skipped. They smiled and giggled, happy for each other, happy to be playing in the brook. He realized his vision was historically inaccurate since there would not have been girls, at least Caucasian girls, playing in this brook even 150 years ago. It hadn't been settled yet. But then, the brook in his mind could be anywhere, and these girls were just girls and he saw and heard them now, the same as Paul.

Just then, he felt indebted to his new friend. "Can I help you with anything?"

"No thanks. This is your vacation. You're supposed to relax."

Alex sighed. Relaxation was the furthest thing from his mind. He thought about the odd man he met not far from here yesterday morning. "You ever see a short, heavyset man around here before? He's, well, mentally challenged in some way?"

Paul shook his head.

Frustrated, Alex looked up through trees at the late afternoon sky. "Non omnis moriar," he said quietly.

Paul finished fastening two pieces of meshing together in a big circle around the tree. He reached over the top of the screen, grasped the tree trunk and jiggled, testing the strength of his work. With a puzzled expression, he asked, "I will not die entirely? *Who* will not die entirely?"

Shocked that he knew Latin, Alex replied, "John Mead, I guess. You ever meet him?"

"No."

Then Alex had a thought: "Paul? Will you come inside with me? There's something I want to show you."

After a hasty introduction to a still-leery Kate, Alex put Paul to work, and ten minutes later the man had the note properly translated. When he read, his voice flowed thick and slow like honey.

> I will not die entirely. For as long as these words exist and can be read, I remain merely dormant. If you have discovered and can comprehend this note, I thank you, for a portion of me has consequently been reborn and I am again young and shiny—

Paul glanced up from the paper and quickly apologized that *shiny* may not be the right word, that he took liberty in a couple spots where an accurate translation was difficult. He continued,

> —even though my age is old and I am dying. But enough of me. My intent in writing is to present a foreigner.

Kate scrunched her nose. "A foreigner?"
Paul flipped through pages of the dictionary. His fingers moved nimbly and traced to a word halfway down a page. "Stranger, perhaps?"

Alex and Kate had pulled their chairs close to Paul, and Alex looked at the word over Paul's finger and read the definition aloud to Kate. *"Extrarius: outward, external/strange, unrelated, foreign."*

They both thought awhile, searching for a more appropriate word. "No," Alex said. It suddenly seemed obvious. "Mystery. He meant a mystery."

"Ah, that should work nicely," said Paul, penciling in the change. He resumed his translation,

> My intent in writing is to present a mystery. In the year of 1905, a great storm buried a man. The man was lost to the ages as if he never existed; yet he remains here forever. Over this man's chest is the Sailor's Stone. Within his heart is a box that contains a key. To find the key you must be a philosopher, a scientist, an artist, a sleuth. You must deduce potentialities, balance probabilities, and choose your path using intellect and passion.
>
> The discovery reveals a second mystery that opens something deeper and more substantial, for a journey to the past is a passage to the future.
>
> Thus, my dearest reader, you have insights to ponder and clues to consider. Use them together to guide you on your journey.
> - John Mead

The three of them sat in silence, as if they needed to digest the translation before they could discuss it.

Finally, Alex turned to Kate. "We already know the answer to the lost-man part, don't we? He's the sailor who went down with the *Madeira* off Gold Rock Point."

"But what exactly are we supposed to find?" Kate asked. "A box with a key that unlocks something deeper and more substantial? What's that mean?" Just then, Kate sat upright, her eyes wide: "His body isn't still down there, is it? Paul, do you know?"

"I remember the story of the *Madeira*. Whatever became of the dead sailor's body I can't say, but it most likely would have been torn apart against the cliff. If it got trapped inside the wreck they would have retrieved it, though, even in those days. The wreck isn't deep. The largest section of hull rests on a slope—from a depth of about thirty feet to seventy or so."

"So how do we find a body that isn't there?" Alex asked. "Is all this just metaphor, then?"

"It's supposed to be a *first* mystery, so obviously there's more," Kate replied. "Like this is just a start."

"But more what?" Alex asked. There was a hint of disappointment in his voice. "A clue, a discovery, a clue, another discovery? What's the point? What's the prize?"

Kate replied, "Well, he did say there was an insight within the message, too. The part that struck me as odd was where he wrote that because we were reading it, he felt alive, like he was reborn or something."

Just then, Alex perked up. "Like we woke up something in his cottage, or woke *him* up."

"Alex, stop it now. If you get me thinking this place is haunted, we won't stay another night."

"No, I don't mean like that."

"How did you mean it, then?"

Alex paused, organizing convoluted streams of ideas. His thoughts were sometimes like abstract paintings; layered, textured, and visual. Putting them into words oversimplified them, and rarely captured what he was truly thinking.

"By us reading his message, we now have an awareness of John Mead and an impression of the sort of person he might have been. I think he intended for his words to stir us to think of him as a person who not just merely once existed, but as someone who dreamed and, maybe, a person who had something important to pass on, some great piece of knowledge."

Kate stared at Alex blankly from the far end of the table. Paul was scanning the walls of the cottage, listening intently. Alex knew he was following.

"Because when you think of someone who has passed on," Alex continued, "you tend to dismiss them, don't you? They're gone, they're a memory."

Alex saw Kate's face flush. He knew she was thinking of Michael because he most assuredly was. He was hitting a nerve, a big nerve. They had admitted to each other on more than one occasion that when their son died, they felt him slip away. Really, truly, slip away. And Kate said the same about her mom. "So John Mead," he continued, "is trying to keep in touch."

"Why?" asked Kate. Her arms were crossed.

"I don't know, to keep the essence of himself alive? His beliefs, hopes. Insights." Alex thought of a ship like the

Madeira drifting and rocking helplessly just offshore, in its hold a treasure John Mead had placed there.

Finally, Paul spoke up from his position by the windows. "I didn't know Mr. Mead. But since he didn't have children, at least according to my mother, maybe he felt that whatever meaning he had attained in his life would be lost forever." Paul paused, looked down at his hands. "And isn't that a more troubling notion than the prospect of actually dying … being forgotten? Leaving no legacy, no lasting impression?"

"So he's still here," added Alex. "Even though he's dead, he's still here."

"For starters, he better not still be here," Kate replied. "But what exactly is his point?"

Alex exchanged a fleeting look with Paul and then said carefully, "Kate, I think an insight he wishes us to grasp is … how do I say this … is that the human spirit is transcendent. When the heart stops beating, the spirit goes to heaven but it can also remain behind. Let's say John Mead had secrets. Unconfessed sins, perhaps, unrevealed talents, whatever. For a reason we do not yet know, he felt a connection with the dead sailor. To him, maybe this Sailor's Stone could represent a history or a fate that they shared: men lost to the ages, hearts weighed down by despair, something like that. The key could represent his hope for redemption. All we know is that if I'm correct that this is the insight he wanted to share, it is linked with the clue."

Kate shook her head. "How the hell do you get all that from just a few sentences?"

"I don't know," Alex replied. "Because, for me, it's there."

"Well," Kate said, "be that as it may, how do we find a man buried by a storm if we don't even know where he was buried?"

Alex opened his mouth then he closed it. Despite feeling frustrated by their apparent dead-end, he also felt relieved. He had expressed himself well; he had brought up the memory of both Michael and his mother-in-law and Kate did not berate him, did not chide him, did not stomp away in disgust.

"So," continued Kate, "this is what's meant by 'handing on to others the fruit of our contemplation'?"

Alex smiled. He could not help himself. "I suppose it is."

Chapter 5

When Paul left, it was after 4:00 p.m. As they watched his little pickup disappear around the bend, Kate said, "Let's hike up to Gold Rock Point! See what we can see."

"You sure?"

"We can eat out tonight. Come on, Alex. Paul said you could see the *Madeira* from the cliff on a sunny day if the water was calm. Let's go look real quick, okay? Before it gets too cold and dark."

With the sun setting, Alex and Kate emerged from the shadow of the cottage into pinkish-orange light that made everything look leaner and taller. A stand of birch in the backyard was a thicket of elongated sticks, and their white bark took on an eerie phosphorescent glow. Following Paul's directions, they took the overgrown trail to the southwest. It was the same trail that the strange little man had taken, at least until he disappeared. Alex searched for him, and for anyone who might be the Tin Man, but saw no one. He thought about mentioning the incident to Kate but decided against it. It would only freak her out.

At one point, they had to brush through evergreen branches. Further on, they walked past more of the ever-present birch and some aspen. A breeze swept through the trees, and the dead leaves that still clung to branches brushed against each other in parched whispers.

The grade became steeper, their steps shorter. Up and up. Finally they reached a lookout point high over Lake Superior.

Gold Rock Point.

To the southwest, less than a mile away, Split Rock Lighthouse perched on its own mighty cliff. On the horizon, dark clouds were gathering. A cold breeze chilled their faces as they walked with care right up to the edge of Gold Rock.

A solitary, wind-twisted pine stood next to Alex, and he wondered how long it had been there. No taller than he, it was gnarled, misshapen, and bore only a few meager clumps of needles. It would have been a pitiful excuse for a tree had it not survived here, alone, on this inhospitable precipice. As such, it had an appearance of defiant pride, like that of a boxer. Its branches: arms, its tufts of needles: gloved hands. And the seasons: rounds of a never-ending match. The little tree had faced its adversary head on.

Looking down into the water below, they found the surface already in shadows so the massive *Madeira* was hulking out of sight. Over a century ago, ten drenched, exhausted sailors stood in the same spot watching with horror in predawn light as their trapped mate sank with the ship into the heaving, violent water.

Kate took his hand. "This mystery business—about finding a key inside a heart and everything else—it scares me, Alex."

"I think I'll call Dad when we get back," he said, not wanting to let it go. "He has a book on shipwrecks that might have info on the *Madeira*."

Kate shivered; Alex felt it in her hand. "Let's go, then," she said. "It's getting dark and we don't have a flashlight."

"Hi Dad, how's it going? … Oh yes, it's fantastic … uh huh … Say, Dad, I'm on the cell, can you just grab that Lake Superior shipwreck book of yours and look up the wreck of the *Madeira?* … 1905. In a storm known as the Big Blow … Yeah, no problem, just give me a call back … yep … Sounds good, Dad. Thanks."

Alex hung up. Kate sat down next to him at the dining room table, looking worried. "If everything sounds normal, if this 'man buried by a storm' was retrieved and is not, for some un-Godly reason, buried right here … can we just put all this to rest?" She perched on the edge of her chair. "Because the more I think about it, the more bizarre this all seems, Alex. That note in Latin—I just don't know. I like mysteries well enough, you know that, but I don't like strangers—*dead* strangers—telling us to find the body of a man who drowned in Lake Superior a hundred years ago so we can find a creepy key. I mean, we're deep in the woods at a big, old cottage. This could be dangerous. Maybe all this stuff is part of some serial killer's twisted game: whoever's ignorant enough to get sucked in ends up in a scuba diving outfit handcuffed inside the *Madeira.*"

Alex twirled a pencil between his fingers. The Tin Man was on his mind.

"You know?" Kate said, pressing him.

"I know."

Kate put a hand over her husband's. "Lord knows since Michael we've been broken—*I've* been broken. But I'm ready for us to start over now. And you mean too much to me to lose you, too. You do. We have five days left here. Let's relax and enjoy them. We're doing good, Alex. Aren't we? We're close. We haven't been like this at home since, well, you know. With Michael and Mom gone ... I can't lose you, too. Deal?"

The phone rang.

"Deal?" she repeated, before he could answer it.

"Sure. Deal." He picked up: "Hi, Dad. Okay, yes ... yep, just the part about the *Madeira*."

As he listened to his Dad read the account of the accident, he jotted notes. Finally, the answer came and his heart sank. "*Cleveland?*" he asked his Dad. "He was buried in *Cleveland?*"

So they were done; done with this sticky business. A character like John Mead, he thought, was of the past, of the twentieth century, but he didn't even fit in then. A character like John Mead was not of any particular time. Whatever obscure, tarnished key he had to offer would remain buried. Layers of time would settle on it until it was too deep to ever be found.

When Alex hung up, Kate walked behind his chair, massaged his shoulders. "I'm sorry." She bent down, kissed his neck, and whispered in his ear, "Come on, Alex; let's go eat."

The restaurant was up the North Shore in the small town of Tofte. It had started raining—large, splattering drops pocked the windshield—and Alex did not see the entrance until Kate touched his arm and pointed to the sign that read *Bluefin Grill*.

Inside, as they waited to be seated, an older woman asked Kate to take a photo of her and her husband standing next to a wood-carved statue of a bearded, wrinkly sailor who, according to a sign, went by the name of Salty. To Alex's disappointment, Salty did not have a Sailor's Stone over the chest of his yellow rain coat. That would have been way too fortunate. As Kate conducted her customary photo shoot when asked to take a simple picture, Alex turned his attention to a framed print of Split Rock Lighthouse at night, an amazing photo taken by a photographer named Bryan Hansel. Oddly, the lighthouse and keeper's quarters looked like they were leaning in to the lake but what captivated him most was the fog bank beyond the tall cliff of Split Rock. The fog completely concealed Gold Rock Point and its Shipwreck of the *Madeira*. It left the impression that Gold Rock was always in the midst of a storm, even on clear days. As if the Point had secrets. As if—

"Alex, come on," said Kate. She and the waitress holding two menus were both staring at him, waiting for him to come back to the real world.

The upstairs dining room was dark. Chandeliers with clusters of tiny bulbs like bunches of grapes glowed under a ceiling that was barely visible. As they were escorted to a window seat overlooking the lake, he noticed that each table had a single lit candle. Faces of couples floated at the edges of their pools of light, speaking in hushed tones.

After ordering, they sipped wine and Kate talked enthusiastically about a morning hike up Oberg Mountain and lunch at the Koho Café that was just beyond Bluefin Bay at the end of a scenic boardwalk. She talked about walking the shoreline, holding hands.

And for a while, Alex thought it sounded nice. She was wrong: they weren't doing okay here; they were doing great. Their relationship was how it used to be. Tomorrow, he could skip rocks from the beach and she could sit on a driftwood log to count the skips. They could talk about having another child, about their future. On a walk, he could help her up the tricky, steep parts, and when she made it, he could grab her and hold her tight. They could spend their evenings inside at Stonebrook, in front of the fire. In bed.

And she would welcome it. That was the best part.

As they dined, they reminisced about their wedding day. After the plates were cleared, Alex dipped his head into their own little pool of light and reached across the table to hold Kate's hands. "So what was the most romantic night of our honeymoon?"

She stared at him, wide-eyed, thinking. Alex had attended college in England on a six-month study abroad program and had taken her to Europe after they were married. It had been a whirlwind of castles and cathedrals, quaint towns and sprawling cities. "I think Prague. At the opera, and walking the Charles Bridge."

"Not the Shakespeare play at The Globe?"

"Alex, it was The Two Noble Kinsmen. That friendship versus love theme and all that fighting and killing doesn't do it for me. Too twisted. Honestly, I don't know what men see in Shakespeare.

"But Prague, Alex," she continued, her voice thickening, "The castle and St. Vitas cathedral on the hill—how gorgeous! I couldn't get enough of it." Then she added, "I couldn't get enough of *you*.

"So what's your most romantic night?"

"Kingussie," Alex replied.

"Scotland?" Kate sounded incredulous. "The Highlands? Why?"

"I don't know exactly. It felt *right* there. Comfortably romantic, if there is such a thing. Like how an older couple might feel if—"

"If you're saying we're old, that's certainly not romantic."

"No, I mean it was as if—when we were all alone next to that loch—Loch Gynack—and there was nobody around, and hills all around us, it was as if...." Alex grabbed his glass and twirled it gently, looking for the right words.

Kate took a long sip of her wine, leaving him hanging.

"It felt like we had been together for years and years, like we already had a lifetime of accumulated experiences within us." He remembered the ruggedness of the area; the land and lochs were inseparable. "Anyway, those two days and nights, I felt a tighter bond with you, as if we had already been through ... our trials. And we had made it. Right then I felt that we would never part."

He looked at her sheepishly. "Strange, huh?"

"No, beautiful," Kate replied, her eyes moist. "That's beautiful." She dabbed at the corner of an eye. "So it had nothing to do with making love under the stars that night?"

"You got me there," Alex replied, with a smile. "You know me well, my dear Katherine."

Kate lifted her glass. "Well then, here's to comfortable romance … and making love next to lakes."

"I'll drink to that," he replied, getting aroused. He lifted his glass to hers. "We better head back. Lake Superior beckons."

Chapter 6

On the drive to the cottage, the rain had eased. As Kate waited for Alex to unlock the front door, a mist in the air felt silky wet on her skin, like dew-covered spider webs.

Alex had decided against making a fire, asking instead to conclude their romantic evening upstairs. So Kate ushered him up and went into the kitchen for one last glass of wine for them to share.

The pantry door was open a crack, yet she swore it was closed when they left. *Old houses do this*, she told herself. *Don't they? Creak and shift? Latches can unlatch?* She dismissed her concern and, for a moment, thought of surprising Alex with a glass of Tang from the ancient Tang canister he had found in the pantry. She reached for the door but decided against the idea: *too cruel*, she thought, and instead pushed the door closed.

With the wine and a bowl of grapes, she made her way past the dining room table where Alex's notes from his conversation with his father caught her eye.

She switched on the light, set the glass and bowl on the table, and brushed her fingers over the paper. She remembered having once admired her husband's penmanship, not for its neatness—it was an ungainly scrawl that even a doctor would ridicule—but for the way it revealed his creativity and uniqueness. The letters, nearly unreadable, looked as if they floated over the paper; the slants and swirls were choppy and uneven like the fleeting strokes of one of those impressionistic paintings he loved.

Her husband was perhaps the most right-brained—and to her mind, the least-organized—thinker she had ever known. He could be oblivious to so much, yet could imagine and comprehend things in a way that astonished her. When they had visited the Minneapolis Institute of Arts last year, he had become so engrossed in a painting that his unblinking eyes watered. It was the world-famous *The Scream* by Edvard Munch. She had glanced at it, dismissed it with a wince, and then moved on to the next painting. When she noticed he was no longer at her side, she saw him transfixed, his head cocked to one side. She returned to him, and he pressed a thumb and finger between his eyes, trying to stave off tears and to hide the impact the painting had on him. She looked again at the wretched figure in the painting with hands held up to cheeks, evidently, in the act of screaming. It had given her an edgy, uncomfortable feeling, and that was all.

"That's torment, Kate," Alex had told her. "The artist, this Munch fellow, he knew torment like nobody's business."

Her husband knew torment, too. They both did. Life after Michael had been … hell. She knew he was ready to move on, start over, and have another child. She was the one who had been holding them back. She could not get past blaming him.

While Alex's preferences leaned toward lush harmonies and subtle rhythms, in capturing the unusual in the usual, she was nearly the opposite: a "just-the-facts ma'am," her father had always joked. To her, life was action, a process, cause and effect. For as hard as she had tried, she had not been able to forgive.

Until they came here. And thank God for that.

She focused on her husband's jottings, at the details his father had relayed to him from the shipwreck book. She remembered watching him on the phone listening to his father, laboring to get down every pertinent detail.

She made out words here and there in the notes: "schooner-barge … grain, lumber, iron ore … Nov. 28, 1905 … 3:30 a.m., towline with *Edenborn* snapped; *Madeira* to drop anchor, ride out storm … Anchors discovered intact on bow? … 5:30 a.m., *Madeira* strikes Gold Rock … 10-man crew; Fred Benson—hero—clambers to top of cliff, saves all mates but one … Survivors suffer exposure … rescued two days later by tug, *Edna G.*—tug also recovers body of lost mate, remains returned to Clev. Ohio."

The last notation, "remains returned to Clev. Ohio," Alex had underlined, circled, and then crossed out. Kate saw just how disappointed he was that John Mead's clue turned out to be a dead-end.

Before she turned away, a sense of uneasiness chilled her. It was from something she had just read, something out of place. She reread his notes, and there it was:

10-man crew.

Alex had dictated from his father that according to the shipwreck book, the *Madeira* had a ten-man crew and one man went down with the ship.

She opened the guest book, flipping pages until she found the portion of the entry that pertained to John Mead's version of the *Madeira* wreck:

> The night of the massive storm called the Big Blow was over one hundred years ago. Less than a mile from this cottage, the schooner-barge *Madeira,* a vessel half the size of the *Titanic,* separated from her steamship consort, the *Edenborn.* The 11-man crew of the unpowered *Madeira* was to ride out the storm at sea …

Eleven-man crew? Kate wondered who had it right, John Mead or the history book. She recalled a related bit of information, so she continued reading:

> When the toll was tallied, the Pittsburgh Steamship Company had on its ledgers the loss of two men: one from the *Madeira,* one from the *Edenborn.*
> This is all according to historical record.
> Yet with respect to the *Madeira,* with respect to Stonebrook, ledgers and records … are dead wrong.

Kate's heart raced and she held a hand to her chest. *Dead wrong.* If the *Madeira* had another crewman who was killed, what happened to him? With a sense of foreboding, she looked at Paul's translation of John Mead's Latin message. What had once been a subtle nuance, now seemed to stand out as if suspended above the paper like a hologram:

> The man was lost to the ages as if he never existed; yet he remains here forever....

The line reverberated in her mind.

So who was right? She knew, she knew. John Mead was right. There were eleven men on the *Madeira* that night and not only the first mate died. There was a second man.

> Over this man's chest is the Sailor's Stone.
> Within his heart is a box that contains a key.

With a trembling hand, Kate picked up her wineglass and then set it back down. She clenched her eyes shut, afraid that John Mead might descend upon her like a ghost and stroke her neck with hands as cold as the lake. Worse, he might whisper horrific secrets. Secrets of the dead.

In her heart, she knew that whatever was here was real. She knew she had to tell her husband about this little detail he had missed. And then he would get immersed. No more romantic nights, no more relaxation for relaxation's sake. She would tell him that there were *perhaps* eleven men on the ship and *perhaps*, therefore, a man was buried here with a stone marker over his heart and a key in it.

> To find the key, you must be a philosopher, a scientist, an artist, a sleuth. You must deduce potentialities, balance probabilities, and choose your path using intellect and passion.

Just then, she heard a noise from the kitchen. A *click*. She held her breath and listened. The refrigerator kicked in, hummed loudly. *Just the fridge*, she told herself, exhaling. It was a noisy unit. But it seemed like there was something else, too—a rustling at the side door of the house that led to the patio with the gas grill. She checked it out, saw nothing. The deadbolt was unlocked but Alex would often forget to lock doors at home so she figured he just didn't lock up when they left. She opened the door, peaked outside, and then stepped out into the wet, dark night to grab a pair of tongs Alex had left on the table next to the grill.

She saw the outline of Paul through the trees ten yards away. He was staring at her. "Paul? What are you doing?"

The man stepped forward; it was not Paul. This man wore a long, black coat. He had a beard and was smirking.

Before she could scream, he said "Shh, shh, shh," holding fingers to his lips. "We are fine, we are fine. I mean you no harm." The man had a harsh accent—Eastern European or Russian. He maintained a calm expression, yet seemed about to jump out of his skin. He openly stared at her chest then the rest of her body. "I am out for a walk from nearby park and got lost."

The man was too far away for Kate to attack, yet too close for her to make it inside and lock the door if he chose to stop her. She felt a surge of adrenaline and was prepared to kick the man in the groin, gouge his eyes, punch him in the throat; she was ready to wrench his arm behind his back until he screamed.

"Did I see you and your husband in town at the restaurant?" asked the man. "Your husband had the Latin dictionaries, right? What was he doing with the Latin dictionaries?"

Kate swallowed. Instead of retreating, which might draw a rapist to lunge, she stood her ground. "We are on vacation," she replied firmly. "None of that is your business. Whoever you are, leave us alone or I will call the police."

"Your husband," the man started, but paused when his head twitched. "Does he have the synesthesia?"

She thought of her son. *Why do numbers have color, mommy? How does time move in a circle? Why does the violin play such beautiful blue music but drums sound brown?* She thought about Michael's head slamming into the back of Alex's.

"What is synesthesia?" she asked, playing dumb. "If it's a disease of some kind, then no. Alex is perfectly healthy and capable of kicking your ass."

For a moment, the man looked amused, but then his smile disappeared. Kate figured it had nothing to do with her threat. He seemed unsettled by Stonebrook.

"The road's that way," Kate said, pointing.

The man nodded, and smirked again. He turned away and headed around the cottage for the driveway.

Chapter 7

Carrying the bowl of grapes and their wine upstairs, Kate paused on the landing. She didn't want Alex to see her hands shaking.

"Are you coming up?" Alex asked. "What's taking you so long?"

"Be right there," she replied, taking a swig of wine. She decided that here at Stonebrook, against all reason and better judgment, she would not give in to her fear. She would not let the man in the long black coat scare her into running and she would not let him take away her night. She would tell Alex about him later. If he ever returned, she would fight.

When she entered the bedroom, Alex spotted her concern before she was able to tuck it away. "What?" he asked, sitting up in bed. "What is it?"

"Nothing," she replied. Tonight was *their* night, she had decided. Tonight would not be dictated by the likes of dead men and shipwrecks. Or even Michael. It would be her night to love her husband, her time with him before he shoved out to sea in the morning to fight the battles in his mind. Her one consolation was that she could go with him. A lover hidden in the knapsack of her sailor—her sailor sleuth. She could whisper in his ear, explain the details that were lost to him.

She could protect him from the man in the long black coat.

"Here," she said. "Have some wine." She wanted him drunk. Wild.

She handed him the glass and kept the bottom tipped when he was going to stop drinking. When it was gone, she set it down on the table.

And she stripped for him: her sweater and jeans, her bra, her panties, her socks. All that remained was her shame and her fear; it gave her goose bumps and made her naked body shiver, but she did not cover up. She wanted him to see her standing there completely exposed. Somehow, it was a confession, an apology, an expression of vulnerability; it was her way to tell him she needed him to love her. She wanted him to see all this and hoped desperately that he did.

She plucked a grape from the bowl, pressed it between her lips, nibbled, and swallowed. And at last she shed her shame and her fear. At least for tonight.

She slid under the heavy quilt by Alex's feet and kissed her way up.

Her passion was a fire.

"They who dream by day are cognizant of many things, which escape those who only dream by night. In their gray visions they obtain glimpses of eternity, and thrill, in waking, to find that they have been upon the verge of the great secret. In snatches, they learn something of the wisdom which is of good, and more of the mere knowledge which is of evil. They penetrate, however rudderless or compass-less, into the vast ocean of the 'light ineffable'."

—Edgar Allan Poe, Eleonora (1842)

Monday: Mr. Mead's Lantern

Chapter 8

Lying under a tree on a bed of warm, spongy grass next to a river, Alex felt tranquil. Then a lousy fish interrupted the scene. It had caught his eye because each time it sprang from the water, it turned to face him. Its round eyes looked spooked; its mouth opened and closed as if mouthing words; its tail flailed. A heavy rain began to fall with gusting winds and he felt tightness under his armpits—he was lifted by sprouting tree limbs—leaves closed in on him—they whispered, whispered louder and louder. In the rising tempest, it was a raspy, full-throated message that became nearly intelligible:

Shhhhuuumaaanoooo—shhuuumaaaallleeeeavvvv— heeeeereaaarre—sorrrrryyyyseeeeeeeeas.

He had tried to decipher it but could not.

Then he fell. He splashed into water, swallowed by silence. Sodden with weight and ice cold, he tried to swim straight up, but his foot had caught on something—no, something had caught his foot. He kicked frantically—*No! Please, dear God, Enough!*—and he opened his eyes to see his son Michael standing at the foot of the bed. He was wearing the hospital robe that he wore the day he died.

"Dad, you have to find it!" His high-pitched little boy voice sounded thrilled, like he was talking about a pirate's treasure.

"Michael, I'm so sorry," was all Alex could manage in reply. He meant to say he was so sorry about the accident, and that he missed him, but didn't know how to get it out without breaking down in tears.

Michael frowned, dismissing the sentiment. "The Reflectory," he exclaimed. As if that one word held all the answers and made everything better. He ran from the bed to the window. Little hands pressed against glass. "Can't you sense it yet?"

"No, son. What is it?"

"I'm not supposed to say." Michael came back to the bed but turned to look at the bedroom door. "Mom just came in. She's come to wake you for breakfast. Just remember, Dad. Find it. Find the Reflectory."

Something—someone—grabbed Alex's foot. He heard, "Morning, sunsh—" then he kicked and heard, "Ow!"

The cloak of sleep lifted with the smell of bacon, and he opened his eyes. There was Kate, a look of concern on her face, her right hand drawn back defensively. "Alex, you're shaking. What's wrong?"

"Sorry, Kate," he replied. "Just. Just a strange dream, I guess." He didn't want to tell her that he had just dreamed about her son standing right next to her in the room.

On the way to the kitchen, Kate took the tray of dirty dishes out of her husband's hands and set it on the dining room table.

She pointed to the notes from his father's conversation—"Look here,"—then she pointed to John Mead's guest book entry—"here,"—then she slid over Paul's translation of John Mead's Latin message—"and here." She carried the tray into the kitchen, leaving him baffled.

When Alex finally figured it out, he went into the kitchen where he saw Kate at the sink. She turned to him.

"You knew all this last night?" he asked.

"Yes."

"Before dinner?"

"No. Not until we got back from the restaurant. When you went upstairs, I looked at your notes."

He nodded at her. He was about to ask why she hadn't told him last night but decided against it. Last night had been great. They needed a night of passion. It had been their anniversary, after all, and it had been their best day together in over three years. He walked up to her and wrapped his arms around her.

"Thanks, Kate," he said. "Thanks."

Sitting again around the dining room table, Alex told Paul that the body of the sailor who went down with the ship had been sent back to his hometown in Ohio, but that there was a second sailor on the *Madeira* who had died. He told Paul about their fruitless search for a conspicuous stone earlier that morning on the grounds. They had looked down by the beach, all around the cottage, but did not know what this particular stone would look like, so were at a loss.

After listening in his customary silence, Paul said, "If you're telling me we're looking for a different man, perhaps we're supposed to look for a different storm, as well. Have you considered whether John Mead meant that the storm in question was perhaps not actually a meteorological storm?"

Alex shook his head.

"Well," continued Paul, "he must have figured that whoever would go to the effort to translate his message would at first deduce his 'man buried by a great storm' was one-and-the-same as the sailor who went down with the *Madeira* during the Big Blow...."

"Sure," Kate said. "Makes sense."

"But that sailor—he's not the one we're looking for. A body sent back to Cleveland is not a body 'lost to the ages as if he never existed,' and it certainly is not one that 'remains here forever,'" said Paul.

"So why do you think his 'great storm' means something other than The Big Blow?" asked Alex.

"John Mead directed us to the *Madeira* and the events of the night she went down. But the sailor known to have been killed by the Big Blow is not the one he wishes us to find. I'm just saying, what if the mystery sailor was not killed by the Big Blow that night and did not go down with the *Madeira*."

"So he made it to shore?" asked Kate. "What killed him then?"

Alex spoke for his friend: "Another kind of storm ... a metaphorical one—a *struggle*—among men. Even the word *bury*—that the man was *buried* by a great storm; it might mean what we assume, that his body was buried at sea or put in the ground, but *to bury* can mean *to cover or conceal, to hide*. And this key that's inside his heart—"

"So wait—is there literally a body buried here," interjected Kate, "or just metaphorically? Because if there is, what are you guys saying? Would you two dig it up? Would you reach inside his chest cavity and expect to find a box with a key?

Alex glanced at Paul. Paul stared at a point in space.

Alex said, "There is literally a body, Kate. I think there is."

"And which of you two would reach inside the man's remains to retrieve it?" The idea seemed so otherworldly, so ludicrous. To sit around a table and talk about it was one thing, doing the dirty work was something else entirely.

Alex looked his wife in the eye. "There's something more here than a story of a tragic event in 1905...."

"But would you reach inside, Alex?"

Alex recalled the vision of his son begging him to find the Reflectory. "I would, Kate. Truly."

"Wow," Kate said. She took a deep breath and exhaled. "Wow…. Okay, boys, what's the next step, then?"

Alex shrugged. They seemed stuck. An old song came to Alex's mind: "The Wreck of the *Edmund Fitzgerald*," Gordon Lightfoot's haunting song of a Lake Superior storm and a tragic shipwreck that had killed an entire crew.

The lake, it is said, never gives up her dead,
When the skies of November turn gloomy.

The dead on the Fitzgerald, he remembered, were the entire crew: twenty-nine sailors. They were still entombed inside the *Edmund Fitzgerald* at the bottom of the lake because they were too deep to reach.

But in this case, Superior had done more than keep her dead. She had swallowed a man's existence. Other than an allusion in a cottage guest book and a cryptic message in Latin written by a dead man, there seemed to be no other reference to the sailor and no trace.

That evening, Alex sat on one end of the couch with Kate's feet on his lap. She lay across the couch munching the final morsels of toasted marshmallow, chocolate, and graham cracker. "Sure you don't want a s'more, too?" she asked.

Alex was staring into the glowing embers with eyes wide open. "No thanks." The question that burned in his mind was how John Mead knew of this man buried by a storm. Even if he died at a ripe old age, he still had not even been born when the *Madeira* went down. So he must have heard about the sailor's existence from the previous owner of Stonebrook.

It had been such a small crew. The ship was 436 feet long, longer than a football field, but certainly the survivors would have noticed a stowaway and reported the fact. Or if the shipping company's records were inaccurate and there were, say, eleven crewmembers and *two* had died, why would the crew not have said so?

He had already checked the library shelves and the rest of the cottage for old journals or diaries. He had spent hours scouring the cottage grounds for a conspicuous stone but there were stones everywhere—big ones, little ones—the North Shore was full of them.

His thoughts turned to Tudor House, the cottage by Split Rock River where the survivors of the *Edenborn* had found shelter from the storm. Perhaps John Mead had mentioned it by name for a reason; perhaps there was something there that might tell them more about the night of the Big Blow and the wrecks of the *Edenborn* and the *Madeira*.

"Well, you sure have been quiet today," replied Kate, a hint of agitation in her voice.

Alex forced a smile, squeezed his wife's foot. "Just thinking, I guess." They had to find Tudor House. Tonight. According to John Mead, the owner had moved into a nursing home. Only a 'Duke' remained behind—an old dog, perhaps—cared for by a park ranger. There had to be something of interest there.

Kate licked some melted marshmallow off her fingers. "Well, not me. I'm done thinking."

"Kate, we need to pay a visit to Tudor House."

She stopped mid-lick: "You can't be serious …"

Alex glanced at his watch—it was already 10:45—and decided that with or without her, he would go. He had to go. He moved her feet from his lap and then stood. "Tonight's the night. We depart at twenty three hundred hours—just enough time to get ready."

A smile came to the corner of Kate's mouth.

He was taken aback, then remembered she loved action over inaction.

"I love it when you're decisive," she said.

"Oh, and dear," he added, "wear that black sweatshirt of yours; it should be fetching in the moonlight."

Chapter 9

One at a time they scuttled down the steep embankment to the bike path that skirted Minnesota 61, Alex first, and then Kate. At night, the narrow break in the forest from the road toward the lake looked like an opening to a cave. The tall, barren trees cast shadows across the path, tearing moonlight into shards, illuminating nothing beyond.

"Okay," whispered Kate, "before we take another step, will you *please* light that lantern? If a ranger or someone spots us, so be it. I don't want to stumble upon anybody in the dark. I'm liable to have a heart attack.

Alex lit the brass watchman's lantern, which he had found in the study closet, and it cast a sickly yellow glow.

Kate looked from the lantern to the darkness ahead and then back to the lantern. "That's it?" she asked. "Come on, Alex, crank that baby up."

"I did already. The wick's as high as it'll go. You sure you want to come?"

Kate took a deep breath, exhaled, and slid her arm through his. She did not want to stumble upon the man in the long black coat again.

They walked side by side into the night, their feet crunching leaves, their hearts pounding fear.

About fifty yards in, they stepped over a *No Trespassing* sign on a low cable strung across the path. Past that, a short wood-planked bridge spanned a swampy patch of ground. Moss and tufts of grass blanketed the rotting wood. Deep grooves down the middle showed decades of use from carriages and automobiles.

Around a curve and up a hill, they arrived at a clearing where the moonlight returned, and in the eerie white light at the end of a circular, weed-covered court, they saw an ivy-draped house. A steep-pitched gable jutted toward the sky like a sword, while a black chimney stood tall over the roof like a sentry. The place was immense, almost as large as Stonebrook, and had a commanding view of Lake Superior below.

"Tudor House," whispered Alex. There were no lights on and the place had an aura of being abandoned, but he extinguished the lantern anyway so they would be less visible.

Despite the cold, Alex felt sweat in his armpits. The option to turn tail and run, he knew, would receive no argument from his wife, but he willed himself to keep walking.

He rapped lightly on the door.

Kate spoke into his ear, "Why the hell are you knocking?"

He frowned at her. After a moment, he tried to turn the handle. "Locked."

They made their way around to the side and found a second door. Alex checked it. "Locked."

They headed around back, found a third door. "Last one," Alex said. He set the lantern on the ground, and tapped on the door.

"Oh, *Alex*, I swear—"

He reached for the handle, saying, "Well, you never know."

"Shhh!" Kate hissed in his ear. "What was that?" She grabbed his arm, fixated on the door.

"What?"

"That noise. That *thunk*."

"I didn't hear anything," Alex replied. He grasped the knob, turned it. The door creaked opened.

"Bingo," he said. "We're in."

He felt Kate's grasp on his elbow tighten. "Turn on the lantern, Alex. I'm just not going in without it."

"Light it, you mean?"

"Whatever, Alex. Just give me some light."

Unlike his wife, the shadows ahead of them were steady, and not until they walked into a room with a high ceiling did the shadows part, as if begrudgingly allowing entry. Then in the middle of the great room, the shadows grew and closed in behind them, blocking the exit.

In the farthest reaches of the lantern's glow, a grandfather clock ticked the passage of yesterday's time, and suddenly it chimed loudly, warning them again and again, twelve times, that they were not welcome here.

Alex held the lantern over his head and scanned the walls, taking inventory of a multitude of mounted animals. There were the heads of a deer, a bear, a moose on one wall, while waterfowl, hawks, and a great owl suspended from the ceiling. All these had been arranged in positions of flight, except for the owl, which perched wide-eyed in the rafters, looking very much alive.

The large manor, unveiled in such a way, was overbearing and hushed like a museum at midnight.

Alex walked around while Kate stood in the middle, holding herself tight, gaping at the display of wild animals. "Let's check another room," she said, her voice sounding thin. "I don't like it in here … too many eyes."

The French doors off the great room, Alex assumed, would lead to a study. The left door did not budge, but the right creaked open easily. Inside, near the far wall, was a massive flattop desk, behind which hung a boar's head.

As they walked toward it, their light seemed to bring the hairy beast's black eyes to life. Alex had a vision that its body was poised behind the wall and as soon as they got close enough it would break through, and gore them with its tusks.

"Icky," Kate said, peering from behind Alex.

Alex pointed to a bookshelf on the wall. "There." On the shelf was a collection of leather-bound journals between a pair of gargoyle bookends.

"Well, hurry up," whispered Kate, "I don't want to hang around here forever."

Wondering when the journals began, Alex handed the lantern to Kate and reached for the leftmost one. It was a large, ledger-like book. The brown spine and cover contained no dates, no text, no pictures. Thumbing through it, he stopped at a page that contained a folded newspaper clipping. Kate held the lantern close as Alex unfolded the yellowed paper.

Sunday, April 4, 1841

New York City Gazette

A True Description of the Lake Superior Country, Its Rivers, Coasts, Harbours, Islands, and Commerce

By John St. John

To the traveler, let me say a few words. Take a bark canoe, which two or three trials will make you at home in, for they are much easier to get the "hang" of than most persons suppose; go to adjacent islands or along the coastlines, run into the caverns and grottos, which cannot be reached in any other way. If you are in pursuit of pleasure, whether lady or gentleman, you can find it in the Lake Superior region provided you can be pleased with grand scenery, water-falls, lakes and mountains...

The entry where the clipping had been inserted was in small, meticulous quill-pen writing. The ink was blotched only in a couple spots and was legible despite its age:

May 23rd, 1895,
It was another dreary day of gray clouds and rain, and my anguish is still so fresh. I see that I have not written since mother and father's funeral.

I would have been first to suggest that an architect's wife has no place on a site until the work is complete. Whether father's secret project inside the Henry Stapleton Manor would have been his greatest achievement, as he had professed, we shall never know. Samuel believes he can finish it and he did inherit father's brilliance, so perhaps he will. As long as he stays in the good graces of the eccentric benefactor, at least funding will not be a concern, as Stapleton was a former senior executive at Standard Oil and has only slightly less money than John D. Rockefeller.

I enclose herein the excerpt from the news article that father had tacked to the wall near his favorite office window that overlooked The Green. I remember always seeing it there and know of its significance to him since he was a young man. I daresay, if it were not for the opening of The Green, through which father had strolled weekly, he likely would have left Boston years ago in pursuit of his wall-tacked dream and built his secret project on his own in some rustic location.

Alex and Kate exchanged a look before Alex flipped randomly through routine entries that described the author's daily events and reflections.

But the final entry in the book held something more, and they could see it in the first sentence.

May 7, 1899

I write tonight with renewed melancholy. Father and mother died four years ago this very day. That the accident happened on my birthday compounds my despair. Christine has put on such a grand affair yet here I linger, alone in my office.

My poor brother … It had been our good fortune that one client, our dear and wealthy Henry Stapleton, had remained not only tolerant of Samuel but thrilled with his obsessive, grandiose ideas that he brought with him back from Scotland.

But Stapleton is dead and his manor is gone now. Burned to the ground a month ago.

And either angels or demons have poisoned Samuel's soul. He had always sensed things that are beyond me: the circle of time, the links between sound and color. But he now claims to have finally passed into something called Newton's Realm from within father's secret project before it went up in smoke. I tell him I will not hear such crazy notions because to speak of them risks a sentence to a lunatic asylum.

As I conclude this journal, I turn yet again to the page with father's newspaper clipping. The beauty of the Lake Superior Country beckons Samuel, and since he was bequeathed the entire estate of Henry Stapleton, he will move there and start his project anew.

Ruination is upon the Tudor firm of architects.

He wants me to come with him. He says I keep him grounded. Alas, I must join him. I have no alternative but to join my brother.

"Wow," Alex said. "Couldn't you just read through all these? Amazing that both Samuel Tudor and John Mead had synesthesia."

"Let's find the book with 1905 in it," replied Kate. "I want to get going." There were nine books on the shelf; Kate pointed to the third from the left. "Try that one."

Alex returned the first book and pulled Kate's. He checked the date of the first and last entries: 1899, 1906.

"Bingo, Kate."

"Shhh!" hissed Kate.

"What?"

"Shush! … That!"

After a moment, Alex replied, "I can't hear any—"

Kate punched his arm to quiet him and together they listened to the sounds of the cottage. The grandfather clock ticked. Outside, leaves rustled across the ground in a breeze. Then Alex heard the new sound, too. It was like the faraway clink of two wineglasses or the ring of a tiny bell.

"That! You heard it didn't you?" Kate's fear was piqued, and she started to click her fingernails together. "What is it, Alex?"

"Probably wind chimes or something."

"*Or something?*" Kate replied, her voice a high-pitched whisper. "What *or something?*" She set the lantern on the desk, held onto Alex's waist with both hands, and looked up at him, her face contorted by anguish and shadow. "It's not wind chimes," she said. "It's inside the house."

Jingle, jangle. The sound was now closer, clearer.

Kate buried her face in Alex's chest. "It's moving—oh God, it's moving," whispered Kate as softly as she could because whatever caused the sound now seemed to be in the nearby great room.

"It's a bell from a dog collar," Alex said into Kate's ear, hopeful, trying to calm her. "It's just Duke."

"Where's the thing poop, Alex? Wait. Duke's a cat." Kate sounded hopeful, like she was trying to convince herself.

Alex considered this possibility but the jingle-jangle was too regular, too even.

A realization hit him that caused his heart to lurch. He extinguished the lantern, shoved Kate underneath the desk, and crawled in behind her.

"What, what?" whispered Kate.

Alex pulled the desk chair in as close as their bodies would allow and then cupped his hands to her ear: "Duke's not a cat. Duke's a man."

A split second before each jingle-jangle, they now heard dull thuds.

Thud, jingle … thud, jangle.

"How do you know?"

The sound was getting closer to the study.

Thud, jingle … thud, jangle.

"Grandfather clock," Alex replied in the lowest audible whisper he could manage. It was all he had to say. Kate's own grandpa had a grandfather clock. He had to tend to it to keep it working; he had to pull down a balancing weight at least once a week.

"Maybe a ranger ... "started Kate.

Alex shook his head: a ranger would not tend to a clock used by nobody. Duke tends to it. Duke was a man. And Duke was coming.

Chapter 10

Thud, jingle … thud, jangle.
Thud, jingle … thud, jangle.

For a few eternal seconds, all was quiet. Neither of them spoke.

Then the door, which was already ajar, slammed loudly against a doorstopper.

Kate jerked; Alex cupped a hand over her mouth and grabbed her hands so she couldn't click her fingernails. It dawned on him that the jingle-jangle sounded like cowboy spurs and the thuds were footfalls of boots against the hardwood floor. As if the Duke was looking for bandits; bandits cowering behind the bar of a saloon.

They heard a click—a light shone about the room—a flashlight.

Alex saw the light play upon the wall behind them, across the shelf with the missing journal. He braced for the moment of their discovery. Kate was curled into a fetal position. He would do everything in his power to protect her.

But the moment did not come.

The *jingle-jangle* retreated from the room.

When they heard a distant door open and close Alex dared to peek over the top of the desk. Through the window in the front of the house, he saw the flashlight beam. The figure holding it was a silhouette, an outline of a cowboy hat and a holster with a pistol.

"Dear Lord," he said to himself. Then to Kate, "Let's go—out the back."

They crawled on the floor underneath the window, and at the door to the study, Alex said, "Wait—the journal."

Kate reached for her husband, but he was already dashing across the room to grab it when the flashlight shone into the study from outside. Alex tried to scamper back on hands and knees under the window but the beam caught his face then the light that played on the study's interior wall started to jiggle, its circle of illumination getting smaller. The man was approaching the window.

Alex and Kate bolted through the house to the back door and spilled out onto the patio. They paused to scan the grounds in case the man had run around the side of the house to stop their escape. But clouds had rolled in and concealed the moon—if the man had turned off his flashlight, he could be anywhere.

They could see nothing.

Kate whispered, "Where's the lantern, Alex?"

Alex cursed under his breath. He had forgotten it. "It's behind the desk. Come on, there's no time." He grabbed her hand and stepped tentatively across the patio, afraid he'd hit a tree or trip on a rock. Kate stutter-stepped behind him, groping with her free hand.

Together, they felt their way through a thicket of trees and part of the way down a hill until a patio light clicked on behind them. On the patio was a man dressed as a cowboy.

Alex stared back in amazement. It was the little man he had seen running through the woods on their first morning. The man who donned the John Wayne hat and warned him about the Tin Man. *John Wayne aka the Duke. Of course!*

Kate tugged Alex's sleeve. "He had us trapped in the study. Didn't he know we were in there?"

"He let us go, Kate."

"Why doesn't he follow us?"

"I don't know. He just, he just let us go."

As their eyes adjusted to the darkness, the expanse they had been heading toward turned out to be Lake Superior. After a short walk southwest along the sandy beach, a tall outcropping of rock forced them back up into the woods. There they found a park trail that lead back to Split Rock River. Near the footbridge, they trudged up the embankment to the road right where a white car was parked. They peered inside and found it empty.

Across the bridge, they came to the small lot where their SUV was parked and climbed into the vehicle with two big consolations: they had the journal and they had their lives.

Not until they had driven safely back over the bridge and past the entrance to Tudor House did Kate speak: "Alex, the lantern—it had an inscription on it, didn't it?"

Damn, thought Alex. "I think so." *But it did, he knew it did.*

"What did it say?"

Alex grimaced. "Something, something, John Mead, something, something."

"Oh, Alex," Kate said, deflated. "How could you? You might as well have left your wallet or a trail of crumbs back to Stonebrook." She saw her husband's hand brush his back pants pocket to make sure his wallet was still there. She shook her head.

"Sorry," he said again.

Alex set the journal on the dining table and they stared at it. It was so plain looking yet it was the reason they had committed burglary. It was the reason, it now seemed, that they had risked their lives. Perhaps tomorrow, someone would come around, the cowboy with his gun or the police. He wondered if they should burn the journal to get rid of the evidence or if they should turn themselves in to the police and plead for leniency. He wondered if they should just go to bed because it was 2:30 in the morning.

He did none of these things. He sat down and opened Edward Tudor's journal.

December 1, 1905
This evening I returned from Samuel's, exhausted from our business on the point.
Samuel had ridden here yesterday to inform me of the shipwreck upon Gold Rock Point and to

solicit my help. I had news of my own to share of the wreck of the Madeira's consort, the Edenborn, but Samuel's account of the Madeira and her crew was certainly the more riveting tale.

When he took me to Stonebrook and I looked down from the cliff to the tranquil lake below, I could not believe what I saw: shards and debris scattered about the base of the cliff, but the Madeira itself was gone! Sunken in the waters off Gold Rock!

Then, because the ground was nearly frozen, we started a large fire at the top of the cliff but further back in the center of Samuel's Circle of Trees where the soil was deep enough, where he thought it was appropriate, and let it burn through the night.

This very morning, we trudged back up the hill as the pink-orange glow of the sun broke over the lake's horizon. It was an unsettling task, but we set to it with resolve.... I am tempted to document the events that took place at Stonebrook on the 28th and 29th but Samuel has requested my silence. As he had stated, it is his own conscience that will bear the weight of what transpired. So in the interest of many, and for my dear brother, I will heed his request and not risk noting them, even in my own journal, save that my meandering thoughts should ever fall into the wrong hands.

When Alex finished reading the entry to Kate, they knew who had built Stonebrook cottage and what had transpired on top of Gold Rock Point that morning so long ago. Samuel Tudor, the synesthesia-addled genius possessed by either angels or demons had built his estate, while his brother, Edward, built Tudor House just a few miles away. And on December 1st, Samuel and his brother buried a body on the point. In the center of a circle of trees.

Then they placed a stone on top of the poor man's heart.

Faith and love are apt to be spasmodic in the best minds. Men live the brink of mysteries and harmonies into which they never enter, and with their hands on the door-latch they die outside.

—Ralph Waldo Emerson, from a letter to Thomas Carlyle, March 12, 1835

Tuesday: Pancakes on a Tuesday Night

Chapter 11

Waiting for the better part of an hour for Paul to return, Alex had been reading Edward Tudor's journal entries and glancing out the front windows of the cottage for a police car. Earlier, he had tossed and turned until around 6:00 a.m. when he awoke from a dream that had the same distinct phases as the dreams from his first two nights at Stonebrook. Like the first two, this one did not continue after his fall.

Nervousness turned to excitement when the sound of an approaching car turned out to be Paul's truck. Alex stepped outside, excited to share his news. "Kate's made coffee," he said, walking up to the little yellow truck as Paul unfolded his tall frame from the driver's seat. "Come on in, we know where the man with the stone over his heart is buried."

At 9:15 a.m., the three of them sat together at the dining table. Alex explained what happened at Tudor House, then opened the journal to the December 1st entry. "Here, Paul, look at this."

As Paul read, Alex studied him closely. The man was like no one else he had ever met. He was so pensive. His intense eyes, magnified by his thick glasses, held a sparkle that hinted that they could be expressive, yet they were not. His face, his mannerisms were also constrained; he was a spirited man screwed up tight. Paul talked about the essence of life captured in a brook, the laughter of little girls flowing in its cascades—he without a doubt felt such things, he took them in. However, he did not release them. He was a butterfly trapped in a jar. The man just needed someone to open the lid.

When Paul finished reading, he set the journal aside with a slight frown. "What sense do you two make of this?"

"They buried a body," Alex replied, thinking it was obvious, "Samuel and his brother Edward. Up on Gold Rock Point." He gestured with his coffee cup in the direction of the cliff. "Then they marked the grave with a stone."

"But why?" asked Paul. "Why way up there?"

Alex had been contemplating that question. "Something bad happened," he said with a shrug. "Something very bad. And they did not like this person they buried."

"What makes you say that?" Kate said. "Because they buried him up on the point? They had to bury him somewhere, Alex."

"Because they placed a stone over his heart."

"So? That's just a marker," argued Kate. "A tombstone."

Alex crossed his arms. "Tombstones are placed at the head of the body, not over the heart."

"What are you saying, then?"

"I think he was murdered."

In the ensuing silence, the first raindrops pattered against the window behind him.

"That's ridiculous," Kate said at last. "Paul, tell Alex that's ridiculous; it's a marker for heaven's sake."

Paul cast his eyes to a knot in the table. "Well, it's certainly not the proper thing to do. That is, if they really did place it over the man's heart. Even if it was intended as a tombstone, it's a rather unusual one. A rock should only be used in a pinch."

Alex got up from his chair and walked over to the window. "Or if you were hiding the grave," he said. A fog had drifted in from the lake and mist was reaching toward the cottage. The woodshed was already a gray haze. He looked in the distance to the trees on the back slope of Gold Rock Point. Half of them were in the fog. It looked like a rainforest canopy. "We have to go up there."

"It's raining," Kate said.

"We can bring the umbrella."

"No, Alex. It's slippery; we'll break our necks. Let's go to Split Rock and see what we can find out about our cowboy friend. We don't have to say we were trespassing on Tudor House grounds, just that we saw a guy in a cowboy outfit walking through the park, and that it looked like he had a gun. Maybe we'll be able to figure out if we're fugitives."

Alex nodded. "Paul, want to come?"

"You guys go ahead. I have some restoration work to do in the boathouse."

The road into Split Rock Lighthouse State Park wound up a steep hill on the lakeside of Minnesota 61. On any other day, thought Alex, the sight of the ranger station would have been inviting, because it meant one was about to camp or hike or visit the historic lighthouse.

On this day, the ranger station was a place with uniformed officers and a stop sign, and the low building looked functional and dreary, like a border crossing.

He pulled up to the stop sign. "Alright, Kate, what are we going to say?"

"Just what I told you earlier: we were out hiking and saw a man in a cowboy getup with a gun."

"Where were we hiking?"

"Alex, I don't care … along Split Rock River."

"What time?"

"Just before dark," Kate said. "Alex, honestly, we didn't murder anybody. It'll be fine. We saw him in the woods, okay? In the area of the manor but on park property. Now, let's go in already. Unless you want to draw attention to us by just sitting here."

They hurried through the rain inside and at the counter they waited for the ranger—Reese, according to his nametag—to finish with a phone call. Ranger Reese was a stocky man with the face of a fifty-year-old and the jet-black hair sideburns of a thirty-year-old. His jaw moved up and down on a piece of gum as he cradled the phone against his shoulder to type something into a computer.

After Ranger Reese hung up, Alex said, "Um, good afternoon." He had rehearsed the line he was going to say but it escaped him.

Kate jumped in: "Say, we were out hiking by the Split Rock River yesterday and—I know this sounds strange—but we saw someone dressed up like a cowboy who looked like he had a gun."

"What time was this at?" asked the ranger.

Alex felt he had a line he could handle. "Five. It was around five."

"In the morning?"

"Evening."

"By the river, you say?" Ranger Reese seemed to be considering something, his mouth sashayed, as if slow dancing with his gum. "Sure you weren't further in the woods, up Day Hill there by the large house?"

"Well, we did see the no trespassing signs; it was when we were turning back to get to the river that we saw him," Kate replied.

Ranger Reese's fuzzy black eyebrows arched. "You walked through the bog, ma'am?"

Kate forced a smile and replied, "Nope, not quite right through but we did get a little wet." Like her unnecessarily nervous husband standing next to her, the man evidently had difficulty determining when little details were pertinent and when they were simply incidental. "Anyway, all we wanted to do, sir, is report it and see if you knew anything about him. Does he work here or something?"

"Oh, I know about him alright but you ought to speak with Millie. She's the one who takes care of that manor place. Done so since the park got that land around it. What's it been, over a year now."

"Is Millie working today?" asked Kate.

"Yes, ma'am. So you know, she's with the Historical Society now, not the park service. Today she'll be up at the keeper's quarters. A middle-aged lady, long reddish-brown hair. Can't miss her…. Say, you guys taking the lighthouse tour?"

"Maybe," offered Alex.

"You might as well since you'll need to pay for it to get up to see Millie. By the way, all those Society folks up there on lighthouse hill are dressed up in 1920s garb like its 1924 and the light is still active. Millie will be in the kitchen of the head keeper's quarters meeting with tour groups as they come through. She plays the part of keeper Young's wife."

They found the middle-aged woman with the long red hair in a small kitchen that smelled like hot-stoked wood, dough and honey. Alex and Kate had sneaked away from their tour group, which had ascended the stairs to the lighthouse and fog-signal building, so they could catch Millie between tours. Her hands were dusty white from flour and her hair dangled in such a way that when she glanced up from her kneading, it appeared her freckly face peeked out from behind curtains. When she stood to greet them, a small amount of flour trapped in her lap spilled to the floor. A big-boned woman, her elbows and finger-joints were large, but she otherwise was slender.

With an amateur actor's over-enunciated, too-loud voice she bade them welcome to her kitchen and exclaimed that she was baking bread for her husband, Mr. Young, head lighthouse keeper.

Alex felt sorry for her when Kate interrupted the woman's recitation of her role at the lighthouse to inquire about the cowboy who guarded Tudor House.

"You saw him outside? By the bog?" asked Millie, in a more natural tone.

Kate nodded.

"Hmm. Well, the man you saw was Erik. Erik Tudor." Millie rinsed her hands in a washbasin and then started drying them with a little white towel. "He's the younger brother of a man named Ben Tudor. Twenty-one years younger, in fact." The woman looked down at her shoes. "You see, Erik is disabled. Spent most of his youth in an institution until his brother brought him to Tudor House.

"He has these old walkie-talkies that we use. In the morning on my way in to work I pull off 61 and check in with him, and this morning he told me somebody's been in the study again, reading his great grandpa's journals. Most often when he tells me this he says it's someone who I know is dead, so I don't make a big deal about it—I just try to calm him down."

"I'm so sorry if we scared him," Kate said.

"Well, it's just that he's been real lonely lately. And he has psychological issues—he was born without some big piece of his brain, I've been told. The corpus something."

Alex raised his eyebrows, flabbergasted. "The *corpus callosum?*"

Kate looked at him for an explanation.

"It's the wide, flat band of tissue beneath the cortex that connects the left and right cerebral hemispheres."

"Is that important?" asked Kate.

"Well, yeah. He's pretty much missing out on a bundle of about 250 million axons that connects his hemispheres."

Millie continued, "But there's something inside Erik, you know? Something he's hiding, like he knows much more than he lets on. He's very high functioning in some areas. One of those savants, you might say. I read him a book once, cover to cover—Sherlock Holmes, it was, *The Hound of the Baskervilles*, one of my favorites—and he recited it back to me from memory."

"So why the strange outfit?" asked Alex.

"Well, Erik, the dear, sometimes fancies himself a cowboy. That's his other personality. It's like a buffer for him so when he feels threatened, he hides behind his hero." Millie smiled, her eyes warm with fond reflection. "He becomes John Wayne. *The Duke*. The gun you saw is a toy, of course, so there's no need to worry. He's the shyest, least dangerous person I know."

"I saw Erik in the woods on our first morning. He hiked to Stonebrook and was carrying his Duke outfit in a bag," said Alex.

"Oh, that's quite impossible," replied Millie. "Must have been someone else. Duke never leaves Tudor House, let alone Erik. I have to sedate him just to get him to the dentist or the doctor."

Alex, who had been worried about being arrested, was finally feeling more at ease and had in mind a return trip to Tudor House to return the journal and retrieve the lantern. "Does he like visitors? We could check on him for you."

Millie looked hopefully at each of them. "Well, I could sure use a break tonight. If you'd be willing, I have a few days of food and supplies for him in my truck …"

"We'd love to," Kate said.

"There's a few rules you'll need to follow …" started Millie. "At precisely 4:30, you need to scratch lightly on the back door—it's the only way he'll let you in before he runs upstairs. When he comes back down, if he's Erik, you need to serve him Spam and Tang. But if he's Duke, you need to serve him his beef stew in a tin bowl and Folgers coffee in his dented tin cup with hot water from the stove. And so you know, seventy percent of the time he comes down as the Duke."

They heard the voice of the tour guide approaching outside.

Hurriedly, Millie added, "Look, I'm off work in a half hour. If you can stick around until then, we can head down to my truck together and I'll give you the supplies."

Instead of waiting for their tour group to hear Millie the actor explain her role as a keeper's housewife, and perhaps receive a questioning glance from the guide they had ditched, Alex and Kate retreated through the first floor of the house, nodded hello to the man dressed in a sleek black uniform at a desk, and sneaked out the front door into the rain that had turned back into a light mist.

The octagonal tower of Split Rock Lighthouse stood on the unyielding shoulders of a 130-foot-high cliff. On this gloomy day, its exterior looked bruise-yellow and the housing for the light was a black eye. As lighthouse towers go, she was short and fat, just fifty-four feet tall, according to the assistant keeper standing inside at the base of her winding stairs. She had a one-thousand-watt bulb and a bivalve Fresnel lens that rotated on a 250-pound bed of liquid mercury. Her official beam range of twenty-two miles was limited as such only because of the curvature of the earth. It had been reported by men perched high on large ocean-going freighters that they had seen her beacon as far away as Grand Marais, more than sixty miles distant.

From the top of the lighthouse Kate looked outside to wave down at Alex, but it was not the lighthouse that held his attention. Instead, he stood at the cliff's edge with his back to her and looked away from Split Rock up the shore to the northeast, to neighboring Gold Rock Point.

The cliff face of Gold Rock extended all the way from the shoreline of the adjoining bay to about three hundred feet into the water and was at least eighty feet high. The outer-most point curved out of the water like the stern of a giant ship run aground. *A ship with dirt and grass and trees as cargo and, for the past century,* thought Alex, *a dead man.* Underwater, off her rock stern was the ruined *Madeira*. Alex looked for the Circle of Trees on the cliff where the body was supposed to have been buried and wished he had a pair of binoculars.

Behind him, Split Rock's fog signal blasted for a tour group. Its sound was a loud, two-second-long "BE-YOU," that scared off the three seagulls that had perched on the fence. Alex glanced at his watch; twenty-five minutes had already passed.

"I don't understand this Erik/Duke character," Kate said, shaking her head as they walked back to the keeper's house.

Alex did. On their first morning at Stonebrook he had rummaged through the pantry and found an old, large canister of Folgers coffee and a collection of dusty old stew cans on one shelf. On another were relatively new cans of Spam and Tang. The Duke had long ago been a visitor to Stonebrook Cottage. He must have been afraid to venture from Tudor House to Stonebrook. More recently, it had been Erik who came. It meant that Erik felt comfortable to be himself with John Mead.

"Kate. Millie's wrong. Erik's been to Stonebrook. So has The Duke." He then told her about all the Stonebrook pantry discoveries and Erik's warning about a dangerous Tin Man.

Kate, for her part, finally admitted to running into the man in the long black coat and they agreed that he was likely Erik's Tin Man. She also told him she wasn't afraid, that she wanted to stay, despite the danger.

"Are you from around here, Millie?" Kate asked as they walked toward the parking lot.

"Two Harbors, born and raised. My folks had a place right in town. Dad was a teacher at the high school; mom worked at the nursing home."

"Did you ever know a man named John Mead?"

"Funny, he's one of the dead people Erik talks to," replied Millie. "I know he owned that Stonebrook place up the shore and he died not too long ago but can't say as I knew him."

"Has Erik ever mentioned seeing a guy in a long black coat or talked about a Tin Man?" asked Kate.

Millie knitted her eyes together. "Hmm, nope."

"Do you know a guy named Paul Kransberg?" continued Kate, "Real tall guy?"

Millie stooped to pick up a gum wrapper on the path. "Yeah, sure. The Shepherd."

"That's him," Kate replied, trying to hide the excitement in her voice.

"As far as I know he still lives in the woods. Nobody in town ever sees him or his mother since she got sick—except for at the grocery store or gas station. Not that we saw much of them beforehand, though."

"What do you know about him? How'd he get the name, Shepherd?"

"Shepherd went to my elementary school, in my class as a matter of fact, until his mom pulled him out. Fifth grade, it was. Mr. Barreiro's class. That poor boy was picked on so bad that I don't know how he took it." Millie shook her head. "But he did, he took it every day. At recess, they'd rough him up and make fun of how he and his mother had a few sheep, and the boys would bleat at him. You know, sheep noises. So they

104

took to calling him The Shepherd. Everyone called him that, I guess."

"How could someone do such things?" asked Kate, her voice sad and angry. "Paul's so innocent."

"Wasn't his dad ever around?" asked Alex as they reached the parking lot and headed toward a green pickup truck.

"His mom was never married as far as I know. It was always just the two of them. I'm not even sure what he did for schooling after he dropped out. Didn't have any, I imagine. As for a job, the only one I knew about was that he taught violin for a while and maybe still does. How or where he had learned the violin, I have no idea. And not fiddle fuddle stuff, either, but *real* stuff, *good* stuff. The classical sort, you know, like Mozart.

"Jasper Jacobson's boy, Emil, took lessons from him for several years—a few other kids in town, too. Emil's now at some prestigious school for violin out east. A couple of the others play in orchestras. Funny, huh?" Millie paused. "I mean, how can an elementary school dropout living with his mom out in the woods teach the violin as well as that? And Jasper, he has nothing but good things to say about Shepherd nowadays. Says Shepherd has a gift and not just with the violin either, because he used to worry about his little Emil something fierce—he told me so himself. But after spending time with Shepherd, Emil changed."

"Changed how?" asked Alex.

"Oh, you know kids," said Millie with a sigh, "how some of them don't care about anything except themselves. That was Emil. Well, Emil started to care." Then Millie shrugged, matter-of-factly, as if there was no other way to describe what happened to the lad. "I wish Shepherd would stop into town more often. I'd love to chat with him and sort of apologize for all the bad stuff life brought him."

"But you had nothing to do with that, Millie," Kate said.

Just then, Millie looked at the ground. "Look, I liked Shepherd—*Paul.* I liked Paul because he had smart eyes and talked to me in a way nobody else has since. That's why he was picked on, because he was different like that. The reason I had a crush on him was the reason he was ridiculed and I did nothing about it. I avoided him. I was afraid to be Paul's friend. Worse than that, I was embarrassed."

At her truck, the three of them stopped. Millie took off her slicker and handed it to Kate: "In case it's still raining on your hike in." From the passenger's seat, she pulled out a heavy backpack and handed it to Alex. "Just leave the slicker and pack in the kitchen—the spare key, too."

She then perched herself on the edge of the passenger seat to pull a sweatshirt on over her dress while telling them how to find the path that used to be a driveway. She told them about the no trespassing signs, too, about how to get around to the backdoor at Tudor House.

Alex and Kate did their best to listen as if they had never been there before.

"Alex," Kate said from the passenger's seat when they climbed into the SUV, "we scared the bejeezus out of Erik. I mean, we broke in during the middle of the night, for Pete's sake."

"Except we didn't exactly break in," Alex replied. "He let us in. When I knocked at the back door, we were whispering. He must have thought it was the safety knock and we were Millie. Either that or he saw us coming and remembered seeing me from our first morning."

Alex started the SUV and wondered what it would be like going back to Tudor House. And, who was the Tin Man that Erik warned him about?

He switched on the windshield wipers and took a right onto Minnesota 61.

Chapter 12

When they returned to Stonebrook, Paul was out back, even during this inclement weather. From the dining room windows, Alex scanned the grounds for Tin Man, steaming the windowpane with his breath, as Kate emerged from the bathroom with a towel to dry her rain-soaked face and hair. He didn't think the man would return so soon. More likely, he would come around when their SUV was gone, if he came back at all.

"Whatcha thinkin'?" Kate asked.

Alex turned from the window and frowned at his wife. He didn't want to worry her, so he changed the subject to something that had been bothering him since learning Paul taught violin. "What instrument was it you played when you were a girl?"

"Alex. You can never remember. *Cello*. It was the cello. I played it for three years."

"Why'd you stop?"

Kate drew a heart shape in the steam on the window and then an arrow. "I got bored with it. I wanted to be a cheerleader. Too busy. You know how it goes."

Alex leaned against the wall next to the window with a blank look on his face. Paul, he thought, had been planting peonies his whole life. He had been playing the violin his whole life. "I wish I played something. I wish I played something now."

"Sure, but you know what? You would have stopped, too. There are other things in life, Alex. You played basketball; you played baseball. You were in the Latin club. I still can't believe that your school even had a Latin club, not to mention that you were nerdy enough to join." Kate smiled at him while towel drying her hair. "All those things—you know why you stopped doing them? Because you moved on. I no longer play the cello; you no longer study Latin. It's the same in our careers, same in everything."

After a pause, when Alex did not reply, Kate announced in a chipper voice, "I'm going to take a hot bath."

"You just dried off."

"Yeah, but I'm cold," Kate replied. She leaned up, kissed her husband on the lips and then grabbed his butt. "And what the heck, I'm moving on. I wish they had a radio here."

"Maybe you should mention it in the guest book when we leave. Something like: 'Loved it here, weather was nice, but a radio, now *that* would have been great.'"

"You're a funny man, Mr. Fitzgerald."

"Hey, you okay if I go visit Paul in the boathouse?"

"Knock yourself out. As long as you lock the doors."

Alex hurried in the rain to the boathouse, but by the time he reached it his wool jacket was sopping in the shoulders and his hair was wet. Opening the side service door, he was hit with the smell of dead fish. Gray light filtered in from two open boat doors and revealed an antique boat on a lift. About twenty feet long, the boat was all wood except for white upholstered seats. Behind it, he saw an even older boat that looked less luxurious yet had a class and character of its own. Alex walked to the aft of the first boat, admiring it. The sound of his boots hitting the wooden planks echoed.

"That you, Alex?" Paul asked.

"Where are you?" Alex squinted into the boathouse.

Paul stood up. His head loomed over the top of the boats, a lock of his gray-black hair hanging in his face. "Come here," he said, and then popped back out of sight.

Around the corner, Paul lay on the floor, peering with a flashlight under a small door in the back wall. "I had always figured that behind this door was just some storage shelving, but there's a draft," he said, reaching into a pocket for a matchbook. He struck a match, held it down to the half-inch crack under the door. The flame danced and flickered away from the opening. "See?"

Alex rapped on the door. It felt thick. "Isn't it a closet? For storing oars and lifejackets? The draft could be from a crack in the wall to the outside."

"But this wall is where the boathouse ends. There's nothing behind it but earth and rock—at least in theory. The air smells stale, like air from underground, not outside. Like there's a tunnel."

"Could be whoever built it dug out a little recess to keep things cool."

Paul blew out the match and moved to a sitting position. He pulled his knees up and rested his hands on them with a skeptical look on his face.

"Well, anyway," continued Alex, "we'd need a battering ram to get through that." The stocky door looked like a miniature entry to a castle. The wood was a deep reddish-brown—mahogany, he thought—and carved into it was an engraving of a violin. It had a large iron ring for a handle and an old-fashioned keyhole. Alex grasped the ring and tried to turn it. "I guess we'll have to assume they wanted to keep their boat supplies extraordinarily safe."

Paul latched his toolbox as Alex sat down on the wooden planks alongside him. "Anyway, good news," Alex said, and he told Paul about meeting the woman at Split Rock who cares for Erik the Duke and that they were going to visit him that night to return the journal and retrieve the lantern.

Paul folded in his long legs to sit cross-legged and stared at the little boat in front of them. He seemed preoccupied, as he often did.

"Guess we won't be arrested after all," added Alex, trying to get a reaction. For a moment, he wanted simply to ask Paul what he did for a living but such a leading question would feel clumsy, contrived. More likely than not, the response would be a short sentence and then the man would pick up his toolbox and make haste to his little truck. While most people started conversations with such idle chitchat, this man did not do chitchat. He would listen, but participation was another matter. To converse with him, it was necessary to busy oneself so that the talk was secondary, almost incidental.

Alex stepped over to the older boat; the one Paul was looking at. He rested a hand on its hull. "What kind of boats are these?" he asked.

Paul lifted an index finger from his knee, pointing to the big one first. "That's a '57 Chris Craft. Twenty footer. Beautiful boat. Great condition except for dings in her hull." Paul paused. "And this one here's a Dispro…. Otherwise known as a Dippy."

"Looks old."

"Ancient. 1922. Made by The Disappearing Propeller Boat Company out of Ontario. Haven't been any of these made since sometime during the 50s."

Alex tilted his head to look at the wooden boat from a different angle and then ran his hand along its smooth side. "Looks like a long, wide canoe with big benches and a motor."

"It is," Paul replied with a smile. "Except for one ingenious little difference. The propeller can disappear right up into the interior housing. It'd even retract automatically if it struck a shoal or a rock."

Alex loved the little boat. He felt John Mead inside it and smelled sweet pipe smoke. "Paul, can I ask you something?" Alex swallowed hard and kept his eyes riveted to the Dispro. "Who are you? What is that ingenious little thing that makes you different?"

In the ensuing pause, Alex regretted asking the question that now seemed to resonate lamely in the smelly air of the boathouse, and yet he refrained from trying to take it back. He noticed from the corner of his eye that Paul had reopened his toolbox and was inspecting its contents.

At last, Paul spoke: "Literally everything a person experiences, Alex … everything a person absorbs, nourishes their mind. But most people, when they see or hear something—and to a lesser degree when they smell or taste or touch—they process the stimulus quickly, literally. A cottage is a cottage." Paul lifted his gaze. "A lake is a lake…."

Despite the coldness in the boathouse, Alex felt hot. He sat down on the wood planks next to the slip with the suspended Dippy and dangled his feet over the edge.

"I do not think in such a way," continued Paul, sounding embarrassed.

Alex started to untie a shoe—it was the only thing he could think to do. "You mean, you think, how? Figuratively, then? Only figuratively?"

"Not exactly. Alex, have you ever known anyone who was so into something that it consumed them?"

"Like a hobby?"

"Sure. Have you ever known anyone like that?"

Alex smiled. "My father-in-law. He's into hunting big time."

"What does he tell you about hunting? I mean, if you were to ask him what it's like for him sometimes when he's hunting."

"He talks about it all the time. He goes on and on—"

"No. I mean, if you were to sit him down and look in his eyes and ask him; ask him how he feels about hunting, what would he say or, at least, try to say?"

"I don't know. That he loves it, I guess."

"*How* does he love it? Do you understand, Alex? If he isn't the sort of man to put it into words, do it for him. What does hunting do for your father-in-law?"

"I went with Ed once after his wife died. Deer hunting," Alex said. He had pulled off a shoe and a sock and now he set his bare foot on top of the cold, dry sand at the bottom of the slip next to a wooden runner. He undid the laces of his other shoe. "At my wife's uncle's cabin. That last night before we drove home, after Ed got his buck, we sat around the fire and he stared into it for the longest time. Then he said something out of character. He said, 'I saw that deer before I saw him. I knew he was there and then he just—he was there.' He took a sip of beer and told me and Charlie that he saw the world through that deer's eyes, felt its muscles in his, felt its heart in his. Which was interesting because Ed has a bad heart. Then he shot it."

Alex paused and then added, "That was pretty much what Ed said. So I guess that's my answer. That's how hunting makes him feel."

Paul looked pleased with the story; his eyes were vibrant. "So after that day, when your father-in-law sees a deer, he no longer sees *just* a deer, does he?"

"No, I suppose not. He feels the deer at a deeper level, sort of like he's one with it. One with nature."

"There are many people, Alex, who have never had such an experience as your father-in-law. Of those who do, it is usually within the confines of one activity, one pursuit."

"What sort of experience? You mean like a one-ness with something?"

"Seeing the deeper, richer perspectives."

Alex sank his other bare foot into the sand and wiggled both feet back and forth. He knew what Paul was getting at. "You're not talking only physical things are you? You're talking intangibles... The texture of ideas. The contour of thoughts. The color of emotion."

Paul leaned forward, looked Alex right in the eye. He did not say a word but seemed to speak with all his being: *Yes. Yes. That is precisely what I am talking about!*

With welling awe and sympathy, Alex held his gaze to his friend's. "That's how you're different. My God, Paul. You have synesthesia, like my boy had."

This time, Paul did answer: "Synesthesia is on the surface," he whispered. He leaned back against the wall, looking exhausted. "What's here is beyond that. And what you have is beyond that, too."

Alex opened his mouth; he wanted to disagree but no words came out.

"I saw it in you when we first met. You carry it in your shoulders because it weighs upon you."

Alex thought of Michael. Before this week it was Michael who weighed upon him. Michael's birthday, Christmas, every day. But ... not this week. Somehow, not since they'd arrived at the cottage. In the past, whenever he had forgotten about Michael, if only for an hour, he felt pangs of guilt for having done so. He felt as if he owed it to his son to never forget him, to always and constantly remember that he had forgotten to strap the boy in his car seat. But Paul was right, something else weighed on him now.

The Reflectory. Whatever that was.

"You suppress your gift of comprehension," continued Paul. "You force yourself to perceive life the way you think others do. You fear that to do otherwise would set you apart and you would be labeled as different. *Kooky.*"

"Maybe I am *kooky.*"

"Kooky like Wolfgang Mozart? Like William Shakespeare? Albert Einstein?"

"What?" Alex had to laugh. "Paul, those people were geniuses. I'm no genius, ask Kate. Those guys focused all their energy on their work and did amazing things. I can't even think straight enough to hold down a job."

"Alex, I've read enough books in my life—biographies and autobiographies of great innovators, creators, and thinkers— and the ability, the *willingness*, to loosen the binds on the human mind is the common thread among them. So, Alex, do not be afraid to loosen the binds. It is a great gift.

"This door behind me … this whole cottage. It has me baffled, Alex. Help me. Tell me what you see at Stonebrook."

Alex hesitated. "Well, it was built in 1900. It—"

"No," replied Paul, actually looking upset. "Tell me other things."

Alex opened his mouth to speak again but then closed it. His suppressed thoughts about Stonebrook seemed to gather excitedly, all straining to be the first to spill out of his mouth.

"Loosen the binds," Paul prodded.

"The screen door—the one on the side of the house to the kitchen—when I first opened it, it squeaked and then snapped closed behind me and when I heard this, I snapped back in

116

time. I had a vision of back then, of 1905. When the door bounced a second time, lighter, I bounced to a time in the fifties or sixties, and in those fleeting moments I was transported, I saw Stonebrook as it might have been during those times."

"What did you see?"

"It was just a visualization, Paul. Something I conjured up."

"What did you see?" pressed Paul.

"Things that aren't there now. In the kitchen, in 1905, I saw, I *smelled*, loaves of bread cooling on the stove. There was a woman at the sink with her back to me. She had on an apron and I know she was scrubbing something because I saw her arms working back and forth. I saw rhubarb preserves in the Kerr jars that Kate and I use for glasses. The windowsills were lined with spice jars. In the sixties, I saw a different woman, but it's the same scene with her at the sink.

"Elsewhere in the cottage—the bed … on the bed, Paul, is a quilt of a lake and forest, and it comes alive every morning. Sleeping under it, I've had the most vivid dreams of my life, dreams about Stonebrook but I cannot make sense of them. Each night they get more vivid, each night they excite and scare me more than the last.

"The library. In the library I imagine it's sometime in the 1940s, and I see silhouettes of two men sitting in the high-back chairs reading. Smoking pipes. Between them is that lamp with the green shade and in front of them is the low table with the globe and maps and books. They are talking quietly."

"Who are they? What are they talking about?"

"I don't know."

"*Who are they?*"

Grimacing, Alex absently brushed sand from his feet. The men were merely a fantasy. You see an old library and you try to imagine the people who might have used it, nothing more. To speak of such things in a heavy, serious manner assigned them too much relevance, made them too real. "I wouldn't know them by sight … but I imagine they are an old Samuel Tudor and a young John Mead."

"What are they talking about?"

"I don't know, they're whispering, I can't hear."

Paul drummed his fingers on his knees, waiting patiently. He was sure becoming a bossy introvert.

"Okay," Alex said with a sigh. "I can't hear them but they're discussing something that's here at the cottage: The Reflectory." He stood, surveyed the two boats, and took a couple of steps away from Paul. He looked through the open boathouse door into the fog and mist. The lake disappeared in a gray shroud twenty yards out. He envisioned Samuel Tudor and John Mead out there now, in their antique wooden Dippy. They, with their boat, were dark shapes in his mind, yet somehow were still clear. Samuel Tudor wore clothing from 1905: a houndstooth vest, an ascot, a derby hat, a watch chain dangled from a watch pocket. John Mead wore clothes from the fifties: a white dress shirt with suspenders and trousers and his hair was slicked back and parted neatly on the side. They faced each other in the boat but they looked into the boathouse as if they had been huddled, discussing a matter of secrecy and were interrupted by Alex and Paul. The pipe tobacco he smelled earlier seemed sweeter, fresher, as if it wafted in from the lake. They were watching and listening to a conversation taking place in their boathouse decades later, in a new century. He could see all this and yet could not interpret their faces to know whether they were pleased or displeased.

"Samuel Tudor and John Mead," Alex continued, "they whisper about much more than a man buried in a storm. That man is insignificant, Paul." He felt the Reflectory was a place where color and sound play together as elements in a symphony of a profound new world ... a world he desperately wanted to explore. Then he added in a whisper, "He's the tip of things. He's ... the way in."

"Good. That's good."

Alex turned to look at Paul. "Tell me what *you* see."

"There is cohesion here, an undercurrent of something just out of reach. This cottage has contours so deep I cannot make them out; textures so fine, I cannot feel them; colors so vibrant, I am blinded by them.

"This is why I tinker about the property the way I do, why I walk up to the cliff sometimes to think; I'm trying to make sense of this place, but there are massive pieces missing."

"There's something grand here, isn't there, Paul?"

"Yes."

"The Reflectory."

"Yes."

Alex stared at the rain. It had picked up and pelted the lake harder. The fog was retreating out into the lake. Whatever discoveries that lie ahead were locked by a key that was in a dead sailor's heart under a stone in the middle of a circle of trees. He sat down to put his shoes and socks back on. "Let's head back, Paul, if you're done here. Kate's probably wondering about us. It doesn't look like it's going to let up anytime soon so we might as well make a dash for it."

The man in the long black coat entered Stonebrook cottage. He pulled the wet hood off his head and blew lightly into his hands to warm them.

The bathroom door was open a crack and he heard a splash. He wanted to see the attractive woman naked. He wanted to feel her breasts, be inside her. But there was more important business at hand. He walked across the squeaky hardwood floor to the library and found Edward Tudor's journal on the map table. He opened it and smiled. As he thought, they had taken the book with the December 1, 1905 entry. Erik had hidden it from him, except for the one time he found it back in its place with the others under the boar's head. He had already dismissed it as a decoy. He had been told that Samuel Tudor and John Mead were notorious for secrecy and elaborate tricks to hide their Reflectory. After all, there was no circle of trees on Gold Rock Point and the word "tree" was a metaphor for hierarchy and a circle of trees had no hierarchy: each in the circle was an equal. It made no sense.

He stroked the whiskers on his chin, turned his attention to the Latin dictionaries, and opened one to a bookmarked page.

There were more splashes in the bathroom, and then he heard water drain. Now was not the time to explore the woman's body, and he had time to slip out; the gurgling water provided cover. He took a step toward the front door—the floorboard squeaked. The water kept draining so he took another step. This part of the board squealed even louder.

The draining stopped yet he knew the tub could not yet be empty.

The wife called out tentatively, "Alex?"

He waited.

"Alex!"

There was fear in the woman's voice. *As there should be*, he thought.

Chapter 13

Dripping wet, Alex and Paul slipped off their shoes inside the kitchen door.

"Alex?" Kate called his name but her voice was distant, scared.

"Yep, just got back—" he yelled out.

"Come here! Alex, be careful! Come here!" She screamed.

Running through the kitchen, Alex heard Kate cry out again and he picked up speed cutting the corner in the great room to the bathroom and shoved the door open.

"Kate, what happened?" Alex grabbed a towel from the rack and draped it around his naked wife. She shivered in the middle of the emptied tub, her legs drawn up to her chest, her arms wrapped around her knees.

"Someone was here. Inside the cottage. I heard footsteps on a loose board in front of the bookshelves, but the water was draining so I wasn't sure. I plugged the drain and heard the board creak again but then it got quiet—I said your name because I thought it was you but you didn't answer. You didn't answer!"

At last, Kate took a breath as she pulled the towel tight around her body.

Alex got into the tub and sat behind her. "I'm here, I'm here, I'm here," he said, caressing her back. He wanted to ask her if she was sure it was footsteps she had heard but he knew now was not the time. "Let's get you into your robe, okay? How about some coffee to warm you up? How's that sound?"

"Nice," Kate replied with a sniffle. "Where's Paul?"

"He's here. Should I ask him to leave?"

"No, that's okay. Maybe he can make a fire?"

"Sure," Alex replied. "Paul?"

From outside the bathroom, Paul answered. "On it."

As Alex closed the bathroom door and helped Kate out of the tub she asked, "Who was it, Alex? Was it Tin Man again? Did you lock the doors like I asked?"

"Yes, I locked them. Are you sure it wasn't the cottage settling that you heard? Normal creaks and groans?"

"I'm sure." Kate sat on the toilet lid and Alex held out her robe for her to put on. "Someone was walking on that spot by the bookshelves where the wood is all warped. It only squeaks when you put weight on it. When I plugged the water I heard it for sure and I hollered your name. Whoever it was, stopped. I didn't know what to do so I unplugged the water again and let it drain. I hoped he would use the noise as an opportunity to leave. All I could do was stare at the door and pray that I didn't need to kick someone in the balls."

Alex smiled briefly.

"After the last of the water gurgled away," Kate continued, "I prayed. It was so quiet, all I heard was my own breath and I prayed that he had left and that you would come …"

She turned and looked at her husband who was kneeling on the floor in front of her. He pushed her hair from her eyes.

She broke down and added, "And you did."

With a cup of hot coffee and Alex's arm around her, Kate started to relax on the couch in front of Paul's roaring fire.

She got up and walked to the library, her steaming coffee held in front of her as if to ward off evil spirits. Near the bookshelves, she took small steps, pausing after each one. On the third step, the floor creaked; on the fourth, it groaned. The fifth step squealed.

"That one," she said, pointing at it accusingly. She looked back and forth between Alex and Paul who still sat by the fire. "Come here, guys. It was that one. Without a doubt." She rocked back and forth on the spot—*squeal, squeal, squeal*—it sounded like an angry pig.

Alex and Paul walked up to her and the three of them looked down at her slippers.

"Who is it, guys?" she asked. "Who's been here?"

After they scrutinized the floorboard, they scanned the bookshelves, trying to pinpoint what the intruder had been after.

On the map table, Alex saw Edward Tudor's journal where he had left it. The Latin dictionary was open to the page marked with the bookstore receipt. "Okay, I had closed the dictionary," he said. "The last time I used it, I closed it. I'm sure of it."

Kate picked up the receipt and stared at the open dictionary. "But why would he open your Latin dictionary? And why does he care if you have synesthesia?"

"Our intruder knows that Stonebrook has secrets," replied Alex. "And if he's been watching us, he knows that we're aware of the secrets, too."

"Where's the sheet with Paul's translation?" asked Kate.

Alex saw it lying on the coffee table. He also saw the Latin note from John Mead and his own scribbles about the *Madeira* wreck. "Looks like nothing else was touched but who knows. He could have read everything."

Paul sat down in one of the library chairs. "I've seen him. Four times, in fact."

"Paul," Kate said, agitated. "Why didn't you mention it earlier? Did you ever call the police?"

"No. I thought he was someone from town, that's all. Someone playing a prank; out to scare me. I didn't connect him with the cottage."

Kate said, "He definitely has a Russian accent, though, so if it's the same guy, he's not from Two Harbors."

Alex figured that this at least explained why Paul always carried a tool or blunt object around with him: self-defense. He remembered Millie's sad account of Paul's troubles. Sometimes schoolyard bullies never grow out of being bullies and then they raise new bullies so that people like Paul are hounded their entire lives. "If he's a foreigner, any clue who he might be?" asked Alex.

"I was never able to make him out. He keeps to the woods, and he wears a hat pulled down low—or maybe it's a hood, and glasses. Once, I led him along the brook, pretending to take a stroll, and he followed."

Kate continued, "Paul, did Alex mention that we talked to a woman named Millie at Split Rock? She said she went to school with you until your mom pulled you out."

"I remember Millie," replied Paul. "Millie Sparks. She was nice."

"Millie told us that you teach violin," Kate said, apparently forgetting about Tin Man for now to get Paul to open up. "She said that your mom has cancer. She told us about the bullies, too. Do you want to talk about any of this?"

Paul did not take his eyes off his hands, and he did not blink.

Alex rubbed his forehead. He knew his wife meant well but he did not want to see his friend suffer.

Kate stepped around the squeaky boards over to Paul and leaned down to speak softly to him. "We're your friends, Paul. We care."

With a hitch in his voice, Paul replied, "What do you want to hear?"

Kate, pleaded Alex silently, *he's not a talker, he's not like other people.*

"Well, I don't know. Where are you from?"

"Saint Paul. Born in '45."

Kate waited for him to divulge more but Paul did not continue. "What about your mom? What's she like?"

"Mom was the first female violinist in the Minneapolis Symphony...."

Paul seemed to be struggling so Alex had an idea to help him. He jumped in: "That's the physical, isn't it? The tangible. Loosen the binds, Paul. Tell us how you really see her."

Paul reflected for a moment and then smiled sheepishly. "Mother is pancakes on a Tuesday night."

Alex loved that: *Mother is pancakes on a Tuesday night*. It told him that Paul's mom was eccentric and fun loving, yet lovely and warm. It told him that Paul loved her dearly and that they had a close relationship. It told him that Paul's mother lived life uniquely, unapologetically.

Paul's eyes followed the chimney stones up to the ceiling and seemingly beyond. "When I was growing up, on weekend mornings Mom always slept in and left me to my own devices. It was Tuesdays—Tuesday nights—that she made pancakes. With sugar or jelly on top. We'd drink milk and maybe have a piece of meat or some fruit."

Paul smiled a distant smile. His eyes, still cast skyward, narrowed to slits.

Alex knew what was happening to the man: cherished feelings and memories were like grease: they lubricated one's thoughts, made them flow.

"On those nights, we'd sing and dance and laugh. We had to, though, because of her rule."

"What rule?" Kate asked.

"To quote Mom, 'Tuesday night pancakes are not to be eaten with a serious face or a heavy heart.' That's why Marek usually went to the bar on Tuesdays. He could smile, even laugh on occasion, but his heart … it was too heavy. Mom and

I could see how he labored with life, trying in vain to get out from under it, if only for a moment."

"Who's Marek?" whispered Kate.

"Father. Marek, Marek Majewska. A depressive alcoholic. He was Polish but grew up in Budapest. Mother met him when she was on tour in Italy and he was filling in for a cellist. When he joined the orchestra permanently, he moved to St. Paul and lived with us. Mornings on the days they didn't have practice sessions or a concert he would play his cello in his underwear. Afternoons were for drinking brandy and smoking cigarettes, evenings were for vodka and more cello. He had no existence outside of this. For supper he ate cold soup right out of the can.

"Until I was seven, my life was Tuesday nights and music. Going to concerts to hear Mother and Marek and the others in the symphony was my greatest joy. I'd close my eyes when they played and have the beautiful music seep into me. 'A bath for your soul!' Mom always said backstage afterwards. And she was right: on the walk home, holding her hand, I'd feel all fresh and clean. I had no friends, really, no social life, but I still thought it was the best childhood a boy could hope for."

"What happened to your father?" asked Kate.

"In the middle of the night one night, Marek sat down on my bed, and he never came into my bedroom so I knew right away that something was wrong. He said in his broken English, 'Paul good lad. Paul good lad.' He kissed me on the forehead and walked out. Not until morning when I saw his cello was gone did I know he had walked out for good. He went back to Europe—to Budapest, or to Poland, maybe.

Mother said that she and he—they really didn't love each other. She loved his music but that was the only thing they shared. Sometimes, even music isn't enough.

"After he left, the symphony let my Mother go. She said it was for political reasons, but I think she lost her desire to play. To this day I don't understand why we moved up here of all places. She had said she wanted to disappear for a while…. I guess she wanted to disappear forever.

"Anyway, for the first six months after we moved, Mother didn't even touch her violin. We did not have Tuesday night pancakes. We did little of anything. Then one weekend she decided to treat herself to a weekend up at Nanibijou Lodge. When she got back things got better. We started having our own concerts. We called them concerts, anyway, and we held them on Tuesdays and ate our pancakes at intermission." Paul smiled. "But they were really mother playing violin and me making a horrible racket. Now, because of Mother's uterine cancer and hearing loss, it's just me who plays."

Paul took off his glasses and rubbed his eyes with a thumb and forefinger. "She's eighty-six. She's been saying since she got sick that it's my concerts that sustain her. She tells me: 'Little Paul, if you stop playing, I'll stop living. Keep playing, Paul. Keep playing.'"

"Tonight's Tuesday night," Kate said softly. "You play for her tonight?"

"Yes."

"Could we host your concert? If your mother's up to it? We can even make pancakes."

Paul looked away, at the fireplace. "You know, when I started working here she used to ask about the cottage: what it looked like, how it was decorated…. Sometimes I wonder if she's told me everything she knows about this place and how I got this job.

"Why?" asked Kate.

"She told me that a man in a suit stopped by our house one day when I was at the library, a lawyer from Boston, Massachusetts. He was executing provisions for the will of John Mead and according to the will his cottage was to be turned into a rental property upon the event of his death. A handyman was needed. Mother quickly offered my services, and a month later the checks—checks large enough to cover her medical expenses—started arriving. We'd never seen so much money."

Alex couldn't help but think he had received an invitation to stay at John Mead's cottage from the same firm, probably the same attorney.

Paul put his glasses back on and exhaled, puffing out his cheeks and lips. Talking seemed to exhaust the man. "I think before she dies," he continued, "she'd like to visit Stonebrook. So yes, Kate, we'll come. I'll play for you tonight."

Chapter 14

Unlike their first two trips up the hill to Tudor House, their third one was not a clandestine operation, so they walked right up to the cottage's back porch. Standing in the rain at the door, Kate held Edward Tudor's journal in a plastic bag and Alex wore the backpack of supplies for Erik. They stared at Alex's watch: 4:20 p.m.

"Can we do the safety knock now?" asked Kate, as Alex tried peeking under a closed blind of a porch window.

Alex shook his head. "It's not 4:30."

"Do you suppose he's right here, behind the door?" Kate was anxious.

"Like Boo Radley?"

"Boo who?"

He rolled his eyes at her but saw that she did not mean her 'boo who' question as a joke. She looked anxious. The hood of Millie's waterproof slicker kept her face dry, so when another drop formed near the tip of his nose he could not resist the urge to blow it at her face.

"Hey!" she said, wiping her cheek with a dry hand she pulled out of the sleeve. "Quit it."

"My apologies, Your Dryness." Alex tried the doorknob and found it locked. With a quick nod at the door, he added,

"Well, go on, then. If you're so eager to get in ... go on and give it a knock. See if he'll let us in again."

Kate hesitated as if unsure how one properly did a "safety-knock"—and then lightly scratched and tapped on the door.

They both listened, heard nothing.

She tapped again and said softly, "Erik? Hello, Erik, this is Kate and Alex. We're friends of Millie's. We brought your dinner for tonight and some supplies.... Will you please let us in?"

Nothing.

"We'd love to meet you, Erik. If you could unlock the door …"

Nothing.

Kate cleared her throat. "You see," she continued, talking louder at the door, "we're staying up the road at Stonebrook Cottage—"

Thunk.

The door twitched as a deadbolt popped back into the door. They heard faint rustling on the other side—hurried footsteps moving away.

"Magic words, Kate," said Alex, wiggling his eyebrows. "Magic words."

Inside, Kate whispered, "Erik? Erik?"

"He's on his way upstairs by now," Alex said. "Let's hit the kitchen. We have to put all this stuff away and start his supper."

After stashing the food items in their proper places, they anticipated seeing the Duke and got out his tin bowl and the dented kettle. Overhead, they heard an occasional groan of floorboards.

"When's he going to come down, Alex?" Kate asked. "Should we start the stew yet?"

"Let's see what he's wearing first." Alex picked up a can of Spam and a can of stew and wondered how much of each Erik had eaten in his life.

At last, the faint and familiar *jingle, jangle*.

The Duke. The Duke was coming.

Two cans of stew, right?" Kate asked. "That's enough?"

"Should be. What did you do with his pills?"

"Right here in his bowl. I'll ladle the stew on top like Millie said."

Precisely at 5:00 p.m., the jingle-jangles stopped outside the kitchen. The brim of a cowboy hat poked around the corner. Then they saw an eye peek at them. It was blinking rapidly; it darted back and forth between Alex and Kate and then popped back behind the corner.

Alex whispered, "Talk to him Kate. A woman's voice will be familiar."

Kate said, "Hello … Erik, I mean Duke. We're Kate and Alex. Millie asked us to come out to meet you."

No response, no movement.

"We're making stew and coffee for supper. How does that sound?"

Again the hat emerged from behind the corner and this time he stuck his entire head out. Wide-eyed, nose sniffing, mouth pursed, Alex thought he resembled a rabbit tempted by offered morsels.

Finally, he stepped out entirely; his deliberate moves into the kitchen evidently were meant to resemble his hero's swagger. He stopped a few feet short of the table and struck a classic John Wayne pose—the one that resembled Michelangelo's David sculpture—with one hand poised in front of his chest, fingers curled around the end of a small, ratty blanket draped over his shoulder, and the other hand dangling loose at his side. One leg was bent at the knee.

Erik's face was wide like it was made of silly putty and someone had stretched it horizontally until his features—his eyes and nose and mouth—became elongated from ear-to-ear. He looked more like the hobbit Bilbo Baggins than John Wayne.

Alex thought Erik's stoutness somehow looked new, as if he had up until recently been much thinner, perhaps even fit from running and hard, physical work. Alex's eyes were drawn to his plump belly. The brass buckle on his belt was propped underneath and looked to provide much needed structural support.

The man had an unwashed smell that neither Alex nor Kate could deny.

Kate spoke softly to him: "It's all ready, dear. Have a seat and I'll dish you up."

Millie had told them that as The Duke he did not talk, so she asked no questions.

"I'll get your coffee in a second."

With food on the table in front of him, it seemed that Erik the Duke no longer noticed his new visitors. He shoveled stew into his mouth spoonfuls at a time until his cheeks bulged and then he dabbled at the mess on his lips with a napkin as he chewed and swallowed. This process repeated through two large bowls and culminated with a belch. He then blew on his coffee vigorously even though it had already cooled, and he gulped it down pausing just once, with the cup still held to his lips, to breathe through his nose.

When Erik finished, he stood, undid his belt a notch right in front of them, retrieved his blanket from the back of his chair, and did his quick-step-swagger out of the kitchen.

Alex was slack jawed.

"What the hell was that," Kate said. "Was that not the most bizarre experience of your life? Where did he go?"

"John Wayne movie," Alex replied, remembering that Millie had said after supper he often went back to his room to watch one.

"Is that it, then? Are we done with him?"

Alex shrugged. "He's done with us, anyway." He looked at his watch: it was only 5:17 p.m. They had plenty of time to look at Edward Tudor's other journals before the concert.

After nearly ninety minutes of reading, Alex decided to skip ahead to the final entry of the last journal before they left for the grocery store for pancake mix. Alex first read it to himself, then aloud to Kate.

December 4, 1918,

On our drive home from Doc Hammerstein's in Duluth, we could see that a thick blanket of fresh snow had covered the road, but before turning in I told Christine that I wished to walk the remainder of the way. When she drove off, I closed my eyes and tried to accept my diagnosis. I plodded up our Cragside Hill alone. At the top, when I caught my breath, I looked not ahead at our stone chimney that had been my guide, nor did I look at the lake in the distance below. No, I turned to look at my footprints that had brought me there … and they were as straight as straight can be. Thanks be to God.

"What's that mean?" asked Kate, wrinkling her nose.

After having learned so much of the man's life in his own words, Alex felt like he understood him somewhat, but this last entry was unique. It was the only one that Alex thought could be construed as profound, nearly poetic. It was also the only one that managed to encapsulate Alex's sense of the man's life in a few sentences. On its surface, it sounded regretful but it was, he figured, the opposite. It was an expression of contentment.

"I think he came to accept himself that day," Alex said. "Embrace himself, even. He realized that he did not look at the world with an eye for appreciating its beauty, its mystery. His place in life, his accomplishment, had been making a path, plodding forward, enduring. My take is that when he was still back in Boston, he had deluded himself that he was a visionary like his brother Samuel. But to his core, Edward was just too regimented with structure and common sense."

Alex stared at the date of the entry; he could not imagine how different life would have been back then. "But, at least on December 4, 1918, he was finally pleased with who he was. I think that's what he meant by his last entry."

Alex and Kate did not notice Erik standing in the doorway until he spoke.

"Mr. Mead's lantern." His voice was breathy and his eyes were timid behind lids that fluttered as if blown open and closed by his own voice. He wore gray sweat pants and an untucked white Rugby shirt with an embroidered blue violin on the breast. The shirt was stretched tight over his belly.

He was no longer the Duke. He was Erik.

Alex looked at the oil lamp on the desk. "That's right," he said as calmly as he was able. "That's John Mead's lantern."

"Mr. Mead, he's gone."

"Yes, he is, Erik." Alex did not move a muscle so as not to startle the man. "We're staying at his cottage this week. We borrowed his lantern."

Erik waddled into the study and inspected it. He touched a finger to its glass then jerked away as if it were hot.

"You talk like him," said Erik, still looking at the lantern.

"Like who?" asked Alex.

"You talk like him. You will find him and take him away in the boat. Just as he planned. You're not like the other seeker. I left him for *you*."

"What do you mean, Erik?" asked Kate. "Is the other seeker Tin Man? Alex will take who away in a boat?"

Erik retreated from the study as unexpectedly as he had entered, and they saw on his back a large, black numeral one. In the great room, he walked at right angles around throw rugs and furniture and plopped down on a massive pillow on the floor in a corner next to the grandfather clock. Alex and Kate approached as he was crossing his legs but he did not look up at them.

"Did you know John Mead, Erik?" asked Alex.

Erik gave no response except for a twitch of his chubby jowls that might have been a nod.

"Erik, honey, we need to know more about John Mead and the Tin Man," prodded Kate.

"It's not finished. It's never finished. It needs someone."

"What does, Erik?" Alex pressed.

"You talk like him."

"What will never be finished?"

"You talk like him."

Chapter 15

Speeding around the bend in Stonebrook's drive, Alex was relieved to see that Paul's little yellow truck was not in front of the cottage. They had all but run through the supermarket and now they zipped into the cottage to straighten up as best they could before their guests arrived.

"They're here!" announced Kate, glancing through the front window. She grunted as she hoisted up a heavy suitcase full of scrapbook supplies and stashed it in the entryway closet. She saw her yoga matt draped on the back of the couch, ran for it, and tossed it on top of the suitcase and closed the closet door. "What do we need to do? Chill wine? Light candles? Arrange chairs?"

Alex was picking up the sitting area around the fireplace: "I don't know. I've never hosted a classical concert before."

Kate flicked on the outside light for their guests and glanced outside.

"They're getting out, Alex. Oh my! Paul's wearing a tuxedo!" Kate stifled a giggle behind her hand. "Okay, I'm officially freaked out. But, how handsome. And his mother … he's helping her out now … she's wearing—yup, black evening dress."

Alex walked up behind his wife and she turned and stared at him.

"What?" he asked before he realized how disheveled he looked. He had not shaved in two days. His left sock must have caught on something because it was halfway off his foot; the dirty underside of it had flipped up over his toes. His hair was still damp and messy from the drizzle on the long walk back from Tudor House to their SUV.

"Oh, Alex, you look like hell—go upstairs and do something with yourself."

"Do what?"

"I don't know—just make yourself presentable."

"New socks, it is."

His mother, Paul explained to them when they stepped inside the cottage, had misplaced her hearing aid, so the introduction that took place was brief, informal, and loud.

In lieu of a handshake, Elsa extended both her hands to Kate and then Alex. She held his hand in hers: her fingers felt warm and airy-light, like fresh-baked bread sticks.

"Pleased to meet you, Alex, dear," she said with a wink. Her voice crackled with enthusiasm. "Paul has told me what a wonderful boy you are."

"The pleasure is ours," Alex replied. He found himself surprised by Paul's mother. To say that a woman can be physically beautiful at the age of eighty-six struck him as unusual, but that was how he saw Elsa. Beautiful. The fact that she was likely bald underneath the burgundy bandana from chemotherapy treatments did not matter. The rigors of time and advanced cancer were present—wrinkles framed her eyes, mouth, and high cheekbones; her skin was pallid—but they did not detract from her beauty as much as they added a timeworn, stubborn dignity. She looked like the late actress, Jessica Tandy.

Kate led Elsa to the couch while Paul brought his violin case to the dining room table and sat down.

"You ready?" Alex asked, sitting down next to Paul at the table. He finally looked at Paul: "Hey, you okay?"

"I don't know how to play for you."

"Play however you want."

"I can't." Paul shook his head. "It's hard to explain."

"We're not picky, Paul. Heck, play violin chopsticks if you want. We're just happy to listen."

Paul glanced at his mother who was laughing with Kate on the couch. His voice was soft when he spoke: "For a long time now I've been playing to soothe. Remember our discussion in the boathouse? Textures, contours, and colors? In music, they're rich. Mother taught me that. Since her cancer, I play reflectively for her. I let the notes linger so she can separate the sounds like colors onto her own palette, colors for her to dab at and apply to whatever musical scenes she wishes to create in her mind.

"When I play, Alex, she smiles a far-away smile and her eyes fix on a point in space, like she's neither here nor there … she's just, released. See?"

Alex nodded. He did see. Paul knew his mother thoroughly: her passions, her happiness, her faults, her fears.

He would tap them on their shoulders. The fears and anguish he could dupe for a short while; get them dancing with each other in a corner like marionettes on a tiny stage. Her passions and happiness, he would untie and unmask so they could sway and pirouette, if only for a short while, unencumbered by strings. By cancer. "Play in a way that comes to you, Paul. Just let it come."

While Paul checked his appearance in the bathroom, Alex served wine, lit candles and the oil lamp, turned off the lights, and added logs to the fire.

Alex sat quietly on the couch with the two women, anxiously sipping wine, listening to them chitchat, until the lanky musician appeared. In Paul's hands, he thought, the violin and bow looked like small toys, yet they also suited him.

Alex had placed a chair at the rear of the great room, and Paul now nudged it with his foot. Then he nudged it back again, where it was. He sat, then stood. He brushed his pants, sat again.

Paul closed his eyes, and when he finally opened them again, he seemed to be a different person—there was no aura of bashfulness. He gazed not at his audience but into them.

Autumn from Antonio Vivaldi's *The Four Seasons*, he announced, was to be the first piece of the evening. His mother, he explained, had cherished *The Four Seasons* since she was a little girl learning violin. When Paul was a boy, she had once played it for him solo in the empty, ornate concert hall in Minneapolis. Thus began their tradition of playing it together four times a year: Spring in spring, Summer in summer, and so on.

"On this occasion," he added, "I will play Autumn as I have never played it before. The *Allegro* will be for mother and will represent the autumn of her cherished tour of Italy, before I was even born. The *Adagio Molto* will be for Kate, the *La Caccia: Allegro* will be Alex's, and both of these pieces shall offer a flavor of a North Shore autumn."

Kate turned to smile at Alex, and he could tell she was giddy with joy, even though neither of them knew what "allegro" or "molto" or any of those other words meant.

Then at last, but only for a moment, Paul eyed the violin in his hand and it sprang under his chin as if beckoned there.

Music had captivated Alex in the past, but in this silence before bow touched string, his head felt like it was at the end of taunt ropes, like a hot-air balloon waiting to be released. He knew Paul would take him on a ride. His scalp tingled, and his mind was ready to feel air.

The first strokes seemed to violate the strings and they cried, begging for more. Alex's mental tethers were not loosened; they were slashed. The voice of the violin was silky blue, wood scented and cold. It was a great gust that lifted him into a rich and vivid scene: he saw two peasant girls, the ones he had imagined laughing and playing in the brook, only now they were young women with long black hair. Riding the violin, Alex's mind swept down a cobblestone lane on the outskirts of an old Italian village—the women, walking ahead, had turned a corner and the violin sped up to catch them.

They were naked.

Breasts swayed, hips rotated, bare feet padded the stone path. The violin passed them and turned for a look.

The violin blew autumn winds incessantly, chilling them: faces braced, arms crossed, nipples hardened.

Swirling leaves scraped against the path.

A foggy, horrible realization came to Alex: *Paul, why do you treat these girls so? Your music is warm but you play it cold.*

Paul's violin slowed, and he brought the women to a beautiful country garden complete with a grand water fountain and hedge maze. The women hugged, like sisters trying to keep warm.

Paul's playing ended as abruptly as it began, and Alex's eyes popped wide open.

He was not in Italy; he was inside a cottage in Minnesota.

Next came *Adagio Molto* of Vivaldi's *Autumn*. Alex closed his eyes again. But with this piece no strange scene enveloped Alex. It was like a simple study of color and time: a green leaf turning to yellow, to rust. Its life drained by a beautiful rigor mortis until a breeze plucked it from its branch and it fell into a brook.

Alex filled his mouth with more wine and let its oaky-dry taste rest on his tongue. He had poured too much and now he drank too fast.

The last piece, *La Caccia: Allegro*, Paul had said was for him.

Alex swallowed.

Rhythmic and steady, the violin hinted at something but kept coming back to itself, repeating, stressing, and then trailing off for more consideration at what else might be.

He rested his head on the back of the couch and felt his mind squeeze between the bow and strings; it sailed into the air of the great room, higher and higher.

And in his mind he saw that they were not alone.

In the library, two men sat in the high-back chairs.

Samuel Tudor and John Mead. They were not whispering; they were staring intently at Paul. Their ashen faces and pale eyes made them look like wax figures, yet they also looked very much alive.

To his horror, the men tilted their heads up and they looked into the open air of the great room right into Alex's own mind, into his soul.

They saw him, they saw him … they saw him!

When Paul finished, the applause from Kate and Elsa startled Alex from his dream and his mind plunged back into his body on the couch.

The three pieces of Vivaldi's Autumn could not have been more than fifteen minutes long but it seemed to Alex that he had been absorbed for hours.

His heart pounded, his palms were sweaty. Frazzled, he absently studied his empty glass as Paul introduced the next piece as solo violin material by Italian composer, violin virtuoso, Nicolo Paganini.

Elsa said, "Paganini, dear? Since when have you played Paganini?"

"Since here," he replied. "I found some sheet music in the cedar chest so for about a year now when I'm cleaning up between renters, I play it."

Alex did not know Paganini from Panini, but he figured his music would be extraordinary. Next to him, wrapped in a shawl, Elsa looked proud and surprised. And next to her, Kate simply looked radiant. Her face, backlit by low flames and bright-orange embers of the fire, was aglow with excitement.

He did not share her excitement: he had just returned from a chilling autumn day in rural Italy and saw a solitary leaf reveal its vibrant colors at the moment before its death. He had just floated near the ceiling and saw dead men behind them in the library.

"Paganini was master of the G string," Paul added, and the first piece he would play would be entirely on that one string.

Alex clutched the arm of the couch with his left hand and grabbed the seat cushion between his legs with his right.

Please, no.

Paul sat with limbs akimbo in the chair. His face was a sweaty glow, and when his tapered fingers started the Paganini piece, Alex imagined it was like watching the composer-violinist himself. Paul's face contorted so acutely he looked like a demon.

The sound of the G string was dark-hued. Played on its own, it was a day of gray skies and rain. It was waves crashing. Stormy, yet contemplative.

And it finally struck Alex what was happening to him at Stonebrook.

He was transforming. The person who he was deep down since Michael died was finally coming to the surface. The haze that had been thickening over his soul was blowing away.

At Stonebrook, the binds on his buoyant mind were more than loosening, they were popping free.

He had always felt that ideas had texture, thoughts had contour, emotions had color, but here he could no longer dispute this. With his enhanced perceptions came not just greater appreciation but exploding passion: life was not a mere existence. It was a struggle to understand and express; it was a challenge to explore and discover.

Life was a calling to the helm of one's own ship, and the voyage was one of enlightenment. No previous sailing experience required.

Paul was right when he had told Alex in the boathouse about the ability, and the *willingness*, to loosen the binds on one's mind. Alex had the ability within him but never the willingness. It was the mystery of Stonebrook and the friendship of this man who played Paganini that had given him that. He only hoped—prayed—that it would stay with him and result in something worthwhile.

Although Paul's music offered somber impressions, the pieces he chose to play were full of excitement and vigor. Perhaps Paul himself struggled to understand his own calling, his own muse.

Alex rested his emptied Kerr jar on the floor.

Next to him, Elsa began to cry. They were good tears, tears that flowed from love and raw emotion. They were inconsolable because they did not desire consolation.... He understood that.

He understood many things now.

After the applause and his awkward bow, Paul tried to convince his tired-looking mother it was time to go home but she would not hear it.

Kate offered to make pancakes and Elsa seized upon the idea. "My dear," she said, clasping her hands together, "that would make an already lovely evening even more special."

"Well, it's all settled, then," Kate said. "Why don't you boys head out to the woodshed for more firewood? We ladies here will take a little break before I fire up the stove."

In the kitchen, with Paul on his heels, Alex poked his head out the door. "Stopped raining," he said. He turned to Paul, an idea coming to him: "Let's go."

Paul shrugged. "Where?"

"Gold Rock Point."

"What about my mother and Kate? What about pancakes?"

"You don't know Kate," Alex replied. "She'll ask your poor mother questions for an hour before she even thinks about starting the pancakes."

Paul rubbed the back of his neck, doubtful. "I'm wearing a tuxedo."

Alex continued, "Its fifteen minutes up, fifteen back. We have time. All I want to do tonight is see the stone. Find it quick then head back and eat pancakes. Easy as that."

Kate and Elsa sat side by side on the deep, low couch. The old woman's fragile body looked draped upon it. It was as if her muscles had atrophied to mere weight-bearing capacity and they could do little more than support her bony frame. They talked about Paul's playing, but Kate could only hold back expressing her concern and curiosity for so long. "I don't mean to pry, Elsa, but—well, I hope you're doing okay, with your cancer."

"Oh, I get by, dear. I quit the chemotherapy a couple weeks ago. The doctor figures I have a month, maybe less."

"I'm so sorry … Paul never said—"

"Paul doesn't know yet. I guess I'm waiting to tell him."

Kate looked into the fire, unsure what to say.

"Do you want to know what it's like? Knowing I'll die soon, I mean?"

Kate shrugged.

"I'm untouchable. The cancer, I've beaten it."

Kate tried to understand but felt like she had no idea. "I'm sorry?"

"Allow me to demonstrate something," Elsa said. She inhaled as deeply as she could and then straightened her legs. They quivered after a few seconds and then gave out. Breathing heavily, she added, "That's the limit for me now.

Used to be—just a month ago—I could hold my legs up for twenty seconds.

"So I ask you, dear: should I feel trapped in this body? Condemned? … I often do, mind you. I am human, after all. But—and I'm aware this might not make sense—I am free to feel as I choose. Having cancer has taught me that my true self is … exquisitely … *beautifully* detachable from my physical self."

Elsa's voice was tinged with emotion, her eyes sharp on Kate's. "*Who* I am is not the sickly woman you see before you."

Kate's mouth felt dry, and she swallowed. She was reminded of her great uncle Brody who had died of lung cancer when she was a girl. Uncle Brody was an English professor who, after having broken the news of his impending death to the extended family, confided secretly to his inquisitive grand niece that life was what happened on the shelves of God's library. *You get to add stories,* he had said. *You have a bookend that's birth, a bookend that's death. When you reach your death bookend, you get to take all the stories of your life with you; you get to check them out forever, but they're the only ones you're allowed to read.* To Kate, as she grew up, this struck her as an acquiescence, as a coming-to-terms: unappealing, yet not exactly horrible, either. In fact, she thought it was brilliant.

"So who are you, then? What are you?"

"I am spirited," Elsa replied. She pressed her shaky hands to Kate's cheeks. "I am spirited." Her voice was now a passionate whisper. "And I am not what you see. Because—guess what?" Elsa paused to glance around as if she were about to reveal a big secret. "I leave this here body untended on occasion. Close up shop, if you will. And while I'm checked out I don't have to listen to any frazzle-snap status reports of its old-body, arthritic sensations."

Elsa looked down at her legs with a frown. "I'm sure not still alive for the physical experiences, but I don't subsist off my memories, either."

Kate wondered what was left, then: after all, the old woman's memories were Uncle Brody's books. They were one and the same. Why not start reading early?

"What I cherish is my true self," Elsa explained. "It's where I go when I leave my body. And that is better than withdrawing inside memories. It's what sustains me, keeps me looking forward to each new day."

"I don't understand," Kate replied. "You don't look back on your memories?" She figured every elderly person did that, especially if they knew they were dying.

Elsa smiled grimly. "Kate," she said, "I love memories, but at my age they're like everything else: shaky and fleeting. Entire years can drop out of sight. Precious events can bleed into one another, making even the sweetest of them bitter. Memories should be a support structure for who you are, not the other way around. Even at the end, you should not let them become you. I don't."

Kate reached for Elsa's hand to comfort the woman, but also to try and move on to something less somber.

Elsa bristled, withdrew her hand quickly: "You don't think this concerns you, do you?" She brushed at her dress, picked off a stubborn piece of lint. "Because you're young?"

Kate shook her head. Her own mother just died, her son died. The conversation was becoming too painful. "I'm sorry, no. I'd just rather talk about something else."

Elsa's face softened into a look of apology. She returned her hand to Kate's.

Kate looked away and cleared her throat. "So. Who is your true self, then?"

"I am a musician, dear. A person who knows how to filter beauty from a tarnished existance, stretch it taut on violin strings, release it back to the world as clean and bright as a rainbow. I am a mother who turned a mistake into a blessing, into my Little Paul."

"So you're a violin player and a mother?" asked Kate.

Elsa nodded. "In the end, it is my music and my son that define me more than anything else. They're also my medicines that keep me breathing…. So, Kate. Who are you?"

Kate felt her face flush. "Well, it has nothing to do with my job…." She thought of Michael. "I don't know, I guess."

"What defines you doesn't have to be illustrious. My own mother's was a simple one: she was always there for her kids. *Always*. Precious few women can say that, especially nowadays. I loved her dearly for that."

Kate was quiet. *Michael.* She was there for him at the hospital when he died. She wanted to tell Elsa about their son, but it was too unbearable, and she did not want to break down tonight. So she turned her attention back to Elsa and Paul.

"What did you mean, you 'turned a mistake into a blessing?'" asked Kate. "Was Paul an unplanned pregnancy?"

Elsa attempted to stand but found the effort too taxing. Kate offered assistance, but she declined with a wave of her hand and remained seated. She cupped her hand over her mouth, holding back emotion.

"I'm sorry," Kate said. "That's none of my business, Elsa. Here …" She stood up and put the last log on the fire. She bent to her knees and retrieved the blanket underneath the coffee table. "Just lie down and rest; I'll go start the pancakes."

"Oh my dear, it's okay. I've wanted someone to know the truth for years and years. But you mustn't tell anyone, especially Little Paul."

"You should confide in a friend, Elsa, not me."

"No, dear. *You*. I want to tell you. The couple intimate friends I once had—well, they're dead. My sister, she would judge. I deserve judging, but hers … hers is blind. I'm from a generation whose morals do not bend."

"But you don't know me," Kate protested.

"Ah, my dear, you are a stranger *and* a friend. You are a fresh breeze off the lake, and I like you. When we part, you'll go your way; I'll go mine. My heart lighter, and yours I pray, fuller."

Chapter 16

Wet leaves slicked the uneven path and Alex and Paul chose their steps carefully. The oil lantern turned everything sickly yellow, and objects beyond its reach seemed to scurry until, at last, the small light carved out a tree, a rock, a bush. At the narrow stretch, they brushed through pine boughs that flicked water at them and onto Paul's tuxedo like wet brushes.

Alex was certain that Kate would have objected to their hike up to Gold Rock after dark, especially after a rain, but if they could return with news of finding the stone, he thought all would be forgiven.

As they walked, Alex asked about Paul's violin, having noticed how delicate it had looked.

"It's a treasure," Paul replied. "A gift to Mother from a friend in Italy, someone she met in a little seaside village called Monterosso who had it delivered to our house after she returned to Saint Paul."

"From your father?"

"No. Marek joined mother here in Minnesota when he became a full-time member of the orchestra, before I was born. The violin arrived later. Its maker was a man by the name of Bartolomeo Guarneri, one of the finest violinmakers in history. Paganini himself played one," Paul announced with pride.

"Mother—she never touched it. She insisted she was saving it for me."

"She never told you who sent it?"

"Believe me, I pressed her but she would never tell. 'Just a friend,' she always said. 'Just a friend.'"

"It was when I was touring in Italy with the orchestra," Elsa began, "In Rome. 1946. We had a two-week break before heading to Venice and I decided to spend a week on the Italian Riviera. That's where my grandmother was from and that's where I met him: in Monterosso."

Kate wanted to ask, "Met who?" but she held her tongue. The blanket from under the coffee table now covered both of their legs. She vaguely wondered what was taking the boys so long as she snuggled under the blanket to hear about the man from Monterosso.

"He was the most amazing person I had ever met. I can still see that first day so vividly. I was practicing my violin outside at the fountain, near the beach behind my hotel. I saw him through the window at the hotel bar, speaking with a couple of Italian men wearing suits. He was ... tall, like a basketball player. An American, I had assumed, a former Army officer, maybe—a hanger-on from the war who preferred Europe to the U.S. He had brown hair, a light blue shirt, cream slacks, and sandals. But what caught my eye most was how he carried himself. The Italians gestures were so quick and expressive, which made it even more pronounced: he moved so deliberately. And he swayed, as if he had been drinking; yet there was no glass in his hand. He commanded the attention of those Italians; they couldn't take their eyes off him. When they shook hands and parted, he ordered a drink then sat down next to the window and looked right at me. I knew he would be able to hear me through the open door and so I put on a little show.

"After I finished and was putting my violin in its case, he came outside. He sat on the bench across from me and lit a pipe and then stared at the sunset. He had the most beguiling smile and his eyes were brilliant gray, like polished stones. Oh, they were intoxicating! And he said, 'music is color and perspective … it can offer the musician's soul.'"

Kate finally broke down. "Who was it? Marek?"

"My dear," said Elsa with mock anger, "it's the nature of my confessions to save the actual confessing part for the end of the story."

Where the hill got steep, Paul slipped once but regained his footing. When they neared the top, they stopped, side by side. Alex cast the lantern back and forth. There were trees everywhere.

Leading the way around trees and under branches, Alex whispered, "What do you suppose it looks like? The stone?"

"Maybe we'll know it when we see it."

As they made their way and reached the clearing near the edge of the cliff, Paul added, "Let's turn back, we're running out of trees. Edward's journal entry said they lit that fire in the center of a circle of trees."

Backtracking, they veered to the right, to cover new ground.

Alex saw it right away. Finding a pattern out of something seemingly random had always been up his alley. It was one of his fluky, useless abilities that Kate had always teased him about.

He touched Paul's elbow and pointed. "There...."

In the lantern glow, he made out three trees among others that looked to be equidistant from one another, about seven feet apart. If one drew a curved line from one to the next they would, in fact, form a segment of a large circle.

Paul gave him a quizzical look.

They walked to the nearest tree and considered the next one.

"No offense, Alex, but this would be one mammoth circle. You sure?"

The Circle of Trees reminded Alex of Stonehenge. In his mind, all the trees inside the perimeter were not even there, because he envisioned the circle as it had existed one hundred years ago. "This is it."

Paul dropped a coin on the ground as a marker and they started circling clockwise, one tree to the next. Deciding upon the forth tree was difficult and then the fifth tree in the arc was much smaller, much younger than the others. Paul wrapped his arms around its trunk. "This one wasn't here at the turn of the century. It's fifty, sixty years old, at the most."

Alex cast the lantern on a couple older, larger trees outside the arc that they had been following, but excluded them. "We'll go with the young one. It's in the pattern."

They kept on. Seven feet, tree. Seven feet, tree. Seven feet, tree.

Forty-nine trees later, Paul picked out his quarter on the ground and bent to retrieve it. "You did it, Alex. I don't know how … but you did it."

Alex felt a chill, and his heart pounded in his chest.

They had found it.

The Circle of Trees.

"We ended up seeing each other every day until I returned to Rome. He had just come from there and was headed farther north somewhere—oh, where was it now—to Prague, I think … or maybe Edinburgh, Scotland. I can't remember. Anyway, he took me to a small concert—Mozart and Paganini, it was. He held my hand during the last Paganini piece and I let him. The next day was our last and we spent it together. We walked along the beach and through the vineyard slopes overlooking the Mediterranean Sea.…" Elsa was smiling distantly and she brushed her fingers across her temple and behind an ear as if taming wind-blown hair even though she had none. "And, Kate, that afternoon we were overwhelmed by the attraction between us. We strolled through the olive trees.… We shouldn't have done what we did, I know. But we did. It was just that one time that we made love. It was then that Little Paul was conceived."

Kate was entranced, waiting for more, but Elsa went silent. "So why do you want to keep this from your son? That's a nice story."

"Because. That man. He was not Marek. I was engaged to Marek in Rome three weeks prior but he did not join me on my little trip to Monterosso. Kate … Little Paul's father was someone else."

The trees, young and old, were perfectly spaced the entire way around. Inside the circle, none of the trees appeared to be as large as the oldest batch that formed the circle. "It's as if whenever a tree died that made up the circle, a new one grew right in its spot," Alex said.

"Yeah," Paul replied, "but it's not natural. Mother Nature can do many things but being precise in her tree distribution is not one of them. How do you explain that?"

That trees too young to have been written about by Edward Tudor composed some of Samuel's Circle of Trees did not cast doubt on Alex's resolution. Someone had planted them to replace the dead ones to keep the circle unbroken and alive. John Mead had.

"Who was Paul's father?"

Elsa looked past Kate to the dying fire. With the lights still off in the cottage, her watery eyes reflected the glowing embers.

"My dear. It was John Mead."

They aimed for the center and strode right up to the stone. There were other stones but Alex walked right past them. He had a hunch about this one. It was the size of a bowling ball; it would be moveable. He handed the lantern to Paul and knelt to the ground. Water soaked through the knees of his jeans. He cleared away some leaves and pulled grass from around the base of it, exposing dirt. The moss-covered stone was only partially buried. He almost decided to rock it loose but changed his mind. It could wait until tomorrow. "What's this about, Paul?"

Alex's question was rhetorical but he looked up at Paul anyway.

The man stood over the stone, over him, swaying in the stillness.

Pancakes on a Tuesday night, Alex and Kate had learned, were not to be eaten with a serious face or a heavy heart. That was the rule.

Alex's heart was feathery light; he devoured his pancakes as he shared the news of finding the stone.

After eating, Alex and Paul washed and dried dishes—their punishment for hiking up to the cliff at night—and started making plans to head back up first thing in the morning. Kate put dishes away, listening to them. Elsa had excused herself to the library and sat in one of the high-back chairs, an old travel book of Italy in her lap, unopened. Her hands rested on it as she dozed in the chair.

When the Kransbergs left and Alex had locked all the doors, he went upstairs to the bedroom where Kate was already getting her pajamas on. "You okay?" he asked, resting a hand on her shoulder.

"A bit tired, I guess. It's been quite a day."

"Just since Paul and I got back from Gold Rock, you've seemed …" Alex struggled for a word and added, "preoccupied."

Kate looked down at the floor. "Elsa told me some things. But I'm not supposed to tell you."

Alex was well aware of his wife's tendency to share the secrets she was supposed to keep from him so he went about undressing without saying a word. She usually divulged faster when he did not pursue things.

Kate sat on the bed and started to cry. Alex sat down next to her.

"Alex, it meant the world to her to come to Stonebrook … to watch Paul play his violin here. I mean, because of her cancer."

Alex nodded. "She did seem to get pretty choked up, didn't she?"

Kate put her hand on Alex's knee. "Are you really going up to the point tomorrow?"

"Yep."

"To dig up that body under the stone?"

"Yep."

Alex stood and walked around to his side of the bed. Tonight was the night to get further in his dream, he had decided. *Tranquility, Interruption, Tempest, Falling.…* This recurring dream had been in the back of his mind all day. He would have a similar dream again tonight; he knew he would. Tonight he would let it flow; he would make it past *Falling*.

He saw Kate watching him from the bed. He took off his watch, put it on the nightstand and got into bed.

"Alex?" she said.

He looked at her; she waited for his face to clear, for him to fully hear what she was about to say.

"Alex, I changed my mind. I'm going up there with you. Whatever's here on this property—I'm in, same as you guys. We're a threesome from start to finish."

"You sure?" Alex was more than a little surprised.

"Look, you guys need me. I can't explain why right now but you do. And this place—it touches each of us and we each have our own motivations, our own dreams … myself included."

If you can force your heart and nerve and sinew
To serve your turn long after they are gone,
And so hold on when there is nothing in you
Except the Will which says to them: 'Hold on!'

—Rudyard Kipling, *Rewards and Fairies (1910)*

Wednesday: Silver Moon over Monterosso

Chapter 17

Floating on his back in a small pool, Alex felt intoxicated by a silky, warm liquid that enveloped him. High above was a ceiling fresco of forest and sea—roaming beasts, soaring birds. He inhaled deeply. A rapping sound from far off, like the dull sound of knuckles on a wooden door, interrupted his tranquil bath. Except instead of stopping to wait for an answer, the echoing sound continued unabated. It became louder, faster, as if some creature was approaching. He heard a *snort*, loud and guttural. Slushy raindrops started to dapple his bath, dropping down from clouds in the painting on the ceiling. He dropped his legs under him but could not touch the bottom of the bath. Sleet pelted his face, slapped the water, and then a spiraling undertow tugged him down, spun him around and around. As he started to spin, he caught a glimpse of a boar's head, each rotation bringing to light bits of horrific detail: black eyes … yellow tusks … coarse, brown-black hair … snarling teeth. In the swirling tempest, the boar spoke, its throaty voice loud and urgent:

"Shhhhuuumaaanoooo—shhuuumaaaallleeeeavvvv—*heeeeereaaarre*—sorrrrryyyyyseeeeeeeeeas."

He spun down through the eye of the whirlpool into complete darkness, splashed into water and sank fast until his feet hit something hard. He reached down and felt the object. It was a stone.

Just then, he heard his name whispered: "Alex."

Again: "Alex."

There was something over him, holding him down. No, it was … covers. The quilt. The quilt at Stonebrook.

He felt his dream evaporate, but it had not been a dream, not a regular one anyway. It was something more.

"Hey, Alex," said a familiar voice. Someone nudged his shoulder.

He opened his eyes and saw Paul holding a flashlight, its beam cast aside.

"Jeez, Paul, what are you doing?" mumbled Alex, disoriented. When it dawned on him that he had made it through *falling* and had been on the verge of the next phase, he became disappointed.

"Sorry. But you're the one who wanted to be up on the cliff at sunrise." Paul shined the light on his watch. "Sunrise is forty-five minutes."

"Well, you shouldn't have taken me seriously," replied Alex with a yawn. He leaned over and nudged Kate.

"Wait, Alex, Kate's not coming, remember?" whispered Paul.

"She changed her mind."

Just then, the lump under the quilt-lake moved and an arm emerged and clicked on the bedside lamp on the far side of the bed. "That's right," announced Kate, sounding more awake than Alex. "Someone has to keep you two dreamers on task."

Alex said to Paul. "See? You heard the lady. We have some digging to do."

When they reached the top of Gold Rock Point, Alex set his shovel and pack on the ground next to the stone. He walked past the far end of the Circle of Trees toward the edge of the cliff. The sun was still tucked under Lake Superior and the horizon was turning beautiful shades of pink and purple. Far overhead he saw the Northern Lights.

The morning was clear and still. Alex exhaled and watched the plume of his breath dissipate. He tried to locate the wreckage of the *Madeira* but it was out of sight. He scanned the lake. There were no ore boats, no fishing boats. To the right, on the neighboring cliff to the southwest, stood Split Rock Lighthouse. She was now a sentinel of the past, watchful over nothing. Redundant since the advent of navigable radar, she had been decommissioned on January 1st, 1969. From her new museum, tourists bought posters and bookmarks with her likeness. Hordes of them trampled onto her grounds and entered her. Cameras clicked, video cameras whirred. Children with sticky fingers clambered up and down her circular steps, making a game of her, uninterested in her significance, her past.

"Whatcha see, honey?" asked Kate. She had walked up behind him and curled an arm through his. In her other hand was a steaming hot mug of coffee from the thermos she had brought up for them.

"I just wanted to be up here at the same time as Samuel and Edward. See what they saw that morning."

A shooting star zipped across the sky as Kate handed the mug to Alex. "Beautiful."

Alex took a swig of the coffee; Kate had made it strong. It tasted like hard liquor. "And here we are," he said, "over a century later, unearthing what they buried that morning. Between then and now, Lake Superior was a wealth of commerce and fishing … it rose and fell."

Alex looked over his wife's shoulder behind them and saw Paul leaning on his shovel. He returned his gaze briefly and then looked down at the stone. He was anxious; he wanted the job done. They all did.

"It'll rise again," Kate said, squeezing his elbow. "Come on, let's get this over with."

Three feet deep, Paul's shoveling became lame and he stopped.

Alex kept at it, hard. Adrenaline and the strain on his muscles gave him a sweet rush.

166

The sun now over the horizon made everything look brighter except for in their deepening hole.

Kate stood back with her arms folded in front of her, watching her husband pitch soil up and out, up and out, up and out.

Paul sat cross-legged at the edge and started pushing dirt away to keep it from spilling back into the hole. "Go easy now," he said. "We're digging straight down from the spot of the stone—we'll hit his rib cage."

Alex grimaced at the thought of cracking a rib with a shovel. The sound of it would be ghastly, like cracking a lobster claw.

"Shouldn't we dig down by his feet or something?" asked Kate.

"We don't know which direction he's lying," Paul replied.

Alex paused for the first time and leaned on his shovel. Between deep breaths, he added, "If we dug to his left or right, we'd miss him completely."

Kate walked over to the dislodged lichen-covered stone and nudged it with her foot. Holding her mug with both hands, she looked for the perimeter of the Circle of Trees that Alex had pointed out to her and tried to connect one tree to the next. Even with the daylight she could not do it.

Alex, covered with dirt and sweat, dug relentlessly until at last he tossed his shovel aside and doubled over with exhaustion.

Kate looked in the hole and held a hand to her mouth. "Oh, God."

In the bottom of the hole, a portion of three ribs was exposed. Human ribs. They were grayish white and poked through shreds of a ratty material that might have been the remnants of a shirt or coat.

"Kate—" started Alex, looking up at her.

"What are we doing?" She looked flustered, almost panicked.

Alex held his hands out to her, palms down, to calm her.

To Kate, the brown-red dirt on his fingers looked like caked, dried blood. "He's for real," she said. "Oh, God."

Alex made a motion to get out of the hole and she backed away from him.

"We have to call the police," she added.

"But we don't know—"

"He was murdered!" She glared at her husband. "We *know* he was murdered, Alex. We can't go digging up murdered people! There might be evidence here, and what about respect for heaven's sake?"

Alex got out of the hole, walked up to her, rested his dirty hands on her shoulders. "This man died in 1905, Kate. If he was murdered, whoever had killed him is long dead, too. This is no longer a matter for the police."

"Well, it *should* be a matter to the police," Kate replied, defiantly. "It should be a matter to somebody!"

"It does," Alex said. "It matters to us. We'll find out what happened to him. I know we will."

Sitting at the edge of the hole, Paul piped in, "After being pinned underneath that stone for so long, unknown to the world, this man deserves to be discovered. He deserves to be exhumed so his story might be known."

Kate wiped her eyes, irritated by her sympathy for a stranger who had died more than a century ago. "Okay," she said. She exhaled, calming herself. "Alright."

Alex and Paul kept staring at her, as if making sure she was okay.

"Well?" she prodded at last. "Get back to it, then."

Loosening hardened soil with a trowel and brushing it away with his hands, Alex gained access underneath the ribcage from the area that at one time had been a stomach. He reached into the cavity and felt for a small box as if he were groping inside a store-bought turkey for the giblets.

"Nothing," he announced with a grunt. "Wait. Wait!" He started pumping his arm in and out of the hole, scrapping and pulling out clumps of death-soil.

He grabbed at something and pulled, but his fingers slipped and his hand came out empty. Then he tried wiggling it.

"Be careful," Kate said. "Don't break anything."

At last, Alex pulled something out, the size and shape of a cigar box. He brushed off the lid and then froze. He blew on the remaining dirt to be sure.

"What's it say?" asked Kate, leaning down into the hole, trying to see.

Alex held the box up for her and Paul to see.

Burned into its lid were three words.

Contemplata aliis tradere

"Who wants the honors of opening it?" Kate asked as Alex hopped out of the hole. "How about you," Kate said to Paul.

Paul shook his head. "Alex."

Alex grasped the lid between his thumb and forefinger then Paul stopped him. "Wait," he whispered. "Don't move. We're being watched."

Mindful not to turn and look, Alex asked, "How far away?"

"Straight back from Kate, fifty yards out. From the path."

"Same guy that you've seen before?"

"No," Paul replied. His eyes narrowed. "Somebody else."

"Maybe they're together," offered Kate. "This one watches us while the other one breaks into the cottage."

"Could be," Paul replied, scanning the area around the man without moving his head. "There's nobody else up here, anyway."

"Does he have a weapon?" asked Kate.

"Not that I can see. He's just ..." Paul flicked his eyes back to peer directly at the man again. "Standing there. He's ... *fidgety.*"

"What do we do?" asked Kate, not hiding the fear in her voice.

"He keeps looking over his shoulder," added Paul. "Like he's worried that he was followed by someone. This one—he's really, really chubby. And short."

Alex raised his eyebrows.

Kate said, "Duke?"

Shocked at the prospect of The Duke being so far away from Tudor House, Alex asked, "Is he wearing a cowboy hat?"

"No. He's not your cowboy. He's wearing a Rugby shirt."

"Erik!" shouted Kate so loudly she startled Paul.

She and Alex turned and spotted him right away: a big white marshmallow amid the grays and browns of a Minnesota autumn. Erik, who could barely step outside of Tudor House even as Duke, had managed again to hike to Stonebrook and then follow or find them way up on Gold Rock Point.

Alex stood and waved but the man only continued to stare without any acknowledgement. Alex cupped his hands to his mouth and shouted, "Erik! Erik, it's okay, it's us. Look, Kate's here …"

Erik glanced behind him down the hill, back at them, then again down the hill. Trepidation, it seemed, ruled his existence.

Suddenly, he lumbered away.

"Where's he going?" asked Kate.

"The path only leads to Stonebrook," Alex replied. "We better go after him; make sure he doesn't hurt himself or get lost."

Leaving the gravesite open and the shovels behind, they ran downhill, and within a minute they were upon him. Alex and Paul stayed back as Kate trotted up alongside Erik.

"Hi, Erik. It's nice to see you. Where's The Duke?"

Erik continued his snail-pace, belly-rocking jog. "Duke doesn't come to Stonebrook today," he replied between gulping breaths. "Erik comes to Stonebrook." His eyes looked shifty, like he was trying to glance behind him, but he could not take his eyes off the path for longer than a moment for fear of tripping on a rock or root. "Tall one *not* Mr. Mead," he said, sounding upset, "not Mr. Mead one bit," and then he veered off the path and blasted his way between two evergreens.

The three of them paused. He was heading west, away from the cottage, through dense forest.

Alex had initially assumed the man was simply trying to shake them, but his progress through the maze of trees and bushes was so deliberate, so efficient, that he realized Erik knew exactly where he was going. He was on a path that only he could see, a path that went back to Tudor House.

"Go after him, Kate," he said to his wife. "Find out why he came."

"Erik, honey. Where are you going?" asked Kate when she caught up.

"Tall one a trick," said Erik. He had slowed to a walk and was laboring to catch his breath. "Trickery dickery on Erik! Erik change his mind about you!"

"No, no—tall one *not* a trick," Kate replied. She knew what was running through his mind. Paul obviously bore a strong resemblance to John Mead. "He's not Mr. Mead, Erik, but he's not a trick, either. His name is Paul, and he's a good friend. A good friend who wants to help Erik. I promise.

Erik stopped but looked unconvinced.

"Honey, there's just a resemblance, that's all."

The man's expression softened but he turned a leery eye on Paul who stood with Alex a safe distance behind them. "Erik take secret shortcut," he confided. "Long way dangerous now."

"Why is the long way dangerous?"

"Tin Man lurking. Tin Man visits Duke, again last night. Erik comes to Stonebrook to warn you."

"About what? Who is Tin Man?"

"Losing patience with Duke." Erik stabbed a finger at her: "Losing patience with *you*. Tin Man is angry." He wagged his finger in the direction of Alex and Paul: "Very, very."

"Who is he?" pressed Kate. "Is he real, or can only you see him?"

"Tin Man comes after dark. Trying to find John Mead."

"Why do you call him Tin Man?"

"He says so but he's wrong."

"What does he look like?"

"Eyes behind glasses, face behind beard."

"Did he find your great-granddad's journals like we did?"

"Duke hides the clue journal when Tin Man comes to confuse Duke with pretty talk and twisty questions."

"What does he say?"

"Quackery dackery," replied Erik, shaking his head. "Not the Tin Man; not the bones under the stone."

"What do you mean by that?"

"Tin Man wants badly the key to the Reflectory. Wants The Duke to tell him where the key is but Duke doesn't answer him." Just then, Erik's face broke into a mischievous grin that showed crooked, dingy teeth. "Duke doesn't know where the key is; only Erik knows where it is. And John Mead."

"Where is the key, Erik?" asked Kate. While she was curious where he thought it was, she thought he would really have no clue.

Pointing to Paul, Erik said, "Tall man. In his hand, in the box, is the key."

Kate tried to swallow a lump that welled in her throat, and then in a nervous voice she asked, "Where is the lock the key fits into?"

Erik squinted as if perplexed by the question. "Outside the Coliseum," he said at last.

"Where is the Coliseum?"

"Everywhere. Nowhere. The coliseum is a bridge but it is really a vessel. It needs someone. It needs your husband."

Kate thought for a moment and decided on a different approach. "You said yesterday that we will find Mr. Mead. And take him away in the boat…. What did you mean by that?"

Erik touched his belly with both hands and rubbed briskly, like an anxious otter. "Not to say."

He looked uneasy, she thought. He knew more than he was letting on. "What did you mean?" she pressed, testing her influence over him. "*Erik*. Where is Mr. Mead?"

Erik glanced around, perhaps to see if Tin Man was spying, and then his broad face scrunched into a concentrated scowl. He leaned forward, appeared to wait for Kate to do the same.

She stepped close to him, bent down.

Even before she felt his warm breath on her face, she got a whiff of it. It was horrific.

Erik whispered into her ear, "Mr. Mead...." His lips puckered repeatedly and his eyes darted about. "In the mind that Sam Tudor built. All ready. You can find him there. All ready."

"In the *mind* or *mine*?" asked Kate. "Did Samuel Tudor have a mine here?"

Erik shook his head in quick jerks, his cheeks jiggled. "Min*d*," he said, emphasizing the *d*. "Min*d*-min*d*-min*d*!"

Startled, Kate asked, "Erik, do you speak with him? With Mr. Mead, I mean?"

"Yes."

"But he's dead."

"Not entirely dead."

"His spirit is alive?"

"Yes."

"Is his spirit with you right now?" asked Kate. Her skin pricked at the idea.

Erik, his face a couple inches from hers, tilted his head and gazed over the tree line in the direction of Gold Rock Point. He craned his neck in the direction of the cottage as if his beady eyes were tracking a soaring gull. "Mr. Mead has spread his spirit all over Stonebrook to protect it from Tin Man but you do not yet see him. Under the Circle of Trees ... in the cottage." Erik again shifted his gaze and looked straight down at the ground. He looked to be studying a leaf that had fallen on his tennis shoe. "He is waiting. Waiting at the end of the mind that Sam Tudor built."

"But where exactly is the mind that Sam Tudor built?"

"No more questions, no more answers," replied Erik, taking a step back. "Questions from Reflectory seekers are to be referred to Duke."

Of course, thought Kate. Duke never spoke, so questions were not to be answered.

Just then, Erik turned and ambled away muttering, "Tin Man lurking … Tin Man lurking … Tin Man lurking…"

Alex and Paul walked up to Kate just as Erik's white shirt disappeared through the trees.

"What was that all about?" asked Alex.

"According to Erik, John Mead is not entirely dead. And he's waiting for someone. Waiting inside the mind that Samuel Tudor built. He said we should watch out for Tin Man."

"Waiting inside the mine?" asked Alex. "Like a coal mine?"

"No, min*d*. Mine with a *d* at the end: min*d*. As in, the activity of your brain," Kate replied, knocking on her husband's head. "But he must have meant a mine, don't you think?"

Alex shrugged. "Wish we knew who the Tin Man is."

Still looking at the spot where Erik had disappeared, Kate replied flatly, "He's Paul's watcher in the woods. He's my bath-time intruder. Tin Man visits Tudor House at night and reads Edward's journals like we do. He's searching for the key to the Reflectory."

She turned to look up at Paul—her husband was tall, Paul was even taller—he was like a tree to her. "And according to Erik, the key is in your hand. Right there in that little box.... Oh, and guess what else?" added Kate. "Tin Man is angry. Very, very."

With the cottage locked, the three of them gathered around the dining table.

Alex opened the box. Inside, as promised, was a key. Underneath it was a slip of paper. He picked up the paper, unfolded it. Relieved that it was in English, he read it out loud:

> On the edge of reason and before the cliff of providence, you have discovered Timothy Mann, the sailor buried by a great storm.
>
> Over earth tended and wild, a stone weighed upon his heart. The same stone weighed upon our greatest regrets and our utmost hope.
>
> You have cast that stone aside.
>
> For the man, his bones shall forever remain perched over the wreck he brought upon his mates, but his soul, according to the lore of those whose storm ended his life, is now free of its earthly penitence to receive everlasting judgment.
>
> For my predecessor, for myself, the struggle for redemption lies buried in the heart of sin. What you seek is the wellspring of our spirit; what you must find is the Reflectory.
>
> At its opening are revelations; at its core, enlightenment; at its end, deliverance.

My Dearest Reader, within this message there are insights to ponder and clues to consider. Use them together to guide you on your journey.
As Always,
John Mead.

When Alex finished, Kate asked, "That's it? No explanations? No answers? Read it again."

Alex reread the message for her, pausing after every line. When he finished, he picked up the heavy key and scrutinized it, rubbing his thumb against its teeth. To him it represented those ambiguous elements of his life: that fluttering uneasiness that taunted his psyche, that sense of abstractions nearly coherent, almost perceptible. He felt like kissing the key, but he also wished to curse it, and hurl it off Gold Rock Point. He had assigned to it unrealistic expectations, and as a result, it now felt as if it locked up his soul. If they never unlocked the mysteries of Stonebrook, this magical, potent aspect of his mind would also remain sealed, tormenting him forever.

"How can that be it?" pressed Kate. "I mean; we found the man buried in the storm. We dug up this Timothy Mann's skeleton, for heaven sake. Aren't we entitled to know who the man is and how he brought about the wreck of the *Madeira?* Because how could he have? The storm wrecked it, the cliff wrecked it."

Alex sighed. He slid the key across the table to his wife. "All our answers. Everything. Is unlocked by this key."

She didn't pick it up. She frowned at it.

"Are you sure Erik doesn't know what it's for?" asked Alex. He had already pestered her about it on their walk down from the point, but he couldn't help from asking one more time. "I mean, how could he have known where it was buried but not know what it's for?"

"I told you already. He thinks it unlocks the mind that Samuel Tudor built and that John Mead is waiting inside—"

"But that has to be the same thing as the Reflectory," interrupted Alex. "It has to."

"Maybe," Kate replied with a hint of agitation in her voice, "but Alex, he talks nonsense, you know that. He says it unlocks a door to the coliseum but that the coliseum is really a bridge or a vessel—or something. Either he doesn't really know what it fits into or he just won't tell us."

Paul was examining the note as his friends bickered. "Something's missing," he said.

"See?" Kate said. "Even Paul thinks there should be more."

"Their regrets," continued Paul. He picked up the empty box, felt inside and out for a secret compartment. "The stone weighed upon their greatest regrets and their utmost hope. Their 'utmost hope' must be the key. But their 'greatest regrets' … where are they?"

Alex said, "The box in his heart, it was an afterthought, anyway. When Samuel buried the man in 1905, I'm sure he didn't gut the man's innards so he could shove a box in his chest. I don't know how long it takes a body to decompose but John Mead must have buried the box decades later when he wrote this note."

"Oh my," Kate said. "That's it!"

"What's it?" Alex asked.

"Don't you see? Their regrets—you found their regrets. I mean, they did have feelings, guys…. If John Mead buried the box, what's the only thing that Samuel Tudor buried?"

"Timothy Mann's body," answered Paul.

"And, other than his note, what's the only thing that John Mead buried?"

"The key," answered Alex. "He buried the key."

"There you have it," Kate said. "Samuel's greatest regret was, for one reason or another, the body he buried. He must have had a hand in Timothy Mann's death—"

"And John's?" asked Alex.

"How can I explain this …" Kate tilted her head, thinking. "Haven't you ever found, oh, I don't know, good and bad in the same thing? John's regret evidently had something to do with the Reflectory itself; the Reflectory is represented by the key."

Alex reached for the note. "But the key—that's their hope. Not regret."

"For John Mead, maybe it was both," Kate said with a shrug. "It has to be. It's the only thing he buried, Alex."

Paul nodded. "A person's passion in life, a person's dream, can end up being their greatest regret; especially if it's all consuming or if it doesn't pan out. Mr. Mead buried the key in 'the heart of sin'—the heart of Timothy Mann. That alone says something. Mead's sin must have been tied to his involvement here at Stonebrook."

"Okay," Alex said, "let's say that the key represents regret, but if it also represents hope—a 'struggle for redemption' is the phrase I think he used—then it doesn't belong in the heart of sin. Does it?"

"Why not?" Paul asked.

"Because. Hope and redemption, they're good things, they don't belong in the heart of a sinner," Alex replied. But he doubted his own point. He was starting to sort things out, starting to understand. An idea was coming to him that at first revealed itself in shades of gray. In his mind, he held the idea up to light, turned it slowly to see what patterns might appear from a deeper set of abstract grooves.

"Sin," Alex said loudly, as if he had figured out a challenging clue to a crossword puzzle. And he had done just that: checked all the known intersections to what he was trying to grasp: a buried key in the heart of a sinful man; a stone keeping it in place until removed; a circle of trees tucked back from the edge of a cliff. "It's like sin. Redemption represents man's salvation, our solace to keep trying even though we're mired in our own failures … so isn't sin the wellspring of human toil? Wouldn't that be the wellspring of their spirit?"

Kate's eyes were wide. "Huh?"

Alex stroked the long stubble on his cheeks. "If sin represents a fall from grace, it should also be considered a source of goodness."

"Okay," Kate said. "If I can play the devil's advocate here, you've either taken this too far or you just plain have it backwards. Sin isn't a source of goodness, Alex. That's not what we're saying. All we're saying is that the key can represent regret and at the same time represent a hope for redemption."

Alex shook his head. "According to John Mead, a person's sin shouldn't be shunned completely but kept nearby. Conversely, hopes shouldn't be held too close; they should be kept at arm's length, too."

"And how do you know he thought that?" asked Kate, challenging her husband.

"He told us. He wrote that his and Samuel Tudor's greatest regrets and utmost hope were buried 'on the edge of reason and before the cliff of providence.' *Reason* is within their control; it is where they live. *Reason* is Stonebrook. But the cliff—Gold Rock Point—is beyond their control; Gold Rock is in God's hands only."

Alex paused, then added, "Translation: John Mead did not hide the key in the cottage because he thought it bad to fixate on hopes. Likewise, he did not destroy it or throw it off the cliff, because he did not wish to forget his sin. Metaphorically and literally, he kept the key—a reminder of his own sin and a symbol of his struggle for redemption—in the heart of a sinner, on the border between that which he controlled and fate. The Circle of Trees."

Kate reached for the note on the table and read it to herself. "Okay. As usual, I don't know from where it is you pull all this stuff, but, yeah, that makes sense now. So if the key was a reminder for Mead, even a motivation, what does it mean for us? Are we just supposed to recognize that Samuel Tudor and John Mead were not angels and were motivated by their regrets? Is that the insight that's supposed to help us find the Reflectory?"

Kate turned to Paul who sat with his hands folded on the table. He had taken his glasses off so his large eyes looked naked and vulnerable. "You've been quiet," she said. "Is all this a bunch of nonsense or does it make sense?"

"Oh, it makes sense. But there's more."

"More?" asked Kate.

Alex could tell that *more* was not what his wife wanted to hear; she wanted *less*.

"When I read Mr. Mead's message," Paul said, "it feels as if he's speaking to me directly. Personally. Like he's telling me that a stone rests upon my own heart." He reached for his glasses. "He's telling me that I should cast my own stone aside; dig up my own buried regret and hope as we have dug up the key representing his. I should pull them from my heart and find meaning in them, and purpose. I should work toward my own redemption as they had worked toward theirs. If I do that, if I understand how my shortcomings can serve as motivation toward my own salvation, then I might better understand whatever it is that's in the Reflectory."

"Wow," Kate said. She looked at the notepaper that, for perhaps half a century or more, had been buried in a man's heart like a deranged time capsule. "Wow, Paul," she repeated.

"My sins aren't many," continued Paul, "but my regrets, they're—well, they're not small. Exposing them to such scrutiny is a frightening prospect."

Alex nodded, recalling the discussion with Paul in the boathouse yesterday. His poor friend had become so accustomed to hunkering down next to his comforting little brook of life, sifting its shallow waters for nuggets of meaning, that he had become afraid to look for meaning within himself. "You mean, what happens if you come up short? What happens if you find the worst within yourself but are not able to uncover your 'utmost hope'?" Alex could relate to Paul. They were very different people, yet similar in many respects. "You can't struggle toward redemption if you don't know where redemption lies."

"Oh, come on," Kate said. "Pa-lease. You guys can't be serious. You two are the most introspective people I know. If *you* can't find redemption, what chance is there for the rest of us?" She finally picked up the key that Alex had slid across the table. "Anyway, this key opens the Reflectory but what is that exactly?"

"There are only three doors in the cottage with locks," Paul replied, "and they all take the same key—the key I leave for you renters in the flowerpot next to the front door. The carriage house has much smaller locks for the service door and the stable door is padlocked."

"How about a closet or a drawer?" asked Kate.

"Nope," Paul replied. "Not at Stonebrook."

"A secret attic? Crawl space?"

Paul shook his head.

Kate frowned. "Well, we're looking for the wellspring of their spirit? What's that even supposed to be? I mean, how big is it?"

When nobody answered, she sat back in her chair, lacing her fingers behind her head. "The bathroom. I'd hide the wellspring of my spirit in the bathroom."

Alex laughed; even Paul chuckled.

"*What?*" Kate asked, defensively.

"Why on earth would you keep it in the bathroom?" asked Alex.

"I'd want to relax with it. In a nice, hot bath. Well, before my bath yesterday, that is. Whatever the hell the wellspring of my spirit is, I'm sure it's something lovely that I can pull out and enjoy."

Paul jumped in. "I know where mine is."

"For real?" Kate asked.

"For real."

Kate leaned forward. "What? Where is it?"

"Your violin," Alex interjected.

"Close. But no."

"Your music," Kate said, "when you play your violin, I mean."

Paul said softly, "Yes. The violin, Alex, it is the box. The bow is the lock. Yet nobody else can open it. Only I can find what I find when I play."

Alex nodded: it fit him perfectly. "Okay, so where might Samuel Tudor and John Mead have put theirs? Where at Stonebrook is the lock for this key?"

After a moment of silence, a faint smile creased Paul's mouth.

"Where, Paul?"

"You know where."

Chapter 18

The day was still sunny but a cold wind blew off the lake as Paul led the way through the long grass of the backyard toward the long, gentle slope to the boathouse. The man's strides were long and quick, and Alex kept pace right behind him, his soreness from the dig went suddenly unnoticed. Kate, who carried the key and John Mead's note, struggled to keep up.

Alex kept looking over his shoulder to talk to Kate. "And wait until you see the door," he said, "It looks like a miniature version of the door at the Barbican Gate of Alnwick Castle."

Alex could name every section, every tower, of Alnwick Castle. Tucked in the far northeast corner of England he had lived there for six months on a study abroad program in college and later had taken Kate there during their honeymoon. It was where they had filmed portions of the *Harry Potter* movies, and he and Kate had even taken the train from London's King Crossing station up to the castle just as Harry left Kings Crossing for Hogwarts … except they had departed from track 6, not 9¾.

"The barbican was the main entrance, right?" asked Kate.

"Yep."

"What do you suppose we'll find? A treasure?"

They emerged at the clearing above the lake and paused to look at the boathouse below.

"Nothing personal, Paul," said Alex, "but I hope the wellspring of Sam Tudor and John Mead's spirit is not like yours. If it's something that only they could open and use, it certainly wouldn't do us much good."

Kate asked, "What if he's in there now?"

Alex looked at her. "Who?"

"Tin Man."

"Come on, Kate," replied Alex, taking her hand. "It'll be fine."

In the rear of the boathouse, they gathered around the door. Five feet wide by six feet high, it might have passed for an ordinary storage locker if not for the fine wood into which the likeness of a violin had been engraved and the ornate iron-ring handle.

Without a word, Paul kneeled and inserted the key in the lock. He tried turning the key but met resistance; he jiggled it to the left and right, pulled it out, slid it back in; tried again.

It did not turn.

Paul and Alex looked at each other, bewildered.

"It should work," Paul said. He inspected the key to see if a tooth was bent. "It should work."

Alex tried it, too, and then Kate.

Frustrated, Alex grabbed the key back from her, shoved it in. The *clicky-click-click* noise wore quickly on Kate. "It doesn't fit, Alex!"

"Where, then?" he asked, disappointed. "Where does it fit?"

"I don't know. Back at the cottage, maybe?"

"And if it doesn't? I mean, what if it fits into something that isn't even located at Stonebrook: a safe-deposit box at a bank in town, a vault in Switzerland. We have no idea. We have to leave Friday, Kate. We're running out of time."

"Can you stay up any longer?" asked Paul. "It only rents by the week, I'm sorry to say, but you could stay another week."

"I have to work, Paul," Kate said. "I don't have any vacation left. And Alex needs to decide on a job offer."

Alex absently rubbed his stubbly chin; he would have a full-fledged beard soon. To him, their life back at home seemed so remote, so foreign. It was the first time in days that he even thought about his job offers. "Let's rent it another week, Kate. We can at least stay through Sunday, then Paul could use it for the rest of the week without anyone here and keep searching."

"You better call when we get back to the cottage," Paul said. "It was still vacant as of yesterday, but sometimes I get a call right before the weekend that someone will be staying."

"Who calls you?" Alex asked, confused. He had called the 1-800 number from John Mead's attorney and spoke with a young woman.

"The rental agency, usually a gal named Anna. I'm the caretaker, remember, so they need to let me know when someone's coming and for how long."

"Where's the agency, Two Harbors?"

"Minneapolis. They're just a service, though. They have nothing to do with Stonebrook except for taking reservations."

"Who gets the money when people stay?" asked Kate.

"I don't know that people are even charged but the law firm, I suppose."

Alex shook his head. It still seemed like such an odd setup to him: Stonebrook had a maintenance man, a rental agency, a behind-the-scenes law firm. That was it. There was no apparent owner.

"What's the deal with this place, Paul?" asked Kate. "Same with Tudor House. Why do they exist the way they do?"

"I don't know … I guess they were just never sold."

"But why?" prodded Kate. "*Why* were they never sold? This place, its land, is worth millions. It would sell in a day."

Alex touched the hull of the Dispro next to him and rubbed it in a slow circular motion, as if applying a coat of wax. "They're not for sale," he said at last. He liked the feel of the little boat; it was his favorite of the two. He wondered what stories it could tell. "What's here," he continued, "it's not for sale." Just then, a palpable sense of urgency struck him, as if passed to him from the Dispro. "Let's head back up. We better reserve for another week."

Sitting on the couch in the great room, Alex discovered that his now painful muscles were merely discomforting if he did not move them. He watched Kate dial the 1-800 reservation number.

"Yes, hi," Kate said into the phone. "We'd like to reserve Stonebrook Cottage for next week…. You're kidding … you're kidding. By who? … When's the first opening, then?"

"Alex," Kate said with her hand over the receiver, "the first opening's not until January 6th. Should we take it?"

"There's nothing earlier?"

"Someone has it from this Friday through New Year's week. It booked up twenty minutes ago."

Alex rolled his eyes and shook his head. "Damn."

"Alex, I need to know. She's waiting—"

"Yes, yes," he replied, smacking a hand to his forehead. "We'll take it."

As Kate made the reservation, her credit card in hand, Alex got up from the couch and walked over to the dining table where Paul sat with his elbows on it, his palms cradling his cheeks, staring at the key in front of him.

"If we don't figure this out by noon Friday, are you able to do anything while there's another renter here?"

"I can't come and sneak around with someone here," Paul replied, "if that's what you're asking."

"How about you close down Stonebrook for awhile—say it needs fixing or something."

"I need to give advance notice to the agency so they can schedule around it."

"I mean like an emergency, like it flooded out or something."

"Can't do it, Alex. One time, a renter left the bathtub running and I had water all over. The reservation agency notified the law firm, and in a day insurance guys were out, and in two days it was fixed, everything taken care of good as new. We'll just have to wait."

Kate hung up with a grumble. "Can you believe that? Some loser just called! I mean, *just* called! It's now rented for the remainder of November and all of December."

"Did they say who it was?" Alex asked.

"She won't give that out."

Alex rubbed his eyes and leaned back in his chair. "Okay, so what now? We've already looked behind paintings, checked every closet and scrutinized every square inch of the ceiling. We've been through the note so many times I can recite it with my eyes closed."

Looking more troubled than tired, Paul still had the key in front of him on the table and he proceeded to flick it with a forefinger from each hand so that it spun counter clockwise in a circle. "When I put mother to bed last night she told me that she had a premonition. She said that if we found what we're looking for, she figured it would change my life, that I'd see everything in a new light. This place, John Mead, even her and me."

Kate sat down next to the man and touched his wrist.

"Do you suppose that whatever is here could really be so significant?" asked Paul.

Kate bit her lip, and looked away from him. She pulled the box over to her.

Alex replied, "I wish we had a better idea what, physically, we were looking for. It could be another little box or a big vault. He says our revelations can be found at its doorstep but we're fresh out of doors."

Kate screamed.

She had flipped open the lid of the box, then jumped out of her chair, pointing inside it.

It had been empty when they left for the boathouse.

But now, it contained a folded slip of paper.

"Someone read it," Kate said, still with a hand over her mouth. "We have to see what it says."

Paul reached across the table, grabbed the slip out of the box and unfolded it. "It's in Latin. It says:

Get out of my house

Kate moved her hand away from her mouth, stepped sideways to Alex, reached out for his arm.

Alex swallowed. "Is it signed?"

Paul nodded, his face looking pale.

"Who, Paul? Who signed it?"

"The signature is John Mead's."

"My God, he's alive!" Kate said. "He's alive! Erik said that John Mead is 'not entirely dead'—he's alive!"

"No, it doesn't fit," replied Alex. "He's dead, Kate. He's gone."

Not ready to let go of the possibility, Kate retorted, "But Erik said that John Mead is waiting at the end of the mind that Samuel Tudor built. Alex, Samuel Tudor built Stonebrook Cottage. Erik speaks to Mr. Mead so maybe he's here."

"Kate," Alex said. He looked into his wife's eyes, held her arms. "Someone is trying to scare us, that is all. This Tin Man person, whoever he is."

"I agree," added Paul. "He's dead, Kate. John Mead is dead."

"Hey!" Kate said. "The signature. We have two notes with John Mead's signature. Let's compare this one to those."

Using the note they had dug up for a side-by-side comparison, they scrutinized the penmanship of the signatures: the lettering was tiny, scrawling, except for the large swoop of the *J*, the swirl of the *h*, and the arching, graceful *M*. But these letters in the warning were less grand, and gave the impression of deliberateness. "They're comparable," announced Paul, "but they are different. The warning is an imitation so whoever wrote it clearly knows Mr. Mead's signature."

Alex said, "Tin Man."

"How did he even get in?" asked Kate. "We locked it up."

"He must have been a renter and knows I keep the key in the flowerpot," Paul said.

Kate sucked in her breath loudly.

"What?" Alex asked.

"If he knows Latin … he knows what *Contemplata aliis tradere* means." She tapped the lid of the box with the slogan on it. "He saw this box on the table here and now he knows we found something important inside. And he got mad. He hasn't been able to solve the mystery on his own so he watches other renters. Waits for someone else—for us—to do the work for him. He cheats."

"Why?" Paul sounded surprised.

"He doesn't get the insights," Alex said. "He can translate Latin, he knows John Mead would use Latin, he's even figured out he's looking for the remains of an unknown sailor from the

Madeira …" Alex looked at the man's stiff reproduction of John Mead's signature; he touched the letters with a finger. "That stuff's the tangible. This man's smart, probably very smart, but he's lost here because he doesn't get the insights. John Mead wove them into the clues as a safeguard against the wrong sort of person finding the Reflectory. An evil man would be blind to the true significance of this key; that it represents sin and a struggle for redemption. The insights are a security measure, a means to screen out undesirables, because figuring them out is necessary to finding the Reflectory."

Just then, Kate's eyes got big. "No!" she said. "No, no, no."

"What now?" Alex asked.

"I'm afraid to say this. Guess who rented Stonebrook right out from under us for the next two months."

Alex's heart sank. "Tin Man."

"Paul, call," pleaded Kate. They had been trying to get Paul to call the agency back but so far he was unwilling. "You have to call. We need to know who this guy is. She'd tell you because you work here."

Paul finally caved: "Okay, hand me the phone."

"Here, I'll even dial for you," Kate replied, before handing it to him on the first ring. The tiny phone was small in his hands. "Yes—" he said into it, "Hello? Hello? … Anna, sorry, this is Paul Kransberg from Stonebrook again … fine, fine. Well yes, I was wondering who might have the cottage starting Friday … and who's that? … Is that right? … No. No, that's all, Anna … You too. Thank you."

When he was done, Kate reached across the table and took it from him and hung up. "Well?" she said.

"It was reserved, as Kate said, less than half-an-hour ago by credit card. According to Anna, 'same customer as usual.' A man by the name of Nicolai Petrov."

Kate gave Alex a knowing look that he did not reciprocate. "Alex?" she said, prompting him. "The guest book?—*Loved it here. Weather was nice*—Sound familiar?"

Alex looked dumbfounded. "You really think it's him?"

Kate rolled her eyes and got up to retrieve the book from the couch in the great room.

Carrying it back, she opened it to the page with Petrov's name. She sat down, studied the entry, and then leafed through additional pages trying to find other entries from them.

She flipped back to the Petrov's page, saying, "Oh, Alex…." She then flipped ahead, page by page. "Alex. Paul. Many of the entries … actually, *most* of them…." She finally looked up at her husband. "They're fakes."

She thrust the guest book on the table as if it had burned her. "They're written with different colored pens; they say different things with different names. But they're in his writing. This *Tin Man*. He stays here all the time. Paul, come on, don't you ever see this guy?"

"I almost never see the renters," Paul said defensively. "I don't come until after they check out."

"You've seen us almost every day," Kate said, pressing him.

"I was getting the cottage ready for winter. Otherwise, I only come after they're gone. If I get a call for something and stop in while someone's here, I don't bug people—I go about my business and leave whatever it is they need on the doorstep."

Kate looked frustrated. "So, why does he do it? Make up entries?"

"I don't know," Paul said.

Alex picked up the book and flipped a few pages, looking at the recent entries himself. "Maybe others were invited to visit like we were but they didn't leave an entry so he writes in the journal using their names to encourage others to do the same in the hope they'll give away a discovery that might prove helpful to him."

"Like clues?" asked Kate.

"Yep. Except most people wouldn't perceive a Stonebrook clue as anything but a quirky thrill that makes their stay more interesting. I mean, normal people, if they found a handwritten note in Latin tucked inside a book in the library, they probably wouldn't bother deciphering it like we did, but what they'd probably do is precisely what he wants them to do: write about the discovery in the guest book. Something like, 'We absolutely adore this cottage! And that mysterious little Latin note tucked inside the Monk book that my husband stumbled upon sure added some intrigue to our stay…. We had so much fun imagining who might have written it and what it might say. We hope to come back again for our anniversary next year!'"

Kate nodded. "I get your point. So we're up against a man who stays here off and on for weeks at a time, is willing to forge entries, sneak into the cottage at will, not to mention threaten poor Erik at Tudor House. And threaten us."

"He's playing for keeps," Alex said, shrugging.

"Question is," replied Kate, "are we?"

Chapter 19

Kate pleaded to go into town alone for groceries with the argument that they needed food, and the two men should refill and conceal the gravesite on Gold Rock Point sooner rather than later. They had less than forty-eight hours until the official checkout time on Friday, she had told them, so they had to start thinking about covering their tracks and splitting up to make efficient use of the rest of their precious time.

Before trudging back up to the point, the men followed Kate in Paul's truck to the end of Stonebrook's drive. She saw in her rearview mirror that they watched her until she rounded a bend.

Eagle's Nest Road was almost a mile southwest down Minnesota 61, before Split Rock River, and Kate made the turn.

Paul had told them that he and his mother's place was a half-mile up Eagle's Nest, which Kate clocked with the car odometer. She came upon a faded sign that read *private drive* beside a dirt road. She glanced behind her to Minnesota 61, to make sure she had not been tailed, and then took a right and turned in.

The drive was narrow and skirted the hillside. Where it carved through a particularly steep incline, it offered an impressive view of the lake in the distance below. Three quarters of a mile in, as she began to wonder if she had the wrong road, she drove past a wooden gate then under a tall trellis draped with brambly vines.

The narrow ridge widened into a plateau. She saw late-fall remnants of raised flowerbeds and a vegetable garden. There were clipped box hedges; a barn; and a bench next to a small, drained pond. A cobblestone path meandered through the gardens, across the drive, and along the panoramic ridge overlooking the lake. At the far end of the plateau, a house of faded rose brick with a roof of moss-covered wood shingles clung to the edge. It was a timeless setting, thought Kate, as she pulled the car forward. The home had the charm of an Italian villa.

She parked in front, in the worn grooves in the grass that must have been from Paul's truck.

A wisp of smoke from the chimney trailed into the blue sky. Beyond the vegetable garden, a deer emerged from tree trunks and froze to stare at the SUV. Kate got out and closed the car door; the deer retreated several feet, then turned again to stare.

Kate heard the unmistakable sound of a waterfall nearby. She smelled the crisp, cold air and rubbed her hands together to warm them. Minnesota autumns were unkind to North Shore gardens and she tried to imagine the colors that would sprout in the spring and summer; the flowers and vegetables; the pool filled with water…. She pictured Elsa sitting on the bench beside the pool, sipping lemonade, lost in a book of poetry, or her eyes closed, her head tilted toward the sun. But Elsa, she remembered, would not see another spring.

At the door, Kate stared at a brass knocker of two cherubs: one wore a welcoming smile while the other had a knitted brow and a tight scowl. She wavered in her resolve to disturb Elsa. Perhaps the woman was napping or feeling sick. Kate averted her eyes from the contradictory angels, grabbed their knocker, and rapped it lightly.

She fidgeted, glanced over her shoulder to check on the deer but it had gone. As she was trying to decide how long to wait before knocking again, she turned back to see that the door had already opened.

"Kate?" said a woman, peering through the opening. It was Elsa in a wheelchair. "I was expecting my nurse—what a pleasant surprise." She pulled the door open and wheeled backwards. "Come in, come in."

Kate paused in the doorway. "I'm sorry to bother you, Elsa. I just—well, I wanted to stop by for a little visit, that's all."

"Come in, dear," Elsa repeated, motioning with both hands, "but if you're looking for Little Paul, isn't he with you today?"

"He's with Alex. They don't know I'm here."

With a puzzled expression that melted into a smile, Elsa replied, "Very well. There's hot water on for tea."

The house was tidy but haphazardly so. It reminded Kate of her grandmother's house, clean and welcoming but cluttered in the corners. The living room had burnt-yellow plaster walls and was lined with landscape paintings.

Leaning forward in her leather chair in the corner, Elsa poured hot water from the kettle into two cups on a tray at her side. "Anything in your tea, dear?"

Kate stared at the steaming cups; she never drank tea. "Sure, cream. And sugar. Two lumps." She was trying to make it into a latte.

"I can no longer stand the suspense, dear. How did the dig go this morning?"

Kate thought back to the morning on the point. She remembered the bones so vividly—the ribs, the spinal column, the box where a human heart had once been. "We found the key. And a note, too. From John Mead."

Elsa's eyebrows went up. "A note?" she asked. "What sort of note?"

"It said we're supposed to use the key to unlock the Reflectory."

"And where's that, dear?"

Kate took her first sip of the tea that Elsa had placed in front of her. "We have absolutely no idea. And it turns out someone else is looking for the Reflectory, too. I guess that's why I'm here. I was hoping you might be able to help us somehow."

"Oh?" Elsa added a lump of sugar to her own cup and stirred it with a spoon—she did this instinctively without even looking down.

"Elsa … this morning, Paul told us that you had a premonition. Can you tell me about that?"

At first, the question did not seem to register; Elsa stared blankly into space. The swirling tea in her cup came to a stop. "You're wondering if I know more about him, aren't you? More about John that I haven't told you."

Kate nodded but felt ashamed. She was asking a dear old woman to relive bittersweet, exhaustive memories.

Elsa reached for her tea. Her shaky hand and wispy thin arm lifted the cup to her lips. Before she took a sip, she said, "Best to show you, I expect." She set her cup down and winked at Kate, a smile spreading across her face. "Come along, dear. We're going downstairs."

Elsa sat on the second step from the bottom once they had made it down. "Go on ahead, dear. Stairs are my exercise." She was wheezing, trying to catch her breath, still grasping the railing with both hands. "It's in the room off to the right. I'll join you in a moment."

Kate hesitated, uncertain about leaving the woman in such a state. "Go on," repeated Elsa, with a wave of her hand.

At the end of a short hallway, Kate entered the specified room and quickly held out her hands to brace herself—it was pure reflex—because to her it seemed as if she had stepped out into the sky.

Kate heard the voice of Elsa behind her but the woman's words were slow to register.

"It was back in 1953. I didn't know who I was buying this house from or why it was such a steal. John had written me about it and enclosed some photos. He wrote that he knew it was for sale and that he could make the necessary arrangements for me with the owner, if I was interested. But this room—this room wasn't in any of the photos because it did not yet exist. It was built after I agreed to buy this house but before we moved up in late spring. So when I brought the first box down to the basement here … that was when I knew."

"Knew what?"

"I did not buy this place from a stranger. I bought it from John himself because—this room—he built it for me."

With her mouth still open, Kate turned and saw Elsa leaning in the doorframe. The woman was so alive with excitement, she looked years younger.

Kate was breathless: "It's like … a *fantasy*."

Elsa smiled, proud.

Kate walked back to her, offered an arm. "Is this a sun room?"

Elsa laced her arm through Kate's. "Sun room, sitting room, parlor—whatever you want it to be."

"Is it—are we—entirely over a cliff?"

"Three quarters of the room hangs over. The support beams are sturdy, don't worry."

Kate eased Elsa into one of a pair of thick-cushioned chairs in the middle of the room that oddly faced the interior wall, and then she stepped tentatively to the semi-circle wall of glass and touched a hand to the pane, figuring that if it felt real, the room and view must be real.

With her hand pressed against the cold, honest glass, she regained her equilibrium and focused on the world outside. Over a patchwork of treetops below, she saw the lake in the distance. A few miles out she saw the outline of a ship. Just to the left of the room, a brook spilled over the cliff, and at the bottom it flowed like a brown snake through the forest of pine and birch. "Is it Stonebrook?" asked Kate.

"Yes. You should hear the waterfall in the springtime; it roars like a lion. Look down toward the lake. Can you find Split Rock Lighthouse?"

"Yes, how beautiful! That hill to the left of it—that's Gold Rock Point, right?"

"That's right. And there's one more landmark of note."

Kate scanned up and down the shoreline but did not see anything noteworthy.

"A chimney? A rooftop?" offered Elsa.

Finally, Kate spotted it: "There! Yes, Stonebrook Cottage! This is amazing, Elsa. You can see *everything* up here."

"Oh, I can, Kate. I can … but what you see in that direction is not why we're down here."

Baffled, Kate turned her gaze northeast up the shoreline. "What direction?"

"Dear … behind you."

Kate turned and saw that Elsa had gotten out of the chair on her own and stood along the back wall between the door and a long burgundy curtain. She pulled hand-over-hand on a cord and the curtains drew open from the center to reveal an oil painting. More than large, it was imposing. A classic, Renaissance-style painting, it was a good four feet high by fifteen feet wide, with a thick, dark frame.

From left to right, Kate noticed, it told a story in pastoral scenes: girls—sisters, perhaps twins— growing up.

"You see, this painting here captures my life, Kate. It reveals the essence of who I am." Elsa glanced over her shoulder, gesturing with an open palm. "In this first scene, I'm a little girl—"

"But this," interrupted Kate, "it must be hundreds of years old. How can it symbolize *your* life?"

"It was painted in 1947, dear."

Struggling to get past the notion that the artwork was little more than sixty years old, Kate scrutinized the girls for a resemblance.

"I was much younger then." Elsa pointed to her neck: "See my mole? It's on the girls in the painting in the exact same spot."

Kate looked from Elsa to the painting, then back to Elsa. "But why two girls?"

"*Innocence and Wisdom*, that's the title.... In the first scene, they're toddlers. See how Innocence plays in the brook? She has jumped from stone to stone out to the middle of it, to the center of the scene. She's eyeing the other side even though it is clearly out of her reach. But Wisdom: she hasn't strayed from the bank; she's painted less vividly, like a shadow."

Moving to the right, Kate was drawn to the behaviors and expressions of Innocence. She became increasingly mischievous, it seemed. "Oh my," Kate said, turning her attention to the next scene, "you're naked here."

"Nude, dear. I prefer *nude*."

Kate felt embarrassed viewing the woman's young, vibrant bodies in the painting. She held a hand over her mouth and avoided staring directly at them.

"It's art, Kate," said Elsa, noticing her reluctance. "Study them; what do they say?"

Walking on a country lane toward a village, both bodies were statuesque, lovely. They were not chubby like most Renaissance-era depictions of beautiful women, but were slender, true to Elsa's form. The body and even the breasts of Innocence were tan while Wisdom's body and breasts were ivory. "Why is Wisdom nude here?" asked Kate. "It would be wrong for her to be nude, wouldn't it? They're in public. And both of them look so … seductive."

Elsa nodded but remained silent.

Wishing Alex were here for his interpretation, Kate reviewed the previous scenes. She focused more directly on the relationship of the pair, and on Wisdom, in particular. In the first scene, her eyes were opaque and were fixed with concern on the wet rock under the feet of her playmate, but her expression, Kate thought, also offered a hint of curiosity at her frolicking counterpart's behavior. In the subsequent scenes, as the girls grew up, Kate was intrigued to see that Wisdom became more active, her expression more enlightened, her eyes more animated.

In the scene after the one that depicted them as blossoming young women walking nude toward a village, they were still nude and embraced each other in front of a fountain. A man wearing nothing but a mask and a loincloth was draping a cloak around Wisdom as he exchanged a lustful gaze with Innocence. Wisdom looked sad, as if she were saying good-bye to her girlhood friend.

After a moment, Kate thought she understood the scene. "John Mead," she said quietly. "That's John Mead, isn't it?" To confirm her suspicion, she looked ahead at the next scene and, indeed, Wisdom stood alone with the cloak draped around her and a hand poised over a protruding belly—she looked lonely—just as Elsa might have felt after their real-life tryst in Monterosso. At her feet was a violin; behind her was a hedge maze. "He took your innocence. When you were … with him. Because you're pregnant in this scene. And you're alone, except for your violin. Where's Marek in all this?"

"In the maze, I suppose. The inspiration for the painting did not include Marek."

"So John Mead left you and Paul—his *son*—to journey through the maze of your future all by yourself?" asked Kate, sounding irritated. As captivating as the nude scenes were, they were nothing but promiscuity and consequence. John Mead had been an irresponsible playboy; Elsa had been his plaything. It flattered neither.

Elsa reached toward the painting and, with her hand an inch from its surface, traced her fingers lovingly across the scene of the three nude figures in front of the fountain. "There's more to the painting. Do not rush to judgment based on what you see on the surface. It is the deeper meaning that molds the initial impression into something wholly different.

"That woman in me who is Wisdom, you see? She was ready to make her own way. In the first nude scene when the pair strolled down the lane: for the first time, Wisdom bares herself to the world. In her eyes, there's intelligence, but she also has the look of Innocence from the first scene in the brook: a twinkle of playfulness. As for Innocence—her breasts are already quite tanned, aren't they? She's outgrown herself; she has lost herself.

"But their nakedness, while seductive, is not a sexual metaphor. It means that John thought I had the wisdom, the courage, to be vulnerable. To reveal myself to the world. To him. It means he saw in me a woman who had the wisdom, well before I met him, to take a final stroll with my own fading innocence before she was gone."

Elsa paused, allowing time for Kate to think.

"When I was with John, I did say a final good-bye to my Innocence. But I did so willingly and of my own accord. Innocence dwindles and dies in all of us, and she was already dying in me before I met John. That's life. What's vital is to have the insight to recognize that fact so that when she's gone, you may retain something of her spirit within your Wisdom.

"See here?" Elsa pointed at the painting. "Do you see what the man in the mask does in front of the fountain? He offers his cloak to Wisdom for her journey and leaves for her the violin. In the painting he makes the statement that he would care for us—me and our unborn son—exactly as John has done in real life."

Kate tilted her head. Perhaps she was starting to perceive the painting in this new way. "Well, how did John Mead see all this wisdom and innocence in you if you were only with him a few days? Did you tell him all this in Italy?"

Elsa shook her head. "I hesitate to share this …"

"Please. I'd like to understand."

"Remember last night? When I told you how I met John? I was playing violin on a patio between my hotel and the beach and he listened?"

Kate nodded.

"The scenes for this painting, they came to him then."

Dubious, Kate laughed and then frowned. "Are you serious?"

Elsa smiled. "That first night in Monterosso, after he listened to me play my violin, he smoked his pipe and explained to me what he saw in my music." Elsa pointed with her forehead to the painting. "And he explained this. He moved me to tears. Years later, I never expected in my wildest dreams to walk in here and discover a visual representation of who I am so accurately depicted in a such a grand painting as this, in such a grand room as this. And within my own house he had all but given me!"

"But how did he do it? How did he see all this in your music?"

Elsa shook her head as if frustrated that Kate was not grasping something. "Because it was there, Kate. I put it there. There was no mind-meld, no mingling of our psyches. When I play—I mean, when I *played*—I did more than recite, I did more than interpret: within my playing, I *did* reveal my Innocence and my Wisdom, I *did* show my frivolity and intelligence. I infused my sensuality, my desires. It was what made me so good. People enjoyed my music because they felt my heart in it. But John. He was so sensory and insightful, so gifted with perception. Not only with music, but with life.

And he peeled my music, tasted its pulp. He wasn't psychic; he just experienced things differently than most of us."

Kate felt a lump in her throat. "What was it you played for him?"

"Vivaldi, dear. *The Four Seasons.* It was one of the pieces the orchestra was playing on our tour of Europe. Since then, as you know, it's been one of my favorites. I can't tell you how much it reminds me of Italy. That's why Little Paul and I play a season every season, why he played *Autumn* last night at Stonebrook."

Elsa's eyes looked distant. "And wasn't that special? You know, when he played the movement that he dedicated to me, he played it as I had played it for John. It reminded me of my painting here."

"Elsa … is Paul like his father?"

"Yes," she said, nodding. "And Marek. Because he thinks Marek is his father, I suppose the poor boy figures it's in his genes to be somber. I think Paul has the capacity to see the world as his father saw it. He just lacks gumption."

"You should tell him the truth, Elsa. About John."

"Kate…." Elsa touched her young confidant's arm. Her breathing was labored. "You came here asking if I might know where the Reflectory is. I do not know where it is, but consider this: John had this poignant piece of art painted, he gave me this villa, and he added this spectacular room before I moved in. After his death, he supports me and all my expensive treatments—he supports *us*—under the premise that it's wages for the one who minds his cottage. I'm sure Little Paul has mentioned to you how he got the job at Stonebrook, but let me tell you, it was no coincidence that John's lawyer stopped here to inquire about a handyman. It was also no coincidence that Little Paul was not home at the time.... John chose Paul to mind the cottage. I know this. So now, with all this business about the three of you looking for the Reflectory—well, it dawned on me during Paul's concert, when he was playing Paganini ..." Elsa paused to catch her breath. "John chose Paul ..." She looked as if she might faint; she had been standing and talking unaided for quite a while and had overexerted herself.

Kate put her arm around the woman, helped her back into the chair. Then Kate grasped what Elsa was about to say and said it for her. "John chose Paul to mind the cottage because he wanted, he hoped, for his son to be the one to discover the Reflectory. So inside it is the truth."

Elsa clutched Kate's hand with both of her own, evidently overcome with emotion, yet still unable to speak. Finally, she said, "Yes, yes, yes. That is what I believe. And that is why I will leave it in the hands of John. I owe him that."

Kate sat down on the floor in front of Elsa. She felt like a little girl again at the feet of her grandma, listening to her tell one of her fascinating stories. "Did you love him?"

Elsa blotted a tear from her cheek with the back of her hand. "In my painting—did you notice? A brook is there again in the last scene at the end of the hedge maze, as Stonebrook is here now at the end of my life right out these windows. The reason he included it in the painting was because of the night of our walk in the hills over Monterosso. After we made love that night we stopped at a brook that flowed through a grove of olive trees. John started a fire there to keep me warm because I didn't want to head back down; I didn't want the night to end.

"Right there, right then … with a silver moon over Monterosso, I experienced the most extraordinary moment of my life. With his warm body wrapped around mine, we sat together on the ground in front of the fire next to the brook. I remember gazing far away at the dark line that separated the Mediterranean Sea from the starry sky above. I was physically there, but my mind was adrift, and I'll never forget the gentle, reassuring sounds of that brook as John whispered in my ear his theory that a brook captures the essence of life."

Kate had been staring at the last scene of the painting behind Elsa as she listened to the woman's story. "There's a little fire on the bank of the brook, too," Kate said softly. "Within the smoke trailing from it into the sky—is that a faint outline of two bodies?"

"Ah, now you are really spotting subtleties. What he had painted in the final scene of my life was the single moment that I had most cherished in my life. The bodies, they are women; they are me. My long-lost Innocence reunited with my Wisdom."

"As your soul? Going to heaven?"

"I sure hope so."

"You should come down, Elsa. Help us find the Reflectory."

"Oh, no; what's there is not for me. I'm … tired. It's for you younger folks: you and Alex and Paul. That husband of yours, Kate, he's like John, too. I've watched him; I know he is. And you, well, you remind me of myself when I was young.

"Can you do me a favor, dear? When you find what you're looking for, could you please light a fire down there next to the brook for me? It would mean a lot to see it."

"Certainly," Kate replied. She could see that Elsa was exhausted. "Can I help you back upstairs before I go?"

"I think I'll rest here a while. My nurse will come soon."

Kate leaned down and gave Elsa a gentle hug. "I can let myself out."

Upstairs, as Kate walked alone through the living room, she heard Elsa's voice on an intercom speaker next to the front door. "Kate? … Kate?"

Kate pressed the *talk* button and leaned down to speak into the thing: "I'm here, Elsa."

"This other person you mentioned, who's trying to find the Reflectory…." Elsa's voice sounded distant. "Do you know who it is?"

"No, but Paul called Stonebrook's rental agency and got a name," Kate replied. "Nicolai Petrov."

There was no response so Kate pressed the intercom button: "Why?"

"A couple months back, a man stopped up here at the house. A stranger. Paul wasn't home so I was afraid to answer the door, but I did anyway. Guess I was too curious."

"What did he want?"

"He asked to come inside. It was so strange: he had a Russian accent and he said that he knew someone who had stayed at my villa once, many years ago. He said it would mean a lot for him to see where this man had lived while in America."

"What did you do?"

"I shut the door and turned the lock."

"Did he tell you his name?"

"No. But you know; I almost changed my mind and invited him in. He looked so cultured and proper. I was lonely for someone to talk to."

Kate now stared at the same closed door that Elsa had stared at with the stranger locked on the other side. "So why didn't you?"

"Well, he seemed pleasant enough and was really quite handsome…. But—I don't know, dear. It was his eyes, I suppose. They looked so intense. They gave me the impression that he *needed* to come in, as if he could barely restrain himself from slamming the door open and knocking me to the floor."

Kate thought of her own run in with the man and remembered Erik's description of Tin Man: *Eyes behind glasses, face behind beard.*

She looked at the unlocked door and felt the man's presence behind it. *Pretty talk and twisty questions.* She focused on the doorknob, almost expecting it to turn. *Losing patience….*

"Kate?" Elsa's intercom voice sounded even farther away now and more stifled—as if she was trapped in a tomb instead of downstairs. "Are you still there?"

Kate wanted to go home. *Losing patience with Duke, losing patience with YOU!* Just go home and leave the North Shore behind.

She pressed her button: "I'm here." And then she pressed it again, hard: "Do me a favor, Elsa. Keep this door locked. And never let that man in."

Chapter 20

At the grocery store in Two Harbors, Kate was supposed to get enough food for the rest of their stay so they could focus exclusively on finding the Reflectory. Aisle after aisle, though, she could not take her mind off Elsa's painting and the image of Tin Man standing behind the front door.

In the canned goods section, Kate frowned at the contents of her nearly empty cart: three tomatoes, a bag of salad greens. She rolled her shoulders, tried to crack her neck. She had to stop worrying.

When she glanced up at a food shelf, it was the first item she saw: Spam. Stacked between cans of tuna and beef hash. She grabbed a can and smiled. She read the ingredients: pork with ham, salt, water, sugar, and sodium nitrite. Calories per two-ounce serving: 170. Fat calories: 140. Carbs: 0. She shook her head; Erik ate massive quantities of preservative laden calories and fat. She set the can into her cart and then wondered what had prompted her to do so. *For Erik. You never know.* Not that the Spam that was already in the pantry was bad, she thought, but why not have something fresher on hand. She picked up a second can, a third, a fourth. They clanged loudly in the cart, prompting a glare from an elderly woman in a bright green coat shuffling past.

Kate spun her cart around on a mission that dawned on her only as she rushed around the end of the aisle. She was in search of Tang.

Back at Stonebrook cottage, as Kate grabbed the two grocery bags from the rear of the SUV, she felt a sense of returning home. It had been, she was sure, the most intriguing morning and afternoon of her life, and yet it all struck her as just another day of a bizarre new normal.

Smoke puffed out the chimney and she noticed Paul's shovels were in the bed of his little truck so she knew they were back from the point. Inside she found the men on the couch near the fireplace, filthy from their work refilling the grave. Paul, a piece of chalk in his hand, was at a chalkboard detailing a map of Stonebrook's grounds, and her husband was scribbling something onto a large sketch pad.

They reported no problems, no run-ins with Tin Man, and they scattered leaves over the fresh dirt to conceal the site.

At the kitchen sink, Kate tied an apron around her waist and began scrubbing potatoes as she looked out the window. The men agreed to pull themselves away from their work to take turns in the shower while she made supper, and now her eyes were drawn to the spot where the path disappeared into the trees at the right side of the backyard. It was the path to Gold Rock Point, the path that led to Erik's secret route through Split Rock Lighthouse State Park to Tudor House. She wondered what Erik must have looked like ten years ago, twenty years ago, thirty years ago, emerging from that spot.

Did he come only for dinner? *No,* she thought, *he came over for more than that.* It was, after all, his secret path. She got a mental picture of a hidden laboratory with peculiar equipment and bubbling, frothing concoctions in beakers. In the middle of it was a man in a white lab coat with Erik at his side. Doctor Frankenstein and Igor.

Kate heard the shower shut off in the bathroom. Paul would be out soon. She spotted Alex outside, pacing the cottage grounds like a surveyor. His brow furrowed, he stopped to write something in the notebook that he had brought out with him.

He had told her that the longer they stayed here, and the more they learned about Stonebrook, the clearer yet more bizarre his mind became. He had even pictured her at the sink: wearing an apron, scrubbing things or washing. She had scoffed at him because she hated aprons; she thought of them as too domestic, too grandmotherly in a stereotypical homemaker sort of way. So she had put the apron on because she was curious. And when she had tied it around her waist, it felt good, like being at Stonebrook was starting to feel good. At the sink, when she had wiped her wet hands on it, the rough cloth was comforting. In the dining room mirror, when she had glanced at her reflection she marveled at how differently she was starting to perceive herself. It had felt emotional, like … nesting. She had leaned close to the mirror and her eyes there had a searching, yearning look to them and she remembered thinking that her perception of everything was changing, even of physical things. For a moment, her reflected eyes had looked like someone else's so she had touched her cheek and looked real close: *Who am I? Who am I really, this woman in the mirror?* Then she smiled because she liked who she saw. It was a face good and firm. Caring. And yet it was the same beautiful face she had been fretting over her entire life.

Kate sighed. Her husband's vision was not a coincidence. Not quite.

She knew that Alex was putting Michael's death behind him this week and she was surprised at herself that she was okay with that. Before, despite her love for him, she had always wanted him to feel remorse for taking their son away. She hated herself for thinking this, but she had wanted him to never let the shame go. But now, he was slipping free of his self-made prison. She felt shame now because she did nothing to help him escape his pain. She had let him suffer. Then when her mom died she compounded his misery all the more because she did not let him console her. The poor, lovely man—she had made his life *hell*.

Kate rapped on the window and waved him in so he could shower before dinner and when he opened the kitchen door, she said, "Paul's done with his shower."

She stacked the last potato with the others, set down the peeler. She wiped her hands on her apron. "Alex?" she said, turning around.

He stood inside the door, looking haggard and exhausted.

"Alex?"

"Hmm?" He could get lost in his own mental world so easily. "What?"

Kate remembered Elsa's comment that she thought Alex was like John Mead, and she found herself intrigued by his unruly imagination. She had often tried to picture people who might have lived in an old house back in its heyday: on their honeymoon, when they had stayed at Alnwick Castle in England, every time they strolled through the courtyard, she contrived in her mind a scene from the past, complete with a Duke and Duchess, knights and peasants, and she was the Duchess. Now—and *finally*— she thought of her husband as the Duke. "I love you."

Alex slouched in his chair in the library, motionless except for his eyes, which darted from one large sheet of paper to the next that they had taped to walls and bookshelves. After his shower, he had put on his tattered University of Minnesota sweatshirt and gray sweatpants with a hole in the knee. Paul sat in the other chair; he had brought a fresh change of clothes and wore a red and black flannel shirt, blue slacks, and beat-up tennis shoes. They were a modern-day Odd Couple.

They had brainstormed diligently, filling sheet after sheet with anything they could think of that might be of use, but they were still at a loss: the Reflectory was still out of their grasp.

Alex closed his eyes and imagined himself perched on top of the chimney above the roof. He envisioned himself there because it offered room to breathe and think, as if by its height and view he could examine all of Stonebrook and zoom in like a camera to wherever he wished. From his perch, he surveyed the grounds, eyed the lake, and considered Gold Rock Point in the distance.

When Kate finished up the dishes, she came into the library and handed Alex a beer. She stood in front of the Stonebrook map he had drawn on the chalkboard. It was complete with descriptive terms such as *boathouse, beach, cottage, backyard,* and *woodshed*. He had even drawn the path to Gold Rock Point. Underneath it all, he had written, *STONEBROOK GROUNDS.*

"What are all those lines?" asked Kate.

"It's a topographical map. They're slopes."

"That's a pretty big woodshed," she joked.

Alex smiled, pulling the tab on the beer can that made a loud *pssht*. After a few gulps, he said, "It's not exactly drawn to scale, Katherine."

She smirked at him, turned to examine the large sheets of paper. "What's all this, then?"

"Anything—everything—that might be a clue," Alex replied. He held his can so that it perched on his stomach and regarded his wife with half-closed eyes. After a big meal, he always got tired, now he felt nearly unconscious.

The sheets of paper on the walls were broken out into topics. Excerpts from their two written messages from John Mead were on one sheet. On it, they had added their own brainstorming notes here and there, drawn arrows between key words, circled others. It was a hodgepodge mess that looked as if they had been trying to break a secret code. Another sheet, entitled, *Profile of John Mead*, had categories such as *Skills,*

Events, Other. Under biographical, it listed an approximate age and *no children.*

Alex noticed Kate fidget when she was looking at it. "What?" he asked.

"Nothing. It's just—nothing."

The next sheet was titled simply, *Erik.* On it, they had written just six points.

1. Erik knew the Key to the Reflectory had been buried in the heart of sin, within the Circle of Trees.
2. Erik said the key unlocks the mind(?) that Samuel Tudor built (same as the Reflectory?).
3. Erik has a secret path from Tudor House to Stonebrook.
4. Tin Man visits Erik/Duke, threatens him. Demands to know where the key is.
5. Erik thinks he talks to the spirit of John Mead.
6. Erik knows more than he's letting on.

Alex saw his wife staring at the sheet and said, "Erik helped John Mead on a regular basis, Kate." He yawned, rubbed his eyes. "I mean, he has a secret path between the cottages; there's Tang and a butt load of Spam in the pantry for heaven's sake—Paul, we forgot to add that to our list—and even old Folgers and stew."

Kate walked behind Alex and rubbed his shoulders; his head lolled forward, his chin rested on his chest. "If only we knew his role," continued Alex. He tilted his head toward

Paul, "Anything else here you suppose is Erik's besides the food?"

"There are some items in those boxes in the entryway closet."

Alex nodded. He had already searched through the boxes.

"Like what?" asked Kate

"Mail order junk, mostly," replied Paul. "A Ginsu knife, a chia pet, some old records, a walkie-talkie...."

"A what?" Alex asked, furrowing his brow. He lifted his head. "A what?"

"A walkie-talkie. Army surplus, if I remember right. Must be forty years old."

"I never saw that," Alex replied. "Why didn't I see that?"

"It's in the big box on the floor, underneath the records. There's a record player in there, too."

Alex craned his neck to look at Kate behind him. "Hey, remember? What Millie said?"

"Of course."

"Paul," continued Alex, his voice rich with a burst of enthusiasm, "Millie from the park said she and Erik use old walkie-talkies. She calls him on one from the road sometimes. They could use telephones, but Erik—he prefers the talkies. John Mead and Erik—I bet they used walkie-talkies and that's why he likes them so much."

Alex leaned forward in his chair. "We have to try it. Right? Call Erik on the walkie-talkie?"

"What for?" asked Kate. "He won't answer anything; I've already tried."

Alex looked up at his wife with a mischievous smile. "But you're not John Mead."

Sitting on the floor in the entryway, Alex had the big box pulled out. Inside were the items that Paul had mentioned and an assortment of other knickknacks. He pulled out the walkie-talkie and brushed off some dust. Encased in dark-green leather, he thought it looked like a clunky stage prop, but it was heavy with outdated realness. He turned the on/off dial and heard a click but no hiss of static. "Needs batteries," he said, turning the thing over, looking for the battery compartment.

Standing over Alex, Kate had an uncomfortable look on her face. "You really think it's a good idea to pretend to be John Mead? Sounds pretty *trickery*, *dickery* to me."

"It can't hurt, Kate," Alex said.

"Well, when? Tonight?"

Alex checked his watch. It was nearly 8 p.m. and they had been awake since 5 in the morning. Paul looked exhausted, and they needed batteries for the talkie. "No, not tonight. It's too late anyway, huh, Paul?"

Paul nodded, looking grateful. "I can pick up batteries on my way down in the morning."

In bed, Kate gave her husband a rigorous massage with some of her hand lotion that smelled like apricots. She worked his shoulders and neck, his lower back, his arms. To Alex, it was pain-tinged bliss.

As he drifted off, Alex's last semi-conscious thought was of himself crouched in a dark, dank hole, reaching into a chest cavity of human remains. He was squeezing a cadaver's heart, attempting to coax it back to life until he discovered that the cold object in his hand was not a heart at all. It was a stone.

*The mind is its own place, and in itself
Can make a Heav'n of Hell, a Hell of Heav'n.*

—John Milton, Paradise Lost (1667)

Thursday: Gales of November

Chapter 21

Lying on the bank of a small brook, Alex watched sunlight drain over the hills to the west. His head was on a pillow of leaves, his body on soft moss. The whole scene was beautiful and he felt such serenity that he thought he was in heaven.

Downstream, across the brook he noticed an untended campfire. A gust of wind blew life into the meager fire and sparks buffeted from it upstream, and when they sped past Alex they turned and swirled around him and they seemed to not be sparks at all but tiny, bright holes, as if the air around him was not air but a fabric of some sort and the holes exposed this bizarre truth. Overhead, clouds rolled in, thickening the fabric-air, and big drops spilled from them. The sparks danced, evading the missiles as best they could, but one-by-one they were caught with extinguishing hisses until the last was snuffed. Lightning flashed and in its brilliant blue light, Alex saw Paul only a few feet away. Paul looked like a frightened deer—thunder peeled—and his friend bolted, setting off for the cover of his northern white cedars. The brook swelled and Alex was swept away by the engorged water as if grabbed and thrust in. He flailed, horrified, and was about to scream when the tempest changed pitch. It sounded like a nearly decipherable voice:

"Shhhhuuumaaanoooo—shhuuumaaaallleeeeavvvv— *heeeeereaaarre*—sorrrrryyyyseeeeeeeeeas."

The stream ahead disappeared into a gaping hole in the side of a cliff. He fought against the current but was carried inside then straight down into an abyss.

Drenched and ice-cold, Alex stood in chest-high water and found a long stick that he tapped around in the water until he found a shore. When he pulled the stick from the water, the end was on fire and he saw that the water was actually swirly red and orange paint. The long stick in his hand was a large torch or paintbrush—the bristles of the brush fed the paint-fire, yet did not burn down. Exploring, he found no walls, no doors. He lifted the torch above his head but saw nothing. The end of his torch darkened to amber. If it went out, he would be in absolute darkness again.

Anxiety set in, and claustrophobia. "Where am I?" he shouted. But finally he had an idea. As if in response to his excitement, the color of paint at the tip of his brush brightened a shade.

"My mind!" he proclaimed. "This is my mind!"

The end of the brush sparked—exploded—into a hot yellow-white flame. He averted his eyes and nearly dropped it.

He cast the flame all around him, desperate to catch a glimpse of something, anything. But there was nothing. His exhilaration morphed into horror as the shades of paint darkened, then turned black.

The clock on the nightstand read 4:55 a.m. and it was still dark outside. He was grateful to be awake but also sad. He had at last made it past Falling but then nothing happened. The dream was still fresh in his short-term memory and he did not want to lose it. He clicked on the night lamp and, with a pen and paper from Kate's purse, started writing:

> A river.
> Sunset.
> Comfortable. *Too* comfortable.
> A fire on the other bank, downstream.
> Sparks … bright holes? Are the sparks bright holes? Holes to what?
> Rain…. Flooding.

But what did these things mean? He touched the pencil to paper then lifted it, leaving a black dot. All his dreams here started somewhat the same, had the same flow. He quickly jotted down *Tranquility*. That was how they started, so peaceful, so restful. Then the tranquility always ended—*Interruption*. There was always a storm and he always fell. What was new in this last dream was a period of reflection and then a struggle. He wrote these down, numbered them, and then reviewed his list:

1. Tranquility
2. Interruption
3. Tempest

4. Falling
5. Reflection
6. Struggle
7. ?

Something came after *Struggle*. Something had to. He sighed, rubbed his eyes. Stonebrook, it seemed to him, was the place at the end of one's dreams, a place where laws of nature might bend and the human condition itself might be pinned down for proper examination. There was something at Stonebrook that existed at the edges of the sensory spectrums: where light waves disappeared for the human eye, where sounds silenced at the upper edge of human hearing. He sensed all this because it tickled the tiny hairs at the nape of his neck. This realm between the physical and non-physical invaded his dreams.

Alex stroked the quilt, felt the stitching between the squares. *Poor Kate*, he thought. *I'm such a crackpot.*

He pulled the quilt up to his armpits, folded his hands over it. His body was essentially ashore of the quilt lake; his wife was out in the middle of it. The light from his lamp cascaded over the folds and creases between them, making it look like sundown on a wavy day. His body made the hills steeper and at his right side the quilt-land plunged straight to the water like a cliff. This thought gave him a chill. He slid a hand under the quilt just offshore and pushed it up. At first, he did not notice anything but when he peered closer, it was unmistakable. There were flecks of rust color in the dark blue there and on the quilt square over his chest he noticed a pattern to the trees—they were in an oval, almost circular pattern—and in the center of them was a small gray piece of cloth—a stone.

Only now did it dawn on him that John Mead and even Samuel Tudor had slept here in this very bed, perhaps with their hearts also under the stone, their wives out to sea. The quilt had caught his eye on the first morning of their stay when he had the silly notion that Kate's breasts created great waves that destroyed a Lilliputian world each night. Alex remembered the night Kate had stripped for him and got on top of him in bed. She had been freezing cold and had pulled the quilt up over her back and draped it over her shoulders as she straddled him. *Gulliver Love*, thought Alex with a smile. She had wanted more romance this week, more passion. But he had been preoccupied, as he often was.

He felt desire now; he wanted Kate now. He slid his hand under the covers down her warm body. She opened her eyes, parted her lips. His hand continued to explore.

Afterward, Alex's aching muscles were spent and he was hot. He did not want to lie on top of the quilt so he pulled his side down and lay naked on the sheet. He wanted to talk to Kate about his dream while it was still fresh, but she had already kissed his shoulder and rolled over.

Wide awake, Alex slipped away from his wife and went to the kitchen to make a pot of coffee. Wind rattled the screen door in its frame, and from outside he heard big waves crashing. Through the window over the sink, he saw tree branches sling back and forth as if they were seeking escape from the wind as much as being blown by it. He cracked open the kitchen door to lock the screen, and a cold gust blasted his face as he heard a deep roar that seemed to come from all over, yet he knew must have been the lake. He shivered. He closed the door.

There would be storms today.

Chapter 22

Paul arrived promptly at 10:00 a.m. with batteries and a latte. When Alex opened the door, he noticed the man's wispy hair had been tousled by the wind, and with his large eyes and stiff gait, he resembled a stunned zombie.

Kate had been sitting alone on the back porch, and when she saw the coffee cup, she instantly brightened. "For me?" she said, striding toward Paul. "How nice."

Paul handed her the cup—"I hope you like chocolate"—and gave the batteries to Alex. Flattening and straightening his hair with his freed hands, he added, "I had them add some syrup to sweeten it up a bit and they went ahead and added the whip cream, too. I didn't ask for it—I hope it's okay."

"It's perfect, Paul. Thank you." She took a noisy slurp that left whip cream on her upper lip. "Say, how's your mother doing?"

"This morning the basement stairs were too much for her. I had to help her down to her sitting room."

Alex was already occupied at the dining table putting the batteries into the talkie. He snapped the battery compartment of the talkie back in place and then clicked on the unit, which crackled to life. He played the volume up and down and the hissing static made him think of the crashing waves on the lake. "You guys ready?" Alex asked, his finger already poised over the talk button.

"No, wait!" Kate said, startling him. She bit her lip. "Paul should call."

Both men stared at her, perplexed. "I just figured—" started Alex. "Sorry, Paul, I just thought you probably wouldn't want to."

"I'm not sure I do," agreed Paul.

"But it has to be you," protested Kate. "You're older, closer to John Mead's age. You're from this area and know this cottage better than both of us combined. Look, we can help you." *And you're John Mead's, son*, thought Kate. *And Erik thinks you sound and look like your dad.*

Alex held the hissing talkie across the table. "She's right."

Paul hesitated then reached out to take it. "What do I say?"

"Don't introduce yourself," Kate said. "Just say Erik's name—who knows, maybe he's on."

Paul depressed the talk button: "Erik," he said, then released it.

Several seconds passed.

He pressed the button again and repeated into the talkie: "Erik, it's me."

As they listened to static, Paul said, "Should I try a different frequency?"

"No," Kate replied. "Mr. Mead would have left it on the one they used."

After a few more seconds of waiting, Alex said, "He's not on. I mean, what were the chances, anyway?"

Just then, a voice emitted from the talkie; it was a crackly sound over the hiss: "Hello?"

They all stared at it, amazed. Paul pressed the button. "Hello? Erik?"

"This is Erik, this is Erik," came a quick, excited reply.

Kate said to Paul, "Ask him how much longer you must wait. Ask him when the boat will come to take you away."

"Wow, talk about trickery-dickery," Alex said, impressed with his wife.

Paul said into the talkie: "Erik, how much longer must I wait? When will the boat come to take me away?"

"You are here," came Erik's response. "You will never leave."

Kate said to Paul, "Tell him you must—you *must* leave."

"But I *must* leave," Paul said into the talkie.

There was no response on the other end—just static.

"Careful, Kate," said Alex. "Don't get him riled up."

Finally, over the static, they heard: "All is ready. At the end. All is ready, as you had instructed. But you mustn't leave Newton's Realm; you must help me defend Stonebrook against the bad Reflectories! If Tin Man finds you, all will be lost. Tin Man will bring the others and they will ruin the mind that Samuel Tudor built…. Please. Allow Erik help the trio before it is too late."

"You have my permission to help them," Paul replied. "What do you need from me?"

"Not here, not now …" Erik's voice sounded hushed, as if he was whispering. "The Tin Man has a walk-and-talk. Meet Erik tonight. At the place, at the time."

Paul and Alex looked at Kate.

She frowned. "We can't ask him where that is because John Mead would know."

Alex nodded. "Just agree to it, Paul. We'll figure something out."

Paul pressed the talk button: "Okay, Erik. I'll meet you tonight."

After Paul clicked off the walkie-talkie, Alex let out a sigh of frustration. Even if they found Erik tonight, to walk up and ask for his help might scare him off. But at least Erik thought he heard John Mead give his permission. The only problem was that Erik expected an actual meeting and John Mead was dead.

When they got back from the Ben Franklin store in Two Harbors with a pair of Motorola Talk About walkie-talkies, they tested their ranges at their stakeout locations: Alex took off for Gold Rock Point with John Mead's talkie, Kate drove to the end of the driveway, and Paul headed down to the boathouse. Despite background noise from Paul's waves and Alex's wind up on the point, they heard each other well enough to be satisfied. The talkies would work.

"What now," asked Kate, when they reconvened at the dining table. It was only a little past noon. They figured they had until at least 5:00 p.m.

Alex smiled. "Lunch, I guess. Then free time."

Paul wanted to be next to the lake. Whenever the lake was stormy, he was drawn to it, compelled to witness its passion. He went to the boathouse to tinker on the boats, tinker in his mind.

On his walk down, he realized he was being pulled in two directions. Not up and down as if he had been strapped to a rack and pulled apart by the hands and feet, but sideways. Except it wasn't his limbs that were bound but his brain, only his brain. It was separating, incrementally, and his identity was tearing. That was fine with him, he thought, as he opened the boathouse door. He was tired of the confusion and insecurity. Sick of the melancholy. Those were the parts he wanted torn away. There was more to him than that, he swore that there was. Perhaps he would not be reconstituted, his brain forever bisected into two sad, separate halves, but that was a risk he took willingly. Who he had grown to be he felt was not who he was meant to be. It was as if sorrow had been attached to him without his doing, as if despondency had suctioned itself to him. Like barnacles on his soul.

He pulled the tarp off the Dispro and inspected her thoroughly. She had been well maintained and required nothing in the way of restoration to make her seaworthy. Her life vests were there; her oars were there, too. There was a little gas in her tank, but he didn't know how old it was. With winter coming, a time when people pulled their boats from the lake and emptied their gas tanks, Paul decided to go into town for fresh gas.

Upon his return, he filled the tank and tried the motor. It buzzed to life. The boat was ready.

Alex spent much of his time on the porch in an Adirondack chair, the key to the Reflectory in his hand. He fidgeted, crossed his legs, un-crossed them. He was trying to make himself relax but could not. His body ached, but it was his mind that caused him distress. It felt overburdened. For too long it had toted around cynicism and apathy, and a bevy of other negative thoughts, as if someday they might come in handy. These thoughts, though, were heavy, and here he needed to be light. He needed to cast them away.

He saw Paul walk up from the boathouse with a gas tank and head around the side of the cottage. *For the Dispro,* thought Alex. He remembered Erik's words: *You will find him and take him away in the boat. Just as he planned.* Paul was going to fill the tank for the Dispro.

Alex stood and walked over to lean against the doorframe between the porch and the great room. Kate was sitting cross-legged on the floor in front of the couch, her dead iPhone in one hand. She reminded him of a little girl the way she sat there with her legs crossed. She was so stable, he thought. Stable within herself, sure of so many things, yet still a little girl, still innocent. *Why did she love him*? Their son was gone because of him, he was gifted yet undecided about his career, he was forgetful, sloppy; he was anything but an ideal man. Yet she stayed with him and she still loved him. He knew she did.

Just then, Kate looked up at him. She was listening to one of her favorite songs from when she was a girl on Erik's record player and was bobbing her head to the music. She smiled and waved at him before closing her eyes to listen more intently to her music.

He was grateful for her beyond words.

Kate mourned the death of her iPhone. She touched the black screen, hoping to poke it back to life.

She had plugged in the record player, attached the speakers, and played Erik's old records—The Beatles, The Tokens, The Monkeys. And others. She thought about a younger Erik playing these same records here, and she also thought about herself as a little girl listening to her parent's records in the den of their house on Delmont Street. The most current record in Erik's collection, she figured, was Queen's album: *News of the World*. Perhaps he had stomped his feet and clapped his hands to "We Will Rock You," as she and her classmates had done in elementary school music class.

She flipped over an album cover by The Tokens. It had the song "The Lion Sleeps Tonight" that her mom had loved. After she put it on, out of the corner of her eye, she saw that Alex was staring at her. She waved at him and then closed her eyes.

She imagined that she and Alex and Paul were on a safari. And Tin Man was really a lion.

At 5:40 p.m., the three of them stood together on the porch. All afternoon the clouds had been darkening, the wind worsening.

Alex had the farthest to go so he was first to leave. Kate kissed him on the lips: "Be careful up there," she said. "If it starts raining, come back down, okay? No need to risk life and limb."

When Alex checked in for the first time on the walkie-talkie from Gold Rock Point, it sounded to Kate from her quiet position inside the SUV as if he was in a wind tunnel. Paul's background noise sounded better because he was inside the boathouse, but it still seemed as if both men were calling from the far corners of earth.

Every fifteen minutes, she checked in with them; Erik would not come by the road, she thought, he would take his secret path. She rolled her window down and glanced up at the black sky. She wondered if it was going to snow instead of rain.

Paul would stay dry but Alex was exposed. And poor Erik should most certainly not be out hiking on his maze of a path. If he twisted an ankle, they wouldn't be able to search for him until morning.

At 7:30 p.m., the rain had already started, so if Erik had in fact left Tudor House, he would be turning back. He had his issues, but he could still recognize when a situation was dangerous. She pressed the button on her talkie: "Nothing here …"

Paul checked in: "Same here." He sounded like a surfer shouting from the funnel of a breaking wave. "No sign of him."

"Alex?" Kate said.

No response—just static from her own talkie.

"Alex?" she said louder.

Just then, she heard a blaring hiss from her talkie that must have been wind but it no longer sounded like wind. It sounded like a hurricane. She heard deeper sounds, too. Alex's voice.

It sounded like, "Kate—Kate," but whatever else he said was drowned out.

"Alex! Come down now!"

She waited for a reply but didn't think she heard one.

"Alexander, come down from there!"

The rain pelting the windshield started to thicken and splatter like juicy bugs. It was sleet.

"Alex!"

She pressed the talkie to her ear and after a few seconds heard Paul's background noise and a strained voice over the elements: "I'm sure he can't hear you, Kate. The wind is incredible—coming straight off the lake. The waves—they're rolling into the boathouse."

"He'll come down, right?" She wanted to hear Paul say her husband would have enough sense and that he would be safe. "Right, Paul?"

"I don't know, Kate."

Kate gripped the talkie like a vice. She pressed the tip of its short, plastic antenna into her chin, thinking. She knew her husband. He was staying put.

Just then, she caught movement outside. It was something big and slow. And close.

The whatever-it-was had moved right down the drive to Stonebrook. Her rear window was covered with sleet, so she opened her door and looked behind the SUV.

Taillights. Moving away toward the cottage.

For a split second, the lights seemed to stop but it was hard to tell. Then the lights were gone.

"Paul," she said into the talkie. She was already sick of speaking into it. "Somebody's here, a car drove past." She hated the noises on the other end, hated waiting for the replies.

"What kind of car?"

"I couldn't tell; I only caught a glimpse of it."

"Did they see you?"

"No … I don't know. It's dark and sleeting and I'm off to the side, but maybe. I thought it might have stopped but I bet it rounded the curve in the drive."

She heard Paul's urgent voice: "Get out of there, Kate. Just in case. Lock your doors now and drive away."

She stared at the sleet-covered windshield, debating: it could be someone looking for Split Rock Lighthouse; it could be a wrong turn. She locked the doors, started the SUV, ran the wipers.

Instead of driving out, she shifted into reverse.

"Paul," she said into the talkie, "I'm heading back to see …" and then she tossed the talkie on the passenger seat.

"No, Kate …" Paul replied. His background noise was different; he was outside. "Drive out to the road and wait there. I'll check it out and give you a status on the talkie."

She took her foot off the brake, backed up, and angled on to the drive.

Behind her, the dark silhouette of a vehicle loomed. She pulled alongside the car and tried to peer inside it but saw nothing. She scooped up the walkie-talkie: "Paul, you there? The car is parked in the bend but I don't see anyone."

"Hang on, I'm coming ..." Paul replied, sounding out of breath.

Kate could not suppress her sinking feeling. *Tin Man is angry. Very, very.*

She wondered how many other times he had parked in the bend like this, how many times he had parked here and sneaked up to the cottage to watch them. Late at night, or anytime, if he was bold.

Watch out for Tin Man, watch out for Tin Man, watch out for Tin Man.

Kate jammed the talk button with her thumb. "Paul, stop! Just hide, okay? In the carriage house. Hide there. I'll meet you there and we'll go get Alex together ..."

She waited for Paul's reply but her talkie remained silent. She pleaded with it to offer Paul's voice, "C'mon, c'mon, c'mon," until she realized she still had her thumb squeezed over the talk button. If Paul had already replied, she would not have—

Something outside caught her eye. Near her face, through the driver side window, a small object glinted; it looked like a silver ring suspended in the air. Then it moved, tapped against her window.

She blinked, tilted her head. It baffled her, entranced her.

It tapped again.

She focused past the ring and saw a dark figure wearing a slicker with the hood pulled over his head and then she realized what the ring was: it was the business end of a pistol.

Tin Man tried to open the door then gestured with the weapon up-and-down.

Kate popped the lock as the man motioned her to open the door and get out.

With the door open, she looked furtively at him. His black beard was wet; his eyes were dark in their sockets: all she saw of them through his glasses was that they were unblinking. He held the pistol in his right hand; his left held something up to his ear.

Just then, she heard Paul's voice from her talkie but also, inexplicably, the sound of it came from the man: "Kate? Kate? You there? I'm in the carriage house."

His beard widened at the cheeks; he was grinning. Smirking. From under the hood then, the man revealed a walkie-talkie and she heard Paul's voice from it: "You want me to come for you?"

The man's head moved side to side as he depressed the talk button on his own talkie for her to speak.

Kate leaned forward. Her chest felt tight as if the breath had been knocked out of her. "No, Paul" she whimpered too softly for Paul to have heard.

The pistol leveled close against her forehead.

She shut her eyes tight. "No, Paul!" she repeated, louder. When she opened her eyes he nodded and gestured with the pistol toward the carriage house. Kate knew what she was supposed to say. "I—I'm coming. I'll be there shortly."

The smirk widened into a grin.

Chapter 23

Alex checked his watch: 7:28 p.m. He was out near the edge of Gold Rock Point watching the massive waves roll in. Caught up in the excitement, he didn't care that it had started raining. In fact, he welcomed it: *Bring it on,* he thought. *Bring. It. On.*

He cupped his hands around his mouth and yelled: the sound seemed to collect in front of his face, halted by the wind, and then disappeared.

Across the bay to the southwest, waves pounded Split Rock. He saw them through the storm only because of their sheer size as they slammed against the cliff, exploding white water nearly up to the top where the mighty lighthouse stood.

Turn on the lighthouse! thought Alex. *Someone turn her on! She deserves nights like this!*

He heard his talkie crackle—Kate's voice—she was checking in again. He could not make out her words but she sounded fine. With the talkie pressed tight to one ear and a finger pressed into his other, he waited for Paul's reply because he had been checking in second. After he thought he heard him, Alex shouted, "Nothing here, but Kate—Kate! You should check out these waves! They're beyond belief!"

"Why are you and your husband here?" the man asked in his harsh accent, walking a step behind Kate.

"We're celebrating an anniversary," replied Kate, talking over her shoulder.

"Your husband is a budding architect. Did John Mead invite you?"

"My husband," Kate replied, "hasn't even built anything yet, so I have no idea why you think the previous owner might invite us." Hoping to change the subject, she asked, "Why does Erik call you Tin Man?"

"Erik is an idiot-savant who talks to dead people. When I first visited him I claimed to be Timothy Mann, the sailor supposedly buried under a Sailor's Stone with the key to the Reflectory." The man laughed. "I asked him to tell me where my body was buried."

Relieved that the man was still looking for the key and didn't know they had already dug it up, Kate recalled her conversation with Erik when he said, *Not the Tin Man; not the bones under the stone.* "So who are you, really?" She regretted asking these questions, because if he replied with something that sounded truthful, she feared it meant he planned to kill them.

The man put his hand on Kate's shoulder. She stopped walking and turned around. In addition to the pistol in his hand she saw the muzzle of a rifle strapped behind his back.

"I am a Percipient," he replied. He said the words slowly, as if waiting for her to fawn over him. "I'm from another Reflectory."

Kate didn't like this. It sounded far too truthful.

"Do you know what a Percipient is, dear?"

Kate shook her head.

"Save for the handful of individuals known as Blue Violins who can pass into Newton's Realm, Percipients are the most enlightened people in the world. Would you like to know how smart I am?"

Kate wanted to roll her eyes but refrained. She also wanted to ask what a Blue Violin was and what Newton's Realm was, but she didn't want to fuel his ego. Instead she replied, "No."

The man smirked again. "When I first entered the Reflectory in Moscow, known as Bunker Deep, my IQ was 145. Nothing wrong with that, no? I was considered a genius, after all. However, after four stints inside the Deep, my IQ is now 190." The man snapped his fingers. "I am beyond gifted."

The man was full of himself yet seemed on edge. He also did not seem to grasp that there was a difference between enlightenment and intelligence.

"So the ones you call Blue Violins," replied Kate, "they're a lot smarter than you?"

The man's smile disappeared.

She felt she was dead anyway, so she might as well piss off the arrogant bastard. "And John Mead was a Blue Violin, right?"

"John Mead had a cognitive ability beyond your understanding," replied the man. He seemed defensive, yet in awe of the man, like he was talking about a revered archrival. "He would have to translate his thoughts to an excruciatingly rudimentary level for you to even grasp his intelligence. He was a five-sense synesthete: in his world, music and words have color, numbers have texture, and emotions like love and hate are three-dimensional scenes in his mind. Synesthesia is a toolbox for any Blue Violin to open Newton's Realm, and his was by far the largest. He spends more time in Newton's Realm than any Blue Violin in history."

"You talk about him like he's still alive," replied Kate. Then, taking a stab: "As if your little group from Moscow didn't kill him to steal his Reflectory."

"His presence is still thick in this world. His protective veil over Stonebrook is starting to weaken. It won't be long—"

"Oh my God, you did kill him!" Kate swung her arm to slap the man's face, but he bobbed his head back and turned enough that she missed entirely.

"*You*," replied the man, "are not protected within his veil! I know what you will do before you even think it so I warn you to not try that again. It is your husband I can't read. I will ask you again, does he have the synesthesia?"

"Yes," she gloated, realizing that while he no longer had a sensory form of synesthesia her husband's gifts also cast a veil over this Percipient from Moscow. The man feared Alex for some reason. She should use it to their advantage. She added, "And you will die trying to read my husband's mind."

"Keep moving," replied Tin Man and gave her a push. "I will kill him just like my associate killed John Mead."

Kate turned and continued walking, pleased that he was no longer smirking.

Alex tried to reach Kate and Paul: "He's here, guys!" he shouted. "Erik is up here, on the point!" It was Erik, he could not believe it: he had hiked from Tudor House after dark in the wind and rain, without even a flashlight, around fallen trees, over slippery rocks, up the steep hill to Gold Rock. The rain was turning to sleet, so a return trip to Tudor House was out of the question. "I'm going to try to talk to him, see if he'll come down to the cottage. Meet us back there."

Instead of wasting his time listening for a reply that he would not be able to hear, Alex clicked off his talkie and slid it into his jacket pocket. He approached Erik who was walking through the other side of the Circle of Trees toward him. The man's head was down, staring at his feet; the slicker he wore was too long for him and it brushed across the undergrowth.

Kate stopped in front of the carriage house and heard the man's voice in her right ear. "If you attempt to warn your friend, I will put a bullet in your head before you even get his name out. Now slowly, let's go inside. You will whisper and call him over."

Erik stopped in the center of the Circle of Trees and thrust his arms in the air. He closed his eyes and his lips started to move as if he was mumbling something.

Alex moved in closer, straining to hear, until he was just ten feet away.

Erik dropped to his knees, placed both hands on a stone. He bent down until his forehead touched the backs of his hands.

It was the Sailor's Stone in the center of the Circle of Trees.

Erik's belly heaved up and down as he breathed. His lips continued to move but he spoke silently.

Kate opened the door and stood in the frame. She could not see inside anyway, so she clenched her eyes shut tight, pleading that Paul had not come. "Paul," she whispered. "Paul?" she repeated. No reply.

When Erik finally stood, he looked right at Alex without a hint of surprise. "You will find him and take him away in the boat. Just as he planned."

"Kate?" she heard someone say from inside. "Is that you?"

She wanted to tell Paul to run but felt the gun at her neck. "Yes. I can't see you Paul."

She heard movement and then saw a silhouette approach. She tried gesturing with her hands that there was someone behind her but it was no use.

"Are you okay, Kate? What is it?"

Tin Man shoved her inside and pointed the gun at Paul.

Alex swallowed. "Did you speak with Mr. Mead, Erik?"

"It's not finished … it's never finished … it needs someone."

Unlike the last time he had heard Erik utter those words, Alex knew what he was speaking about: the Reflectory. "We need to find it soon, Erik," he replied, "by tomorrow."

"Erik can help; Erik has permission from Mr. Mead now. The other two are in danger."

"Kate and Paul? What sort of danger?"

"Tin Man has come calling. Tin Man is at Stonebrook."

Alex smiled reassuringly as he held up his walkie-talkie for Erik to see. "I just heard from them … they're fine, Erik. They haven't seen a thing."

"We must go to Stonebrook but we must take a secret path. He will come here for you. He will come to Gold Rock Point."

Alex was about to protest when Erik turned and started walking. Then he realized that as long as they were heading back to the cottage, it didn't matter. Pleased with his luck, Alex followed a couple steps behind.

In a gully that ran parallel to the primary path, Erik pressed ahead, negotiating obstacles with ease, plodding through the overwhelming density of trees and bushes in the dark as if he moved entirely from memory.

They came to the brook and in front of them water spilled over a rock wall twenty feet across and perhaps five feet high.

Erik pointed downstream and Alex looked in that direction. In the distance, through the sleet that slanted upstream into their faces, a flashlight bobbed. Someone was heading from the cottage over the footbridge on the main path toward the point.

Vague concern entered Alex's mind. He turned to Erik and found he was unable to take his eyes from the man's emotionless face. "Who?"

"Tin Man," replied Erik.

Alex remembered the talkie and reached into his pocket for it. *Kate.* He had to try to reach her. He clicked the unit on—Erik snatched it from him and tossed it into the brook.

"What the hell—what are you doing?"

"Tin Man has a walk-and-talk."

Alex was flustered. "But he can't know our frequency—"

"He knows," interrupted Erik. Then he waddled away and stopped, his back to Alex, several feet away.

Stunned, Alex figured the man had to urinate. If Tin Man had been listening, he would have heard them check in with each other, heard where Paul was, where Kate was.

"Erik," said Alex, "where do we cross?" As far as he could tell, there was only the footbridge farther down, but that was out of the way. "C'mon! Where do we cross?"

Just then, the noise from the waterfall changed pitch, and then the sound stopped altogether. The water level at the base of the falls started to drop, and soon three holes near the base of the falls were visible—water surged through them, like horizontal geysers.

Alex looked back and forth between Erik and the waterfall. *What the hell is he doing?* The man stood in front of a metal box, holding a long lever in both hands. Water, that had seconds ago shot through the three holes, eased up. Erik's eyes seemed focused on the dropping water level above the falls, and with a sudden movement he wrenched the lever with both hands, putting his weight into it. He adjusted his grip and pushed it down until the lever was within inches of the ground.

The water that was pouring through the holes in the wall slowed to trickles and then stopped.

Erik loped back to Alex, "Cross here, cross now," he said, as he continued past and stutter-stepped down the slope into the emptying brook. Water at the base of the wall was draining downstream, retreating at Erik's feet so that he splashed across the brook as if it were a mere puddle. "Hurry, hurry!" Erik said over his shoulder. "Cross here, cross now!"

Alex, stupefied, had not budged.

"Level is rising, time is wasting. Wasting into too late!"

Alex glanced above the three closed holes and saw water cresting again at the top of the wall.

Water started pouring over the lip.

Without thinking, he rushed down into the emptied riverbed.

A new waterfall found its voice, started its roar. Tens of gallons of water, and then a moment later, hundreds of gallons, cascaded at his feet; he ran and splashed for the other side. He slipped, fell backward. Water threatened to sweep him away as he scrambled onto the bank just in time.

While Erik clambered up the bank, Alex turned to look at the falls. "What the hell is that?" he said to himself. He looked up at Erik behind him and yelled, "What is that, Erik?"

The man was rubbing his hands together. And Alex saw a proud grin on his face as he pointed to the base of the falls. "Sluice gates." His lips puckered a couple of times as he dipped a hand down then back up, gesturing the effect he had just created.

Alex climbed up the bank and stood next to Erik.

"Sluice gates," repeated Erik. He stood next to a metal box identical to the one on the other side. He started to pull up on its lever.

"What are you doing?" Alex asked.

"Open … gates." Erik spoke between jerks on the lever that did not budge. "It is time, at last."

"Time? For what?"

"Turbines need water, generator needs turbines."

Alex leaned over to help him. Together, they wrenched the lever up in small increments. Alex's back was to the waterfall, but he could hear the difference in its sound: tighter, higher pitched.

"Enough," grunted Erik when the lever was halfway up. Alex held the lever firm while Erik locked it in place with a thick metal pin he stuck into a hole at the side of the box.

Alex turned around and saw the three jets of water gushing again from the base of the wall. "My Lord, it's a dam," he said. "What's it for, Erik?"

"Power."

"But power for what?" Alex knew that Stonebrook Cottage ran off standard electricity brought in from the line that ran along the road. He had seen the wires himself.

"Power to light the mind."

Of course, thought Alex. A mind needs nourishment and what better source for powering the Reflectory than the brook of life. "The mind that Samuel Tudor built," Alex said.

Erik nodded. "You will take him away in the boat."

"Just as he planned," finished Alex.

Erik looked pleased. "Just as he planned."

Instead of walking with Erik back to the cottage, Alex ran off, yelling, "I'm going for Kate," he said. "Head to the cottage, Erik. Wait there."

His sense of direction was hindered not only from being unfamiliar with Erik's secret path, but also by the wind and sleet. He tripped on slippery roots and rocks, scraped his neck against a jutting branch, and got caught in bramble that blocked his path.

He finally stopped to get his bearings.

He shouted, "Kate!"

It was not more than a quarter-mile from the brook to the clearing along the drive—he had to be close.

"Erik!"

He should have emerged on the grounds by now.

At the top of his lungs: "Kate!"

He shoved wet, cold hands under his armpits. "Kate," he said under his breath, his voice cracking. "I'm sorry." Tears were in his eyes but his face was wet and numb so they barely registered. He pulled out his right hand and blew on it. *Think, Alex. Damn it. Think!* If he had been walking straight, he would have hit the grounds minutes ago. If he had veered right, the main path was there and even if he had somehow missed that, he would have come out over the lake. So he had veered left. Too far to the left. It was a long way to Minnesota 61; he would not have hit it yet.

Alex turned right, about forty-five degrees. He did not run this time; he swallowed his panic and walked. And prayed he was heading northeast.

For a few minutes, the woods thickened, but he stayed on course and came to a clearing where he nearly smacked into a car before he saw it. Next to it was their SUV. He slammed the roof of the car hard with both hands. He had hoped this was all a bad dream; that his hands would have passed through the vehicle, but the sting told him otherwise.

With Stonebrook's gravel drive underfoot, Alex ran around the car to the SUV. All the windows were covered with icy sleet. He opened the driver door. Nobody was there, nobody in the back seat. He looked up and down the drive. *Why hadn't she just driven away?*

Alex shouted as loudly as he could: "Kate!" *Where are you, where are you!* "Kate!"

Then he realized Paul should know if she was still safe. They would have maintained contact with the walkie-talkies. Alex placed a knee on the driver seat and scanned the front seat and glove box for Kate's unit but did not see it. No talkie. No car keys, no cell phone.

How long had it been since he and Erik had seen Tin Man cross the bridge for the point? Ten minutes? Twenty? His sense of time felt out-of-whack.

He wiped the face of his watch and pressed the light button: 8:45 p.m. He got out of the SUV and slammed the door. How long would Tin Man look for him up on the cliff before returning? He started to walk down the dark drive toward Stonebrook and then broke into a run.

Chapter 24

Twenty feet from the cottage, Alex heard knocking and stopped to listen. *Thump ... thump.* A few seconds later, *thump ... thump ... thump.* From the cottage—no, the carriage house. He turned toward the carriage house and listened intently as he walked. *Thump.* It was louder but still muffled. He opened the service door. It was pitch dark inside but right away, he heard the thumping clear and loud, and now it came erratic and fast: *thump-thump, thump, thump, thump-thump.* There were other sounds, too—rustling, and human sounds: throat noises, it seemed, and groaning.

Alex called out, "Kate? Paul?"

He felt for a switch on the wall but could not find one. Then he remembered it was on a pull string, and he groped for it, both arms swiping the air. His left hand brushed against the string and he tugged. In the stark glare of the naked, swinging bulb, he saw his wife and friend on the floor near the large swing-out doors, duct tape over their mouths, hands and feet bound with rope. Their feet had been tied to a bar of what had once been a horse stall. Paul had his head next to the stable door.

Kate's eyes looked panicked—they were unblinking and wide, and she breathed hard through her nose in strained wheezes. Alex quickly kneeled to the floor and peeled the tape off her mouth. She gulped for air and coughed each time she tried to talk.

Alex peeled off Paul's tape but he remained glassy-eyed, breathing deeply. To have heard Paul's head pounding against the door over the howling wind outside, thought Alex, he must have been knocking it hard.

Kate sat and spit out her words between gasps: "That bastard," Kate said, furious. "That bastard … Paul, you okay? Untie Paul first, Alex."

Paul blinked—he was at least awake—but remained lying down as Alex worked at the hay rope around his hands.

"Did you see him, Alex?" asked Kate, but before he could answer she continued: "He was coming for you up to the point. He has a talkie and he heard us the whole time. He has a gun, too, and once he finds the Reflectory I think he plans to kill us. Even Erik. He was watching Erik all day today at Tudor House, waiting for him to leave to meet John Mead and he went to follow, but Erik gave him the slip in the woods so he drove here instead. He's from another Reflectory in Moscow called Bunker Deep. The Reflectory turned him into a super genius called a Percipient. Oh, and guess what: Erik called him *Tim* Mann, not *Tin* Man, because the guy claimed to be the dead sailor we dug up."

As Alex freed Paul's hands, he started to remove the rope around Kate's wrists.

Kate took a breath and gestured with her tied hands to a hacksaw on the wall. "Use that."

Alex started cutting as Kate continued, "He's got my cell, Alex, and my keys and Paul's keys, too. And—oh, he was so flipping smug!" Kate started to cry—not her sad cry, Alex noticed, but her furious one. She wiped quickly at her nose with the back of her hand. "At least he doesn't know we have the key. If he did, I'm sure he'd torture us to get it."

Alex put his arm around his wife. "How long since he left?"

"Over thirty minutes," Paul replied. He sat with his back against the door, gingerly touching the back of his head. "We have to get out of here—he'll be back soon."

"How is it he missed you, Alex?" asked Kate. "Didn't you run into him on the path or up at the point?"

Alex thought about Erik. His life was in danger, too. "Erik came up to the point. We took one of his secret paths back." He helped Kate to her feet as Paul stood slowly, holding onto the stable bars.

"Paul, are you okay to walk?" Alex asked.

"I think so."

"We have to call the cops," Kate said.

"We have to find Erik first," replied Alex. "He saved my life; the least we can do is save his."

At the front door of the darkened cottage, Kate said, "We had left the lights on. He's been here." Kate sucked in her breath. "Or he's already back."

Alex reached for the handle.

"Wait, Alex—"

He opened the door before she could stop him and flipped on the light switch next to the door.

But the great room remained dark.

"He cut the power?" whispered Kate.

Alex made his way in the darkness to the cottage's only phone, the old black rotary on the end table next to the couch, and picked it up. "There's no dial tone," he announced, with the phone at his ear.

"Press that clicky button on the base," Kate said.

He clicked it several times. "Still dead."

"Tin Man," Kate said knowingly.

"Or the storm," added Alex. "We need to find Erik."

"Uh-uh, we need to leave before he comes back." Kate replied. "Erik can take care of himself."

"Okay, look," started Alex. He was trying to keep his head clear; they needed to act rationally. "You two check the boathouse for him. I'll check the woodshed. If we can't find him, we'll immediately head for the road."

In the falling sleet, Alex thought the woodshed looked like a black hole into which he might disappear forever. Closer up, he made out its shape, its angles. He reached for the latch but hesitated. The moment did not seem real—it swirled in the storm. It was a Big Blow sort of storm, a storm that wrecked ships. A storm that sent freezing sailors into sheds.

Paul opened the boathouse door, and he and Kate saw the lit oil lamp on the dock. In the shadows of its feeble light, they saw a man sitting in the Dispro.

Alex opened the woodshed door. "Erik?" He stepped inside. "Erik?" He patted the stacks of wood, groping farther in, feeling for Erik in case he had passed out from fright or overexertion, but nobody was inside.

"Erik," Kate said, with a sigh of relief when she made out his features.

He sat in the bottom of the Dispro, which he had lowered to the wooden runners, holding his head with both hands. Around his neck was an age-faded, orange life vest. The man had also opened the large boat door to the lake and they saw waves rushing all the way up and inside.

"What on earth are you doing, Erik?" asked Kate.

Erik patted his head with his hands and rubbed it as one might pet the head of an animal. "All is ready," he said at last. "Erik will guide you."

Kate raised her eyebrows. "Where?"

"All is ready. Erik will guide you."

"To the Reflectory?"

Erik braced against a rush of water as a wave pounded the back of the Dippy, and then he nodded his head so vigorously that his jowls shook. "In the boat, Erik will guide you."

"Can't we walk, Erik?" asked Kate, trying to keep her voice soothing. "It's—well, it's just that it'd be a bit rough on the lake tonight."

A smaller wave smacked the back of the Dispro; the runners underneath it were already slick and it edged down the slope a few inches with the receding water. Paul grabbed its mooring rope and wrapped it around a pole.

"By boat—by *Dippy* boat—is the only way."

Kate looked at the Dispro with disapproval; it would bob like a gondola in the middle of the ocean.

"Why not the cruiser?" asked Paul.

"Chris-Cross crash. Dippy slippy."

Just then, there was a rap on the service door and Alex poked his head in. "There you are," Alex said, panting when he saw Erik. He came inside and closed the door behind him. To Paul he asked, "Why's the boat down?"

"Erik let it down. He's ready to take us to the Reflectory."

Alex grimaced. "How about we walk instead?"

Kate shook her head and pointed a thumb at Erik. "By Dippy boat, per our guide here."

Alex eyed the dippy and then considered the Chris Craft. It would be by far the safer vessel on such a night. There was no comparison.

"Chris-Cross crash, Alex," Kate said. "Dippy slippy."

Alex returned his gaze to Erik and nodded. Then he asked, "Where is it, Erik? Where are we going?" He reached into his pants pocket and pulled out the key to the Reflectory. "Where is the lock for this?"

"Not to say."

Frustrated, Alex let out a grunt and put the key back in his pocket. Then his face brightened: "Can we pull the Dippy? With the Chris-Cross, can we pull it along behind?"

Erik turned his head slightly, apparently considering the option. He nodded. "Pull Dippy."

Kate put her hand on Alex's arm. "No way, Alex," she said. "Look at it out there."

She was probably right, he figured. It was reckless, plain and simple. *But Erik, he knew things.* If the man could find a path where none existed and make streams stop flowing on command, perhaps he could tame Lake Superior, as well. He met Kate's eyes. "I'm going. I have to, Kate. At least no one is trying to kill us out there. If we walk inland, we might run into your little Percipient friend."

Kate turned to Paul, hoping for an ally. "Paul?"

Paul was staring at the Dippy. He lifted his eyes to Alex's. "There's something grand here, isn't there, Alex?"

"Yes."

"Something beyond our dreams."

"Yes."

Alex nudged the Chris Craft with a hand, and the boat swung gently from the suspension chains. "Looks like you're outvoted, dear. C'mon, Kate, she's a bruiser. A cruiser-bruiser. She'll be fine."

Together, Alex and Paul heaved the cruiser down the planks and outside. It slipped easily until a wave smashed the back of the boat and water spilled inside.

Sitting on the floor in the rear with Erik, Kate screamed, "Ohhh God! Oh my God, that's freezing!"

Paul heaved himself up and into the boat to start her up. "We need to get past the breakers."

Alex kept pushing until the icy water was almost up to his waist, and then he jumped up, hooked a leg over the lip of the boat, and rolled in as it roared to life.

Within minutes, Paul had switched the tank of fresh gas from the Dispro to the Cruiser while Kate helped Erik into the larger craft and Alex tied the boats together.

Now Paul dropped the cruiser in reverse, accelerated.

Their spirits lifted as the boat headed out into the lake, but sank when they saw what was bearing down on them: a wall of water, fifteen-feet high, rolling, looming. There was no time to turn the boat around, no time to get out.

Chapter 25

Kate hit the floor, her arms over her head.

Alex, caught in the front, would get the worst of it. He scrambled to the floor, too, and gaped at the approaching wave.

Paul turned his back on the wave, faced shore. He held one arm straight against the wheel and kept his other hand on the throttle, flooring it, propelling them deeper into the lake and up into the heart of the wave.

The cruiser raced up the wave as it came upon them, the aft rearing first, and then the entire boat. Kate slid against Erik on the floor, wrapped her arms around him.

The boat pushed toward the frothy-white crest that looked like jagged teeth eager to chew them up and spit them back at the boathouse.

Kate pressed her face into Erik's arm.

The whitewater cascaded over the boat—Alex was hit hard, then an odd sensation of buoyancy sprang beneath his torso— the cruiser bobbed out the top backside of the crest—his stomach lurched.

The twin in-board engines droned loudly as the rear of the boat sailed completely free.

They met another wave; the front caught the tail end of the crest, and then the hull slapped the surface hard; the water inside the boat splashed to the back like an aftershock, and Kate sprang up on a seat as the onslaught soaked Erik who remained motionless on the floor.

Alex, drenched, felt colder than he had ever felt before. If they capsized out on the lake, he wondered how long it would take for hypothermia to set in. *Not long*, he thought. *Not long.*

Paul had sustained the pounding wave sitting upright but must have been knocked against the windshield. Blood rimmed his left eye, ran down his cheek, yet his face remained pinched tight with resolve, as it had been when he played violin. He spun the wheel violently, shifted the cruiser. The boat turned as he accelerated into a trough.

Just then, there was a massive drag on the vessel. Everyone lurched forward.

"The Dispro!" Alex stared at the towrope fastened to the rear of the cruiser. He had forgotten about it. *Why had they bothered?* He got up on his knees and then sat on the seat next to Paul. He grabbed the man's arm and yelled over the noise of the storm: "You okay?"

Paul nodded.

The question Alex did not ask was how Paul planned on landing a brittle antique boat on a lakeshore of rocks, during a storm, without smashing the boat and its occupants to bits.

When Alex dared look back at the shore again, it was perhaps two hundred feet behind them—it was the blackness that did not roll, did not rise and fall. The Dippy, he noticed, had survived.

Then he saw a flicker of light. *Tin Man. Searching the lake with a flashlight.* He was sure of it. The man must have discovered the boats gone—the Dippy had probably pulled away just in time—or perhaps he heard the cruiser's engines and knew it was them.

Alex turned around and leaned close to Erik who still sat cross-legged on the floor despite the standing water. "Erik. Where to? Where are we going?"

Another swell rolled in and lifted them. *Up, up.*

Erik held his head, his palms cupped on top, as if he wore a hat he was afraid to lose. His raincoat was open in front. The temperature was near freezing, the northeastern wind bit hard at any exposed skin.

They rose straight to the top where they seemed to perch for an instant before pitching down the backside. On the descent, Alex looked up at the sky—a large drop caught him in the eyeball and he winced.

Finally, Erik removed his right hand from his head and pointed in the direction of Gold Rock Point and Split Rock Lighthouse.

"A little island? ... Erik?" Alex's spirit sank. What if the Reflectory was inside a locked chest on the bottom of the lake. "Where? Shore? What is it? How do we land?"

"No island, no land. Dippy slippy. Dippy slippy into the mind that Sam Tudor built."

"How far, then?" pressed Alex.

"Over tragedy, under fate, through incomprehension...."

Damn it, Erik, just come clean, thought Alex. He wanted to scream at the man. *Tell us before we freeze to death or drown out here! Unless the Dippy is a freaking magic, chitty-chitty-bang-bang boat that can fly and take us to never-never land, the Dippy is useless!* But he knew Erik would not say any more, he would never say any more. He would help, but help would be minimal.

Alex exhaled and shook his head. Kate sat on the seat next to Erik at the back clinging to her life vest with both hands. It would do her no good because they were too far from shore.

Just then, regardless of whether they traveled to the southeast or northwest, whether he lived or died, Alex had decided on a new plan, an addendum to the insanity: he would at least spare his wife. He leaned into Paul who was watching the swells like an anxious seaman and cupped his hands to Paul's ear so Kate could not hear. "How close to shore can you get?"

Paul looked at him briefly as if to determine if he was serious.

Alex continued, "Southwest of Stonebrook's rocky beach and past the rock outcroppings—there's a small cove of sand this side of Gold Rock Point—how close to the cove's beach can you get?"

Paul shrugged as if to say, what does it matter, why would you want to. Then Paul knew why. He glanced behind them at Kate.

She eyed him suspiciously: "What? What are you two talking about?"

Paul leaned close to Alex. "As close as you need."

"Twenty feet? Ten?"

Paul considered it. He nodded.

The swells were coming off the lake from the east-northeast. In order to get where they needed to go, Paul headed nearly straight into them for a ways and then quickly spun the boat around and throttled it. Like a giant surfboard, the cruiser rode a swell at a slight angle back toward shore.

"Where are we going?" asked Kate.

Without lights, all they saw ahead was sleeting rain against a backdrop of black.

The light of Tin Man's flashlight shone bright and uninterrupted—the light was being cast toward the lake. *He can't see us from there*, thought Alex, narrowing his eyes, *We're completely dark.* But the engines of the Cruiser were almost deafening: *He hears us.* "Paul, ease up!"

Paul eased up on the throttle.

"Where are we going!" shouted Kate from the back.

"How much farther?" Alex asked, ignoring his wife.

"I don't know."

The light from Tin Man's flashlight had disappeared. Alex figured the man must have turned away from shore to make his way inland, back up to the footpath so he could cross the brook then take the path up to Gold Rock Point and look again for the boat from the cliff.

Alex blew on his hands and rubbed them. He tried to psych himself up, tried to convince himself that he was about to do the right thing.

The darkness ahead suddenly looked different—fuller, closer!

"Rocks!" Alex shouted, pointing to the large outcropping that seemed to be reaching out to slam them from the right.

"Turn, Paul! Stop!" but Paul had already spun the wheel and they skimmed past the danger.

But they would hit the beach!

Paul thrust the cruiser into reverse.

They saw shore, fifteen feet away.

The cruiser started slowing, her engines groaned.

Ten feet away.

Slower.

Five feet.

Alex rushed to the front of the boat and leaned over to see.

The front of the cruiser bumped, crunched over small rocks—if Alex reached down, he could have touched them—when at last the engines propelled the boat backward.

Alex hurried to the back of the boat—he had to act fast. Kate had one hand over her chest, pressed against the life vest. The other gripped the left side of the boat.

Paul maneuvered the boat around. He looked urgently at Alex, his eyes saying, *do it now—if you're going to do it, by God, do it now!*

Kate, despite suspecting something was up, was caught unaware. Her husband squatted behind her, wrapped his arms around her under her elbows and hoisted her up and over the side of the boat. He did this forcefully; he knew his wife well: if she had had more than a second to consider his intent, she would have fought him with all her might.

She landed on her feet about a yard from shore, the water around her knees. At first, she looked frightened, baffled; he had moved so swiftly. She tried to grasp his hands in hers but he pushed them away.

Her face was right there just inches below his. He could not look at her.

"What, Alex—?" she said. "What?"

She tried to pull herself back in the boat but he held her shoulders, kept her down.

"What?" she repeated. There was no anger in her voice, which surprised him, only fear and sadness. Sadness at not being with her husband.

It broke his heart.

"Why did you toss me over?" she asked. She groped for his hands, but he did not give them to her. "Alex?"

Paul turned the cruiser to face the lake; Kate held the side and stepped with it into deeper water. Alex knew her legs must be freezing, but all that seemed to register in her face was getting left behind. They had come to this cove once—he couldn't remember when—their entire stay at Stonebrook was a blur now, but the cove was hidden from the cottage grounds and was a good fifty yards off the path that led to the point. She would be safe from Tin Man.

"Go, Kate," said Alex harshly, resisting the urge to pull her back in. He pointed to the beach and spoke with emphasis: "Wait a few minutes, let him pass first. Watch for his flashlight and let him pass. Then take the path back to the cottage for dry clothes and take off for the road. Flag someone down. It's just a couple miles to the Split Rock ranger station. Find someone to help."

"No," pleaded Kate.

"You can make it," he said. "I know you can."

When he dared glance at her eyes, he saw the agony there and understood. She did not fear for herself, she feared separation, she feared for him. *Why do this, Alex? I wouldn't want to live without you—if you die, I want to die, too. I don't care about my life if it is not our life—why do this!*

But he also saw resignation; she knew she could not change his mind. She held up a hand. It was an offering; she wanted only to touch him. Their hands pressed together, their fingers locked. Through icy hands and blurry eyes, a great warmth passed between them.

Within seconds Paul had the boat turned around and ready to go.

With her free hand, Kate touched Alex's cheek and said, "Live."

She moved her fingers to his lips; he kissed.

But he did not want his last words to be a broken promise, so he remained silent.

Paul revved the engines, the boat pulled forward.

Kate's hand slipped away.

Chapter 26

Ahead of the cruiser, a swell reared like a rattlesnake.

Paul floored it; the engines groaned. The wave was a giant coil, sucking water, propelling itself over the boat in a deafening hiss: spitting, striking, threatening to make them pay for their delay. And they rode straight up toward the snake's head.

Alex turned, saw Kate scramble to land, and then he could no longer see. When they popped out the topside, drenched, he waved to her to say he was okay. His whole arm felt numb—his mind felt numb.

Paul headed straight out, northeast, pushing it in the troughs, easing up on the crests. The Dispro, Alex was amazed to see, still trailed securely behind them.

"Turn the lights on, Paul," he said.

"What?" Paul looked at him, confused.

"Turn the lights on!" demanded Alex. His teeth chattered, so he unclenched his jaw. "We need to draw him away from her."

Obediently, Paul flipped a couple switches.

The wind blew strong toward shore and so, thought Alex, would sound. He found the volume dial for the radio and clicked it on. He turned it up as high as it would go: static blared from speakers on each side of the boat. He adjusted the tuner and stopped at the first station that came in clear. *Unlike talkies*, thought Alex, *FM radio did not give a damn about foul weather.*

He had hoped to find the rock station out of Duluth that they had tuned into for awhile on the way up from the Cities. He wanted old rock 'n' roll: screaming guitars, testosterone-laden vocals. AC/DC maybe—something to cut the night and carry to shore.

What came out of the speakers was the sound of plucky guitars. Simon and Garfunkel. *Mrs. Robinson.* No longer up against the wind and waves, the boat flew, even with the dead weight of the Dispro behind them. Perhaps Paul Simon had what it took—his voice seemed to make the boat lighter, faster.

Alex sloshed back to Erik in shin-high water. The second breaking wave had been a killer; they now rode low. Too low. Water spilled in intermittently. They did not have long.

"Erik, you have to give us actual directions …"

Despite the standing water, the man still sat on the floor. He had never budged. Alex thought he must have hurt his head because he was still rubbing it.

"You have to tell us where to go," pressed Alex.

Erik replied: "Over tragedy, under fate, through incomprehension."

Alex's entire body shuddered as if trying to cast out the cold. There was no time now for Erik's evasive prattling, no time to solve riddles, no time to huddle with Paul to figure things out. All their effort up until now, all their time: it would soon be for naught. "Where?" Alex asked. He sat down on the edge of the seat next to Erik. "Just point! Where!"

Erik did not reply, he did not gesture. He just kept rubbing his head.

Over tragedy, under fate, through incomprehension, thought Alex. *Like in his dreams!* In them, he ascended high and then fell. He felt a hot rush in his chest.

> On the edge of reason and before the cliff of providence …

It made no sense; it could not be; yet … Alex knew.

> Over earth tended and wild, a stone weighed upon his heart …

He knew where the Reflectory was …

> The same stone weighed upon our greatest regrets and our utmost hope.

It was the most appropriate spot Alex could think of and yet it was also the most unbelievable. *Dear Lord*, thought Alex. The chill he got had nothing to do with being cold. He was amazed.

He felt now that he had known the whole time, that deep within his own soul a flicker of a voice had told him the one place, the only place, the Reflectory could be. But his conscious mind had blown at the voice, extinguished it every time it rekindled, because it whispered the impossible.

Over tragedy: the Madeira.

Under fate: Gold Rock Point.

Through incomprehension: What was that? The cliff itself? Yes, the solid basalt rock of the cliff! Of course. The stone did more than weigh upon a dead man's heart: it weighed upon the greatest regrets and the utmost hope of John Mead and Samuel Tudor. Literally.

Alex sat down in a splash on the floor right in front of Erik. The water felt warm. "It's in the cliff. Isn't it, Erik. Inside."

Erik stopped rubbing his head. There was a spark of awareness in his eyes that Alex had never seen before.

Erik nodded and replied, "Five by six. Dippy slippy."

Alex tried to recall what was unique about the Dispro but his thinking was becoming sluggish. The Dispro was like a big canoe except for one ingenious difference … *the propeller … yes, it was the propeller.* It could be pulled up into the interior housing; it would retract automatically if it struck something hard. The Dispro could float in much less water than the cruiser. "Erik, you take the Dippy into the cliff. There's an opening you steer it into, a sea cave."

The spark in Erik's eyes became a flame. They no longer looked like his eyes but like someone else's. "Five by six. Four over, two under."

Alex's head was thick. Erik's words spilled into his brain and sloshed around inside. "The entrance is five feet wide and six feet high?"

Erik nodded.

Four over, two under, Alex figured, must be the vertical clearance—four feet above the lake surface and two feet

278

beneath. The Dispro could slip into such an opening; the propeller would retract if it struck the bottom. But during a storm?

Because of the loud music, Paul had not heard the conversation behind him.

Alex stood up, dizzy, and spilled into the seat next to Paul. He clicked the radio off. "Turn her back to shore, Paul," he said.

"Where to?"

"Gold Rock Point. Head her straight for the cliff."

Kate inched her way up the crevice that ran between two wet slabs of rock. At the steepest part, she wished Alex were there to give her a hand. Instead, she reached into the darkness above her, found a sprawling tree root, and pulled herself up.

The sleet was turning to rain again.

She walked, she thought, only a short ways, until she realized that she had reached the path. *Where was he? Where was Tin Man?*

And then she saw a light. It was bobbing, coming up from the cottage grounds toward her, moving quickly. *His* flashlight. She stood there for a moment, dazed.

Finally, she dashed back the way she had come to hide in the trees off the path.

She followed the light with her eyes, trying to calm herself before the man got close.

It was a good plan, she supposed: lead the man to the point so she could slip away behind him, but she had almost screwed it up.

Tin Man's pace was hurried, nearly a run.

Yes, it was a good plan except for one thing: they *all* should have jumped out. They would have had time.

Tin Man stopped in his tracks. He held his light steady on the path, precisely where she had stopped.

Kate's eyes widened. What did he see?

The man hunched low, examining the ground.

Had she dropped something?

Footprints. The ground was soft so where she had stood, there were likely two impressions. Her throat constricted. She could not have breathed if she wanted to.

She saw the hood of his slicker move and the light flashed in her direction. She closed her eyes; she could not help it.

With her eyes clenched tight, she thought she heard … music? It came from the direction of the lake. *Mrs. Robinson?* Then it was gone.

"There it is!" Alex said when he saw the faint outline of a couple huge boulders he knew were at the base of Gold Rock Point. "About a hundred yards away, huh, Paul?"

Paul saw them, too, and he eased up on the throttle.

Alex stepped to the rear of the boat and spotted where the towrope disappeared into a swell behind them. The rope was slack. His heart sank. The Dippy. Where was it?

When Kate opened her eyes, the man was flashing the light on the opposite side of the path. She realized that he must be perplexed. She had stopped and stood on the path with her feet perpendicular to it, her toes pointing in the direction he now shone his light. He saw two prints, but then no more. And he heard the music from the lake, too.

Tin Man the great Percipient was more than perplexed. She almost felt like smirking.

Finally, he continued up the path toward the point. His body blocked the flashlight but she could still see the beam of light that it cast. In the rain, it looked smoky gray.

Kate exhaled, stepped out to the path behind him, and watched the light diminish. She turned toward the cottage when she remembered something … something that foiled Alex's plan. She had been introduced to the business end of Tin Man's pistol once already and so had Paul; Alex knew about that. But there was the other piece … the one she had caught a glimpse of dangling from a shoulder strap. It was black and sleek and she had never seen anything like it. Although shorter than the rifles her Dad had owned, it looked much more dangerous. In the commotion, she had forgotten to mention it to Alex and Paul. Now they were her decoys.

Kate clicked her fingernails together but that made her fingers ache even more. She turned and looked up the path in the direction of the point again. The arguments for letting Alex and Paul and Erik fend for themselves had been washed away. The storm might sink them, the lake might swallow them, but if Tin Man, with his fancy weapon that they did not

know about, killed them, their spilled blood would be her fault
… her greatest regret.

Kate shivered. She started up the path to Gold Rock Point.

Chapter 27

Alex caught a glimpse of the little boat as it popped up from behind a wave. "There, Paul!"

Paul craned his neck back and forth; making sure they did not get pushed too close to the cliff, waiting for an opportunity to turn around and look for the little boat.

It was crazy, thought Alex. Because even if they did thread their way inside, what then? Would it not be like being trapped inside a big washing machine? Would the next breaking wave not crush them?

Alex thought of the *Madeira* lying in pieces in the frigid water beneath them and John Mead's description of her fate:

> ... a great crash sent shudders through the steel vessel. To the horror of the crewmen, the *Madeira* was pounding broadside against the base of a cliff.

In a relative lull between two wide, rolling swells, Paul brought the boat around and then straight over the top to find the Dispro. Starting down the backside, they nearly struck the little boat, which, absent the tautness of the towrope, blew and spun like a leaf.

"Paul!" said Alex as they cruised past it, "she looks great—no water in her as far as I can tell." He supposed it was because there was nothing weighing it down that it thus far had bobbed and weaved itself out of trouble.

Paul brought them close a second time; Alex snared the boat with an oar, pulled it next to the cruiser. He jumped in and held it for Paul and Erik.

Stumbling over roots and rocks in the dark, Kate maintained a safe distance between herself and Tin Man. At least she prayed that she did. The flickering light that she had been following disappeared and so she stopped in her tracks. She listened to the rain and her own labored breathing, and tried to convince herself that he had reached the first switchback so he and his light were up above her, pressing on. Not waiting.

Kate swallowed, held her elbows. Her legs and feet were numb but painful, as if she were still standing in Lake Superior. She tried to rub life into them, coax them to go on, to ignore her anxious brain that was telling them to go back.

Erik scrambled over the side of the Dippy, stepped over Alex and plopped into the driver seat. Alex gawked at Erik, stunned by his burst of activity and apparent intent to drive.

Paul was still in the bigger boat. "What are we doing with the Cruiser?"

"Drop anchor, leave her here. Tin Man will be on the cliff soon." Alex stared in that direction but saw no light searching the lake yet. "Turn her lights back on and crank the radio again. Draw his attention. It'll give Kate more time."

"She's going to swamp," announced Paul as he reached for the anchor.

Alex could tell Paul did not want to lose the beautiful boat, but he flipped on her lights and radio, anyway.

On the radio, Don McLean was singing "American Pie"— taking his Chevy to the levy. Alex grimaced; he thought of Buddy Holly crashing his plane into Gold Rock Point.

Paul stepped down into the little Dispro as Alex saw quick flashes of light, like a strobe light, from where the cliff top probably was. Just then, despite the loud music, he heard a spray of whistling around them, high-pitched. He sat up, perplexed. The bow of the cruiser splintered in a hail of woody, popping noises—*tuk-tuk-tuk-tuk-tuk-tuk....*

"Go, Erik, go!" shouted Paul. "Alex—down! Get down!"

Finally, it occurred to him: it was not hail from the sky; it was not the boat breaking apart from the rough water. The splintering bursts destroying the fine woodwork of the cruiser were from a hail of gunfire from the cliff. A fully automatic hail.

The spray of bullets stopped but the boat lights stayed on. ABBA was on the radio now, "Dancing Queen," feeling the beat of the tambourine.

Alex watched water slosh into the boat. Paul said, "I don't think he sees us."

They were stuck with the Dispro—the slippy Dippy—and they weighed it down something fierce. Paul added, "But we have to head straight in, I'm afraid."

He was right, thought Alex. It would take too long and be too dangerous for the Dippy's puttering motor to carry its heavy cargo at an angle away from the cliff. If a wave caught their side, they would swamp; they would die. There was only one direction to go: straight toward the cliff, right underneath the watchful eye of a reloaded Tin Man.

ABBA faded behind them, and ahead loomed the sound of waves crashing against the cliff.

Alex wanted to tell Erik what to do, how to steer, where to go, but found that his strength was waning. Words reached his mouth but sat there numb and thick on his tongue like Novocain.

Alex turned and looked at Erik. His eyes looked brighter somehow, his movements more fluid; his hand moved subtly back and forth, and he kept the little boat straight.

On the edge of reason, before the cliff of providence—that was where they were headed. John Mead had been writing about the location of the key, of course, but he had also been writing about the Reflectory. Whether the cliff would eat them up or allow them safe passage inside, the matter was out of their hands. And even though Erik was at the helm, it really was not in his hands either. It was fate that blew in the wind and sailed on the waves. It was fate that stood on the cliff top and drove the boat. And fate looked grim.

Alex said into Paul's ear, "Sure you don't want to drive?"

Without taking his eyes off the cliff, Paul considered the difficulty of what they intended to do. He shook his head.

"It's been nice knowing you," added Alex. He had meant it as a joke, but it came out sounding serious.

"You, too."

Then he added, "I guess the lake's done gathering now, isn't it Paul? It's venting now."

Paul finally looked at Alex. He smiled.

Kate discovered that as long as she kept her legs moving they stayed loose. She had reached the Circle of Trees and was about fifty yards from the edge of the cliff when she heard the spraying gunfire. Carried on the wind, it sounded muted, harmless. But she knew better. "No," she pleaded. She sprinted through the circle, straight for the cliff. "No, no, no!"

Erik, it became evident, was an expert handler of the Dispro. His hands on the throttle, he did not oblige her sputtering complaints and kept her whines whisper-quiet. He kept her straight when the big swells came.

They were thirty feet from the cliff when they rode high on the next wave. Alex saw Tin Man on top of the cliff and nudged Paul.

They saw another round of gunfire—*heard* it—right from the source. The end of the weapon lit up and spit-sprayed bullets in a zipping noise. Paul dropped to the floor, but Alex did not move—he sat there and dimly wondered why he did not care enough to duck. The hail of bullets was directed elsewhere, still at the cruiser, a long ways behind them now. They could hear the music still, but only when they were high on a wave. From the cliff top, the sound was probably better. The cruiser was probably still visible, too.

Closer in, idling back against the waves, Erik seemed either to be looking for the hole or trying to time the waves. Alex wished he would kill the motor for fear of being heard from above.

A pair of ten-foot high, narrow boulders loomed ahead like sentries. A breaking wave crashed into them—BOOM!—and an instant later hit the cliff itself—BOOM! It sounded like cannons.

Erik found whatever he was looking for and headed straight toward boulders.

This is insane, thought Alex.

Another wave would be looming behind and it would break right on top of them. With one hand he gripped the side wale of the Dispro, and with the other he gripped the bench he and Paul sat on.

Another terrifying thought seized him: *There's not enough room between the boulders! No, Erik—reverse—damn—we're dead!*

But they were not dead. There *was* space. Just enough, and Erik hit it flush.

They glided between the sentries.

Water from the last wave was still pulling away from the cliff. The lake was sucking its own water back out, getting ready to blow another wave at them.

Alex saw the hole—it was right there. *Make it! Make it! Make it!* He felt a surge of elation despite what was next: he hated caves: hated tight spaces.

But the front end of the Dippy bumped. They jolted to a stop.

Alex was incredulous. *It bumped?*

Erik had told them to jump, but it did not register. Alex sat alone in the boat gaping at the hole that was so close yet so out of reach. If the lake were calmer, they would have made it easily. The boat started rising—Alex's heart rose with it: *push me in, push me in!*—but the boat turned sideways and it would not fit that way.

Then Alex was grabbed. Paul had reached up from the water to pull him out of the ill-fated boat right as the wave hit.

BOOM, the wave broke over the sentries and engulfed the three of them.

Alex heard a loud crack then he felt weightless; everything seemed quiet and tranquil. Then water pulled him away from the cliff and he flailed his arms to stop himself from being sucked out. As he shot between the sentries he grabbed for one but his hands were too numb, and he slid past.

He got his legs under him to stand but the water was too deep. "Paul! Erik!" he yelled, his mouth barely above water. "Where are you?"

"Quiet, Alex," replied a low voice near him.

He saw them at the base of the cliff trying to clear a portion of the Dispro's hull lodged in the hole. It was the boat he had heard when the wave hit. It cracked apart on the first wave.

"Swim here," commanded the voice. "Quietly."

It sounded like Paul yet Alex saw in the faint light that Erik was looking at him.

Alex paddled to them, barely keeping his head above water as Erik nudged Paul into the sea cave.

"Come, Alex," Erik whispered, extending his hand.

Alex reached out—Erik's hand exploded. Flesh hung limply, two of his fingers dangled.

Alex's stared at the mess that had just been a hand—his mind was churning in slow motion and he belatedly realized that there had been a crackling sound: bullets spraying the two boulders. He could not help but think that one of the cracks was the shatter of knucklebone in Erik's hand.

And yet, Erik did not scream.

Past the Circle of Trees, Kate slowed. She walked in a crouch, scanning the edge of the cliff ahead. Out of the corner of her eye, forty feet to the right, she spotted a dark shape. She froze, tense, focused on the figure, waiting for movement.

She heard the spraying sound again—this time, it sounded real, like a fuming animal—and she stood up straight. She fumed now, too—anger and desperation ripping through her, making her muscles hot.

When she had last seen Alex, her heart had overflowed for him. That moment had been absolute beauty, undiluted agony. *Live*!

Kate ran toward the figure standing at the edge of the cliff. She had told him that he would die trying to read her husband's mind. She was willing to die to make that happen.

Erik grabbed Alex's arm with his good hand and pulled him toward the hole.

Just before scrambling inside Alex looked straight up the face of the cliff. He saw a red beam of light; it was so bright because it pointed straight down at him, at his head. He prayed that he blended in, that somehow along the track of the laser, the mist and darkness was enough to conceal him….

When Kate got closer to the edge—within twenty feet—she saw the man's black shape clearly. He faced the lake; his "profoundly gifted" mind was distracted enough that he did not hear her approach. His machine gun, she saw by the vertical angle of a red-laser scope, was pointing straight down.

Had they crashed against the cliff? Oh, Alex!

Instead of pausing or even slowing, Kate ran faster. Despite the slush-slicked cliff edge, she ran as fast as her numb legs could go.

The man spun around and only then did she realize that she had started screaming. *Such an odd way to die*, she thought. *Such a very odd way.*

The red light disappeared. Alex winced, expecting a bullet between the eyes, wondering vaguely if he would feel death pierce his skull. Paul pulled him into the pitch darkness—Erik splashed inside right behind him.

"To the rear now," said Erik, nudging Alex in the back. Alex bumped into Paul who was groping for a back wall as the three of them hustled through thigh-high water.

Alex was still distracted by Erik's voice: instead of sounding anguished and unintelligible from the pain of his injury, it was calm and intelligent, and he no longer spoke in sing-songy riddles.

Behind them, a wave exploded into the hole—SHOOOOMMM!

Erik pushed Alex hard and to the right of Paul. "Lean back, feet and arms in front of you!" he said.

Alex did as instructed as a floor-to-ceiling wave pounded him from behind—WOOOOSH. Almost instantly, his feet hit the back wall and then his hands pressed against it. If Erik had not warned him to lean back, he realized, he would have struck his head; if Erik had not shoved him to the right, he would have slammed into Paul.

He thought he was unharmed. And even the frigid air and water that had gnawed at his body had lost its bite. He did not even feel cold anymore.

When the water withdrew, Alex heard gagging on his left.

"You okay, Paul?" asked Alex.

The gagging turned into a gasping cough. "In the shaft—" he sputtered. It was Erik, not Paul.

"The what?"

"Sucked in—" replied Erik, coughing. "Paul. He was sucked into the flowshaft."

Kate's intention had been to push the man over the edge with her hands but because she had been discovered, her impulse was to lunge feet first with all her might. She might go over with him but she figured she was going to be killed, anyway.

Tin Man had a second before the impact and instead of shooting he braced himself, ducking as he did. One of Kate's feet glanced off a shoulder but the other caught the man square in the face. He fell backward, flailing his arms as he tried to grab her but his head and torso were already over the edge. He went down, along with his weapon, out of sight.

Kate landed on her side, jarring her stomach with her legs dangling over the edge. She thought she heard a sound below, a sound like a sack of potatoes hitting concrete. Close by was the dwarf spruce tree they saw on their first hike to the point—she grabbed its trunk and pulled her legs back up. Panting, her body lying on the sleet covered cliff top, she realized that she was still alive only because Tin Man had turned around and had tried to save his own life. The extra resistance he offered by bracing himself was enough to keep her from going over with him.

She peered down. All she saw were two large chunks of wood; pieces of boat, she knew. A wave had smashed it—smashed *them*—against the cliff.

Just then, another wave rolled in, hit the cliff. When it receded she saw three pieces. She pressed the heels of her palms into her eyes. *Too late…. They're gone…. Oh Alex, I'm sorry.*

She sobbed. The tears felt warm on her cheeks, but the wind quickly chilled them.

In her despair, she felt as if she was falling over the cliff, anyway. Falling into a loneliness that had no bottom. And she had an awful idea: she could end the suffering. She could join Alex right now … *a couple feet to the edge,* she thought. *All I have to do is roll back over. Roll back over and fall.*

Then Kate thought she heard music. It was faint, then gone; her subconscious offering false hope.

But she heard it again.

Kate peered into the mist over the lake and saw a bleary, twinkling light. *The cruiser!*

She sat up abruptly and grimaced from the pain in her side. "Alex," she whispered. She tried to stand but only made it as far as kneeling. "Alex!"

She extended an arm, held a hand out toward the boat in the distance, and closed her eyes. At first she was not sure what she was doing, but then she knew: she was reaching inside herself as she had never done before and she was reaching for Alex's warmth. She was not thinking rationally and for the first time in her life, *thank God*, she felt free of rational thought and its encumbering, organized, sequential, linear, confining, confounding logic! Sharp, hard intellect was cutting and, she realized now, she had always shred life's precious, delicate realities before she was ever able to experience them for what they were.

Opening her mind now, she absorbed the reality of how beautiful her husband had been, how beautiful their life together was; their love was robust and true. And she felt him now. Felt his heart, his mind. The most compelling intangible truth she felt was that there was no warmth from the cruiser. Alex was not there.

She felt him though ... *alive.*

Again, she peered over the edge: *Tin Man.* He had been shooting at more than the Dispro boat. He had been shooting at her husband and Paul and Erik.

They were down there.

She cupped her hands around her mouth and shouted down: "Alex!" She winced at the pain in her side as her old, stubborn logic answered: *But they were shot and killed ... or crushed against the cliff.*

"No," she whispered to herself, "they're alive!"

She closed her eyes tight and hit her forehead with an open hand to keep any bit of depressing logic from taking hold. *They had not been shot; they had not been crushed. They had not!* The illogical certainty was as strong as her love for her husband.

Still focusing inward, she barely heard the waves roaring and crashing below.

Dippy slippy, Erik had said. She envisioned it slip into something.... The cruiser out on the lake was a diversion. She pictured it floating empty.

And Tin Man's shooting—it had been desperate because when he had spun around to face her, his body tensed in self-defense but also in frustration. She had interrupted him, interrupted his killing.

Dippy slippy ... Dippy slippy ... What had Erik meant?

Then something in her mind mixed like the ingredients of a sweet batter. Instinct mixed with intuition. Neither one alone would have taken her thoughts to this point, but the two together revealed what had happened. The Dippy was supposed to have slipped into something …. Into the cliff.

Alex, and Paul, and Erik—they had made it inside. They were now underneath her. It made no sense but it was true. Still kneeling, she pressed her hands against the cold ground, the cliff of providence.

They were entering the Reflectory.

She wished them well.

Chapter 28

Alex heard Erik's wading strides along the back wall and asked, "What's the flowshaft? Is he okay?"

Erik either pulled or pushed something because there was a scrapping noise and a sudden gush of water from the back of the cave where Paul should have been.

Then there was light, too, revealing a long shaft. The flowshaft, he saw, was a tunnel with lights—and Paul! Gasping, coughing, looking eerily luminescent, he was washed back toward the two of them.

"Wrong way, Paul," said Erik, "we need to head in."

Paul stopped as the flow of the retreating water eased. "Erik," he said, his voice fearful and raw, "what's going on? What is this?"

"We need to head inside. Our friend Alex is really cold and so will the two of us if we don't dry off and warm up."

Alex looked at Erik's bloodied, disfigured hand. He felt woozy. "I'm fine. Paul, Erik's been shot."

SHOOOOMMM, another wave blasted the cave opening behind them.

Erik said quickly: "Watch your head—hold your breath— let it carry—"

WOOOSH. The wave blasted Alex from behind. His feet caught beneath the lip of the shaft's opening and the force of the wave propelled him into it. He wrapped his arms over his head and was swept deep into the flowshaft.

Trapped under water for what felt like eternity, Alex panicked, stood up, and struck his head against something hard. Disoriented, he saw something glimmering under the water like a light from another world: an eternal lamp from the spirit of the sailor who had plunged to his death with the *Madeira*. Forever vigilant over the shipwreck, he was now perhaps outside, sitting at the edge of the cliff, reliving the night of his death. When he returned to his cave, he would find three new dead men to keep him company.

Then Alex thought he felt a decrease of pressure on his forehead. Air. Water drained below eye level and he saw Erik's head. The man's face was pressed to the ceiling of the flowshaft. So was Paul's. *What were they doing?*

They looked like fish out of water. Sucking, gasping.

They both turned to Alex, mouthing words he could not hear as they approached him. The water continued dropping. At last he heard, "Breathe!"

Alex had been drifting off but now realized that to sleep was to die. *Oh my God, breathe!* He pushed lamely against the hard ceiling with his hands, trying to lift the millions of pounds of basalt rock above him, and then it dawned on him to tilt his face up, too. He inhaled, exhaled, his lungs heaving violently.

He heard Erik's stern voice again: "We need to hurry—it's not far," and he guessed it was a new personality. When at

Tudor House he was the Duke; at Stonebrook Cottage, he was Erik; and when inside the mind that Samuel Tudor built, he was … this calm, collected person. "Alex, are you with us?" he asked.

The water level was dropping quickly now, retreating through the hinged backing behind him. *But another wave will come,* he thought. The certainty was inescapable and he wanted to weep. *The water will fill to the ceiling again!*

Erik grabbed Alex's hand and yanked him deeper into the tunnel.

The water level had receded to their knees when, behind him, Alex heard the next massive wave explode into the sea cave: *SHHHHUAAA.*

It hit the rear of the cave, slamming the hinged backing open: WOOOSH, and rushed into the shaft.

The water level rose instantly: waist-high—midsection—chest. Alex started to whimper. He tightened his grip on Erik's good hand.

A few steps later with the water at neck level, Erik announced, "You guys can stand up now, we're in the antechamber; the water level here cannot exceed six feet."

But Alex saw for himself that he could stand straight: bright lights rimmed the walls of a great cavern. He could have been twenty feet tall and stood up in here. At the far end were steps that led up to a large wooden door.

Erik bobbed and treaded water but still managed to lead the two much taller men through the pool of the antechamber as if they were little children … freezing, bruised, stunned little children.

"Alex, here's a railing." Erik placed Alex's hand on a rail. "Can you feel it?"

Alex groped. It was in his hand but he could not feel it. "Yes," he lied. With his free hand he reached for the key to the Reflectory in his pocket but couldn't get his hand to slide into the crease. "I have the key."

"There are steps. Seven steps up. Can you take them?"

Alex's head was spinning again. He forgot who was speaking to him and where he was. It sounded like Paul but it could not have been him because Paul was up at the top of some steps and the voice he had heard was right next to him, assisting him. Too exhausted to turn his head and look, Alex closed his eyes. His body felt heavenly warm yet his bones felt brittle cold, like they had been immersed in liquid nitrogen. "My insides are cold," replied Alex meekly. "Cold to the core."

Unconscious, he collapsed into the water.

If you have built castles in the air, your work need not be lost; that is where they should be. Now put the foundations under them.

— Henry David Thoreau, Walden

Friday: The Dance of Invention and Harmony

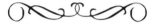

Chapter 29

Lying on a hammock, Alex felt foggy. He had never experienced anything so strangely comforting: his wet body had become dry and warm. There was a recollection of pain and then of numbness but now there was nothing but cozy delirium.

Tranquility …

Yet, his hammock swayed. Curious about his motion, he opened an eye.

Interruption …

He was in the rear of a pilothouse on an old ship. Alex saw a man facing away from him at the helm. The man looked old. In his day he must have been a towering figure because his decrepit body was still tall. His hair was gray-white but was still thick with streaks of black. His large hands embraced the wheel as though it were an extension of him. He looked natural, an old traveler, journeying even in his waning years.

Alex cleared his throat. "Hello …"

The man did not reply. He did not even turn around.

"Hello," Alex repeated.

The waves outside must have picked up because the swaying of the ship intensified.

"Hello there!" Alex said, louder.

No response.

The boat rocked; objects and equipment began to teeter; the old man anticipated every movement so that he always stood perfectly straight, perfectly balanced.

Rain splattered the windows. But it had always been raining, thought Alex, and the sea had always been heavy—the calmness earlier was a mirage. The sailor at the helm knew of these true elements that never let up; it was the reason he could not turn around.

Alex spilled out of the hammock, stumbled over to a side window, and with hands pressed to the glass, saw that the ship deck was at least fifty feet below the pilothouse.

When he turned back, the old man was not there. Without direction, the un-manned wheel spun violently and the boat heaved toward a cliff.

Tempest …

Where was the old man?

The boat dipped in a trough. In another dozen waves they would meet the cliff.

Where's the old man!

Alex looked about frantically and found him slumped on the floor in the back of the pilothouse. The man's right hand rested on a knee. His left hand was balled in a fist, and he held it straight out to Alex.

"We're approaching a cliff!" Alex said, running over to the wheel. He grabbed it to keep himself from falling and it took all his strength to hold it steady. "What do I do?" he asked over his shoulder. "Which way do I steer!" he shouted.

The man did not answer.

Alex scanned the pilothouse for a navigational device that might be of service and noticed the compass on the panel in front of him but inside the round glass ball the letters—N, S, E, W—were jumbled at the bottom like a pile of jacks. He looked down at the wheel in his hands. A brass plate at its center read, *Madeira*.

He was doomed. His fate was sealed. Sealed inside the past, inside the Wreck of the *Madeira*.

And the old helmsman, he was sitting on the floor in the corner! Alex turned to glare at him. "I'm going to die," he said hotly. "Aren't I?" The pilothouse lurched and he tumbled to the floor and slid against a wall, smacking his head against the low window there. "I don't want your fruits, John Mead!" fumed Alex.

The wheel spun so fast it blurred like a roulette wheel.

Alex rubbed the back of his head. "Your fruits are spoiled. They're rotten. Rotten!"

John Mead opened his left hand and revealed a small glowing sphere. It was a hot orange-red and hovered untouched, an inch from his palm. His long, bony fingers extended underneath it like brittle sticks that might ignite.

"What is it?" Alex asked, curious despite his anger.

John Mead lifted his hand up and the sphere, still levitating over his palm, moved with it and illuminated his face. Finally, Alex saw the man's eyes. They were dark-gray and tired, and unlike any he had ever seen … except, one other's. But whose? Tenderness was there: at the corners of his eyes and in the gentle way he blinked. Profoundness filled the circle of large irises; intelligence was in the gaze that contemplated the sphere.

The man lowered his hand, and with it, the sphere, to the floor. He slid his hand away and the sphere hovered on its own near the rocking pilothouse floor.

In the dark pilothouse, its brightness was startling.

The object floated across the floor; it stopped at the wheel.

A soul? Was it the old man's soul?

Handing on to others the fruit of our contemplation.

The sphere moved higher. It levitated over the wheel. Alex hoped it would magically calm the storm outside or at least control the wheel and steer the boat away from the cliff but it did neither.

Waiting. It was waiting.

"Old man …" said Alex softly. "Mr. Mead. I'm afraid. Your contemplations … they're too strong for me, too rough. I cannot see through them; I cannot steer within them. I cannot even understand them!"

"You can," replied John Mead. His voice flowed like honey. It was deep, sweet and smooth.

"How?" Alex asked. "How?"

"The intangible portion of our universe is not constrained by logic, at least logic as you understand it today. But you already suspect this. You will endure the storm and enter Newton's Realm; you will thrive. I have faith."

Alex stared at the sphere, mesmerized. "I can't," he said meekly.

With a nod to the helm, the old man replied, "Find your soul's base."

The sphere moved again. It hovered toward the broken compass; closer, closer, then with a hiss and a sparking flash like that from a welder's torch it seared its way inside the glass compass. The N and the S instantly popped to the glass surface, opposite each other. The W and the E popped into their places, as well. In the center of the sphere, the light shone bright, and it held the directions in place. The letters of the compass started to spin. North, East, South, West, North, East, South, West. Faster and faster, the compass spun. N-E-S-W, N-E-S-W, N-E-S-W … If left unmanned, the boat below would crash against the cliff. Alex stood and staggered back to the wheel. He grabbed it for the second time just as the pilothouse lurched again.

The compass letters were a humming blur; it seemed on the verge of exploding. The floor cracked under his feet—the *Madeira* had struck the cliff!—and in an instant, the compass shattered on the floor into thousands of tiny sparks that all spilled down through the crack.

The wheel of the boat snapped away from its support and Alex, wheel still in hand, fell.

Falling …

Down he went.

He heard crashing waves below.

Down.

Where were the sparks? Had they extinguished on the descent?

Reflection …

Alex shut his eyes tight. There was a sudden change in pressure and a gurgling noise, like the rush of displaced water and bubbles heard by a diver splashing underwater. He tried to swim to the surface but something held him down.

Struggle …

He felt cold yet hot with adrenaline. Feverishly hot.

Alex woke up. He did not open his eyes but knew he was in a strange bed because it felt so soft. He was hurt: the back of his head throbbed with pain, his skin felt as if it had been pricked with pins.

A recurring sound had petrified him: *Shhhhuaaa … wooosh.* It was a real noise from last night but he had heard it before. He had heard a sound like it in his dreams at Stonebrook, in every one. But none of his dreams here felt like dreams. They were … walks within his mind.

Before he dared open his eyes, he recalled something else from last night that was still quite fuzzy; it had been his final thought before passing out on the steps and falling backward into the water: there had been someone next to him there, supporting him. Erik, but not the bizarre Erik that he was accustomed to. Not the Duke, either. Someone else.

Alex opened his eyes a fraction. He rubbed his forehead and found it drenched with sweat. He coughed, tried to wet his dry lips with his tongue. He slipped a hand gingerly under the back of his head and felt a fresh, throbbing wound at the base of his skull. He fumbled with a bed sheet and some wool blankets that had been wrapped cocoon-like around him and discovered that he was wearing someone else's pajama pants and nightshirt. On the little table next to him were a glass of water and a bottle of aspirin. He grabbed both but gulped down all the water before he even opened the aspirin.

The room had a pair of 1950s-era radiators along the walls that were ticking, spreading old warmth. Four wall sconces glowed, casting antique yellow light. He wondered where the electricity came from and then remembered the dam at the brook. The room was powered by hydroelectricity. The brook that gurgled with the laughter of little girls and captured the essence of life also powered the Reflectory.

Near the door, shelves were filled with art supplies. There were brushes, palettes, paints, drop cloths, sponges, and buckets. Collapsed easels rested against a wall; wooden crates and burlap sacks were stacked in corners on the floor. One crate read that it was from *Italia,* but the other words on the crate, which also were in Italian, he could not read. Others were from Denmark, England, Indonesia, and elsewhere. The plump burlap sacks had tiny numbers and letters on them— they could have been from anywhere, contained anything. Alongside the supplies area were carpenter tools, a couple workbenches, and machines for drilling and sawing, and a large kiln. There were stacks of lumber, boxes of ceramic tiles, metal framing … so many gadgets and tools, the function and purpose of some he could not even guess.

Near him, in addition to his own bed, were two others. Both had disheveled blankets and indentations in the downy pillows—from Paul and Erik?

There was a refrigerator, too, and a basin sink and a stove. Two leather chairs and two couches were in the center of the room. There were no books, though, and no paintings.

Alex tried to stretch. At first it felt good but then he got a hitch in his rib cage and he doubled over, coughing. On the sofa table in the center of the room, he spotted a pitcher filled with water. He lowered his feet to the floor and stood. Lightheaded, he paused for a moment and then carried the water glass and aspirin over for more water.

Details came to him one by one. He had survived hypothermia. Erik and Paul must have somehow carried his body up some steps to this room, stripped off his drenched clothes, and swaddled him in blankets. With each barefoot step, the events of the night before, if it was indeed morning now, came back to him. He hoped Kate had made it back to the cottage and away to the road for help. Maybe she had already returned to the cottage with the entire force of the Two Harbors Police Department and they were now combing the grounds for him. But Paul and Erik—where were they? Where was Tin Man?

Alex sat on the couch next to a neatly folded stack of clothes and slippers. On top of them was a note. It read: *went for Kate.*

That was it. Just, *went for Kate.*

Erik's right hand, he remembered, had been blown apart. Alex had seen his fingers dangling. If Erik was left-handed, it might have been his writing, especially since his mental abilities greatly improved once they were inside the cliff.

He poured water into his glass, opened the aspirin bottle, tipped out four pills into a shaking hand. Perhaps the two of them went to get Kate. He considered the pills in his hand, popped all four of them into his mouth and chased them with another gulp.

He tried on the navy pants; they fit at the waist but were too long. He rolled the ends up into cuffs then put on the slippers. The T-shirt and tan button-down shirt fit nicely, as well, after he turned the sleeves up.

Time to explore, he thought.

In case he needed to leave his own note later, Alex folded the slip of paper and tucked it in the breast pocket of his shirt along with the pen.

At the door, he turned the handle and pushed it open into the middle of a cold passageway. To his left and right were mammoth wooden doors; straight ahead was a plain, small door. He figured he would work left to right, and so he walked to the first door at the left, the only one with dead-bolt locks and a security bar. He slid the bar away, flipped the deadbolts, turned the iron-ring handle and pulled. He had to pull hard to budge the massive door, and as it swung inward, even colder air coiled around it.

Alex shivered. His fingertips and ears throbbed hotly—they remembered their frostbite.

He peered around the door and saw a great cavern with a pool of water. The lights, positioned several feet above the water, were affixed to the cave walls with an electrical line running from light to light. At his feet was a square landing with mooring poles.

The antechamber, thought Alex. *Where we came in.*

Twenty-five feet away was a dark hole: the long flowshaft. Beyond the shaft was the sea cave and beyond the cave was Lake Superior.

Alex stepped out onto the landing. The water before him was like dark, smooth glass. The storm had passed—waves no longer broke into the flowshaft. There were no dripping sounds, no sound of distant waves, only the electric hum of the old lights.

But how do we get out?

He saw something at the bottom of the pool, about six feet long. His eye had been drawn by a white glimmer at one end of it. He kneeled on the stone floor of the landing, held onto a mooring pole, and then leaned over the edge of the pool. The glimmering object was not a discarded piece of metal or a white rock; it was a face. Tin Man's.

Unlike Alex's dream, which had taken him inside the hull of the *Madeira,* face to face with the haunting spirit of a man who had been killed by the horrific storm a century ago, this man was an honest-to-goodness *dead* man … from *this* storm. He was real, and he was really dead.

The man must have slipped off the cliff into the lake, his body pushed through the sea cave and flowshaft by the waves. The eyes would not pop open because they already were open. They still had in them the transfixed terror from what must have been an abrupt, horrific death. Alex nearly had ended up the same way—in the flowshaft he had lifted his head and gulped air just before it was too late. Later, in his dream, he had felt the rise of death twice more. He felt now that if he had chosen to remain ensconced in the pilothouse instead of taking the helm, he would have drifted up into his own oblivion. And if he had chosen to swim up through the opening of the *Madeira*'s hull, he would have swum to his own death.

For a moment, Alex was perplexed: bodies in water, they floated, did they not? Scenes of war came to mind: footage from Pearl Harbor, from D-Day. In the aftermath of those battles, bodies floated by the hundreds, the thousands.

Why did this body not float?

Then he remembered, as he had in his dream. This was Lake Superior. Things were different here. With water so cold, bodies will not float. And submerged, the bodies are preserved; oblivion is captured. While studying abroad in England, Alex had spent a week in Moscow, Russia, and had seen the body of Joseph Lenin lying in the glass case of his tomb in Red Square. If Lenin had had his eyes open instead of closed and was twenty years younger with a beard, he would have resembled this man now.

Despite Alex's revulsion, he knew he should retrieve the body and look for identification to see if Tin Man's real name was in fact Nicolai Petrov. The man also might have their car keys, and Paul's, too. But even with a long stick or pole he doubted he could reach the body to pull it over. He would have to wade in.

To keep his pants dry he decided to take them off. He never wanted anything to do with wet, *ice-cold* clothes, ever again.

When his foot touched the water, he grimaced and sucked air through his teeth. The water, when he was all the way down, threatened to get his boxer shorts wet so he cinched them up to his crotch with his hands. Not until he had waded up to the body did he discover that he had no idea how he intended to accomplish his task of moving the thing. He did not want to put an arm down there because his shirt would get wet, and he did not like the idea of grabbing the man, anyway. He was so cold already: his teeth were chattering again and his legs felt like icicles.

Only one thing to do, he thought, staring at the submerged body's vacant eyes. *Just—please, oh please—if you blink or open your mouth, I'll scream!* Alex grimaced and nudged the torso with his bare foot. Even though it was under water, it felt extremely heavy. Dense. The man's arms and head lolled back and forth but otherwise the body did not seem to have budged. He nudged harder. The body moved a few inches.

Then he noticed the broken left leg. From just above the knee, it bent sideways from the body. Alex felt sick. The man must have struck one or both of the sentry boulders when he

312

fell. He saw now the horrific damage sustained to the side of the head: the ear was a mess and the mottled cheek was concave, the cheek bone clearly shattered.

He pushed the man over to the steps and then hooked his foot under the man's good leg and lifted it onto a step where he could reach it with his hands. He stepped out of the water, grabbed the ankle with both hands, and pulled the leg to the surface up to the man's waist. Crouching next to the body, he felt around the man's waist and padded the back pant pockets. From the right-rear pocket, he retrieved a wallet. Inside was some cash, a credit card, an identification card.

The ID card was in Russian and English. The man's name, of course, was not Tin Man. It was Nicolai Petrov.

Alex patted the front pant pockets for keys but did not find any, so he stepped back into the water and reached into the trench coat to feel for pockets. In a breast pocket, he found Kate's keys and another set. He recognized the little violin attached to the ring—they were Paul's.

Alex's legs were still wet when he put the socks, pants, and slippers back on. Standing with the ID card and wallet in one hand and the two sets of keys in the other, he regarded the dead man at his feet. The upper torso and head were still below the water and both arms dangled straight over the head like he was signaling a touchdown.

At last, the anger came. It had been pent up but now it rushed in like water through a dam. This man had tied up Kate and Paul. This man had shot Erik in the hand … he had tried to kill them all. And for what? Why had he been so desperate? Alex kicked the man's foot and it flopped down a step. "Serves you right," he said. He threw the emptied wallet at the face—it splashed into the water, struck the man's forehead, and sank to the bottom of the pool.

"Serves you right," Alex repeated in a whisper.

Back inside the hall, Alex opened the small door across from the original door he came out of and found it completely dark with a loud electric hum. He felt for a light switch on the wall, but found none, so he retreated and closed the door behind him.

The last door was the grandest of all. It looked exactly like the door in the back of the boathouse except it was well over twice the size. The engraved violin on this door was a bright blue—the detail was stunning.

This was it, he knew. The door that led to the Reflectory, or as Erik would say, *the mind that Samuel Tudor built.*

Alex grasped the metal ring and turned it. He pulled the door wide open.

Chapter 30

A ringing telephone startled Kate awake in the master bedroom of Stonebrook Cottage. According to her watch on the nightstand it was 8:37 a.m. After a disorienting moment of wondering why her husband was not lying next to her, she sat up in bed. Despite her exhaustion, she marveled that she had fallen asleep without him. She had come upstairs to get out of her wet clothes and had lain down for a moment.

So, Tin Man had not cut the line after all. It must have been out due to the storm.

The phone continued to ring and she ran downstairs to pick it up.

Before answering, she knew it was not Alex or even about him. There would be no telephones where he had gone. It was someone else who was calling. And something bad had happened, she feared. Something very bad.

Tucked deep inside the Reflectory, inside the small keeper's quarters, Paul Kransberg could not take his eyes off an eerily familiar scene in a painting on the wall. Erik—or whichever personality Erik had been inside the cliff last night—had instructed him how to find the quarters after they took care of

Alex. All that the peculiar man had told him was that inside was "a truth."

"A truth" that, according to Erik, would "sear your soul, brand it into a new, larger whole."

And he had been right. Absently, Paul scratched his temple below the bandage that now felt tight and hot. He did feel something of a searing, because his eyes started to burn and his nose began to run. He wiped at them with a shirtsleeve and began blinking rapidly. He wondered if he was about to cry. He had not cried in a great many years so he did not remember how it started.

Upon hearing a distraught, uncertain voice introduce herself, Kate knew precisely what had happened. She dropped to the couch. It was Elsa's nurse calling. Calling with the news.

The first thing Paul had noticed inside the keeper's quarters was that it smelled faintly of pipe smoke like the library of Stonebrook Cottage. There was a leather swivel chair behind a desk and two foldout chairs in front of it. On a table next to the desk was an old computer. Overstuffed bookshelves pinned a recliner chair and a small bed into a corner. A washbasin was in another corner. To the right of the basin was a space heater. On the basin were a toothbrush and a tube of toothpaste. Eyeglasses rested upon an open book on the nightstand.

When he had stepped inside and picked up the pipe from the ashtray, he noticed that a flame had charred the tobacco in the center of the bowl, but then it had gone out, seemingly not smoked. The perimeter of the bowl was lined with brown tobacco as if a person had just left and might return at any moment.

There were two paintings on the wall opposite the desk. Treasured paintings, Paul supposed, given that they were inside this personal space. According to the title plate underneath the one on the left, it was of the central park in Boston, Massachusetts: *Boston Green*. It was dated 1871 and the scene was of a boy and a man sitting next to a pond. Samuel Tudor would have been a little boy then. Perhaps the man was his own father.

But now, what held him riveted was the painting on the right, the one entitled *Moon Over Monterosso*. It was of two figures on a hilltop at night. The figures, so tiny within the grand scene, sat next to a small fire near a brook. They looked away toward a seaside village below. Monterosso, Italy. A full moon loomed large over the coastal Italian town, casting silver light.

Kate pressed the phone hard against her ear as she listened to the woman explain that Elsa spent the night before not in her bed, but in her favorite chair in her favorite room. "She'd been looking out at the lake, I guess," the woman said. "When the storm came, I told her we should get her up to her room but she refused so I brought down a cot and blankets and a pillow. I stayed with her through the night because Paul wasn't there, and, well, I was worried.

"This morning—Elsa—when I went to wake her for her pills, she was already sitting up and had her eyes open. So I thought she was awake, you know? But she didn't—she didn't take her pills when I offered them to her. She didn't … take them."

Just then, Kate heard an abrupt silence on the other end, a silence broken by hitched, heavy breathing.

"Elsa's gone," said the woman at last. In a flurry, she added, "She's gone—I'm sorry—she wrote this phone number down and left a note that I should call it to get hold of Paul. Tell Paul, won't you? I'm sorry. Tell Paul?"

"I will," Kate replied but the woman had already hung up.

The brushstrokes of this painting matched his mother's favorite painting.

Paul stooped close to it and studied the two figures huddled close like lovers. He recalled easily his mother's description of her most exhilarating experience in her life, because he had been surprised that it did not involve playing violin. She had described an experience of "intense peace, intense pleasure." She had described the scene in this painting: the brook, the olive tree grove, a small fire. The moon.

He remembered that she had been especially smitten with the silver moon.

Except there was one blatant omission from his mother's description: the man. The man in whose lap she sat, whose chin perched on her shoulder, who looked to be whispering in her ear, pointing at something down the hill.

The woman was his mother. There was no doubt in his mind. And the man was the one who had given her the painting. It was her "dear friend" she had met in Monterosso. Her dear friend who had given Paul his beloved violin after he was born.

But these figures were not merely friends. The implication was undeniable: this man whom his mother had never spoke of was the truth that Erik told him he would find here, inside one of John Mead's personal spaces deep inside the Reflectory, it was the truth that seared his soul, branded it into a new, larger whole.

The man was his mother's lover.

The man was John Mead.

The man was his father.

Kate knew that Elsa had not been looking out at the lake. She had been looking for a fire along the bank of Stonebrook, a fire that Kate cursed herself for not having started last night as she had promised she would. By the time she got back to the cottage it was too dark and stormy for Elsa to have seen but she should have done it anyway. With the phone receiver still at her ear, she heard her own hitched, heavy breathing.

Paul recalled vividly all the scenes of his mother's painting. The most eye-catching to him had always been the final one of the intertwined silhouettes of two women rising in the smoke of a fire with looks of great contentment on their ashen faces.

The setting of that scene looked like the setting of this painting. He wished his mother were with him now to see this. How happy she would be to discover that her lover, the father of her only child, cherished the same moment that was most sacred to her. He could not wait to take this painting home to show her. He could not wait to tell her that at last he knew who his real father was.

Kate told herself that she had barely known the woman, really, and that she had been old and had advanced cancer. Her death was not a surprise; in a sense, it was welcome. As Kate cried, she told herself these things so that the woman's passing would not affect her so much. Yet, it did.

Paul sat on the bed in the little room and, at last, he cried. He had not known John Mead. He told himself that he should be furious over the great lie he had been fed his entire life because now his past was false: the shy boy who grew up under a cloud, the morose man he had become—it all felt artificial. And it was not his fault. It was John Mead's fault. His mother's fault.

But the tears streaming down his face had little to do with anger, and they had little to do with grief. He had never known his biological father, and he had been deprived of what might have been a happier, extraordinarily fascinating upbringing, yet his tears were not caused by such things.

Sitting on his father's bed with discordant noises pounding in his head, he finally identified the emotion that was welling inside him. Knowing that his real father was John Mead, should not have triggered such an unlikely emotion. Yet it did.

It was not until a few minutes later, when Kate had started to calm down, that she heard something—*someone*—right behind her.

She whirled around to see Erik sitting at the far end of the dining room table. His right hand was heavily bandaged and he was hunkered down over a bowl. It was Erik, she saw—not the Duke—so in his bowl would be Spam; in his glass would be Tang.

"Hello, Erik," she said. She kept her voice as calm as her emotional state would allow, as much to reassure herself as him. "Alex and Paul," she continued, "they're still inside?"

Erik blew vigorously on a spoonful of food and gulped it down. As she walked up to him, she saw that he had mashed the Spam into small chunks. It was steaming so he must have heated it up on the stove. It looked like dog food to her.

"They're still inside the Reflectory, aren't they?" she asked again. She sat down next to him. "Erik?"

He did not reply but paused in his chewing.

"What happened to your hand, dear? Are you okay?"

Finally, Erik said: "Tin Man."

"Oh my—did he shoot you? From the cliff?"

"Shot Erik's hand," replied Erik. "Missed the tall one, missed Mr. Fitzgerald." A grin spread across his wide face. "Tin Man's dead. Very, very."

She had saved them after all, thought Kate, remembering her desperate lunge. He had been shooting at them, and she had saved them.

"Mr. Mead and the tall one bandaged Erik's hand," continued Erik. "Mr. Mead and the tall one saved Mr. Fitzgerald's life."

"Mr. Mead?" Kate was perplexed. "How did Mr. Mead help save Alex's life?"

"Mr. Mead is inside me when I enter the mind that Samuel Tudor built. Mr. Mead saved Mr. Fitzgerald."

Kate frowned at Erik. She watched him blow on and then shove another big spoonful of Spam into his mouth. She listened to the loud smacking noises as he chewed with his mouth open.

"Where are they now, Erik? Are they still inside the Reflectory?"

"Yes."

"What are they doing?"

"Seeking. Finding."

"Seeking and finding?"

Erik took another huge bite. She wished he would stop. It was making her nauseated.

When she saw he was about to lift another spoonful toward his mouth, she touched his forearm and asked again, firmly: "Seeking and finding what, Erik?"

Erik's spoon stopped at his lips. He tilted his head toward her but kept his eyes on his spoon. "Truth," he said. His lips puckered once, twice. Then: "Meaning."

"What are those things, truth and meaning? What's inside there? Tin Man said he was from another Reflectory in Moscow. A place called Bunker Deep. And he said that John Mead was something called a Blue Violin. What do you know about all that?"

"Not to say," replied Erik, inserting the heaping spoon in his mouth.

"Erik, tell me," Kate replied sternly. "What is inside these Reflectories and what is Newton's Realm?"

As she watched him chew, she felt increasingly worried about her husband's safety. "When are they coming back?"

From Erik's full mouth, came: "Never ever." A hunk of meat dribbled down his chin and dropped onto the ledge of his belly.

"What!"

"Never ever. Cannot shannot mannot."

"You mean they're trapped?"

"Not trapped."

"What, then? Erik, damn it! What's happened to Alex and Paul?"

Erik swallowed and eyed his glass of Tang.

Kate grabbed it, held it at arm's length.

He appeared to be considering something. "Not trapped," he said. "*Delivered*. Given the gifts of awareness. That is what a Reflectory does. To anyone. But only a Blue Violin can travel to Newton's Realm."

Kate shook her head. She really, *really* did not like speaking with Erik. "Take me to them," she demanded.

"In the canoe," replied Erik, to her surprise. "In the canoe, Erik and Kate can go."

Paul lay down on the small bed and rested his head on the pillow. There was something deeper in his mind that caused his tears. He was crying, he figured, because he finally understood himself, his *deeper* self. He had always been a useless ponderer, he thought. He had been a ponderer his entire life and yet inside him not all was placid. There were … ripples. During this past week with Alex and Kate, and now inside the Reflectory, he had discovered that the world was not mirror; it just had a glare on its surface that was difficult to see through. Because he had never jumped in to know any better, jumped in to the world to see how deep it was, see how well he might swim.

He had never given the world a chance. He had never given himself a chance. And his soul had grown stagnant on the bank of its own little brook…. It was time to venture.

After Erik finished eating, Kate led him to the couch to lie down where she draped a blanket over him. He looked too exhausted to leave now. If Alex was fine, if Paul was fine, they could wait a little while longer. And there was something important she needed to do first. It was too late, but it needed doing anyway.

So these were tears of … happiness. Paul rubbed his eyes. Yes, that's what it was: happiness. Because how long had it been since he was truly happy? It had been even longer than since his last cry. The catharsis felt liberating, like had just stepped outside the gates of a self-induced prison called melancholia. Now that he could identify the emotion, he stopped crying.

He was ready to dive now. Dive into the vast ocean of life, instead of meditating on the shore of a tiny, remote brook. He was ready, not because his father was John Mead, but because of what he had learned at Stonebrook with Alex and Kate—that he had passions and gifts worth sharing. He had learned that his greatest regret was simply not doing anything with them.

Finally, Paul laughed. It came out sounding like a donkey bray. It was lame, rusty. *An appalling excuse for a laugh,* he thought, so he laughed even more because of it.

When he settled down, he set his glasses on the nightstand next to the bed and drifted off to sleep. He slept not as Paul the Shepherd but as Paul the discoverer of a great truth, discoverer of his own soul.

He was the son of John Mead and Elsa Kransberg. He was Paul Mead. It made sense; it fit.

Paul dreamed of playing his violin in front of a packed amphitheater. In his dream, his mother and father watched him perform from a balcony far up in the sky. Then, even though his mother had never been a singer, she sang to him in Italian, and her voice was two voices—her Innocence and Wisdom—and it was the sweetest, most sublime sound he had ever heard.

Chapter 31

Inside the woodshed, Kate stacked logs into a cradled arm but then let them drop to the floor. She leaned against a wall, overcome with emotion. She wished that the telephone lines had still been out this morning so that she would not have gotten the call about Elsa. Maybe that would have made her feel less guilty.

With as many logs and kindling as she could carry, she started a small fire on the bank of Stonebrook near the footbridge. It took awhile to get it going—the ground was wet and the air was cold, but it was good wood, perhaps even wood that John Mead himself had stacked, since she had grabbed the oldest, driest logs from the back of the shed.

She stood, cold, with arms crossed, waiting for the fire to grow. The wispy, gray smoke reminded her of the final scene of Elsa's painting, her Wisdom and her Innocence together again, embracing, soaring to heaven.

A brook captures the essence of life, John Mead had told Elsa. There was beauty in that sentiment. Perhaps that was what touched her so dearly here at Stonebrook. It was so simple, so natural. Now the brook that had been quiet and peaceful all week was purging, renewing.

The waterfall upstream from the footbridge roared, and she was mesmerized by it. She felt a tug inside her mind like she did on the cliff the night before when she knew that her husband was alive and right underneath her. Except, this tug was less urgent. She let it take her mind down into herself, something she never used to do. And as she descended, she felt heavier while everything around her felt lighter. The stick in her hand was so light; she let go of it, expecting it to float away but it fell to the ground.

She envisioned—saw, heard, smelled, tasted, touched—a comforting woman hugging her. A woman who smelled of vanilla extract and sugar, a woman with warm, tender hands, a woman with a voice like satin, a voice that whispered, "Let them go…. Let them go."

This woman, she was beautiful. And Kate's greatest regret was in denying the fantastic beauty that had always surrounded her and existed inside her. Life was not an item on a to-do list; it was not a hurdle over which one must jump; it was not a burden. But how often had she felt that's what life came down to? With a great deal of sadness, she knew the answer: every day.

"Let them go," the woman's voice reminded her again. The woman was Elsa and she was Kate's own deceased mom and her son Michael. Their presence was vague yet strong. *But why?* Kate wondered, *Why do you bother with me?* Kate reached a hand out. She felt the warmth of the fire lace through her fingers as if it were from a comforting hand. She felt warmth wrap around her body in a hug. Around her legs, too, like little boy arms holding her legs as tight as they could. She thought she did not deserve them.

Let them go.

Kate felt their lessons, their passions, their love, and their innocence. Finally, Kate screamed, "Elsa, I don't want to let them go! I need them!" She started to cry. She sobbed, "Mom, I don't have the strength." She wanted to sit down—her arms and legs felt like rubber—she wanted to hide. "Michael, I'm so sorry I wasn't there for you when you had the accident with Dad."

The fire crackled, a single spark drifted up.

And a little bit of something sank in: although she had not lit the fire for Elsa while the dear woman was still alive, it did not matter. She lit it now. She lit it anyway. And her cynicisms and resentments and scorn and hate were burning in the flames next to the brook of life. They were burning there because she had just let them go to embrace Elsa, to at last accept her own mother's passing, and her son's.

And at last she saw it. *Beauty.*

Kate closed her eyes. When she opened them, she looked up at the wispy smoke that trailed into the sky.

She whispered, "Thank you."

Chapter 32

Alex saw basalt rock descending. Someone had blasted a stairwell and chiseled uneven steps. The walls and ceiling were untouched native rock so it felt like he was about to enter a cave.

A light was on below and he could see a portion of the floor at the bottom. It was tiled and looked fancy, not like a cave at all.

When he reached the bottom, his breath caught in his throat. A massive room opened up in front of him, or a corridor. It was perhaps thirty feet wide, one hundred feet long, and twenty feet high. Unless there had already been a large cave here, all that cubic space would have been millions of tons of rock. Even if it had been a cave, this was a Herculean feat by passionate, brilliant men, who, it was now incontrovertible, had also been insane.

And to Alex's surprise, he felt deeply touched, deeply humbled. He had survived and he had found the Reflectory. Tears welled; he held them back. They were of relief, weariness and elation, which he understood, but they were also of sadness. Since Michael died, he had felt adrift; he had been searching, endlessly searching.

But for what?

Crying would be okay, he told himself. He was alone; there was nothing to be embarrassed about.

He slumped to his knees and let it out. He doubled over until his forehead touched the cold floor, as he had seen Erik do the night before over the stone in the center of the Circle of Trees. It seemed to excise a great weight from his chest because, for the first time in recent memory, his heart beat strong and unlabored, as if liberated.

But for what had he been searching?

In the car accident when Michael's head struck his own—that was the moment this all started. Along with his boy's synesthesia an awareness of an entirely new level of comprehension passed into his mind and his life since that day seemed devoted to learning to perceive the world in new ways.

He knew that he had inextricably linked the search for the Reflectory to a search within himself. All week long, he felt these searches coming together like merging paths in a dark forest. But what was it within himself that he was looking for? Meaning?

Battered and weary, Alex struggled to his feet. He felt like a medieval knight wounded during an epic battle, who woke up hours later in a foreign, beautiful place. On the walls and ceiling were paintings. The place had the aura of something sacred, like a chapel. The search for the Reflectory was a metaphor, he had figured, but it was also real.

In the silence after his tears, Alex could almost hear an undercurrent of echoing choir music: deep male voices praising, praying, chanting. Yet something was secular about the place, too. He could almost hear Erik's eerie refrain in the chant: "It's not finished … it's never finished … it needs someone."

But what did that mean? What here was not finished?

Chapter 33

Erik sat on a folded blanket in the bottom of the canoe, toward the front. Kate sat in the back seat and paddled. The lake was almost like glass and she made good time. When the canoe passed through scattered debris from the Dippy floating at the base of the cliff, her heart started to race. She did not see a way to enter the cliff nor did she see Tin Man's body.

"How do we get inside?" she asked. Then she saw it: the small opening between two tall rock outcroppings.

"Over tragedy, under fate, through incomprehension," replied Erik without turning around. But his voice was different. It was deeper, now. Smoother.

Kate rested the paddle across her knees. It was a sunny, quiet morning and she heard the drops of water dribble into the lake from the wet end of the paddle.

Erik turned around and looked her in the eye, something he never did. "We have to talk but it isn't safe out here on the water. More visitors from Bunker Deep will be coming. And they will not be pleased. We must get inside." His eyes expressed love and concern, like a father forced to explain some great mystery to a daughter before she was old enough to understand.

Kate scanned the cliff top and looked over at neighboring Split Rock Lighthouse. Sufficiently freaked out, she nodded and resumed paddling. "Why do the people from Bunker Deep want to kill us?"

Erik paused before answering, as if determining how to make things as simple as possible. "There are four Reflectories. Two are in the West: ours here at Stonebrook and also Longbow Castle in Scotland. There are two in the East: one in Moscow and one in Prague. For the entire existence of Stonebrook, over a century now, we have run exchanges with the first Reflectory in Longbow but Moscow and Prague were behind the Iron Curtain. We knew little of their recent work and vice versa. In the first visit between East and West since the nineteenth century, we sent a Percipient—actually a full-fledged Blue Violin and John Mead's heir apparent—to Moscow, while Moscow reciprocated and sent a senior Percipient here. Longbow held their own exchange with Prague."

As they approached the two huge boulders, the Lighthouse disappeared behind the curve of Gold Rock Point. Kate found herself longing for the old Erik, the one who made no sense.

"Sadly," he continued, "it was a preplanned and coordinated slaughter. Three percipients and John Mead were killed here, three were killed at Longbow and, I suspect, our two percipients from the West were likely killed in Moscow and Prague."

"But why?" asked Kate. "Why were they killed?"

"Moscow and Prague became greedy. Blue Violins know the dangers of making Percipients of people who were already geniuses before entering a Reflectory but they evidently couldn't resist the temptation to expand their realms exponentially."

Kate listened, feeling clueless, as she paddled the canoe between the boulders. They passed between them and into the opening. She felt a moment of claustrophobia and grabbed the wall at her left to keep her half of the canoe outside.

Erik continued talking from inside, his voice echoing from the dark interior: "When a genius is sent into a Reflectory there is an increased chance that they will come out delusional, paranoid, or schizophrenic. They can fall through the gap. I've seen it happen here. In short, they can go mad. What I believe happened in the East is that a Blue Violin or a few Percipients went bad and killed off perceived rivals even within their own Reflectories. Their entire facilities have likely been corrupted and any good Percipients are either dead or in hiding. What we do know is the exchanges were a ploy. The Blue Violins in charge of Bunker Deep and Prague want to take over Longbow and Stonebrook because our Reflectories still work. They will send more men, and they will be armed. So paddle yourself in, Kate. You are exposed to the cliff top."

Inside a sea cave that was twice as long as the canoe, Kate figured that Erik must have grabbed something, maybe pulled a lever or handle on the back wall, because a portion of the rear wall opened. She peered into a long, straight, dimly lit tunnel. The water in the tunnel looked deep enough for the canoe and she marveled that the three men had made it all the way inside without the Dippy boat.

Before she resumed paddling, she noticed a diagram etched on the smooth, gray interior wall over the tunnel opening. "What's that on the wall?"

Erik glanced up at it but looked uneasy, like he didn't want to get into that yet. He hoisted himself up from the bottom of the canoe and sat on the front seat, still facing her. "Kate," he said, "you have to trust your heart and soul that everything I am about to tell you is true."

With a hand over her mouth, she nodded. She was still shocked by the way he was speaking. Now he was going to blow her away with something?

"You might remember this cave drawing from art class in elementary school. It's Isaac Newton's color wheel. The Latin words represent the seven colors of the visible spectrum and the capital letters are the 7 musical notes of the diatonic scale. Symbolically and literally, what lies ahead is beyond color, beyond sound."

"I don't understand."

"In 1668, Isaac Newton invented and built the world's first reflecting telescope in part to disprove the centuries old belief that white light was pure. That it was in fact made up of a spectrum of colors: seven colors to be precise. In 1672 he presented his telescope and findings to the Royal Society and they were, frankly, stunned. This is all part of history."

Kate dipped the paddle in the water to keep the canoe steady. She could not take her eyes off the color wheel and she was not ready to go farther inside.

"Later, in his late forties and before his nervous breakdown, Newton isolated himself for years, secretly blending science with alchemy on an invention to disprove an even larger pillar of society: the belief that human enlightenment was pure. For years he had theorized it was in fact made up of—"

"Let me guess," interrupted Kate. "Seven phases?" With a chill, she thought of the phases that Alex described from his dreams at Stonebrook.

"Yes. Seven components, or *phases*, if you will: the phases of enlightenment. Newton worked endlessly on his human Reflectory: an oval structure of a unique configuration within which he would mentally cycle through the phases to enter a greater realm of consciousness. We call this realm Newton's Realm. The mind's capacity is not fixed from birth. It's like a muscle—and intelligence for anyone can be greatly enhanced inside a Reflectory. But there was a problem for Newton. He was a genius before he entered. He fell through the gap and almost didn't make it out."

"What's this *gap*?" asked Kate.

"Aristotle's Gap. The fabric at the bottom of Newton's Realm has a hole. You fall into it; you fall into Aristotle's Gap."

Kate frowned at him. "I'm not following."

"It is the hole in enlightenment. The hole in which madness overtakes genius." Erik seemed baffled as to how to explain the concept to an actual *non*-genius. "Aristotle had famously remarked that a great mind needs a touch of madness," he continued. "So anything more than a touch, pulls a great mind under. This is how Newton suffered his nervous breakdown. Luckily he was balanced enough to pull himself out if it. But then for his own safety, he destroyed the Reflectory."

"How do we know he even built it, then?" asked Kate.

"Letters to his confidante, John Lock, more than implied his belief in this theory," replied Erik patiently. "But decades after Newton's death, the great Scottish philosopher David Hume found documents from Newton hidden at Locke's estate in Essex. The documents contain the complete explanation and detailed schematic drawing and remain private to this day. Newton called these papers 'A Reflectory for the Human Mind—A Treatise on the Soul.' This treatise still exists on the wall at Longbow."

Kate's grasp on the paddle tightened. Erik's story was making her even more anxious to go inside. "What kind of schematic?"

"For his invention. The Reflectory. Just as Newton's prisms and reflecting telescope accounted for the seven components of light, the Reflectory accounts for the seven natural components that lead to human enlightenment. When Hume returned to Scotland, he built the world's first large-scale Reflectory at Longbow Castle. This is where Moscow's first Blue Violin apprenticed in 1741 and where Samuel Tudor apprenticed in 1889, while he was working on The Reflectory at Stapleton Manor."

"The one that burned down," added Kate, recalling what they read from Edward Tudor's journals. "Before he came here to build his own Reflectory, right?" asked Kate.

"Exactly." Erik motioned for her to paddle into the shaft and when the entire canoe was inside he pushed another button and the door behind her closed.

Kate closed her eyes. *Dear God, where am I going.*

Chapter 34

A Reflectory is never finished, thought Alex. He craned his neck to stare up at the ceiling of exquisite, Renaissance-style oil paintings like the ones he had seen on the ceiling of the Sistine Chapel. There were men and women, birds and beasts, planets and stars. But it was the three-dimensional aspect that was astounding. Like a hologram, the figures and objects seemed unconfined by the flat surface of the ceiling. He wondered if painting technique alone could have produced such an effect or if he imagined it. Lighting for the corridor was recessed and emitted from behind a long strip of crown molding that ran the length of the four walls. Perhaps within the strip was a 3D projector of some sort.

Before Alex took another step inside, he noticed some paper on the floor right in front of him. On the top page written in quill pen were the words *Contemplata aliis tradere.* Alex recalled John Mead's note buried in the heat of sin:

At its opening are revelations …

The papers, then, contained answers: *Revelations.*

Alex wanted desperately to snatch them up and read them—*devour* them—but felt obligated to wait for Paul and Kate; they had worked together the entire week, after all.

Nonetheless, it took all the strength of his will to walk around the enticing papers and move farther inside.

In the center of the corridor, a very long cord dropped from the ceiling. At the bottom of the cord, within a couple inches of the floor, a small glass globe hung. Underneath it, on the floor was a shallow bowl with a silver substance that looked like liquid mercury. A single sheet of paper had been left on the floor there, too.

At its core, enlightenment …

At the far end of the corridor was a large vase. There was something on top of the vase that looked like a paperweight.

At its end, deliverance.

Wait for Kate and Paul, he implored of himself, for the papers, for everything. Just turn around, leave this corridor now, and return with the two of them. Everyone well rested, physically healed, mentally sharp; it all might make more sense then.

"So what's going on here, Erik? How is it you can talk to me here but not at Stonebrook?"

"As you know, I'm the great-great grandnephew of Samuel Tudor who built this Reflectory," started Erik, his voice echoing down the long shaft. "I was born missing a significant portion of my brain: the Corpus Callosum. When I'm at Tudor House or Stonebrook I am disabled, sort of a Rain Man, if you will. At least on the surface. But as we approach the Reflectory, my mind connects. It makes me whole."

Still trying to grasp the change in the man, Kate paddled, and they moved deeper into the flowshaft. It felt like she was at the start of a water ride at Disney World and Erik was her guide. She had endless questions but all she could come up with was one. "How? How does the Reflectory work?"

"Nearly every human mind has the capacity to be brilliant, even when attached to a damaged brain like mine. The Reflectory has elements and structures designed to enable the mind to flow within itself and stimulate the billions of connections in the human brain that normally sit idle. Unless you are close-minded, it will change you profoundly. Probably even before you enter it."

Kate nodded. She felt like she had already experienced her change. Her *Beauty*.

At the end of the flowshaft the canoe entered a large antechamber and she recognized the body in the pool right away: the black beard, the deep-set eyes: Tin Man. The smirk had been bashed from his face forever.

Without turning around to look at the body, Erik said, "That was Nicolai Petrov from Bunker Deep. His brother Mikhail is the one who shot and killed John Mead. And the others."

"I kicked him off Gold Rock Point," replied Kate, as they got closer to the body. "Nicolai. I killed him."

"You saved our lives. And I killed Mikhail, but I was unable to save anyone. It was the end of the two-month exchange. The last day, in fact. We were all inside still. Our percipients, he shot in the head. John and I rushed him and he shot John in the shoulder before I wrestled the gun away. I was a spit second too late, I'm afraid."

Erik looked down at his bandaged hand and sighed. "Then, with a bullet hole in his shoulder, John Mead, the most prolific traveller into Newton's Realm who ever lived, stayed alive just long enough to write down what he thought was necessary. We had long ago made contingency plans in the event he died suddenly along with his two possible successors, including the buried key inside the sailor's heart and many of the notes you discovered, so there was little else to do. We had no options short of our last ditch plan to invite potential Blue Violins to stay at Stonebrook to figure out the clues and discover the Reflectory on their own."

Kate understood that part. It was the reason Alex was invited. "One thing I don't get is the sailor with the stone over his heart and the key inside him. What did he have to do with any of this?"

"The sailor's real name was Timothy Mann. Mann claimed to be a seaman but was in fact a scheming card player. A last-minute addition to the crew of the *Madeira*, one of his jobs was anchoring, but during the Big Blow storm he did not follow captain's orders to drop anchor so the vessel could ride out the storm at sea. Instead, they drifted. Two hours later, the

Madeira slammed into Gold Rock Point. Then he held his mates at gunpoint to be sure he was first across the line that James Morrow threw to them from the cliff. The angry survivors found shelter in the woodshed and then Stonebrook. Later, they searched the grounds with Samuel and found the freezing Timothy Mann hiding under the footbridge. Samuel's greatest regret was what happened next. He stood by and let the crew kill the man. He was an accomplice to murder. The Sailor's Stone was not his idea but he was the one who placed the body in the center of the circle of trees.

"Decades later, John Mead buried a key to the Reflectory inside what had been the man's heart as his symbol of regret. The Reflectory, his greatest accomplishment, was in fact also his greatest regret because in his devotion to the cause, he left his son without a father, without direction. So he placed the key in the heart of a sinner, the sinner who was buried directly over the Reflectory itself."

The canoe was right next to Petrov's body; Kate could have reached out and touched it. Erik tied the canoe to a post by the stairs and transferred his bulk out onto a landing. He kicked the body and it floated away a few feet and then reached with his good hand for her to take.

Kate accepted it, swung one foot then the other to the bottom step and stood next to him. "So what exactly is a Blue Violin, then?"

"It's difficult to translate into words but a Blue Violin is someone with the unique capacity of comprehension that Newton had. We are the ones who enter what is known as the Newton's Realm."

Kate swallowed. "*We* are the ones? Are you a Blue Violin like John Mead and Samuel Tudor were?"

Erik nodded matter-of-factly, started up the steps and gestured for her to follow. "But I can't be in charge of a Reflectory because of my disability."

Kate shook her head and grabbed the railing. This was all too much.

Erik turned and raised his big bushy eyebrows. "Do you need help?"

"Are you in Newton's Realm right now?"

"Not quite. That can only happen inside."

"Why is this place a secret? I'd feel much better if we were someplace in the open."

"If we went public, it would be commercialized. The power of the Reflectory would die or it would simply be destroyed like Samuel Tudor's first Reflectory in Boston and others in history. Reflectories have to be hidden. That's why he came here to the middle of nowhere and moved it underground. He had hired someone to search up and down the North Shore to find a cliff face hidden with natural rocks by the entrance that also had a pre-existing cave structure. Gold Rock Point had massive caves, so this place was chosen."

Erik went to the top step and opened a large door.

Kate's head was reeling and she wanted to faint but knew that just wouldn't happen. She had to ask something that was closer to home. She thought about her husband and why they were invited. "What about Alex? Paul?"

"John Mead knew Alex could be a Blue Violin based on the architecture design he had submitted, and while Paul showed potential, and there is a definite genetic inheritance to the capacity, he didn't think he had it in him. I agree. But that is to be determined. A Blue Violin must go through the seven phases and they must understand the true relationship between Invention and Harmony." Erik gently caressed his bandaged right hand with his left. "Within a couple hours, we'll know if either of them is a Blue Violin."

Kate marveled at the little man's strength and endurance but she didn't budge from the bottom step. "Can I see Alex now?" She wanted no more talk about some Blue Violin slaughter or Newton's Realm. She just wanted to hug her husband.

Erik smiled lovingly. "Yes, Kate."

"In the Reflectory?"

"Yes." Erik smiled.

"No more trickery-dickery, okay? No more riddles or stupid keys or stops for Tang and Spam or history lessons." Despite her agitation, she took a breath and smiled back at her friend on the top step to let him know there were no hard feelings. "Deal?"

And Erik laughed. Erik Tudor actually laughed. "No, Kate. No more trickery-dickery." He bowed and gestured through the open door for her.

Kate climbed the steps and then let Erik walk ahead. At the far end of a hallway he stopped at a second great door; this one with a beautiful engraved blue violin.

Chapter 35

Instead of waiting for Kate and Paul, Alex walked halfway around the globe and dropped to his knees to inspect it. In his peripheral vision, he saw the single piece of paper under it. He could barely resist averting his eyes to the paper but managed to keep his focus on the globe. Inside the glass were four letters. There was an E, an S, an N, and a W. It was a compass!

He thought of the jumbled compass on the helm of the *Madeira* from his dream, his mind-walk the night before.

The cord that attached to the compass was as thin as fishing line. He nudged it and the globe-compass swayed, settled back in its original position. He wanted to touch the peculiar compass itself but felt that he should not.

Alex turned his attention to the tiled floor under it. When he had stared at the walls and ceiling, the floor seemed invisible and now when he viewed the floor directly, the walls and ceiling blurred. The tiny tiles were clay-colored, the size of small, unevenly spaced plates, and they captured his eye with their mesmerizing patterns. Woven around these plates, were slender gray tiles that stretched between the long walls the entire length of the corridor. In the area under the suspended globe-compass, around the tantalizing piece of paper, their woven appearance looked denser, stronger, as if the compass was a weighty spider that dropped from the ceiling on a silky thread of its own making, and the gray tiles on the floor were a supporting web underneath it.

In a large circle around the compass, multi-colored tiles had been laid out to spell two words. On his left in a colorful semi-circle: the word *Invention*. On his right, completing the colorful circle: the word *Harmony*.

He sat down to study the paintings on the long walls, comparing them. Indeed, the Harmony wall along the right of the long room had a more natural, flowing tone. Abstract shapes and patterns eased into a pastoral scene of trees and fields and streams.

The setting on the wall at his left, Invention, started with mountains and a sea, as if continuing from the Harmony wall that had ended in foothills at the rear of the corridor. But it also had temples, aqueducts, windmills, crops. It had a sailing ship on which stood a figure holding a telescope up to his eye that was pointed at a rocket-shaped object high in the sky. This scene changed in the center of the corridor into what appeared to be a depiction of the evolution and history of humans, which ran the remainder of the way to the front wall.

Alex frowned. He shifted his sitting position and turned his head to consider the scene on the rear wall over the vase. It had a sun on a black backdrop. Surrounding it—perhaps emitting from it—were sparks and flares of light. The scene on the front wall had a black circle on a muted-yellow background and around the circle were black specks, black blobs.

He rubbed the beard on his chin. *Who would create such a display? Why?*

He walked to the rear of the corridor where the sun was and then took a few steps to the right—the Harmony wall. Upon closer inspection, he noticed writing in the pastoral background—it blended in well but it was there. Proverbs … poetry. Many things.

He recognized the title of a painting by Paul Gauguin that he had studied in a college art history class: *Q'où venons-nous? Qui sommes-nous? Qù allons-nous?* The English translation, he remembered, was: *Where do we come from? Who are we? Where are we going?*

Most of the scripts he could not read—they were in foreign languages. Latin, Greek, German, French, Italian. There was English, too, mostly in the form of old English and, he guessed, Gaelic.

"What is it?" Alex asked himself softly. "This place, this Reflectory … what is it?"

Then he got an idea—from his dreams. *Find your soul's base.* It was what he and Kate and Paul had discussed doing at the cottage on Wednesday when they talked about where they would each hide the wellspring of their spirits. And they had been right; that was exactly what this was all about. It was what he had been doing in his dreams all along: struggling to find something, find his soul's base.

You must be a philosopher, a scientist, an artist, a sleuth.

He wrung his hands, shifted his weight from one foot to the other. He felt confused, overwhelmed. "I don't know," he muttered. "I don't know my own soul." His gift of comprehension would fall short when turned upon himself. He had no center. His soul, it had no base. And was that his greatest regret? He supposed that it was. It was the reason for his ambivalence toward day-to-day living. It made life seem plain, meaningless. Even before the loss of Michael, before he forgot to buckle his poor son into his car seat. It was that incident that he had always thought was his greatest regret but he realized now it was really his greatest mistake.

The difference between the two was profound.

He felt a sudden anxious constriction upon his heart and it beat harder. Because there was meaning here. Thank God.

Without thinking, he said out loud: "Tranquility; Interruption; Tempest; Falling …"

With each of the four words, he turned clockwise a quarter turn—he had faced the Harmony wall for the first two words and then the Inventions wall for the next two. He continued turning. At Harmony: "Reflection." At Invention: "Struggle." He turned a bit more and faced the front wall again. Then what?

His dreams, with their distinct phases, were a tapestry of metaphoric representations of his thoughts from each day at Stonebrook. In them, past and present were woven. He was warned to leave Stonebrook while enticed to stay and he glimpsed abstractions of the future. These dreams—the phases of them—carried him not forward but into himself. As if to test this theory, Alex walked to the center of the corridor and again and he rotated slowly, taking in the four walls, riding the phases of his dreams, trying to sense them—*feel them*—play out on the walls of the corridor.

Tranquility

Interruption
Tempest
Falling
Then,
Reflection
Struggle

After *Struggle*, he stopped. In front of him was the compass. The cord was right between his eyes.

He knelt on the floor next to the bed of mercury, his focus on the little globe with its letters.

At its core, enlightenment …

His head was woozy and it seemed to him that the corridor continued to spin.

"*Enlightenment*," he said to it. "That's the last phase. The seventh phase."

Alex was speaking now, he imagined, to the old man from his dream. "And how can you be … not entirely dead. What is the power that is here, John Mead? What is this place? Why was it built?"

Alex could stand it no longer. The answer he sought was likely inches from his face. He grabbed the piece of paper that was Enlightenment and held it up. But there was nothing written there. He flipped it over: nothing. He stared anxiously at it, as if words might appear and jump or sing or dance but the paper lay in his hands, two-dimensional, lifeless. Enlightenment was … *nothing*?

Frustrated, Alex slid the paper back next to the bowl of mercury under the globe compass. He remembered the Gauguin phrase he had read on Harmony toward the rear and wondered if any more clues could be gleaned from the painting there. When he studied the phrase again, he noticed a long crack around it. It started at the floor, ran eight feet up, four feet over, then back down to the floor. It was a massive door and above it, in nondescript text, was written: *Literature/Arts.*

There was no handle so he touched the crack at the upper-right corner and traced his finger down it to the floor. He could see no way to open it, so he looked straight across the corridor to the Invention side and noticed an outline for a door there, too. Over it, he made out the word: *Inventions.*

Alex dashed back to the center of the corridor where he could view both long walls. Then he ran closer to the entrance back on the right side of the Harmony painting—the same side as Literature/Arts—and saw another door: *Fantasy.* Then the last door, back on the Invention side, was in the history-evolution section of the painting: *Epoch.*

Four doors. Two on the Harmony side—Literature/Arts and Fantasy—and two on the Invention side—Inventions and Epoch.

The obvious struck Alex. Push one.

He walked back to the Literature/Arts door. On the portion of door where a handle would be, a lone sunflower had been painted in a field of green grass. The brown paint in the center of the sunflower, he noticed, was worn; it had been nearly rubbed off. He pushed there. The door was thick and heavy, and it budged just an inch. He pushed harder and the door swung wide open.

Chapter 36

Despite Kate's trepidation, the door captivated her. She walked up next to Erik and gently touched the engraved instrument. When she moved her finger across it, she nearly expected music to play. "What's the deal with the blue violin, anyway? You have a violin on your Rugby shirt and there's one on the storage door in the back of the boathouse." She turned to study Erik closely and asked again: "Why are the keepers of these places called Blue Violins?"

Erik did not reply but instead retreated down the hall to a small door on the left and went inside.

A moment later, he came out with a pair of slippers and set them on the floor at her feet.

Perplexed, she hesitated, took off her shoes and put on the slippers.

Erik again bowed his head and gestured with his hand for her to open the violin door. He was still wearing his leather boots; he would not be joining her.

With her heart racing, Kate grasped the metal ring, turned it, and pulled. She peeked around the cracked-open door and saw the descending staircase. "Oh Lord," she whispered. "It goes deeper." She had hoped to find a cozy little room like a study. She had hoped to find Alex and Paul sitting in comfy chairs reading boring books on philosophy or poetry. She had hoped to find waiting for her a good cup of coffee and laptop with an Internet connection.

She took a deep breath, tried to clear her mind.

Chapter 37

Inside Literature/Arts, Alex heaved the door closed behind him and looked out over an immense chamber. On two of its high walls, there was a floor-to-ceiling gallery of paintings.

He had emerged on a slender platform near the ceiling. Nearby, a spiral staircase wound tightly around a pole like a snake coiled around a tree branch. The platform was really a narrow walkway that spanned the length of two forty-foot-long walls lined with books. He peered over the railing and saw an identical walkway, and then below that, the floor, where a collection of sculptures waited.

It seemed that to get the full impact of the room, he should be down among everything. In the center of the floor, tiles of the same style in the corridor interrupted the hardwood floor. Their pattern here was somewhat wild, yet cohesive. They swirled grandly, harmoniously and yet appeared troubled, on the verge of spiraling into chaos. It reminded Alex of Van Gogh's painting, *Starry Night*. It was like a turbulent sky or sea, scary and thrilling—a perfect visual representation of the whispering wind and water that had permeated his dreams at the cottage.

Shhhhuaaa-wooosh—shhuamaeeeeavvvv—*heeeeereaaarre*—sorrrrryyyyseeeeeeeeeas.

You must know—you must leave—here there are—stormy seas.

In the middle of the turbulent tiles on the floor, he knew that was where he should stand.

Winding down the spiral staircase, Alex had a dizzying sense of turning faster and faster, so that when he reached the floor, he did not let go of the railing until he was sure of his balance.

There was a record player there right next to the staircase and a record was on the turntable. Anxious to cut the silence and curious to hear what music had been left there, he leaned over it, blew off the dust on the record, and then clicked a dial. There was an amplified hum and the record, *The Marriage of Figaro*, started to spin. He positioned the needle over the record and eased it down on the only song he was familiar with, *Sull'aria,* which he had heard in the movie *Shawshank Redemption.* A crackly hiss permeated the room, and then singing. In Italian. Two beautiful, female, operatic voices. Heard in a prison or anywhere else, they would have been serene, but inside this place, this sanctuary, they were transcendental. Alex felt lifted by them, transported. He sniffed the air and opened his mouth, nearly expecting to smell the sweetness of the music, to taste it.

The record, he guessed, was the last one that John Mead had ever played.

He circled a sculpture that was directly in front of him: a mammoth hourglass encased in a clear glass globe with an etched outline of the seven continents of Earth. The six-foot-high globe was fitted into a short, round wooden stand.

Within the hourglass, at the constricted center of the Earth's core a marble was stuck. Bunched on top of the marble were hundreds more. Below it, resting on the bottom of the hourglass, were thousands. The title of the piece, he read, was *Adam Perpetual.* The stuck marble, he figured, was Adam … perhaps biblical Adam, and the hourglass, the history of humanity. But there were marbles—people—above and below Adam.

Alex tilted his head, confused.

If the marbles on the bottom of the hourglass were descendents there should be no marbles on the top and yet right above Adam were two marbles, on top of those, four, and so on. *Perpetual* implied something constant: Adam—Adams—throughout history, as if every person could be an Adam. Alex counted generations on his fingers, doubling the number each time. Ten generations before him, Alex had one thousand direct ancestors—grandmothers and grandfathers—and so merely doubling ancestors every generation, twenty generations ago meant one million direct ancestors, thirty generations ago, meant a billion different people and how long ago was that? A mere five hundred years ago? His math and figuring, even if skewed, did not change the premise: if he and Kate had children who in turn had children and so on, they would be direct ancestors to billions of people.

Adam Perpetual indeed.

Alex's mouth hung open as he took in the rest of the chamber. There were other such pieces—he would have to study them, put them into context.

The paintings and books were also unique, yet served a greater collective purpose.

Alex made his way to the tiles in the center of the room. As if it were sacred ground, he walked around the perimeter and noticed two painted portraits on the rear wall, one on either side of a door. As he walked over to them, he noticed they were the two smallest paintings in the room and they were the only portraits.

The silver nameplate under the one on the left read: *Samuel Tudor: 1858–1945*. Samuel, he saw, was a short man, like his great-great nephew Erik. Otherwise, he looked nothing at all like Alex had imagined. The man's entire body was thick like a barrel, his hands were rough; his face was weathered. He wore a dark suit but looked unnatural in it. Wavy gray hair had been slicked down, on the verge of springing free.

Alex tilted his head to consider the other portrait and found himself staring into the face of a familiar-looking man just as the record stopped playing.

In the silence, his eyes locked with the eyes of the painting and for a moment he felt that the man there was real and that they stared at each other through a window frame. It looked like Paul. Except, the nameplate read: *John Mead*. The face, the build, the hands—it was Paul. And it was also like the shadowy man from Alex's dreams. Tall, mysterious. Gray eyes. Alex half expected to see a glowing sphere painted over the man's left hand.

Alex swallowed hard, he felt confused, like reality had slipped away and would never slip back. He felt he was going

… mad. Dreams and reality, they were blending together and he was not in control enough to stop it.

The door between the two portraits opened.

Alex froze.

It was John Mead. Alive. In the flesh.

"Alex?" The tentative voice was Paul's. There was a large bandage on his friend's forehead, and like Alex, he also wore someone else's clothes and slippers. Paul closed the door behind him. "You shouldn't be up yet, Alex. You need rest."

"Paul, is that really you?"

His friend nodded.

"I'm feeling better, except for some reason you look just like John Mead," replied Alex, rubbing the back of his neck. "Oh, and Tin Man. He's dead."

"I know. In the antechamber. He must have fallen off the cliff. Where's Erik?"

"He went for Kate, evidently. He left a note on these clothes for me to see when I woke up. Did you two talk last night?"

"After we got you inside and into bed, I tended to his hand and he helped wrap this bandage around my head. He set out clothes for all of us to wear and then he pulled a cot up right next to yours and went to sleep. I tried to sleep, too, but…." Paul nodded with his forehead to the door he emerged from. "He told me to go in that little room in there. It's a keeper's quarters and he said that there was a painting I had to see.

"John Mead is my father, Alex. He's mother's Monterosso friend, the one who gave me my violin. There's a painting of the two of them inside the quarters."

Alex nodded. It all made sense somehow. "Your dad hired you to mind the cottage. He wanted you to be the one to have all this. That law firm who hired you, they could tell you something."

Paul rubbed his eyes. "No. This place … it isn't for me. When you stand in the center of the circle of tiles, you'll understand. Have you done that yet, Alex?"

Alex shook his head.

"Go, then. Tell me what you see."

When Alex's slippers padded on the first couple tiles he became lightheaded and felt adrift—*take the helm*—like he was disconnected from time and space, swept into another reality. Unlike in the corridor, where time seemed to draw out, on these tiles it felt loose, like a meandering river that did not have an end. It could pass slowly or quickly under his feet without affecting him because he was stepping from stone to stone into the middle of it.

In the center, he held his breath, turned clockwise, searching for orientation, for balance. The tiles seemed to pulsate and he imagined that the globe-compass up in the corridor was spinning like a top. He felt completely dizzy yet his body stayed upright. "What is the loosening sensation I feel?" he said at last.

"I don't know," Paul replied.

"They … the tiles. They're alive under my feet. The chamber, it feels alive around me. Like when I was in the corridor." He opened his eyes and found Paul. "I mean *really* alive."

Alex cleared his throat. "John Mead and Samuel Tudor, I thought I felt them at the cottage but their presence inside the cliff here is even stronger. John Mead is still in here. Remember when you translated his first clue for us? It's like that. In spades. We're in his ship, Paul."

Paul did not say anything.

"And the boathouse—our little talk in the boathouse? The contour of thought, the texture of ideas, the color of emotions?"

"I remember."

Alex closed his eyes again. He imagined himself at the helm of the *Madeira*. "My thoughts," he continued, "they're taking tangible form; I can see their outlines, now. Literally." Alex reached both hands out and his fingers stroked the air, closed into a grip. In his imagination he had grabbed the wheel of the *Madeira*. It felt smooth and warm as if someone's hands had been at it for ages and only that moment had released it. "I can touch my thoughts."

Alex knitted his eyebrows as if studying something intently, yet kept his eyes shut. "My ideas. They've always been grainy like sandpaper, but they're becoming smoother now." He could see through the pilothouse windows. "We're in a storm, Paul, we're always in a storm, and its dark and I can't see through it…. My emotions, they're pale. I can see now how pale they've always been but standing here they're starting to color…. Right now—amazement and passion—they are lightning blue and orange bleeding into each other. Together, they're like—like Gold Rock Point at sunrise, and we're blowing toward it.

"Everything … the contours, the textures, the colors. They mix. Marvelously. They dip into our sensory reality but they're on another plane. And this Reflectory," Alex continued, "it's a cathedral, a museum, a laboratory, a vessel; it's where Socrates drops apples onto Newton. Where DaVinci invents Magic Flutes for Mozart. It's an essential world within a peripheral one because that is what our day-to-day world is … *peripheral.* Our physical senses perceive only the scantest portion of a greater reality, a greater realm. We live, we exist, in a false sense of sobriety."

Alex was speaking quickly but then he slowed down. "We are angst-ridden poets. We linger drunk upon our own existence. But this place. This place was designed for journeys across great seas—it was built to clear our heads, extend our capacity."

After a long silence, Paul said, "Do you see, Alex?"

"See what?" Alex replied, breaking out of his trance.

"The Reflectory. It's not for me. I feel meaning here, connectedness, but it points my soul toward music. What I thought about when I stood inside the circle of tiles was the joy of playing my violin. My music is the wellspring of my spirit, Alex. My greatest regret has been not sharing it with others."

Paul took off his glasses as if he no longer needed them to see. "This place has taught me that."

"But your dad hired you to care for Stonebrook. He wanted you to discover this so it could be yours."

Paul shook his head. "He wanted me to find out who I am, Alex. He wanted me to learn from my regrets and pursue my soul's calling. Maybe he hoped that continuing the Reflectory was what I yearned to do but only if it was meant to be. It is not. I need to resuscitate my life. Heck, I need to *start* my life."

Just then, the door from the corridor creaked opened and they whirled around.

Chapter 38

Kate peeked around the door. She stared in astonishment at the great chamber below and then spotted Alex standing in the middle of the circle of colorful, swirling floor tiles, and Paul sitting at the edge.

"Alex! He said you were fine but—"

Kate rushed down the spiral staircase, her hair bouncing as she went, and met Alex at the bottom with a bear hug. He grabbed her cheeks, and whispered again and again that he was okay.

Finally, Kate wiped at her eyes and turned to Paul. A look of concern spread across her face as she noticed his bandaged forehead.

"I'm fine," Paul said, touching the bandage.

She tried to hug him, too, but he remained stiff. "I need to tell you something. Your mother. She's—" Kate paused, looked at the floor. "her nurse called. Paul, your mother passed away. Sometime during the night. I'm so sorry."

Paul lowered his eyes but his face remained unchanged.

"Look," continued Kate with a sigh. "I have a confession to make. I went to see her Wednesday afternoon. She showed me her painting in that fantastic sitting room of hers. She told me about her Wisdom and Innocence ascending to heaven in the smoke of a small fire next to a brook going to heaven. And before I left her, she had asked that I light a fire for her next to Stonebrook when we discovered the Reflectory. The fire that I was to light, that she had been watching for from her sitting room last night, would have told her that at last you knew the one thing that would have made her life complete. Did you find that in here, Paul?"

Paul held a cupped hand over his eyes.

"He found out, Kate," said Alex for his friend.

Kate put a hand on his arm, offering a hug, but he did not turn in to her. "Please excuse me," he said, and he walked back into the keeper's quarters.

After he closed the door behind him, Kate told Alex what had happened on the cliff the night before, that she had killed Tin Man. She wanted to tell Alex about her talk with Erik and explain what she knew about the war with the four Reflectories and their Percipients and Blue Violins but Erik had asked her to wait, so she bit her tongue.

Instead, she decided to tell him about her morning. "Alex, before we canoed out here I let Erik rest a bit." She felt a little sheepish but knew she had to share her experience. "And I grabbed as much firewood as I could carry and started a fire down by the brook, right by the footbridge." She started to tear up and her husband held her. "And I felt Elsa there, Alex. And my mom, too. And … Michael. Michael was hugging my legs. They told me it was okay. Not in words, but I felt them and they told me to let them go. Can you believe that?"

Alex nodded.

"How can we feel people who are dead, Alex?"

Alex shrugged. But his wife, he saw, wanted an answer. "Maybe death … maybe it isn't what we think it is."

Kate searched his eyes. "Maybe *life* isn't what we think it is. Anyway, Alex, I forgive you. About Michael, I mean. I do. I'm so sorry for taking so long, for being so hard on you. I forgive you."

After several minutes, Kate tapped on the keeper's quarters door and peeked her head in.

Paul was standing in front of a painting, his arms folded over his chest.

"You okay?" asked Kate.

"Yeah. Just wanted to say good-bye."

Kate looked at the painting. A man sat behind a woman on a tall hill, holding her tight, his head on her shoulder. The scene was grand: the couple looked away toward a seaside village below. A full moon loomed over John Mead and Elsa—a silver moon. "You want for us to leave you alone awhile longer?"

"No," Paul replied. "I'm done." He turned to her and smiled and Kate could not resist the urge to rush up to the dear man and offer a hug. This time he hugged back.

Alex, Kate, and Paul stepped out of Literature/Arts and closed the door behind them.

Kate said, "It's so beautiful. That chamber, this—whatever this corridor is. It's like a museum. Did you two notice … on the walls?"

Alex and Paul stared at her.

"The chamber names? From back to front?"

They looked at the names above the doors.

"Alternating between the right and left sides?" she continued, prompting them.

The two men looked confused. Alex shook his head.

"Literature, Inventions, Fantasy, Epoch?" Her voice hinted that there was something clever about the wording.

Alex knitted his eyebrows. *Literature … Inventions … Fantasy … Epoch.*

It was Paul who got it first. "L-I-F-E," he said quietly. Then: "Life."

Life, thought Alex, *Chambers of life. Like the four chambers of the heart, the four seasons, the four elements. It was like alchemy.*

Revelations were the papers in the front of the corridor. Kate gathered those up.

Enlightenment, the single piece of paper in the middle, Paul stooped to pick up. He turned it over and folded it first so as not to risk reading whatever might have been written on it.

At the rear of the corridor, on top of a vase was a Deliverance envelope. *Contemplata Aliis Tradere.* They had already seen the fruits, at least some of them. Now they needed to find out why they were planted, what made them grow.

Alex reached down to grab it but hesitated because the rest of his life, he felt, would somehow be altered based on what they were about to read. His fate was out of his hands; it was sealed inside an envelope.

Paul and Kate, with Revelations and Enlightenment in hand, walked up beside him. "We need Deliverance, Alex," Kate said lacing an arm through his. "It's kind of important, I'm guessing."

Alex did not move, so Kate retrieved the envelope for him. She tapped it against his arm. "You okay?"

He nodded even though he felt anything but okay.

"Hey," Kate said excitedly, "let's read all this inside one of the other chambers."

"Which one?" Paul asked.

Kate eyed the shapes and designs of the Fantasy wall. "That one."

To Alex, the abstract painting was mesmerizing. He knew he could un-focus his eyes and drift into its flows. It was the most enticing wall; it would also be the most dangerous chamber. "No. I don't think we're ready for that one yet. At least I'm not."

Kate remembered the talk with Erik about how dangerous Reflectories could be. "Sorry. Inventions, then?"

Paul nodded, approving.

Alex replied tentatively, "Sure … Inventions."

On the top half of the Inventions door was a painted image of a pyramid. At the base of it, dead center in the door, was a painted black entrance to the pyramid.

Alex pushed there and they heard a dull click as the door nudged outward an inch.

"Wait," he said, holding a hand up when Kate made a move to push it and enter. If most inventions throughout history had been the result of endless trial-and-error, he thought, most of them ultimately were the result of one last, profound bit of insight. A *Eureka*! moment.

This chamber would be chock-full of *Eureka*.

"Well after you, then," Kate said, apprehensive. "I didn't mean to rush you."

Alex pushed and the entire door slid straight into the chamber and then banked to the left. He stepped inside.

He scanned the room quickly and then shut his eyes. He just wanted an impression, a snapshot of the room that faded to black behind his closed eyes. And as sight yields to memory, he had something for his imagination.

He had seen an ornate, domed ceiling over a chamber that was still under development. A length of scaffolding ran high along the rear wall above a hole near the ceiling. On the floor, iron rods lay strewn about near a huge wooden, harp-shaped frame. The frame had several rods strung across it, and on these rods were large beads the size of a man's head. It had resembled an abacus, because the beads were positioned in an organized fashion, as if something were in the process of being tabulated. He had seen machinery, too. There were platforms and steps and at the rear of the chamber under the hole in the wall was a giant wheel.

In a word, he had seen *Inventions*.

He opened his eyes again and saw that Kate and Paul had stepped around him and stood at a railing. Kate clutched all of John Mead's papers and the Deliverance envelope to her chest and was looking down.

Paul, swaying, was looking up.

"What is it? All this … stuff?" asked Kate. Her words came out in an open-mouthed drawl. "What …"—she swallowed—"is it for?"

Alex emerged between them and put an arm around his wife's waist. He had an idea of what at least some of it was for … in a sense, what all the chambers were for. He thought of NASA at the infancy of the space program. Men with crew cuts, horn-rimmed glasses, short-sleeved dress shirts, dark ties. Sitting in a huge control center. Tracking progress, tabulating distances, gauging fuel requirements. Putting men into space, bringing them home. Something similar had gone on in here, he thought. And would again. This chamber, this control center, had been around for quite some time, longer than the space program, and yet it was still in its infancy. "Exploration," he said, finally answering Kate. "It's for exploration."

In silence, the three of them took the narrow staircase: Alex then Kate then Paul. On the floor of the chamber, they headed toward the circle of tiles in the center. These tiles were all shades of green—green like emeralds. They did not flow like the ones inside Literature/Arts. These were abstract like a Cubist painting yet looked purposeful, as if Pablo Picasso had gotten together with Frank Lloyd Wright.

Alex stepped on the first tile, paused, and then withdrew his foot. "Kate … Paul. Let's just sit here on the edge, okay?"

Seated in a tight circle, Kate set the Deliverance envelope aside and announced, "We might as well read them in order." She caught Paul's eye, then Alex's. They were ready.

Kate picked up Revelations and scanned it. John Mead had used one of his antiquated quill pens that he had used in his other messages. The ink was a vibrant black, the commas goopy, blotchy curls.

The two men looked on as Kate began reading.

Revelations – Part 1

The poem that Samuel had left for me, I leave for you. Any moment now, I shall die. I'm losing too much blood. You must speak with Erik. If he can manage to stay alive....

My bed, Erik has placed for me in the Callosum.

My stone, I have chosen.

I am ready.

The Bequeath of Nevermore (Contemplata Aliss Tradere)
Mine eyes, moist and blinking
Fade upon enduring beauty
Mine ears, tuned and piqued
Hear silence, nevermore, descending

Mine hand, this touching, clutching hand!
Drops this quill, reaches from the page; grasps yours:
Work to be done
Work be done
Work

When Kate finished, she said, "Holy crap, guys." She dropped the paper as if John Mead's hand might in fact reach out from it and grab her wrist. "He sure doesn't mince words in his poetry now does he?"

"Wow," Alex replied.

"But what does Revelations part 1 mean?" asked Paul. "Where is the part 2?"

Kate bit her lip. "The part 2 is Erik. I'm not supposed to say anything yet, but Erik told me that John Mead was shot in the shoulder by a Percipient from a Reflectory in Moscow called Bunker Deep. Let's just say when we're all done here, I think he'll have more Revelations for us than you can imagine. He gave me a taste on the canoe ride in."

Before she could be questioned, Kate asked, "So who's going to read Enlightenment?" She spun her ring, anxious about what Enlightenment could be.

Alex looked down at the floor. "I already looked at it. I'm sorry, I couldn't help myself."

Kate looked angry but her face quickly softened. "Well, what's it say?"

Alex grimaced. "You aren't going to like it."

Kate unfolded the paper. "There's nothing here. I don't get it."

"Neither do I," added Alex. "Maybe that's when he died."

Paul smiled and took off his glasses.

"What?" Kate asked.

"It's personal. You fill in your own answer."

"What do you mean?" pressed Kate.

"What did you find here at Stonebrook?"

Kate thought for a moment. She knew exactly what she found but didn't want to go first. "What did you find?"

"Truth," Paul said.

"You mean discovering that your dad was John Mead?"

"No. That was certainly a truth but I'm talking about finding out what my life should be about. What I'm meant to do, to be. My truth. I need to play the violin."

Kate nodded. "I found beauty. Back at the cottage, even. And with your mother, Paul. Beauty in the world and in myself that I had never seen before."

Kate turned to Alex, waited for him to speak. "So?" she prompted. "What did you find?"

"I don't know…." He took out the pen and paper from his shirt pocket. He wanted to jot something down, maybe draw a picture, but of what, he had no idea. The Circle of Trees far above them grew not in a perfect circle but in an oval. They served as a perimeter for what lay below … they gave him an idea. "Can we head back up? I need to try something."

Back up in the corridor, with Kate and Paul standing off to the side, Alex again sat on the floor with the globe compass in front of him. He set the Enlightenment piece of blank paper on the floor and drew dots in a large oval to denote the forty-nine trees above them. He connected them with a line and then drew from top to bottom two vertical lines that represented the corridor. The globe-compass positioned in the center of the corridor was likely also positioned beneath the center of the Circle of Trees, beneath the Sailors' Stone. He drew a tiny circle in the center of the paper to represent the compass and the stone.

He jotted the word *Invention* on the left side of the paper and *Harmony* on the right. Even though the names of his seven phases were his own invention, he wrote them down, too, fanning each word out and around the globe compass, placing them on the paper in the general directions he was looking when he had said them as he spun. He drew a curving line from word to word, starting at *Tranquility*, turning clockwise, and ending at *Enlightenment*.

Then he added four more words in four quadrants of the paper to denote the four chambers: *Literature* and *Inventions* on the right, *Fantasy* and *Epoch* on the left. He put the pen back into his pocket because there was nothing else he could think to add.

He held his drawing at arm's length. It looked meaningless.

"Take the helm," he reminded himself, feeling a tug. "Deeper. But where is my helm? Where is my base?"

You must be a philosopher. A scientist. An artist. A sleuth.

Alex's body started to shiver; he felt cold … he was on to something. He stood, inhaled deeply, exhaled slowly. *Okay*, he thought. *The helm. Fantasy? Yes.* It called to him.

He walked up to the Fantasy door. The abstract images on its surface filled his desires, defined his emptiness. He imagined seeing Michael inside the chamber playing chess with John Mead.

But when Alex stood in front of it he felt uneasy. It was not … it was not his base. Neither of the long walls held his base. And the center of the corridor was for the compass—it was not his base, either.

Take the helm.

Philosopher, Scientist, Artist, Sleuth. He was not any one of them … because he was all of them.

Deeper.

His soul was not centered on one side of the corridor or the other. Because it was not bound.

Take the helm!

He was like a nomad.

Deeper!

Alex retreated to the rear of the corridor, farthest from the lake, and turned around.

No, not a nomad. An *explorer.*

He found it.

At last.

John Mead's helm.

His own.

A vision flashed in his mind. He was at the helm of the *Madeira,* at the stormy moment before it struck Gold Rock Point. November 28, 1905. Where should he steer her? He eyed the front wall of the corridor where they had entered. Beyond that wall was Lake Superior. The black sphere on that narrow wall painted over the entrance to the corridor was not a hole or void, but a philosophical end—the end of time, perhaps, or death, or the outermost boundary of one's soul. The brilliant yellow sphere over the vase on the rear wall right behind him was a beginning. It resembled a sun or the beginning of time. Or the birth of one's soul.

What exactly was it that they were inside?

The oval had two sides.

An epiphany was gathering, filling his veins with warmth, his head with a chill.

His drawing … it was a top view.

He knew what the Reflectory was. He finally knew.

Chapter 39

He looked at his drawing; it was the outline of a human head and two sides of a brain.

"A mind," Alex said. His mouth had formed the words, but they were inaudible.

With more confidence, he said out loud: "A mind."

He looked from Kate to Paul. "My God. The mind that Samuel Tudor built. That's what the Reflectory is. A mind. Just as Erik told us. Not a mine, at all. A mind. This grand hallway is the Corpus Callosum, the one thing that Erik's brain doesn't have…. So when he's here, he can be whole."

Facing the entrance, the direction of the lake, Literature and Fantasy were on his right—historically known as the mind's creative hemisphere; Inventions and Epoch were on the left—the logical hemisphere. The Reflectory—the mind that Samuel Tudor built—was an integrated, whole mind. It existed, hid, yearned, pursued, created, loved … as every mind did.

On the floor in the center of the Callosum, circling the suspended globe compass, Harmony was in the right hemisphere; Invention was in the left. But that was only where they started. He suspected that the decades-old belief that the hemispheres worked independently would be disproved here.

Earlier, he might have guessed Stonebrook to be a place where those two concepts would have collided but that was not the case. Invention and Harmony, he realized now, pursued and repelled each other like lovers in a cerebral courtship. Intellect paired with Intuition; Deduction with Imagination; Analytic with Relational. They fought. They loved. They created.

They *danced*.

The breakthrough at Stonebrook was embedded in an entirely unexpected philosophy: Achieving equilibrium, or even stability, within one's mind was not the goal. That would be sedating. Nor was having one side dominate, that would be limiting. The goal was to generate a flow between the sides, in a whirling, graceful dance like one's mind flows through the seven phases. Ultimate equanimity.

It was this fluidity, this process, that enabled him to at last find his own soul here.

A brain has billions of axons sending impulses across synaptic gaps to receiving dendrites. A honeycomb of convolutions, the gray tiles on the floor that wove around the circular tiles and stretched between the two long walls represented this activity—activity that makes a brain a mind and makes a mind an individual. "The tiles," he said, staring at the floor, "here and in the circles within each chamber, they're the connections—the mind at work. Like cells in a brain. This beautiful Corpus Callosum … it's the fibrous bridge holding everything together."

Being tucked so far inside the cliff reminded Alex of his last dream back at the cottage. In it, he had wandered through his own dark mind, amazed. Yet he had felt cohesion within it. Expansiveness. Endless possibility.

He knelt to the floor, traced a finger over a tile. As a network of neural connections, the brain was the grandest of all webs. Within its realm flowed rivulets and streams of impulses. And now he felt a flash flood of new streams in his own brain. They fed a new sea.

His mind was inside a new place, in a realm just beyond the senses: Newton's Realm. And he closed his eyes because vision was a distraction in such a place.

He imagined himself in the pilothouse of the *Madeira*. He grasped her wheel, spun it violently, resolutely. The great vessel turned and she steered clear of Gold Rock Point, missed the mouth of Stonebrook creek.

On top of the cliff he saw figures. Two men, strangers, stood in the distance; they radiated a dark blue, almost black color. Closer, a woman he did not recognize stood with Erik and a shadow that looked like John Mead. In contrast to the menacing men in the distance, the woman, Erik, and the shadow were a powerful, luxurious blue.

Alex realized that the *Madeira* had been nothing but a schooner barge but in his mind he turned her back out to sea, her sails full and on her own power, and she was something more now. She went out unescorted by the *Edenborn*. Back out where it was deeper. There would be exploring to do.

Alex heard someone say his name and realized he had been in a trance.

"—Alex," said the person again.

He opened his eyes and noticed that his hands were out in front of him, holding the wheel that he still saw and felt.

"Open Deliverance," said Paul.

"Why me?"

"Because my father meant for you to open it."

Despite all that he grasped, he did not know why he should be the one to open it.

Kate, holding back tears, said, "Alex, do as Paul says. Open it."

With trembling fingers, Alex tore the envelope open. He pulled out a business card for the attorney who had invited them here, along with another single sheet of paper. The writing was much shakier than Revelations. He must have written it after, when he was near death. Alex read it aloud:

> Upon Samuel's passing, he had asked that he be cremated so that, as the next Blue Violin, I could take him away in the boat and scatter his remains in the waters in front of this divine point of Lake Superior.
>
> Upon my passing, a vase at the rear of the Callosum will hold my own cremated remains. Erik will see to this. And he will place a Sailor's Stone over it. If you are willing and heaven help the world if you are not … remove my stone.
>
> And take me away in the boat. Scatter my ashes.
>
> Become the next Blue Violin.

Kate let her tears come. She quoted Erik: "You will take him away in the boat, just as he planned."

Alex considered the stone. Kate had picked it up when she retrieved the envelope and set it back down. According to the lore of the sailors of the *Madeira*, the stone weighed down the soul of John Mead. To watch over the Reflectory ... until the next Blue Violin came along.

Until *he* came along.

Alex removed the stone, for good this time. He tilted his head toward the ceiling of the Callosum. The spirit of a great man had been released and was now free to soar to heaven.

Epilogue

"Um, Alex?" started Kate. Looking over her shoulder, she saw Erik enter the Corpus Callosum. He was running toward them. "We have a little problem."

"What's that?"

"I think more visitors from Bunker Deep have arrived. And I think they know where the Reflectory is."

The End

Did you like The Reflectory?

If it moved or entertained you, please post a quick review. Enter this link in a browser and it will take you directly to the Customer Reviews page for the novel: http://amzn.to/Z8QChn. Other shoppers will appreciate your insights and I sure will, too.

About Dan Cashman

The author in front of the Day Hill fireplace,
location of the fictional Tudor House.

Until this novel, my only published work was an interview I
conducted as a reporter for the Alnwick Advertiser newspaper
in 1986. Yes, that is forever ago and yes, I was a kid (19 is a
kid in my book).

I was an American in England for six months on a study
abroad program—the unpaid newspaper gig was for a class.
My dorm, if you can call it that, was Lion's Tower, part of the
beautiful Alnwick Castle.

Morning classes were one flight of steps down from my room. I'd wake up, grab a notebook, get some hot chocolate from the dining hall (the castle was always cold!) and learn about British royalty and how parliament works. I even got college credits for foil fencing. Foil fencing! Amazing.

Living at the castle was a fantasy (in fact, many Harry Potter scenes were filmed there). I was backpacking Europe, seeing paintings at the Louvre, the Vatican Museum, the Hermitage. I took in a ballet inside the Kremlin and attended midnight mass with the Pope. It wasn't all peace and love, though: I also smuggled military goods out of Soviet Russia (okay, it was an old army coat), slept in parks and train stations with the homeless, and evaded the police in Budapest (don't ask).

When I look back on that time and at the clipping of my lone legitimate article from the Advertiser, I love that it was about a local woman from Alnwick who was (still is?) a painter. She was taking concrete steps toward her dream, her passion for the arts.

My point (yes, I do have one): This Europe experience planted a passion in me, as well. I wanted to blend art and reality, I wanted to build a castle in the air. I wanted to write a novel. There is no other medium that offers such a canvas on which to paint.

I could not stop this novel from happening. Eventually, I wrote and finally finished (after 14 years of setting it aside!) *The Reflectory.*

I hope you enjoyed it.

All the best,
Dan

Want an update when book 2 is published?

Enter this in an Internet browser: http://eepurl.com/1M-qT. I'll add you to my newsletter.

Comments or questions?

If there is something in particular you LOVED so much or you have a burning question and need to reach me directly, I want to hear about it. If you found glaring mistakes that you can't believe I missed, please connect with me, I want to get them fixed.

My e-mail address: dan@dancashmanauthor.com

Sharing with others

This is huge for a first-time author: if you are reading on a newer kindle, when you turn this page you may be greeted with a request from the good folks at Amazon to rate this book and post your thoughts on Facebook and Twitter. This is an easy, fun way to instantly share *The Reflectory* with your friends. And it's the social media stuff from passionate lovers of literature that gives a novel wings. I'd be indebted!

One last thing: After you share on social media, how about taking the Reflectory Tour?

Visit the link below and I'll share pictures, locations, and how they relate to the novel. Call it a guided tour for hardcore Reflectory lovers.

http://www.dancashmanauthor.com/tour

Come on, let's go!

*(While the **tour** page doesn't really contain spoilers, I do mention scenes, so you might want to keep this hidden page a secret from friends who haven't read the novel yet. Thanks.)*

Made in the USA
San Bernardino, CA
28 September 2014